Frothy praise for *Irish Milkshake Murder*!

"Fans of the three authors will enjoy the returns of their favorite amateur sleuths."
—*Library Journal*

"An unconventional St. Patrick's Day treat may satisfy cozy fans who like their murder sweet."
—*Kirkus Reviews*

"St. Patrick's Day and milkshakes link the stories in these three satisfying mystery novellas. Fans of the three series will relish these fun, holiday-themed stories."
—*Booklist*

Books by Carlene O'Connor

Irish Village Mysteries
MURDER IN AN IRISH VILLAGE
MURDER AT AN IRISH WEDDING
MURDER IN AN IRISH CHURCHYARD
MURDER IN AN IRISH PUB
MURDER IN AN IRISH COTTAGE
MURDER AT AN IRISH CHRISTMAS
MURDER IN AN IRISH BOOKSHOP
MURDER ON AN IRISH FARM
MURDER AT AN IRISH BAKERY
MURDER AT AN IRISH CHIPPER

CHRISTMAS COCOA MURDER
(with Maddie Day and Alex Erickson)
CHRISTMAS SCARF MURDER
(with Maddie Day and Peggy Ehrhart)

Home to Ireland Mysteries
MURDER IN GALWAY
MURDER IN CONNEMARA

HALLOWEEN CUPCAKE MURDER
(with Liz Ireland and Carol J. Perry)
IRISH MILKSHAKE MURDER
(with Peggy Ehrhart and Liz Ireland)
IRISH SODA BREAD MURDER
(with Peggy Ehrhart and Liz Ireland)

County Kerry Mysteries
NO STRANGERS HERE
SOME OF US ARE LOOKING
YOU HAVE GONE TOO FAR

Books by Liz Ireland

Mrs. Claus Mysteries
MRS. CLAUS AND THE SANTALAND SLAYINGS
MRS. CLAUS AND THE HALLOWEEN HOMICIDE
MRS. CLAUS AND THE EVIL ELVES
MRS. CLAUS AND THE TROUBLE WITH TURKEYS
MRS. CLAUS AND THE NIGHTMARE BEFORE NEW YEAR'S

HALLOWEEN CUPCA
MURDER
(with Carlene O
Carol

IRISH MILKSHAKE MURDER
(with Carlene O'Connor and Peggy Ehrhart)
IRISH SODA BREAD MURDER
(with Carlene O'Connor and Peggy Ehrhart)

Books by Peggy Ehrhart

Knit and Nibble Mysteries
MURDER, SHE KNIT
DIED IN THE WOOL
KNIT ONE, DIE TWO
SILENT KNIT, DEADLY KNIT
A FATAL YARN
KNIT OF THE LIVING DEAD
KNITTY GRITTY MURDER
DEATH OF A KNIT WIT
IRISH KNIT MURDER
KNITMARE ON BEECH STREET
A DARK AND STORMY KNIT
CHRISTMAS CARD MURDER
(with Leslie Meier and Lee Hollis)
CHRISTMAS SCARF MURDER
(with Carlene O'Connor and Maddie Day)
IRISH MILKSHAKE MURDER
(with Carlene O'Connor and Liz Ireland)
IRISH SODA BREAD MURDER
(with Carlene O'Connor and Liz Ireland)

Published by Kensington Publishing Corp.

IRISH MILKSHAKE MURDER

Carlene O'Connor
Peggy Ehrhart
Liz Ireland

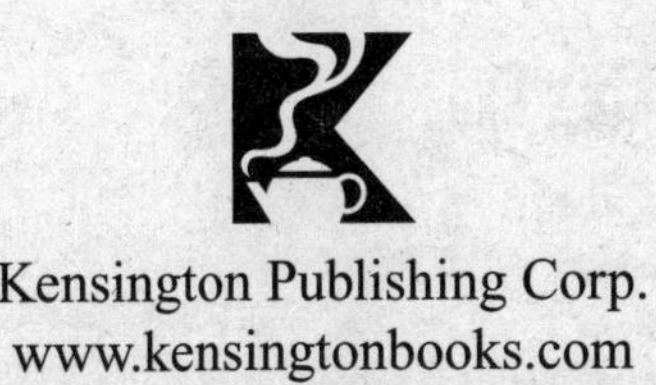

Kensington Publishing Corp.
www.kensingtonbooks.com

KENSINGTON BOOKS are published by

Kensington Publishing Corp.
900 Third Avenue
New York, NY 10022

First Kensington Hardcover Edition: January 2024

ISBN: 978-1-4967-4504-0
First Paperback Edition: January 2025

ISBN: 978-1-4967-4505-7 (ebook)

10 9 8 7 6 5 4 3 2 1

Printed in the United States of America

Contents

IRISH MILKSHAKE MURDER

Carlene O'Connor

Chapter One
Henpecked

Tara Meehan didn't want to disappoint her dear friend Breanna Cunningham, but if she had any doubts about going wild before her wedding, the plastic penis wand Breanna was waving in her face way too enthusiastically solidified her decision. *No hen party for her.* At least Breanna had waited until Tara's last customer had finally left the store (empty-handed) before whipping out the party favors. The customer, an older woman, had picked up a set of antique brass doorknobs, held them up, and put them down again at least a dozen times. "I love these," she said. "If only I had a door for them." Tara knew better than to try and sell her a door to go with them, because then she would say she needed a house, and Tara was not a realtor. That was life in the architectural salvage business. Tara set about closing her shop as Breanna trailed after her, poking her with that ridiculous party favor. "I'm too old for a hen party," Tara insisted. Way too old. Thirty-five. *Ancient.*

Breanna put the wand down on the counter, picked up the doorknobs, and held them to her chest. "Did ya see your one? She was holding knobs up to her knockers!" Breanna wiggled them and howled with laughter.

"You are such a child," Tara said, but she couldn't help but laugh. It was an accurate imitation.

"See?" Breanna said. "It's fun to be silly." She placed the doorknobs back in the old Guinness barrel. Located just off pedestrianized Shop Street, Tara's beloved shop, Renewals, was five hundred square feet of eclectic treasures and had a back patio. Tara had painted the walls a lovely shade of mint green that popped against the bamboo floors. Display cabinets featured hand-picked items, and several old Guinness advertising signs hung on the walls. White orchids topped flat surfaces, sculptures stood in every corner, and fireplace accoutrements were set up near the small working fireplace, which was flanked by stone lions. On the mantel, she displayed brass and iron candle-holders. Pottery from the 1800s was gathered in one section and vases, tiles, and antique fixtures in another. The rustic cabinet by the register was filled with estate jewelry. A small section of crystal glassware occupied shelves in the middle. More old doorknobs and decorative knockers were laid out on an old wooden barrel with *Jameson* carved on the side.

On the patio, larger architectural items, such as old wrought iron gates, were stacked up against the back of the building, along with garden sculptures and fountains. Tara had kept the shop afloat a few years now, and even the locals were starting to accept that the New York transplant was here to stay.

"My work is serious enough. I need to play," Breanna said. She was a clerk at the Galway Garda Station, and to be fair it probably was a stressful job. Tara was grateful every day for the opportunity to do something she loved.

Tara laughed, picked up a glass bowl filled with chocolates, and offered one to Breanna. "Between the knockers and your little wand, I'd say you had a good run at playing today."

"You're never too old for a hen party." Breanna said with conviction as she plucked out several pieces of chocolate. "You won't have to do a thing. I know the perfect venue."

"I'm getting married on Paddy's Day," Tara said. "That's enough revelry for me." She could not believe Danny had talked her into that. Then again, Danny O'Donnell could be quite persuasive. That Irish charm. Tara was starting to think it was more of a curse than a blessing—at least when it came to him getting his way. He'd insisted that Saint Patrick's Day was the luckiest day of the year, and then he added that they would need all the luck they could get. Technically priests did not perform ceremonies on holidays, so this meant there would actually be *two* wedding ceremonies, and even that didn't faze Danny. After years of shying away from commitment, he was now all-in. She was starting to suspect his date of choice was all because of the Saint Patrick's Day parade. Her husband-to-be loved a good parade. The wedding was three weeks away. *Insane.* Tara didn't feel ready. Did anyone ever feel ready?

"You haven't heard the best part of my evil plan," Breanna said as she steepled her fingers and wriggled them, villain-style.

"Listen, I appreciate that you want to celebrate with me. But all we need is each other and boozy milkshakes." Breanna loved boozy milkshakes. Hopefully that would chase all ideas of a wild bachelorette party out of her friend's poor, misguided head.

Breanna was not undaunted. "Don't you want to know the best part?"

"No." Tara grabbed her handbag and gestured for Breanna to step out before she flipped the switch and plunged Renewals into darkness. Outside it was windy and cold; they were still on the lion's side of March. As Tara locked up and headed for Shop Street, Breanna kept stride with her.

"It's too late. Your hen party is already booked, and your friend Rachel is flying in today from New York."

"Rachel?" Tara came to an abrupt stop. "What friend Rachel?"

Breanna cocked her head. "Rachel Madigan."

"Rachel Madigan?" Rachel Madigan was another interior designer in New York City. Tara didn't consider Rachel a close friend. How did Breanna know Rachel?

"And Danny and his groomsman are coming too," Breanna nattered on. "We're going to the Aran Islands, where I've rented a cottage. We leave in the morning."

And that, Tara told herself on her stroll by the Galway Bay back to her flat, was why you never tried besting an Irishman. Or woman. Tara hadn't even bothered to tell Breanna that she hadn't seen or talked to Rachel in years. Why had Rachel even agreed to come?

If Rachel Madigan was just in it for a weekend in Ireland, this was going to be the worst hen party ever.

It was Thursday evening in Doolin, and the last chartered boat of the day was headed out to Inishmore, the largest of the three Aran Islands. The boat, a small ferry, was white with the name CAPTAIN MICKEY emblazoned on it in red. Rachel had only met up with them a few hours ago in Galway, and given they were in a group setting, Tara had yet to ask her why exactly she was here. Was she under the impression that Tara had extended the invite via Breanna? Rachel seemed to be excited about being here and did indeed greet her as if they were long-lost friends. She'd given her a big hug, remarked how amazing she looked, and then proceeded to tell them how she'd followed Tara's progress with her salvage shop online and how utterly thrilled she was that Tara was getting married. There was no mention of the fact that Rachel wasn't invited to the actual wedding. Tara had decided to keep her invites local. She'd been cocooned in her work and family since moving here and didn't want her friends Stateside to feel pressured into attending. And, truth be told, she hadn't worked very hard to hang on to her old life. It almost felt as if it belonged to someone else.

As usual, Rachel was slim and stylish, even in jeans and a sweater. Or denims and a jumper, like they said here. Unlike Tara, who had black hair, Rachel was a platinum blonde and still perky. Breanna, who had wavy chestnut hair and a curvy body, had the girl-next-door thing going for her, not to mention that lovely

Irish accent. The three of them had already made a few heads turn when they walked by.

"Great," Danny said under his breath. "I'll be beating men off ye with a stick, so."

Rachel laughed. "Keep that stick away from my men," she said. "I'm still a single gal."

"You can use it to beat mine into submission," Breanna said. "Then shove them into the boot of a car, and I'll take it from there." She threw her head back and laughed, making her curls bounce.

"I love her," Rachel exclaimed, looping her arm with Breanna's.

Breanna grinned. "What's not to love?"

"There they are," Danny said, pointing further down the dock where his mates Mark and Tom stood, sporting big grins. Mark was lanky and nerdy, Tom was tall, beefy, and, from the mad look on his face, ready to party. He wore a green rugby jersey with the number thirteen on it. Tara found herself wondering if he was just asking for bad luck. Then again, maybe the lucky Irish thing balanced it out.

"Was she surprised?" Mark called out.

"You got me," Tara said. *And you're all going to get it.*

"Wait," Rachel said. "We're going to have a bachelorette party with your husband-to-be and his groomsman?"

"Not necessarily," Danny said. "It's not a big island, but we can still hide." He winked at Tara.

Tom leaned in and wagged his finger at Rachel. He was a bear of a man with a goatee, and his voice was always the loudest in any room. "It's going to be great *craic*," he said. "You'll be begging to join us."

“Crack?” Rachel asked, her expression horrified.

“The Irish word, *craic*,” Tara explained. “It just means they’re going to have fun.”

“Oh.” Rachel seemed to think about this. “I want craic!” she said. “Blondes just want to have craic!”

“In that case, maybe you should join us,” Tom said. He threw his arms open. “You’re tall enough to ride this ride.”

Tara groaned and rolled her eyes at Tom. It just made him grin and wink. She expected a sarcastic response from Rachel, a no-nonsense New Yorker; instead she was shocked when a schoolgirl giggle erupted from her. Tara had forgotten—to outsiders, the Irish accent was a panty-dropper.

“We should join forces, then,” Rachel sang. “This way, Tara can keep an eye on Danny.”

Mark, the lanky one who usually had his nose in a book, even at the pub, pushed his glasses up and cleared his throat. He gaze fell to a pair of lads standing a few meters away. They were drop-dead gorgeous identical twins, tall with dark hair, probably somewhere in their twenties. They were even dressed identical in denim, black T-shirts, black tap shoes, and green blazers. As Tara’s group looked on, the pair began to tap dance in unison, Irish dancing–style. Mark scooted in. “Do you know who that is?” He jerked his head to the lads.

“I’d certainly like to,” Rachel said. “Look how sharp they look.”

“I cannot believe me eyes,” Breanna said. “It’s them!”

“They look like babies,” Tara said.

"Hot babies," Rachel and Breanna said in unison.

Tara couldn't help but feel a little left out. The pair of them were already bonding.

"Hotter than us?" Tom said, patting his belly and looping his arm around a grimacing Mark.

"This is our lucky day," Breanna said. "Do you know who they are?"

"Competition?" Danny said. He grabbed Tara's hand. "Let's elope right now."

Tara laughed and retracted her hand. "Who are they?" she asked Breanna.

"The Irish Dancing Twins," Breanna said. "Oh my word, are they going to be on our boat?"

"No," Danny said. "This is a private charter." He grinned at Tara. "Surprise!"

"How many more surprises can I expect?" Tara said. *None* was the only answer she wanted to hear.

"And you didn't want a party!" Breanna said, clapping her on the back. "You're welcome."

As if on cue, a boat horn sounded from Captain Mickey's. An older man with a long white beard stepped onto the dock. "All aboard!" he said. "That is if you're here for Danny O'Donnell and Tara Meehan's pre-wedding shenanigans!"

Tara groaned as Rachel and Breanna cheered.

"Excuse me?" This came from one of the dancing twins. Everyone turned as the twins approached.

"I'm Dave, and this is my brother, Noel." Dave was standing to the left, Noel to the right. Noel was wearing a gold cross, but Dave was not. That would help keep them straight. Tara bet they hated when people mixed them up.

"We know who you are," Breanna said, pushing her way through the group to get in front. "We love you!"

The twins flashed easygoing grins. "You're too kind," one said.

"They're going to be competing with each other on *Dancing with the Stars*," Breanna said. "Isn't that fabulous?" She squealed. "You're going to be international stars!"

"One of us will," grinned Noel. "My money's on me."

"I take it you follow our Insta," Dave said. From his expression, he wasn't too happy about it.

"I follow you *everywhere*," Breanna said, clasping her hands. "I'm addicted to ye!" She laughed, and then when she noticed they were simply staring at her, she stopped and cleared her throat. "You know. In a cool, noncreepy sort of way."

"We missed our boat," Noel said. "Because this one needs every hair in place before he leaves the house."

"That's not why we missed the boat," Dave said. "We missed the boat because you can't tell time."

"You're the one who can't turn down an autograph," Noel said. "We would have been on time if you hadn't stopped to scribble your name on some woman's cleavage."

Tom shook his head and looked at his feet as if he'd just lost his best friend. "I'm in the wrong profession."

"Wow," Rachel said, craning her gaze to the sky. "Is that normal?" Dark clouds threatened overhead.

"I told ya, Danny," Mark said. "A storm is coming in. A big one."

"A storm?" Rachel said.

Tara studied the clouds. "Maybe we should postpone."

"Not a chance," Breanna said. "You know weathermen. It's never as bad as they predict."

"Don't worry," Tom said, looping his arm around Rachel. "I'll protect you."

Tara couldn't help it—she scoffed. Heads turned her way. "Rachel's a tough New Yorker. She can handle herself."

"When it comes to the Irish weather, I'd say she might need a big man to hide under," Tom said amiably.

"Everyone was right," Rachel said, grinning. "Irish people are so friendly."

Tom grinned. "I'll be as friendly as you like."

"What would your wife say to that?" Mark asked.

Tom shot him a dirty look. "Ex-wife," he said. "At least she will be." His expression turned dark.

"You're not trying to win her back, then?" Mark persisted. "It's over, like?"

"It is, so," Tom said. "But if she thinks she's cleaning me out in the divorce, she has another think coming."

"Anyhoo," Dave said. "Long story short, do you mind if we hitch a ride?"

The wind picked up. Should they trust this Captain Mickey?

"We have to dance tomorrow at the pub on Inishmore," Noel added. "One of our last dances together before *this one* wins *Dancing with the Stars* and leaves me in the dust."

"We'll dance for our passage," Dave said. He broke

into a little dance, and Noel joined in. They were fabulous. Maybe it would be fun to have them aboard.

"Absolutely," Rachel said at the same time Mark and Tom said no.

"Inishmore!" Breanna exclaimed. "That's where we're headed. Of course you can ride us." Tara nudged her. "Ride *with* us," Breanna corrected.

A horn wailed. Captain Mickey stood on the deck, waving them up. "All aboard! We'd better get a move on if we're going to beat this storm."

Tara threw another glance at the sky. "Maybe this isn't a good idea," she said.

Danny looped his arm around her shoulder. "All me best memories start with really bad ideas."

Chapter Two

Row, Row, Row Your Boat

Tara had to hand it to the Irish dancing twins. Even with the choppy waters as the boat bounced over the wild Atlantic Ocean, they were able to maintain their dancing rhythm. *Tap tap tap, tap tap tap.* "Talented and gorgeous," Rachel said. "Can we hire them to follow us around all weekend?"

"Where's the bride-to-be?" Noel said. Tara, shocked, looked up. He crooked his finger in a *come-hither* motion. He had bedroom eyes, dark hair, an athletic body, and dimples. Tara had an inkling they wielded their looks like a superpower.

"How did you know I'm a bride-to-be?" Tara asked.

Breanna whipped out a tiara, stuck it on Tara's head, and shoved a penis wand in her hand. "Hen party!" Breanna shouted. She and Rachel each took an arm, and they dragged Tara to the front-row seats in front of the dancers.

Noel and Dave began to gyrate their hips in unison, and soon their hands reached for their white button-down shirts. Before Tara could inform them it really wasn't necessary, they had ripped them open. Shirt buttons flew in the air and clinked as they hit the deck. A pair of six-pack-stomachs gyrated in front of her.

"What's happening?" Danny said, staring at the twins' muscular physique with the expression one might expect from an old dog when a new puppy arrives on the scene.

"Sorry!" Captain Mickey said, mistakenly assuming Danny's angst was directed at him. "It's going to be choppy for a spell."

"How are those boozy milkshakes coming?" Breanna sang.

Captain Mickey thrust his finger in the air. "Coming right up."

"Shouldn't you be steering?" Tara asked. It was a big angry ocean and a very tiny ferry. He should definitely be behind the wheel—or whatever it was they used to maneuver this thing.

"Don't worry, lassie. I know when me boat needs me and when she doesn't." He winked. The ferry lurched.

"Are you sure about that?" Tara muttered under her breath. It was best not to insult him while he was making the milkshakes.

"It's one of them!" Tom roared suddenly from the corner of the boat. He was pointing at the twins. Danny and Mark tried holding him back, but Tom broke free and charged toward them. They didn't miss a dancing step; in fact, they barely even glanced at him.

He got in their faces. "One of you slept with my wife!"

"You're getting divorced," Mark said unhelpfully from behind. "Remember?"

Tom turned and glared at his friend. "Because one of them slept with my wife!"

"Which one?" Noel asked casually as they continued to dance.

"I only had one wife," Tom said.

The twins laughed. "He meant which one of us," Dave said. They were unbuttoning their pants.

"Stop," Tara said. "We want the PG show."

"You're no fun," Rachel said. She was clutching a euro in each hand. "She's a wet blanket. Come dance for me."

A wet blanket. Once more Tara wondered what Rachel Madigan was even doing here. Taking over, it seemed. Making Tara feel like she was the boring, sensible one. Even if she was, it still stung. Hunting through estate sales and salvage shops or exploring the Aran Islands under better weather conditions (sans drinking games and party favors) would have been more her idea of a hen party. To each her own.

"Tell me," Tom said. "Which one of you slept with my wife?"

"Soon-to-be ex-wife," Mark said again. This time when Tom glared at his friend, Mark's face turned the color of a beet. He mimed zipping his lips shut and throwing away the key.

"How do you even know it was one of us?" Dave asked.

"Exactly," Noel said. "It could have been both of us." He grinned.

Tara stared at the cross on his neck and could only imagine what his sessions in the confessional were like.

"He's joking," Dave said. "For the most part."

Tom held up his mobile phone. "I know it was one of you because I texted her a photo of the two of you—just to rub it in, like—and she said, 'I slept with one of them.' "

"Why are you still texting her?" Mark nagged. "You said you were only going to speak with her if there was an emergency with the kids, remember?"

"We sleep with a lot of wives," Dave said with a shrug. "Nature of the job."

"Your job is ruining marriages?" Tom said. He pointed to the cross. "You should be ashamed of yourself."

"I don't have to conform to anyone else's rules to wear this," Noel said. "I have no shame."

"Morality isn't so rigid anymore," Dave said. "We're not married. We don't seduce married women. They come on to us—believe me."

"From our experience," Noel said, "the fastest way to kill a romance is with marriage." He glanced at Tara and Danny. "No offense."

Tara leaned into Danny. "It's a good thing you aren't very romantic to begin with."

Danny laughed. "Careful. I might toss you overboard. You can commune with all the little fishies."

Tara grinned. "I rest my case."

"Someone needs to straighten the pair of ye out," Tom said, clenching his fists as he stared at the twins.

"No one is straightening anyone out today," Mark said, tugging Tom away from the twins. "You're over her—you swore to me you were over her."

"Did you hire these eejits?" Danny asked Breanna.

"Me?" Breanna said. "I would have if I'd thought of it." Breanna grinned until she glanced at Tom and her smile evaporated. "No. I did not hire them."

Despite Tara's request, the twins' trousers were starting to come down.

Tara waved her arms. "Keep your clothes on," she said. "That's an order." This time they shrugged and buttoned their pants back up.

"You'll still tip us, right?" one of them said.

"I'll certainly tip," Rachel said, dangling her cash. They grinned and moved toward her. Tara turned to Tom. "No fighting on the boat." Next, she headed for the captain, who was making a mess on the bar. Blenders, milk, a big bottle of Irish whiskey, mint ice cream, and whipped cream littered the counter. "Maybe you should concentrate on steering," she said, as the boat lurched again. "Pretty please?"

"Right," he said, scrunching his face. "But she did pay extra for boozy milkshakes."

"I don't think any of us will be drinking in this weather."

"I'll take over," Breanna said. "We're definitely drinking the boozy milkshakes."

Tara turned to Danny, but he was busy trying to calm down his friend. Rachel was flirting with the twins. "Maybe we could continue the show in private," Tara heard her not-really-a-friend say. "There has to be a little sitting area below deck."

"Stay above deck!" Captain Mickey shouted. "No pawing around me private quarters."

"Who wants a boozy milkshake?" Breanna called out.

Nearly everyone raised their hands. Breanna grinned and began blending. Tara sighed. She was outnumbered. "Someone's going to get sick."

"We're all going to get sick," Breanna said cheerfully. "What kind of a hen party would it be if we didn't?" The milkshake making continued. Soon Breanna was forcing one into everyone's hand. The boat lurched, and a microphone screeched as Captain Mickey began to speak.

"Good evening, ladies and germs. I'm Captain Mickey, your humble seafaring captain. This evening we're headed to 'the islands of saints and scholars.' An authentic Irish-immersion experience awaits you on Inishmore, the largest of the three Aran Islands. The presence of *Homo sapiens* on the island dates back to three thousand BC. Stone age and megalithic monuments abound, strewn on grassy hills bordered by meandering limestone walls. The walls—and there are aplenty—were built with stones plucked directly from the fields. And don't forget to visit the cliffs. If you ask me, they rival the Cliffs of Moher. They are approximately two hundred fourteen meters tall—that's seven hundred feet to you Yanks. On a clear day, you can see across to Galway and Connemara." He paused. "I very much doubt you'll be seeing anything this weekend—

not with the storm—so you might as well just imagine it. Everywhere you look is ocean, the Wild Atlantic Way. And it's okay if you don't speak Irish, although many on the island do. The locals will still have a chat with ye, especially if you make sure to visit the fine shops and restaurants the island has to offer. I very much doubt they'll be open in this storm either, but it's still part of me speech. And even though this weekend you're only visiting Inishmore, does anyone know what the other two islands are called?"

"Inishmaan and Inisheer," everyone but Rachel responded.

Captain Mickey's microphone screeched again. "Preaching to the choir," he said. "On the islands you'll find prehistoric forts, and did I mention the cliffs—"

"Let him keep talking," Breanna said. "But we don't really have to listen." She held up a milkshake in each hand. "I've got milkshakes!"

"That's kind of rude," Rachel said. "He sounds very knowledgeable."

Tara bristled. Who did she think she was, calling Breanna rude? If anyone was rude, it was Rachel.

"Oh, he is, like," Breanna said. "But wouldn't you rather drink?" In case Rachel was clueless, she wiggled her eyebrows. Tara got the impression that Captain Mickey was a blowhard.

"You make a good point," Rachel said, accepting a milkshake.

The boat lurched, and Mark went flying. He slammed into one of the twins, and his milkshake spilled all over the dancer's muscular chest and ripped white shirt. He cursed and the other laughed.

"That's what you get, Noel," Dave said, "for sleeping with your one's wife." Noel removed what was left of his shirt. He went to his backpack, which was lying on a nearby bench, and put on a black T-shirt. It said: IRISH DANCERS ARE JUST A BUNCH OF TREBLE MAKERS. Pictured above in white were three pairs of dancing feet. He cleaned milkshake off the gold cross.

Tom pushed his way forward. "Is he telling the truth?" Tom said, poking Noel in the chest. "Are you the one who slept with my wife?" He turned to Mark and held up a finger. "Not one word."

Mark swallowed and nodded.

"I don't even know who your wife is," Noel said.

Tom brought out his mobile phone, scrolled through, and turned the phone toward him. Noel and Dave leaned in to have a look.

"Ah, right, *her*," Noel said. "She was a fun ride." His look was smug, and it was apparent he was thoroughly pleased with himself.

Tom's face turned crimson. He roared in anger as Noel laughed. "I'm going to kill you," Tom said as his hands went for Noel's throat. Once more, Danny and Mark had to hold him back.

Tara approached Tom, who was struggling to break free of Danny's and Mark's grasp.

"Please," Tara said. "It's in the past. You're getting a divorce. Good riddance, I say. Can we just keep the peace until we're on the island? You'll never have to see either of them ever again."

Tom looked her in the eyes, and she could see waves of emotion churning through him. "Don't get married,

Danny," he said, still looking at Tara. "Take it from me. You're better off alone."

Great.

Rachel approached Tom. "Your ex-wife is a fool," Rachel said. "Cheating on a handsome devil like you." Tara was grateful for Rachel, even if she still wondered what on earth she was doing here.

Tom blinked and stopped struggling. "Let go," he said to Danny and Mark. Reluctantly, they dropped their hands. Tom pointed at the twins. "One more snarky comment, and I'll get you."

"We can take you," Dave said. "We've had plenty of practice."

"Are ye gonna knock me down and tap on me head?" Tom sneered.

Noel pushed in front of his brother. "It's not out of the question."

Breanna ushered the twins up to the bar. "Stay here, lads," she said. "Please."

"We never finished our show," Dave said.

"You finish it," Noel said. "I've had enough."

"You're off the hook," Breanna said, the disappointment in her voice obvious. "Besides, it's mighty cold out."

"That's not an issue for us," Dave said with a lascivious grin.

"These milkshakes are divine," Breanna said a few minutes later as she chugged another one down.

"The milk comes from a famous cow on the Aran Islands," Captain Mickey boomed over the speaker. *He could hear every word they said.* "You should pay him a visit while you're there. Ask anyone about her—they'll know who I'm on about."

"I'd love to meet a famous cow," Breanna said. She glanced at Rachel. "Hear that? You probably see a lot of celebrities in New York, but have ya ever met a famous cow, like?"

Rachel laughed. "The only famous cow we have in America is the O'Leary cow, who kicked over a lantern and started the Chicago fire."

Breanna scrunched her nose. "What?"

Rachel hooked Tara's arm. "Sing with me. 'Late one night, when we were all in bed . . .' "

"I'm liking this song already," Breanna said, making eyes at the twins.

Rachel chimed in with the last line. " 'There'll be a hot time in the old town tonight!' "

Captain Mickey appeared and went straight to the bar, where he looked things over. "There's enough for everyone to have one more boozy milkshake," he announced. He held up a plastic cup and a black Sharpie. "I'm going to write everyone's name on the side. There'll be no arguing over milkshakes."

"You're like Starbucks," Rachel said as she watched him write names on the cups.

"Starbuck?" Captain Mickey perked up. "I'm pleased to meet another Moby Dick fan."

Rachel frowned.

They were halfway to Inishmore. The shores of Doolin had long disappeared. Tara was grateful this ride would soon be over. Between the ocean batting the old ferry around like a bathtub toy and the sound of the blender, she could barely hear the twins on the other side of the boat, but they appeared to be arguing.

"We have to do it," one of them said. "It's mandatory."

"It is not—"

Soon Captain Mickey had cups lined up on the counter. Tara gravitated toward the stern and stared out at the ocean. The next thing she knew, Captain Mickey was nowhere to be seen, and all the lads were up at the bar. The focus of their attention seemed to be on a single milkshake.

"It could stand for Danny," Dave said. He held the milkshake out to Danny.

"It could stand for Dave," Danny said. He looked around. "Where did Captain Mickey go?"

Tara wandered over. "What's the story?"

Danny pointed to the cup still in Dave's hand. On it was written *D-A* and nothing else. "We're not sure if this was meant for me or Dave."

"It could stand for *dancer*," Mark said.

"He said he'd write names on them," Noel said. "My name is not Dancer." His mood had turned as dark as the skies above. He pinched the bridge of his nose. "Are we there yet?"

"Your other milkshake spilled," Dave said, holding it out to Noel. "You should take it."

"Looking out for me, are ya?"

"I always do."

Noel eyed the milkshake.

"Just wait for Captain Mickey," Tara suggested.

"One of you can have it," Danny said, walking away

from the bar. "These waves aren't sitting too well with me."

"No crying over spilled milkshake," Dave said as Noel took it. He downed it, then yelped. "Brain freeze!"

"We'll be coming to shore in about thirty minutes," Captain Mickey announced over the intercom. For the next fifteen minutes, Tara stood at the bow with Danny, watching the waves churn. She heard just one of the twins dancing and turned to see it was Noel.

Tap tap tap, slide slide slide, tap tap tap. He seemed off—even a little drunk. How much booze was in that shake? *Tap tap tap, slide slide slide, tap tap tap*. Just as the sight of the shore was coming into view, Noel cried out. "Mark!" When Tara turned around to see what was going on, Noel was bent over, clutching his stomach and moaning.

Mark approached cautiously. "Did I hear my name?"

"Mark," Noel mumbled, trying to point. Tara looked around just as Tom came into view. Noel then pointed at Tom. Tom looked down at his jersey. "What's the story?" Tom asked. Noel continued to point at him.

"He called for Mark, and then he pointed at Tom," Tara said.

Noel lifted his head, sweat dripping down his face. He pointed at Mark. Then Tom. He looked around feverishly, then pointed at the counter. "The milkshake?" Tara asked. He pointed again. Tara went to the counter. She started pointing at items until she reached the egg carton. He nodded. Then pointed at Mark. Then Tom. "I'm so confused," Tara said.

"Brian O'Driscoll," Tom said, pointing to his jersey. "Number thirteen. One of the best rugby players of all time."

Noel was now furiously pointing at his three new obsessions. Was he accusing one or both of something? Did he think there were eggs in the carton and one of them went bad? Tara pointed to the empty vial. "I do wonder what this is." Noel hunched over. His feet had a mind of their own, tapping away. *Tap tap tap, slide slide slide, tap tap tap.*

"Try to relax," Dave said. "Do you want some water?" He looked around. "Is there any water?"

"Mark," Noel moaned. "Mark."

"Why does he keeping saying my name?" Mark asked. "What do you need?" He shouted at Noel. "What can I do?"

Noel looked at his twin and moaned.

"I'm here, buddy. I'm here," Dave said.

Noel faltered and nearly went to the floor. Dave grabbed one side, and Mark the other. They ushered him to one of the benches at the front of the boat. "We're almost there," Dave said. "Can someone call 999?"

"I don't have service," Danny said, looking at his phone.

"Me neither," came from Mark. Soon everyone chimed in that they did not have any service.

"Maybe Captain Mickey has a radio," Danny said.

As they approached the shore, the horn sounded. Dave stayed on the bench with Noel, and the rest of them gathered at the front of the boat to watch Captain Mickey maneuver them in.

"Finally," Tara said. "I hope we can get a medic right away." Just then, a scream was heard. Tara and Breanna looked at each other for a second, and Tara saw the same terror reflected on Breanna's face that she felt. That was no ordinary scream. They ran back inside the boat. Noel was lying across the front bench, one arm trailing off it, the empty cup on the floor below his hand. Foam pooled at the corner of his mouth. His eyes were open and staring. Dave's head whipped around, his mouth open in shock, his eyes filling with tears. "He's dead," he said. "Me twin is dead."

Chapter Three

Body on Board

The group called out for Captain Mickey as Tara and Breanna held Dave back from Noel's body. While everyone was preoccupied, Tara took out her mobile phone. She began to take photos—just in case the storm battered the small ferry and jostled the evidence before the guards could assess the scene. There was a chance this had been a medical emergency, but the foam pooling at the corner of his mouth and the empty vial gave her pause. Better safe than sorry, and she would delete the photos as soon as the guards had copies of them. First, she photographed the counter, both from afar and zooming in. The blender, the jug of milk, the egg carton used for change—she zoomed in on that empty plastic vial. What had it contained? Why had Noel been pointing at Mark and Tom and the carton? Had he seen one or both take something out of it?

Was he sure about what he saw, or was he in too much pain and not even thinking clearly?

Next, she concentrated on photographing the body and the surrounding area. There were a few objects on the floor near the bench: the black Sharpie, a small silver pebble—or maybe it was a metal piece off one of the twins' tap shoes—and the discarded cup with half the milkshake left in it. The photos were done, including zooming in on the one aspect that made Tara worry this was foul play—*murder*—the white foam around his mouth. Wasn't that a sign of poison? Was something nefarious in his last milkshake? Did it have anything to do with the vial and whatever that tiny piece of silver was all about? Danny wasn't going to be thrilled when Tara informed him that she would have to tell the guards about Noel pointing at Mark and Tom. It was hard to accept that this was happening. A healthy young man struck dead. She felt creepy taking the photos, but who knew how long it would take a coroner to arrive? If this was murder—and she was inclined to think it was—Noel's pointing would not be enough to suss out this killer. This crime scene had to tell a story, and Tara wanted to make sure no one would be able to rearrange anything before the coroner arrived. She would show these photos only to the guards.

"He needs me," Dave crooned. "He needs me." Dave wanted to go to Noel's side. She understood the instinct, but once again, their only shot at justice was to preserve this scene.

"I'm so sorry," Tara said. "He's gone. We simply cannot disturb anything. Ask Breanna—she's with the guards." Tara wasn't sure how mentioning this could help, but maybe it would assure him that this was going to be taken seriously.

"I work as a clerk at the garda station," Breanna said. "But technically I'm a member of the team."

"What are you afraid of disturbing?" Dave asked. "You . . . you think . . . someone did something to him?" His head whipped around. "Is that why he kept saying 'Mark, Mark, Mark'?"

"Why would Mark hurt your brother?" Tara asked. It was Tom who'd threatened to kill them.

"I don't know," Dave said. "Why did Noel keep saying his name?"

"He seemed really confused," Breanna said. "He was also pointing at Tom. I don't think we can put a lot into what he said before he . . ." She left the rest unsaid. It was all too horrific.

"You're right, Dave. We don't know if foul play is involved," Tara said. "A coroner will have to decide that. But if it *was* foul play, don't you want the scene preserved?" She was not going to mention the mysterious empty vial, the piece of silver, or the foam at the corner of Noel's mouth. Dave was already in full freak-out mode. "But either way, I know the guards would want us to stay back so they can do an investigation." Tara nodded at Breanna to chime in.

"Yes," Breanna said. "We definitely need to preserve the scene."

"Investigation?" Dave pointed to the empty milkshake. "That must have killed him," he said. "Where's that bloody captain?"

"That's what we want to know." This came from Mark. They turned to find Danny, Mark, and Tom standing before them, looking perplexed.

Tara took a step forward. "What do you mean?"

"He's gone," Danny said. "Captain Mickey is gone."

"Gone?" Breanna said. "He's the captain. How can he be gone?"

"Did you look in his private quarters?" Tara asked.

"We did, actually," Danny said. "If he's on this boat, he must have a really good hiding place."

"And a lifeboat seems to be missing," Mark said.

"Only if there were an even number of lifeboats," Danny said. "Which there should have been. And if that's the case, he's right. One is missing."

"And so is Captain Mickey," Mark repeated.

"He killed him!" Dave shouted. "Why did Captain Mickey kill him?"

"We can't do this," Tara said. "We can't prove Captain Mickey killed anyone."

"Then where is he?" Dave demanded. "Why did he disappear into thin air?"

He had a point there. She didn't have an answer.

"The milkshake wasn't meant for Noel, remember?" Tom said. Everyone startled.

"*D-A*," Dave said. "It was meant for me."

"Or me," Danny said.

"Maybe he was about to write *danger* on it!" Rachel said.

Breanna cocked her head. "Like he poisoned it and then wanted everyone to know?"

Rachel frowned. "Right. Maybe *dancer*?"

"Everyone, calm down," Tara said. "We don't know anything, including how he died. There aren't many poisons that could kill that fast."

"Poison," Dave said, slapping his hands over his face. "He was poisoned?"

So much for keeping her mouth shut. This was going pear-shaped fast.

"Was he lactose intolerant?" Rachel asked.

Dave shook his head. "Why would he drink a milkshake if he was lactose intolerant, like?"

"I don't know," Rachel said. "I'm only trying to help."

"Do me a favor," Dave said. "*Don't.*"

"We need to get off this boat and call the guards," Tara said, gesturing for everyone to move away.

"I'm not leaving him," Dave said. "I can't leave him."

"Come with us," Tara said. "We'll wait right on shore until the guards arrive."

Dave pointed at Tom, who by now was standing on shore. "You killed him. You said you were going to kill him, and you did!"

"I wasn't anywhere near the milkshakes," Tom said. "And it was just an expression. I might not like the two of ye dancing in the sheets with other men's wives, but Rachel's right. Good riddance to her. I wouldn't risk my freedom over the likes of you."

"Do you mean it this time, Tom?" Mark said. "Do you really mean it?"

Tom whirled on him and shook his head. "Is this really what you want to discuss right now?"

"I just . . . want you to be done with her." Mark's expression had taken on a crazed intensity. They were all coming unglued; trauma could do that to people.

"Dave has just lost his brother," Tara said. "Can we all be a little kinder to each other, please?" *And stop squabbling amongst yourselves?*

Tom crossed his arms and stared at his shoes. "I'm sorry for your loss."

"May he rest in peace," Mark said.

"Peace?" Dave said. "Believe me, there will be no peace until I hunt down whoever killed me brother."

Tara and Breanna got on either side of Dave and began coaxing him off the boat. The rest went ahead of them.

"It was a figure of speech," Tom could be heard saying. "I wouldn't even know how to kill a person with a milkshake." There was a pause. "Was he lactose intolerant?"

"If one more person asks that . . . ," Dave said, freeing his arm from Tara's and holding up his fist. His lips curled into a snarl. They finally disembarked and stood on gravel. A fierce wind had picked up, and the first raindrops began to fall.

"If something was slipped into his milkshake, it had to be from Captain Mickey," Mark said. "He's the one who's missing."

"He was also the one making the shakes," Danny added as they finally guided Dave off the boat.

"I was making the shakes too," Breanna said. "But I only used the ingredients that were already laid out."

"It doesn't matter who was making the shakes," Tom said. "Any one of us could have slipped something into his drink. All of us were at the bar at one time or another."

"The guards will get to the bottom of it," Tara said. "We do not yet have a cause of death. That's why none of us can go back on the boat. We must stay off and make sure everything is left exactly as it was." She looked at each member of the group. "I need to see that you understand." One by one everyone finally nodded.

"I still can't get a signal," Danny said, holding up his mobile phone. The clouds were black above them, and the rain was coming down harder.

"I told you the weather report was warning of a storm this weekend," Mark said.

Danny looked sheepish. "I figured it didn't matter, that we'd be in the pubs most of the time anyway."

"I can't get a signal either," Tom chimed in. One by one they checked their phones. No one had a signal. The skies opened up.

"Let's get up to the pub," Danny said. "Maybe someone is around."

He was right. There was no use standing here, hoping someone would come. A gravel path led up to the main entrance of the island. They'd taken the last ferry, and no other boats were docked. Everyone was preparing for the storm. Why had Captain Mickey even taken them? Shouldn't he have known better? *Was* he a killer? Why would he possibly have wanted one of them dead? It was eerily quiet. The rain was now coming down sideways, and as they pushed forward, the wind tried to push them back.

"Run!" Danny said as thunder boomed and lightning struck the mast.

"I can't leave him," Dave said, looking back to the ferry. "I can't."

"Lean on us," Tara said. "You have to." This time, she and Danny got on either side of Dave as they made their way to the island. *No hen party,* she'd told Breanna over and over again. Why didn't anyone ever listen to her?

The storm was raging by the time they fought their way up the path from the ferry to the island. The raindrops stung, and visibility was a joke. The wind was literally tripping everyone up.

"The pub is just ahead of us!" Danny yelled.

"What about the garda station?" Tara asked. With the severity of the wind and rain, she had a feeling it was going to be a while before power was restored.

"Kilronan," Breanna said. "Straight up Cottage Road."

"We have to go there first," Tara said. "How long of a walk?"

"Normally about five minutes, pet. In this wind, might be more like fifteen."

"Let's leg it, then," Danny said. "Before we all catch our deaths."

Dave cried out. "My brother," he wailed. "My brother!"

"We're going to get you some help," Tara said. "Find a medical center—they can give you something to help calm your nerves." They all began to trudge up Cottage Road. Normally this view was lovely, with quaint Irish shops, The Bar, farmhouses and stone walls, rolling hills leading up to the cliffs, and the glorious Atlantic Ocean. Now it was all washed out. Normally, Tara felt a sense of excitement during big storms. But right now it was the last thing they needed. She could see the lads being clueless, but had Breanna even checked a weather report? There was no use whining about it now.

"Are the guards even going to be there?" Tom asked. "There's no one out."

"How do you even know?" Danny said. "I can't see a thing."

"Just keep walking," Breanna said. "As long as we're going uphill, we're headed in the right direction."

"I can go faster," Mark said. "Why don't I run ahead of you?"

"I think we should stick together," Danny said. "This storm is no joke."

"We can probably all go faster," Tara said. "The sooner we get there, the better."

They picked up the pace, leaning into the wind. None of them had even thought to bring a raincoat. Or Wellies. The ground beneath them was turning to muck. They would be lucky if they didn't fall and break an ankle or get sick. Tara felt her teeth chattering. She mustered up her strength and just kept pushing through. Although it felt like forever, it was probably only twenty minutes later when she heard Breanna's voice cutting through the wind.

"Nearly there, lads. It's just up here," she said.

In the distance, Tara could make out a blur of white. The garda station. She hated to admit it, but all she could think about now was getting out of this weather. Soon they were at the door to the Kilronan Garda

Station, and to Tara's relief, when Breanna pushed on the front door, it swung open.

"Jaysus, shut it quick," a man's voice yelled. They piled into the station and shut the door. What a sight they must be, seven drowned rats dripping water and shivering. A stocky guard came out to greet them.

"Don't tell me you're another group of tourists that didn't pay attention to the directive?"

"We're local," Danny said. "We just arrived."

"Ferry service from Doolin was shut down hours ago," the guard said, clearly perturbed. "What do you mean you've just arrived?"

"We chartered a private boat," Breanna said. "Captain Mickey."

"Captain Mickey?" The guard groaned. "His license was suspended. Where is he? He's lost his second chance."

Was that why he was in the wind? Or was it because he was a cold-blooded murderer?

"There's more," Breanna said as she introduced herself and her position as a clerk at the Galway Garda Station. "And you're definitely not going to like it."

After they heard the terrible news, the guards ushered the group into a pair of squad cars. The guards would take them to the cottage Breanna had booked, but they were ordered to stay put until the guards had a look at the crime scene. "Expect a long wait," one of them said. "It might be days before the coroner can make it."

Tara knew it. She was relieved she'd taken photos.

She would have to find a private moment to tell them. The car bounced along beat-up roads, but at least they were safe from the rain. Soon, the blur of a thatched roof came into view. The squad car pulled up in front of a modest stone cottage that Tara probably would have adored under better circumstances.

"Can we all fit in here?" Tom asked as Breanna found the key where she'd been instructed to look and struggled to open the door. She finally got it open, and they all stepped inside. It was dark and smelled damp.

"We need to find the light switch," Breanna said.

A torch flicked on. The guard held it underneath his face, giving his paunchy cheeks an eerie glow. "No electricity, lads," he said. "I can leave this with ye, but I'd suggest rummaging in the drawers for matches, candles, torch batteries—we'll be without power for days, weeks even."

"Weeks?" Rachel shrieked.

"Hen party, woo-hoo!" Tara couldn't help but say.

"You're lucky you have a roof over your head," the guard said. "But I gather it won't be long before she's leaking, so. You might want to scrounge around for pots and pans."

"Alcohol?" Rachel said. "Is there alcohol?"

"You will all need to be questioned about the incident on the boat, so I repeat: you are being advised to remain in this cottage." The guard switched off the torch, plunging them into darkness. "Batteries don't last forever, mind ye," he said.

"We won't go anywhere," Tara said.

"Can we go out for supplies?" Danny asked. "We need food, drink, more torches . . ."

"Maybe you'll get lucky and find that someone left something behind," the guard said. "But all the shops are closed. Did ye really pay no attention at all to the warnings, like?"

"They're getting married," Breanna said, pointing to Tara and Danny, as if this was all their fault.

No hen party! Tara shouted silently. *I said no hen party!*

"Tell ye what," the guard said, his tone softening. "I'll bring ye whatever supplies we have at the station. I'll have a guard drop it off in an hour so. But otherwise, you make do with whatever you have until further notice. Understand?"

"Understood," Breanna said.

"Please," Dave said. "My poor brother."

Tara's eyes were starting to adjust to the dark. The guard removed his cap and held it to his chest. "My condolences," he said. "May he rest in peace."

"He was poisoned," Dave said.

"We don't know that for sure," Tara said quickly. "He died after drinking a milkshake."

"A milkshake?" the guard said. "In a storm?"

"To be fair, the storm only started shortly after we disembarked," Rachel said.

"American," he said. "You are tourists."

"She's a tourist," Danny said, pointing to Rachel. "And she's a transplant," he said, nudging Tara. "But the rest of us are locals."

"Then it's the rest of ye I blame," the guard said as he placed his cap back on. "Eejits." And with the slam of the door, he was gone.

Chapter Four

Truth or Dare

The interior of the cottage consisted of a combined kitchen and sitting area with two bedrooms just off the main room and a small bathroom down a hall. It was perfect for three women; it was claustrophobic with all seven of them—but then again, they were out of the rain and the wind, and as she listened to it rattle the windows and screech outside, Tara was grateful.

"If I weren't soaked to the bone, starving, and thirsty, I'd say this was totally cool," Rachel said.

"We're like survivors on a deserted island," Mark said. "Except for all the other people, on the island, like."

"We all need to change out of these wet clothes as quickly as possible," Tara said. "I'll check the towels in the bathroom. If you brought your own towels—"

"We don't have our luggage," Breanna pointed out. "It's still on the boat."

Tara slapped her forehead. She truly wasn't thinking. Of course. All their things were still on the boat.

"Do you think the guards will bring them to us?" Rachel said. "Should we try to catch him?"

"You think you can run after a squad car that left ten minutes ago in the storm of the century?" Mark asked.

Rachel seared him with a look. Mark's cheeks blazed red as he gazed at his wet shoes.

"We can't stay in these clothes," Tara said. "We'll get sick."

"We get creative, then," Danny said. "Towels, blankets, sheets—we can even use curtains if we have to."

"You're joking me," Tom said.

"There's no choice," Breanna said. "It's a brilliant idea. In the meantime, we can hang our clothes around the place to dry—hopefully get a fire going." She headed to the bathroom and returned with four towels. "We can all take turns drying off, but go easy."

"I'll check the closets," Rachel said.

"Let's all check everywhere," Tara said. "Anything you find that can become a makeshift outfit, put it on the dining table."

"Anything you find that we can eat or drink, same," Breanna said.

"Or smoke," Tom added.

"Even a pack of cards," Danny said. "We'll need something to entertain ourselves."

"Is he serious about smoking?" Rachel said. "No smoking in the cabin."

"And here I thought you were going to be fun," Tom said.

"Let's hope someone left something here of use,"

Danny said. The mission seemed to energize them. They very much needed to focus on something so that the thought of poor Noel lying dead on that boat didn't overwhelm them. Was it possible he died of natural causes? Tara sure hoped so. Otherwise they might be stuck in a tiny cottage on a remote island during the storm of a century with a killer. She was new to hen parties, but she was pretty sure this one would go down in the history books as the worst one ever. She hoped it wasn't a sign of the marriage to come.

Minutes later, they looked as if they had dressed like lunatics on purpose—sheets, old robes, towels, and in Dave's case, a bedroom curtain. Despite the somber mood of a recent death, or maybe because of it, the group took one look at each other, and everyone burst out laughing. Their clothes had been wrung out and were lying about to dry.

But they had found a few things. One more torch, a pack of matches, a can of beans, and two bottles of Bulmers.

They tried the torch. It worked. "We can keep one on and have the other as backup," Tom said. He shone the light from one of the torches around the room.

"What's that?" Danny asked as the light bumped over something in one of the dining room chairs. Tom focused the light. It was a backpack.

"That's mine," Dave said. "I didn't let Captain Mickey take it."

"Why is that?" Rachel asked, her forehead wrinkling as if she was suspicious.

"Because it has my good tap shoes," Dave said. "I always keep them close."

"Is there anything else in there?" Breanna said.

"Anything we can use?" Tom edged forward. Soon, several of them were surrounding Dave and eyeing the backpack.

"I was saving it for a surprise," Dave said.

The wind rattled the windows, making everyone jump. Rain gushed sideways outside. "I'd say we could all use a surprise about now," Mark said, adjusting a very large robe he'd found in the closet.

Dave unzipped the pack and pulled out a bottle of whiskey. Nearly everyone whooped. "I don't want to seem like I'm celebrating," he said. "But I could really use a drink."

"I don't think we should start drinking," Tara said.

"Are you joking me?" Breanna's hands were on her hips, a bedsheet tied toga-style around her. "We're on the Aran Islands in a mad storm, wearing bedsheets, towels, and curtains, after an extremely tragic morning. Not to mention those boozy milkshakes are starting to wear off, it's your hen party and you've literally nowhere to go, and you *still* don't want to party?"

Tara looked around to find everyone staring at her with the same expression: *Come on!*

Tara adjusted her sheet. "You have a point." Cheers went up around the room.

"We should set a few ground rules," Tom said, "before the drinking begins."

"Like what?" Danny O'Donnell did not like rules, and his tone reflected that.

"First of all, until we know what or who killed Noel, we shouldn't ever let each other out of our sight."

Dave held up the bottle. "It's never been opened," he said. "Anyone is welcome to check."

"That seems a bit extreme," Rachel said.

"Actually, it doesn't," Danny said. "One of us could be a killer."

"One of you, you mean," Rachel said. "Because I am not a killer, my bestie is not a killer"—she poked Tara's arm—"and I very much doubt the garda clerk is a killer."

"Thanks," Breanna said. "I think."

Her bestie? Tara had been meaning to ask Breanna exactly what gave her the idea that she'd want Rachel Madigan to join them on this trip. They hadn't spoken in years. And even back in their New York days, Rachel had been competitive. Starting with their first day at FIT, the Fashion Institute of Technology in Manhattan, where they started their interior design education. Friends, of a sort—maybe colleagues, but *besties?* Rachel was driven and a very sore loser. Not that Tara thought she was a killer. Why would Rachel harm one of them? She didn't even know Noel. Or Dave. Or Danny. The letters written on the cup were *D-A*—had it been meant for Dave or Danny? Did Noel just get extremely unlucky? What if someone was after her husband-to-be?

"Poison is a woman's game," Mark said, his gaze bouncing between Rachel, Tara, and Breanna. "It has to be one of you."

"You really think I have it in me to be a killer?" Breanna asked. She sounded almost hopeful.

"Captain Mickey must be the killer," Dave said. "Isn't that what everyone said earlier?"

"It makes the most sense," Danny said. "Unless . . ." He paused as the whiskey bottle was passed to him. He took a drink, then passed it Tara. She stared at the bottle. It seemed no one was worried about germs either. She passed it on without taking a drink. Unfortunately, it was Breanna standing next to her, and Breanna shoved it right back at her.

"We're in this together," Breanna said. "Horse it into ya."

Tara hadn't felt this kind of pressure since high school. She drank, wincing as the whiskey hit the back of her throat, and passed it to Breanna once more.

Dave swallowed hard. "It does indeed seem odd that Captain Mickey is missing. But . . . what if . . ." His voice rose in pitch.

Everyone took a step toward Dave. "What if what?" Danny prompted.

"What if the killer threw Captain Mickey overboard?" Dave blurted out.

Gasps were heard around the room as they considered this.

"Diabolical," Rachel whispered. "Is that whiskey ever coming around to me?"

Breanna handed over the bottle. "Captain Mickey is a big man," Breanna said. "He would have made a big splash."

"It was rather loud on the boat," Tom said. "All that tap dancing. It's possible we missed a splash."

"It's Irish dancing," Dave corrected.

"It still made noises, like tap, tap, tap," Tom said.

"If Captain Mickey was thrown overboard, then who steered the boat to the dock?" This came from Mark.

"Good point," Tara said.

"Anyone here know how to operate a ferry?" Danny asked.

"Like the killer is going to out himself," Rachel said.

"Or *herself*," Mark added.

"Oh, right," Rachel said. "Because poison is a woman's game."

Mark put one finger on his nose and pointed the other at Rachel. She rolled her eyes. "If I was going to kill someone, I would probably use a knife," she said. "Something small and pretty with a pearl handle."

"Rachel," Tara said.

"What?" She put her hands on her hips. "I carry one in New York."

Tara wondered how she could be so glib in front of Dave. His twin was gone. She could only imagine how close they were, even sharing the same passion and performing together. It had to be stressful at times. But from everything she'd heard, they were somewhat famous. They probably made good money. Dave was facing losses on all fronts, although right now all that mattered was that someone he loved had tragically died. Tara turned to Rachel. "Isn't it illegal to carry a knife in New York?"

"I have no clue." Rachel shrugged. "Who cares about illegal when your life is in jeopardy?"

"Are you carrying a knife now?" Danny asked.

Rachel swept her hand down the very short towel

she had wrapped around herself. "Would you like to search me?"

Danny politely declined.

"If the killer threw Captain Mickey overboard, why would he leave Noel lying on the boat?" Tara pointed out.

They all took this in. No matter how they looked at it, this situation was baffling. Breanna began putting logs on the fire. At least they had matches and enough kindling and dry wood stacked inside for one good one. "We're not going to solve this among ourselves," Breanna continued as she stacked wood in the fireplace. "We didn't even examine the crime scene."

Breanna must not have seen Tara snapping photos with her mobile phone. Had anyone else taken any? On one hand, they could compare and see if anything stood out, on the other, short of Danny and Breanna, Tara just didn't know who she could trust.

"The minute there's a break in the storm, we need to find Captain Mickey," Dave said, taking a sip out of the whiskey bottle. "He's either a killer or he ran because he was afraid he'd take the blame."

"The guards will search for him once the weather clears," Breanna said, as she lit the kindling and the fire began crackling.

"I can't just sit around and do nothing," Dave said. "I have to find Captain Mickey."

"If he's on the island, there's only so many places he could go," Mark said.

"What are we going to do? Knock on doors?" Rachel asked.

"He mentioned something about a famous cow," Danny said. "Maybe we start there."

"No one is going anywhere right now," Tom said as he took the bottle. "Shall we play Truth or Dare?"

Tara groaned, then pretended she was coughing when everyone gave her a look. "Yay," she said. "Truth or Dare."

Breanna's shoulders slumped. "I left the penis wands on the ferry."

"How disappointing," Tara said, hoping she was managing to keep a straight face.

"Truth?" Breanna asked, starting off the game. The fire was humming, and they were all huddled around it. Breanna pointed at Rachel. "Or dare?"

"Dare," Rachel said.

Tara had been hoping she'd pick truth. She wanted to know what she was really doing here.

"I dare you to go outside and stay there for ten minutes," Breanna said. The rain was still biblical.

"No," Tara leapt up at the same time as Rachel. "It's not safe, and there's nothing else for her to wear."

"I think I saw a tablecloth," Breanna said.

"It's my hen party, and I say no stupid dares."

Breanna stuck her lip out, but if she wanted to reply, she thought better of it.

"The entire point of the game is stupid dares and juicy secrets," Tom said.

"One tragedy is enough for today, thank you very much," Tara insisted.

"I have one for all of you," Dave said. "Truth! Did

you murder my brother?" He pointed his finger and pivoted until he'd indicated every single one of them. They all simply stared back at him.

"What about Two Truths and a Lie?" Rachel said.

"What's that?" Danny asked.

"We go around and each say three things about ourselves. Two of them have to be the truth, and one of them has to be a lie. Then everyone guesses which one is the lie."

"I'd play that," Breanna said. "Except some of us know each other pretty well—that's not very fair."

"In that case, everyone will need to think of something no one else knows," Rachel said. "A juicy secret or two."

"You start," Breanna said with a nod to Rachel.

"Okay. Let me think. Okay. I've been skydiving. I eloped in Vegas. I'm shocked I was invited to this hen party because I thought Tara Meehan hated my guts." She smiled at Tara as if she had just said something pleasant.

"I . . . I don't hate your guts," Tara said. "But to be honest, I was surprised—"

"No, no, no," Rachel said. "That's not how you play the game. Which one is a lie?"

"You eloped in Vegas is a lie," Tara said.

Rachel stuck her lip out. "No fun."

"Can I continue with my statement now?" Tara asked.

"No," Rachel said. "It's your turn."

Tara gazed out at the heavy rain. "This is the worst storm I've ever been in. If Rachel thought I hated her guts, I wonder why she came, and . . . I love drinking whiskey out of a bottle that everyone else had their mouths on."

Breanna crossed her arms. "You're cheating. Obviously, it's the last one."

Dave popped up. "Me twin is dead, he'll probably go to heaven because he was the devout one, and now I don't know whether or not to go on *Dancing with the Stars*."

"Those all sound like truths," Danny said.

"Oh," Dave said. "They are."

"That's a big deal, *Dancing with the Stars*," Tara said.

Dave nodded. "It's our big break. Was our big break. So close to fame and me brother is dead. They wanted both of us to take turns dancing with the same woman—as if we're literally the same person. It would have been great craic." He lifted his chin. "I'm willing to do it—in honor of Noel—but will they even want me now? Will they want the dancer with the dead twin?"

Chapter Five
On Guard

"This must be so hard for you," Rachel said to Dave. "I'm so, so sorry."

"I wanted to cancel this weekend," Dave said. "But Noel insisted. If the pub was going to stay open through the storm, then we were going to go." He sighed. "He was a man who took his obligations seriously."

"Let's have a moment of silence for him, will we?" Breanna said.

Dave's eyes filled with tears, and he nodded. "I wish I knew a prayer or something. Noel was the one who went to mass."

"We can all say a silent prayer in our moment of silence," Rachel said. They bowed their heads, and quiet fell on the group. Rachel was the first to speak. "You must want to call your family," she said, looking at Dave.

"My family?" For a moment Dave looked startled.

He shook his head. "I'm not looking forward to breaking me mammy's heart. I want her to stay in a world where Noel is still alive."

"If the storm lets up for a spell, we should try and make it to The Bar," Danny said.

"We're going to a pub dressed like this?" Mark asked.

"No one will care," Danny said. "Besides, they probably sell T-shirts."

"What good is a T-shirt without pants?" Mark said. "I'm staying here."

"We're not separating," Tara said. "And the guards told us to stay put, remember?"

"We're not under arrest," Danny said. "They can't force us to stay."

"You really think the pubs will be open?" Rachel asked.

"I bet you The Bar will be open," Danny said. "I'll bet ye they have a generator."

"And food?" Tom said. "I'm starving."

"Maybe they'll know where I was supposed to spend the weekend," Dave said. "Noel always kept track of our accommodations." He wiped away a tear running down his cheek. "We were supposed to dance at The Bar this weekend."

"I really don't want to go outside in this, lads," Breanna said gesturing to her toga-style sheet.

Tara sighed. "I don't think our clothes are going to dry anytime soon."

"There's a hair dryer in the bathroom," Breanna said, perking up.

Rachel shot up. "Why didn't you say so? Let's start drying our clothes."

"There's no electricity," Tara reminded them. They slumped at the realization.

"We can rotate pieces around the fire," Rachel said.

"Good idea," Danny said. "I'll move a few chairs nearby."

"I totally forgot!" Breanna said as the lads began moving chairs close to the fire. "A penis cake was supposed to have been delivered to a shop near The Bar."

"We're definitely going, then," Rachel said.

"I doubt the shops will open for us," Danny said. "But we're going to need more clothes if we don't get our suitcases."

Tara went to the window. "We still have to wait," she said. "And we'll have to wear wet shoes."

"We should place those by the fire too," Rachel said.

Tara continued to watch the rain as Breanna and Rachel set about gathering clothes. Soon, clothing and shoes were all cuddled up near the fire. Tara gazed into the flames, wishing they were here under happier circumstances. Danny snuck up behind her and put his arms around her. "What are you thinking about?"

"Do you know Captain Mickey?" she asked him.

"I do." Danny's voice was guarded. "Why do you ask?"

"Because the twins weren't supposed to be on the boat, remember?"

"Right," Danny said. "They'd missed theirs."

"Which means Captain Mickey hadn't planned on poisoning one of them."

"Maybe it was a spontaneous decision."

"But he did know you were going to be on the boat, and he wrote *D-A* on the cup."

Danny dropped his arms. "Why would Captain Mickey want me dead?"

"Did you owe him money?" Danny was known to play a poker game or four hundred.

"Are you joking me? Captain Mickey wouldn't have let me on the boat if I owed him money. He was a stickler." Danny shook his head. "Maybe Noel had some kind of condition we're not aware of. Maybe it was a heart attack."

"There was foam at the corner of his mouth," Tara said. "And he'd been drinking the milkshake."

"Are there any poisons that kill that fast?"

"I'm sure there are a few." Tara had a question to ask Danny, but she wasn't sure how he was going to take it. "Tom seemed as if he wanted to kill Noel," she said lightly.

"He can be hotheaded, but think about it. If he really planned on killing him, would he have lost his cool like that? Announced it?"

"Maybe he didn't mean it—until he did."

"And what—he just happened to have a deadly poison on him?"

"Maybe he found something on the boat."

"He was with me most of the time."

"Most of the time. But not all."

"What you don't know is that Tom's ex-wife stepped out on him more than once. With other men too. And he didn't kill them."

"Maybe he didn't get the chance."

"Hey, lovebirds," Tom called from across the cabin. They turned, and he threw a shirt their way. It was Danny's, and he caught it.

"Not bad," Danny said. "It's wearable." He touched Tara on the shoulder and whispered in her ear. "If I had to pick one of my friends to be a killer, it would be Mark."

"Really?" Tara hadn't been expecting that.

"What is it they say about the quiet ones?" Danny said. "Still waters run deep?" Tara looked around until she spotted Mark. He was standing by the fire. And if she wasn't mistaken, he had just thrown something into it. He caught her staring and stared back. "Maybe we shouldn't be talking about this here," Danny said. Danny was right, of course. They were stuck together for now. She'd be relieved when they were finally at the pub. Why did Mark look so uneasy, and what had he thrown in the fire?

A knock sounded on the door, making them jump. Tara looked out the window. "I see several men in dark raincoats, but I don't know who they are."

"Don't open it," Dave said. "They could be psychopaths."

"Psychopaths generally don't knock," Danny said as he headed to the door and opened it. They all gathered as three guards stepped inside the cottage. One held a cardboard box that he thunked on the dining table. "There's a bit of grub we rustled up. This should last you until the pub is open."

"When will that be?" Danny asked.

"They're working on getting the generator running. I'd say it will be open by the morning."

"Morning," Rachel said. "Morning."

"We have food, drink, and fire," Tara said.

"Ms. Optimistic as always," Rachel muttered.

Dave stepped forward. "Did you find Captain Mickey? Did you?" He shut his eyes. "Did you see what he did to me brother?"

"About that," the oldest guard said stepping forward. "If there wasn't this storm to deal with, we'd think about hauling you pack of liars into the station."

"Pack of liars?" Breanna said. "What are you on about?"

"Did you or didn't you find Captain Mickey?" Tara asked.

"We found Captain Mickey and his boat," the guard said. "What we didn't find was a dead body."

Chapter Six

The Storm Worsens

The group stared at the guards with open mouths.

"That's impossible," Tara said. "We all know there was a body." Everyone nodded.

"I wouldn't lie about me twin being dead," Dave said. He was choked up and convincing. The guards removed their hats and placed them on their chests.

"May he rest in peace."

"How?" Dave said. "How will he rest in peace when his body, not to mention his killer, is in the wind?"

"With all due respect . . . exactly how much did ye drink on the way over?" the guard standing in the middle asked.

"Captain Mickey likes getting his passengers drunk," another said.

"Especially if there are Yanks on board," added the third.

Dave took a step up. "That's what you're telling me, is that so? You're telling me I'm lying about my twin being *murdered*?" His voice trembled, but his tone was defiant.

"Murdered?" the middle guard said. "Now you're saying he was murdered?"

"He had stomach cramps right after drinking a milkshake," Tara said. "We think it may have been poisoned."

"Not for nothing," Mark piped up, "but poison is a woman's game."

The women in the cabin glared at him.

"I don't have to let ye stay with us," Breanna said. "Didn't you three book a cabin of your own?"

Danny turned red. "I figured we'd be outside or in the pub the whole time," he said. "Bachelor style."

"Typical," Breanna said. "One more word out of Mark about us being the ones who poison, and I'm going to start thinking he doth protest too much."

"You're saying I killed Noel? I'm not the one out for blood." He glanced at Tom. Tom glowered.

"I have pictures," Tara said. "Of the crime scene." Where was her mobile phone?

"You do?" Dave said, whirling on her. "That's disgusting."

"I assure you, it was only to show the guards," Tara said. "You know. In case they thought we were big, fat liars." She grabbed her coat and stuck her hand in the pocket. No phone. Was it in her handbag? Had someone stolen it? Why hadn't she kept a better eye on it? She went for the bag, praying her phone would be there. She dug through her purse, panic mounting. The killer had taken it! The killer must be one of them—and the guards were going to think she was a liar. Just then, she felt it all the way at the bottom. Relief flooded her. She had to watch herself; it was too easy to freak out. She brought it out and poked at the screen. "The battery is dead, and we've no signal," she said.

The middle guard held his hand out. "We'll take it back to the station to charge."

"That is, if our generators hold out," the one to his left added unhelpfully.

Tara didn't hand it over. "How do we know you're really guards?"

"What exactly are you accusing us of, lassie?" said the one on the left.

Breanna stepped forward. "I'm a clerk at the Galway Garda Station," she said. "Breanna Cunningham."

Their scowls disappeared, and the middle one nodded. "I'm Detective Sergeant Kehoe," he said.

"Tara has been a big help to the guards in Galway," she said. "She's only being careful because . . . well, these circumstances are so unusual."

"And you're not wearing your uniforms," Tara said. "Nor did you officially introduce yourselves."

"We're dressed for the weather," Sergeant Kehoe said. "But no offense taken." He dug a badge out of his pocket and held it up.

"It looks legit," Breanna said.

"Does it, now?" Kehoe said. "And to think I got it at the bottom of a cereal box." The guards laughed. "Now will you please hand over your mobile phone?" Sergeant Kehoe continued. "We'll take it to the station and charge it."

"I'd like to come with you," Tara said. "I'm going to need my phone as soon as the power comes back on."

Kehoe crossed his arms. "All of you are sticking to this story?"

Heads nodded, one by one. "It's not a story," Dave said. "It's my brother's *murder*."

"Honestly, there's a chance he had a cardiac arrest or some such, but I did observe foam pooling at the corner of his mouth, and as I said, his stomach cramped shortly after drinking a milkshake," Tara said.

"Get a load of this one," a guard said. "She thinks she's the coroner."

"A milkshake?" Kehoe said. "In this weather?"

"Did it bring all the boys to the yard?" the one to the left joked. Once more, the guards all laughed heartily.

Were they ever going to take this seriously?

"Since when does Captain Mickey make milkshakes any day, let alone on a day like this?" Sergeant Kehoe said.

"Since we're having a hen party for this one," Rachel said, stepping up and looping her arm around Tara. "Although I'd never heard of the term. In the States, we call it a bachelorette party."

Kehoe eyed the men.

"I'm the groom-to-be," Danny said. "We decided to tag along."

"Don't trust her, is that it?" Kehoe said, amused.

Tara felt as if she'd been struck. That couldn't be the reason Danny wanted to tag along. He trusted her. Didn't he?

"That's not it at all," Danny said. "I would just rather celebrate with her than without her." Danny threw her a smile, and she felt her suspicions start to melt.

"Are you really going stand there and do nothing?"

Dave asked. "Before he died, me brother called out Mark's name, then pointed at this one." Dave gestured to Tom. "My brother also slept with your one's wife." Once again he pointed to Tom. "*And* he threatened to kill him."

"Your brother slept with his wife?" Kehoe asked.

"That's the bit you remember?" Dave glowered. "Tom threatened to kill me brother. And by the end of the boat ride, me brother ends up dead."

"You were all drinking the milkshakes, were you not?" Kehoe asked.

"We were," Dave said. "But there was one left on the counter. Captain Mickey said he was going to make one more batch and write our names on the cups."

"Like at Starbucks," Kehoe said.

"That's what I said," Rachel piped in. Kehoe winked at her.

"Anyhow," Dave said in a tone that suggested he didn't appreciate the interruptions, "we didn't know if the shake was for Danny, or Dave—"

"Or *danger* or *dancer*," Rachel said.

"Or Prancer or Vixen," one of the guards said.

"Enough!" Dave roared. "This is not a joke. This is my brother's life. And one of these two killed him." Dave pointed at Mark and Tom. "Or maybe they were in on it together."

"Definitely not," Mark said. "And I'm not the one who threatened to kill anyone."

"It was an expression," Tom said quickly. "And I really don't care that he slept with my wife—soon-to-be ex-wife."

"You keep saying that," Mark said. "But when are you going to mean it?"

"Where did you find Captain Mickey?" Danny asked. "And what did he say?"

"We found him on his boat," Kehoe said. "Doing a bit of cleaning."

"Oh my word," Breanna said. "It was him."

"Cleaning up the evidence," Mark agreed.

"He said one of you was sick on the boat," Kehoe said.

"He's lying," Danny said. "There's your proof right there."

"Wait," Rachel said. "Are we sure he was dead? Maybe he was just really sick."

"He was dead," Dave said. "I know dead when I see it!"

"Besides, did you see a sick twin on the ferry?" Tara asked, turning to Kehoe.

"No."

"Did Captain Mickey say he'd called for an ambulance?" Tara continued.

Kehoe shook his head.

"Captain Mickey's behavior should tell you everything you need to know," Danny said. "He's guilty."

"Given you could all be liars too, lying is not what I would call proof," Kehoe said.

"What did he say when you asked him about a body?" Tara asked.

Kehoe frowned. "How exactly are you affiliated with the guards in Galway?"

Tara hesitated. "I've helped them on a few cases."

"Helped them how? Don't tell me you're one of those psychics."

"That's her aunt, Rose," Breanna said.

"Not helping," Tara said. It was true. Her uncle, Johnny, married a well-known psychic. She wished Rose was here now. "I've been in the wrong place at the wrong time on a few occasions," Tara admitted.

"Translation: everywhere she goes, dead bodies follow," Breanna said.

"Really not helping," Tara said.

"And here you are again," Kehoe said. He narrowed his eyes at her.

Tara held her hands up. "All we have to do is charge my mobile phone. Once you see the pictures, you'll definitely need to ask Captain Mickey why he lied."

"And why he ran away," Mark said.

"And why he was cleaning up the crime scene," Tom said.

"I told you we shouldn't have left the boat. I told you!" Dave began to moan.

"We searched the entire boat," Tom said. "Captain Mickey disappeared at the same time we found Noel's body."

"Noel?" Kehoe said.

"My brother," Dave said. "Noel Carrigan."

"Noel Carrigan," Kehoe said. "The Irish Dancing Brothers?"

Dave nodded. "I'm the brother." He began to tap dance to prove it. They watched him for a while, nodding their heads appreciatively. Most likely, none of them had ever seen someone dance so well while sobbing. Finally, Kehoe held up his hand. Tara was relieved to see him pull a notebook out of his coat. The twins' celebrity status had perked him up. From his coat, he removed what looked like a handheld radio. He clicked a button and static filled the air.

"Yes, Sergeant?" came a female voice.

"Is Garda Collins in the station?"

"Not at the moment. As you know, we have a number of distress calls."

"When he checks in, tell him to meet us at the harbor. And if he gets there first, will ye have him ask Captain Mickey to come into the station?"

Finally. Even if it was because the twins were celebrities.

"Yes, Sergeant." The radio clicked off.

"I'm going to need all of you to stay here," Sergeant Kehoe said. "We'll sort this out."

"We need food," Tara said.

A guard nodded to the box on the table. "We brought sandwiches, crisps, a few apples, cookies, bottled water—it's not much, but ye won't starve to death."

"I see you have whiskey," Kehoe added, eyeing the bottle.

"To be fair, it's been a traumatic day," Tara said.

"If you hand over your mobile phone, I'll charge her up, and I promise to bring her back once we've had a look at these supposed photos." Kehoe looked at Dave. "If you're telling the truth, I'm sorry for your loss." He took off his hat and placed it on his chest. "May he rest in peace."

"They'll be no peace until his killer is caught," Dave said.

"Do any of your friends have a motive to kill your twin?"

"These aren't my friends," he said. "They're clients."

"Clients?" Tara said. "You begged for a ride because you missed your ferry."

Dave's face turned red. "Whatever. The point is, these are all perfect strangers, and one of them killed my brother. I can't sleep here. Noel arranged our stay through the pub. I believe we were to occupy the flat above it. I'd like to go there now."

Kehoe shook his head. "I'm afraid that won't be possible. The publican is staying there because of the storm."

"I can't stay here," Dave said. "What if . . ." He gulped. "What if I'm next?"

Sergeant Kehoe sighed and took a seat at the table. "I've known Captain Mickey all me life," he said. "He's been accused of a lot of things, but murder isn't one of them."

"Why was his license suspended?" Tara asked.

Kehoe looked uncomfortable. "I don't talk out of school." But she'd struck a note, she could tell. Was Captain Mickey really a killer?

"Maybe it was an accident," Breanna said.

"How do you accidentally poison someone?" Rachel said.

Mark pointed at her. "I saw you writing on one of the cups," he said.

"What?" Tara blurted out.

Mark nodded. "Just before Noel drank out of it."

Everyone stared at Rachel. Tears pooled in her eyes. "I was writing my phone number," she said, her cheeks turning red. "To be honest, it was for either of them." She didn't dare glance at Dave, but they all knew who she meant. "But I changed my mind. The cup I wrote on is in the trash can on the boat."

"Women do that all the time," Dave conceded. "Write their phone numbers wherever they can. Desperation is not a great perfume."

Rachel crossed her arms and sulked.

"Come on now," Breanna said, reaching over to pat Rachel's arm. "I'm sure Tara wouldn't be best friends with a killer."

"I think we've established that we're not best friends," Tara said.

"Frenemies," Rachel said. "But I thought that was changing—I thought you wanted me here."

"I had no idea Breanna invited you," Tara said. "I was just surprised, that's all. We haven't spoken in years."

"Why didn't you say something?" Breanna sounded horrified.

"She was already here," Tara said. "And given you didn't listen to the hundred times I said I absolutely didn't want a hen party, I didn't think there was much point." Tara immediately felt guilty. Breanna had become her best friend. She was just trying to be nice. "But it was so sweet of you to plan a surprise. I mean it."

"I was talking to Rachel," Breanna said. "Rachel, when I spoke with you, why did you act like you and Tara were best friends?" Rachel's face turned red, and she stared off into space. Breanna turned to Tara. "It was that day I filled in for you at the shop. Rachel called and asked for you, I said you were out shopping for the wedding—it snowballed from there."

"You made an assumption," Rachel said. "I just didn't correct it."

"But why would you come all this way for a hen party when you aren't even friends with the bride?" Breanna persisted.

"Because I needed to get out of the city, and like I said—I *thought* we were friends." The wounded expression was back. "I heard you were getting married again. I didn't know whether or not it was true. I hoped it was, and I was just calling to congratulate you." Tears came to her eyes. "I'm really sorry. I didn't know I wasn't wanted. I wouldn't have come."

"You're here now," Tara said. "And you're right—we could call ourselves friends. Friendly. I'm sorry for the misunderstanding." Unless Rachel was a murderer, Tara did not want her spending the weekend with her feelings hurt.

"Maybe Rachel came here to poison Tara's husband-to-be," Tom said as he glanced at Danny. "Don't forget the cup had *D-A* written on it. It may have been meant for you."

"Why on earth would I want to kill a man I'd never met?" Rachel said. "Believe me, there are plenty of men I do know that I would go after first." Everyone stared at her. "Kidding."

Sergeant Kehoe turned to his two guards. "I want the pair of ye to go back to the boat. Bring Captain Mickey into the station." The guards nodded and left. Sergeant Kehoe sighed as he took a seat at the dining table. He took out his notebook and Biro. "Now. Let's start at the beginning, shall we?"

Chapter Seven
Open Bar

The next day the storm raged on, but a guard stopped by to inform them that the pub had sorted out their generator and was open. They would serve as a community center; if folks needed help, they could find it there. The grapevine worked just as well as mobile phones, for by the time Tara and the gang arrived at the pub, it was already jammers. Then again, it was a cozy one-room affair, so it didn't take many to feel full. The ambiance was festive, like Saint Paddy's Day in New York City. Tara was startled to see a full-sized cutout of Dave and Noel by the door. In the cutouts they were grinning, and each had one foot up mid-tap and their arms around each other. Noel's gold cross was gleaming.

Sergeant Kehoe had sat with them at the cottage the night before to get their statements, and to his credit he'd taken detailed notes. Tara couldn't help but wonder what kind of sick game Captain Mickey was playing. She had given him the benefit of the doubt earlier—but to lie to the guards about Noel being dead? She could find no excuse for that, other than he had planned on escaping the guards before the truth caught up with him. Where had he hidden the body, and why? He couldn't possibly think his word was going to stand up against all of theirs, could he?

"Electricity," Rachel said, literally hopping up and down. "I love electricity."

"Thanks be to the heavens for generators," Tom said as the lads immediately bellied up to the bar. Mark and Danny followed Tom, but Dave hung back with the women.

"Are you okay?" Tara asked, touching him on the shoulder. He was staring at the cutout, and he flinched when he felt her touch. She withdrew her hand. "I'm sorry. I know that's a ridiculous question."

"You're alright, luv," Dave said. "I'm just not looking forward to telling them that our act is canceled because my brother is not only dead, he's missing." He shook his head. "Usually people go missing before they're found dead, but Noel always did dance to his own tune." He gave a wry laugh. "I know it's not funny, I'm just . . ."

"Coping," Tara said.

"Coping," Dave agreed. "Trying to cope."

Tara couldn't help but scour the crowd for Captain Mickey. His boat was not far from here. She had an urge to sneak out and go down to the boat, but if she was caught, it would only make her look suspicious. Did Captain Mickey really think the guards were going to believe him over seven eyewitnesses? Although there was no captain in the crowd, Tara did catch sight of a priest. He was sitting at a back table with a pint. She tapped Dave on the arm. "Noel was a practicing Catholic, is that right?"

Dave nodded. "I teased him about it. But now I'm so glad he had his faith."

Tara pointed out the priest. "Maybe you'd feel better if he said a little prayer for your brother?" Tara didn't usually disturb priests, but Dave could use any comfort he could get.

"Do you think he would?"

"Let's find out." The two of them pushed through the crowd until they reached the priest. He was sitting in front of a cup of tea.

"Father?" Tara said.

He turned and nodded. He was younger than Tara expected, somewhere in his twenties. "Father Nolan," he said. "How can I be of service?"

"My friend Dave here just lost his brother."

"Poor lad," Father Nolan said. "Shall we pray?"

"If you'd be willing," Dave said. "But I must admit I don't know any prayers by heart. Or Bible verses. But my brother did. He was a big fan."

Father Nolan stared at Dave. "You're one of the Carrigan brothers."

"Pleased to meet you, Father."

"You don't mean—your twin brother—"

"Yes." Dave swallowed through a lump in his throat. "He was killed yesterday, Father. We think it was foul play."

Father Nolan put his hand on his heart. "My child,"

he said, despite the fact that they were very close in age. "Let us go find somewhere quiet to talk."

Tara watched them go, somewhat pleased that he'd understood what was needed. She hoped the guards had seen her crime scene photos by now. Maybe they were grilling Captain Mickey as they spoke. Maybe he would be arrested before the storm was over. That would be a reason to celebrate.

A trad session was gathering in a far corner, and chairs were being arranged in a circle as instruments were lifted from cases. Danny was waving frantically to Tara from the bar, and at first Tara's hopes were raised that he somehow had learned something about the case. Instead, he was jabbing his finger at a table that had just cleared.

"On it," Breanna said, and she practically sailed in the air as she made a dive for the table.

Rachel glanced at Tara. "They're hardcore about their drinking," she said. "I love it."

"You catch on quick," Tara said. "Danny doesn't mess around when it comes to a pint." And for once she was grateful. When life delivered you a warm pub in a storm, you drank. As they gathered around the table and the lads brought over drinks and several bags of crisps, Tara was distracted by a series of framed photographs on a nearby wall. She gravitated over. Most of them had been taken in the pub. Groups of smiling customers with their arms looped around each other, musicians taking the stage, tourists giving thumbs-up for the camera. Many photos depicted customers posed outside with the stunning backdrop of the island. They'd captured folks riding bikes, licking ice cream cones, trudging up hills, standing at the edges of cliffs. One was of a lone cow lying in the middle of a lush green field close to the edge of the cliff, the ocean raging below. Finally, she spotted a photo of Captain Mickey. He was standing in front of his ferry, his arm slung around a young lad who appeared to be an Irish dancer. Captain Mickey was grinning ear-to-ear and holding up a medal. *A proud grandfather?* Tara went to snap a photo when she remembered she didn't have her mobile phone. Who was the young lad in the photo?

She looked around to see if anyone was watching her. She didn't know why, but she felt she had to have it—the more she could learn about Captain Mickey, the better. He was the key to solving this mystery. She couldn't ask anyone in her group because they had all checked their phones when Sergeant Kehoe was there, and none of them had any battery left. The photo was only a five-by-seven. She would return it. She slipped it off the wall, thinking it would be a smooth lift. Instead, it slipped from her hands, and as it did, it began to knock other photographs off the wall. Soon everyone in the pub was staring at her as photos rained to the floor. Tara yelped and was already apologizing as people began to approach, supposedly to help or maybe to admonish her. She was still holding the photo of Captain Mickey, and as others started to approach, she faced the wall, then shoved the photo down the front of her jeans. The frame was cold, and she was hoping its sharp corners wouldn't gouge her thighs, but at least it was hidden. She pulled her shirt down over it, then closed tight her cardigan.

What was she doing? "Sorry, sorry," she said as folks began picking up photos and placing them back on the wall. Would it be obvious one was missing?

Luckily, no one seemed to notice. It was possible the publican or another employee eventually would, but right now they were all too swamped to pay attention. Tara slid into the booth, the picture frame cutting into her stomach as she did. It was official: she'd lost her mind. It was too bad they hadn't been playing Truth or Dare. She was rarely this brazen.

"Butterfingers," Danny said to her with a wink. The frame cut into her again. She winced. Danny gave her a look, then eyed her pint. "Did you want something else?"

"I think I just need to stretch my legs." She slid out of the booth. There was no way she was keeping this framed photo down her pants. Why hadn't she chosen the simpler route to begin with? She squeezed up to the bar, removing the photograph as she went, and waited at the counter until the publican was free.

"What'll it be?" He was in no mood for a friendly chat, and with this crowd she couldn't blame him.

She placed the photograph on the counter. "This was on the floor."

"Some eejit knocked the entire wall of photos down," he said with a shake of his head. "Thanks." He started to take it.

"That's Captain Mickey, isn't it?" Tara said.

"It is indeed."

"Who is he with?"

"That's his grandson. The lad is an Irish dancer." He glanced at the cutout of the Carrigan brothers near the door. "He came close to having his likeness in cardboard instead."

"Oh?"

"He was in the very competition that skyrocketed the Carrigan brothers to fame. Local fame, that is. Although I hear one of them is going to be on *Dancing with the Stars*."

"One of them?" She glanced over at Dave. Had he lied to her? He said they were both invited to dance. "Which one?"

The publican shrugged. "No clue. Mickey's grandson says they only won because they cheated."

It was probably just sour grapes, but Tara wanted the scoop anyway. She leaned in. "Cheated how?"

"Let's just say those lads have a way with the ladies, and they weren't shy about buttering up the female judges."

"I see." *Motive. Captain Mickey had a motive.* Would the publican be willing to report that story to the guards?

"I wonder if yer one ever regretted not going to law school." He clicked his tongue against his teeth. "Heard that was a lifelong dream, but his brother begged him to keep dancing."

Tara couldn't imagine the pressure, the conflicted loyalties. "Which one wanted to go to law school?"

The publican picked up a pint glass and shook his head. "Would you stop asking me which one this and which one that? You try telling them apart." He started to walk away. "Wait." He looked around. "I paid for two of them. Where is the other one?" Tara ignored that question for now. Someone was coming up behind her, nudging her out of the way.

The publican stood suddenly, smiled, and stuck his hand out. "Speak of the devil," he said to Dave. "We were just admiring your cutout. Are you Dave or Noel?"

"Dave," he said, shaking his hand. "I'm afraid . . ." He gulped. "My brother won't be joining me."

The publican gave Tara the side-eye as if to say *told ya.* She shook her head, hoping he'd pick up on her warning.

"But we paid for the two of ye," the publican said, outraged. "Is he the one who doesn't want to dance anymore?"

Dave frowned. "What do you mean?"

"Nothing." The publican straightened up. "I'm just trying to figure out why you're not dancing. Did ye have a falling out?"

"No. We did not have a falling out. I'm terribly sorry. It's just me."

Tara was slightly taken aback. Was Dave really still going to perform? "It can't be helped," she said. "I can vouch for that."

"I see," the publican said, still sounding aggrieved.

"I'm afraid Noel kept our schedule. I don't know where we were staying. Basically anything you discussed with Noel, I need to know." Dave's voice took on a new intensity. Was he that afraid to stay with them? Granted, it was a little crowded. And one of them could be a killer . . .

"I'm afraid there's bad news on that front," the publican said. "Although now that there's only one of ye, maybe it's for the best."

"What now?" Dave said, his tone changing.

"We had to take over the room where you were going to stay because of the storm." He gestured to a booth. "But I can give you a blanket and pillow and you can sleep in the pub tonight."

Tara leaned into Dave. "You shouldn't be dancing. And you're staying with us. We need to have each other's backs."

"You mean stab each other in the back," Dave said. "Funny that none of you are dancers, because they're good at that sort of thing."

"What I'm saying is that I don't think you should be alone. And I don't think you should dance."

"I have to dance. Noel would have wanted it that way." His voice broke, tears once again came to his eyes. "I will honor all the dances that Noel booked. And then I will put me dancing shoes away forever." He bit his lip. "It will be nothing without me brother."

"Story horse?" The publican wanted the gossip.

"He's dead," Dave said. "Noel died yesterday."

The publican gasped. "Lad, I'm so sorry." He lowered his voice. "What happened?"

Tara shook her head. "Please keep this to yourself," she said. "The guards are looking into it."

"The guards?" The publican scooted closer, ignoring cries down the bar for his attention. "Why the guards?" Suddenly he wanted to chat. Typical.

"Someone poisoned me brother with a milkshake," Dave cried. "On the ferry!"

"What?" the publican was truly shocked. His gaze slid to Tara.

"We really don't know yet how he died," Tara said. "It's a police matter."

"This one's getting married and insisted on boozy milkshakes," Dave added.

"I honestly didn't want any kind of hen party at all," Tara said. She should have stuck to her guns. The publican eyed the booth where Danny and the gang sat. "Do you know where Captain Mickey stays when he's not on the boat?" Tara asked, hoping to divert the conversation.

The publican ignored her and looked at Dave. "You don't have to dance, lad," he said. "Everyone will understand."

"I do have to," Dave said. "I want to. I want to do it for Noel." The publican nodded, then pointed to the smallest stage Tara had ever seen shoved in the corner. "There's your platform," he said. "We have your music cued up." Dave thanked him and headed for the stage.

"Dave," Tara called after him. "You really don't have to."

"I really do," he called back, without turning around. The publican turned away from Tara and headed down to the bar to his outraged customers. Tara followed.

"Do you know which ferries were supposed to come to the island yesterday but canceled because of the storm?" she asked.

Maybe one of those captains would know something about the Carrigan brothers. After all, they were supposed to be on another boat. Or was that a lie? She turned to glance at Dave, who was warming up in the corner. It was a marvel to watch him tap dance. He had mega talent, anyone could see that. But it had been mesmerizing to watch the pair of them dance. Identical twins, both with big talent. No wonder they were a sensation. What a sad, sad loss. Dave wouldn't have peace unless they found his brother's killer. Although it was possible a twenty-something lad in the best shape of his life could have had a cardiac arrest or some other medical emergency that ended his life, it wasn't probable. Until a coroner or a state pathologist said otherwise, they had to assume this was foul play. And given the guards didn't even believe there was a murder, Tara felt compelled to do a little bit of digging. Noel Carrigan deserved that. He shouldn't have died on a short ferry ride. And perhaps he wouldn't have died had they not been imbibing boozy milkshakes for her hen party. Someone had taken advantage of a celebration to commit murder. Was it Captain Mickey avenging his grandson over a dancing competition? Or was it the angry husband, estranged from a wife he was obviously still in love with? And then there was Matt, tossing something into the fire at the cottage when he thought no one was looking . . .

"I don't give out personal information about anyone on this island," the publican said. She believed him.

"Not a bother," Tara said. "It's just that the twins were supposed to be on another boat—"

"Impossible," the publican said. "Captain Sara was off yesterday because of the storm. There weren't supposed to be any ferries coming in. Captain Mickey wasn't scheduled either—in fact, he has a suspended license. I suppose he was doing a bit of sneaky moonlighting."

Captain Sara was off yesterday . . . all ferries had been canceled because of the storm. That means Dave and Noel had lied in order to get on their ferry. *Why?* "All the ferries were canceled and yet you didn't cancel their act?" Tara asked.

"I tried to cancel their act," the publican said. "Noel assured me they were coming, no matter what. Said they had an additional gig."

An additional gig . . .

"Captain Mickey said we had to see some famous cow while we were here," Tara threw out.

"Up the hill toward Dún Aonghana, then turn right after your first farm on the left," the publican said. Dún Aonghana, or Dun Aengus, was a prehistoric hill fort situated at the edge of a 100-meter cliff and the main tourist attraction of the island. Tara had been there several times and never failed to be amazed. "But you won't be sightseeing this weekend," the publican said with a shake of his head.

He was right about that. Tara headed for the corner where Dave was still warming up. "I'm busy," Dave said. "Please leave me alone."

"Why did you lie?"

He stopped dancing. "What?"

"You and Noel told us you missed your boat. That's why you wanted to come on ours."

"And?" He raised an eyebrow.

"Why did you lie?"

"Because we were supposed to be a surprise," Dave said. "For you," he added when she didn't respond.

"Oh." Tara felt like a fool. Of course. She had been the additional gig. Dancing, stripping—the whole hen party thing. Someone had paid them to be there. It had to have been Breanna. Why hadn't she mentioned it? Was she wracked with guilt?

"Right," she said. "I'm so sorry. I had no idea."

"That is how a surprise usually works." He stopped tapping. "Wait," he said. "Do you think"—he gulped—"do you think she hired us to kill us?"

"Breanna?" Tara said. "Not a chance."

"Not her," he said. "The other American girl. Rachel."

Tara suddenly went cold. "Rachel?" she said. "What does Rachel have to do with this?"

Dave looked at her as if he pitied her. "What do you think?" he said. "She's the one who hired us."

Chapter Eight
With Friends Like These

"Rachel hired you?" Tara was gobsmacked. She was having trouble trying to wrap her poor head around it.

Dave's eyes slid to the booth, and he started tapping again. "She's watching." He gulped. "Do you think I can stay with all of you after all?" he said. "I don't want to be alone."

"Of course." They should all stay together. Watch each other like hawks. "You're sure it was Rachel who hired you?"

"Of course I'm sure. She met up with us the night before and paid in cash." Sweat glistened on his forehead. "She also swore us to secrecy."

This was upsetting news. Earlier, Tara had assumed that Rachel had simply wanted a trip to Ireland. But what if her reasons for coming were far more sinister? "Have you ever met her before?" Tara asked.

Dave frowned. "No. I can't answer for Noel, obviously, and we've met a ton of colleens in our life. But if we'd met her before, I don't recall."

Laughter rang out from their booth, and when Tara turned to see, it was Rachel who had her head thrown back. She was nestled in between Tom and Mark, apparently flirting her head off. *Blondes have more fun.* Did her idea of fun include murder?

"Nobody on this island cares that my brother is gone," Dave said. "And I don't even have mobile service to call the people off this island who would care."

Tara took his hands. "I care," she said. "And I know others do too. We're going to get to the bottom of what's going on." Tara had noticed that Rachel had her handbag with her, and she was constantly checking that it was at her side. Was there something in there? Or something in her luggage back on the boat? Then again, Tara didn't even know if the boat was still at the dock. Besides, would Tara even know poison if she saw it? She very much doubted it was housed in a plastic bag with a skull and crossbones marked on it or the word POISON screaming out in red. Tara wasn't a guard, and this wasn't her case, but so far they didn't even believe there had been a murder. Had they seen the photos on her phone yet? That should certainly convince them.

"Where exactly did Rachel meet the two of you?" Tara asked.

"We had a show at a pub in Galway," Dave said. "She came up to us after the show, gushing, and she said a little birdie told her we'd be performing on the Aran Islands, and she had the perfect little side gig for us."

A little birdie. What little birdie? "Was your show advertised?"

Dave shrugged. "Noel was a mad social media poster."

And Rachel was too. She had probably pulled out her phone and stalked them the minute she saw them. "The publican said he tried to cancel your show, but whichever one of you he spoke with refused to cancel."

"Really?" Dave said. "That must have been Noel. He was addicted to performing."

"Who else knew you would be here this weekend?" Tara knew it was important to keep an open mind. It was the same with interior design. The most difficult clients were the ones who refused to be open to new ideas. Those were also the projects that were the least satisfying. It always boggled her mind when someone would pay a ton of money to a professional and then dictate exactly what they wanted done.

Dave shook his head. "Not accounting for social media, only the publican knew we were coming." He nodded his head toward the cutout. "Or someone who saw that ridiculous cardboard cutout—or Captain Mickey."

There he was again—Captain Mickey—caught in the spotlight. But Rachel didn't know Captain Mickey or anyone on the island. Breanna must be the little birdie. Tara would keep that to herself; she didn't want Breanna blaming herself for the murder. And despite what Dave asserted, everything was on the Internet. They might not have posted where they were performing this weekend, but it was highly likely that someone else had.

"You have clout here," Tara said. "Do you think you can find out where Captain Mickey hangs out?"

"What about your garda friend?" he asked. "Breanna."

"I can try to do some digging on my end as well," Tara said.

"If she did this," Dave said, his eyes flicking to Rachel. "She knows that I know that she hired us. What if she tries to kill me so I don't give up her secret?"

He had a point. Tara took his arm. "Come here." She dragged him over to the table. It took a minute for everyone to look up.

"Rachel," Tara said, "despite how horrible it all turned out, I just found out that you were behind my big surprise."

Rachel arched an eyebrow as all heads swiveled her way.

"What's this now?" Breanna asked as she sat frozen with a crisp halfway to her mouth.

"It turns out Dave and Noel didn't miss their boat after all. It was just a cover not to ruin the surprise." She waited to see if Rachel wanted to fill in the gaps. But Rachel's complexion had paled—in fact in this light, it looked a little green. "Rachel hired the twins," Tara said, "to entertain us on the boat."

Rachel looked at Dave, tears swimming in her eyes. "I am so sorry," she said. "Obviously I had no idea something horrible was going to happen, but I'm so, so sorry." Then she grabbed her handbag, squeezing it tightly, and asked to be let out of the booth. She then stood trembling in front of Tara. "Happy?" she said. "Now everyone knows that Noel's death is all my fault." Without waiting for a reply, she began pushing through the sea of bodies toward the exit.

"That was . . . ," Danny said. "Not quite like you." He made eye contact with Tara.

She felt a bit stunned. "I'm not trying to be cruel. Dave was worried that Rachel was the only one who knew that she'd hired them." She swallowed. "You know . . . in case." What did Tara know about Rachel, other than the fact that she was a highly driven, competitive designer? "I'd better go after her," Tara said.

"I'm going with you," Breanna said.

Danny stood. "We stick together, remember?"

"We're just checking the restroom," Tara said. "She can't have left the pub." She finished her sentence to find everyone staring at the window situated by the table. And the woman who had just darted past in the rain looked an awful lot like Rachel.

They all agreed the woman dashing past the window was indeed Rachel, but not everyone agreed they should go chasing after her.

"We said we would all stay together," Danny said to Tara as she eyed the door. She was itching to run out after her, and he knew it.

"Let's go, then. Either she's up to something or she needs our help." The storm was still raging. What in the world could have prompted her to flee the pub? Was it a guilty conscience?

"I'm staying here, lads," Tom said, raising a pint. "Good luck to ye."

So much for staying together.

Tara headed for the door with Breanna and Danny right behind her. She couldn't help but feel a bit of anger toward Rachel. They had finally dried off from their walk here, they were safe, and there were people and electricity and food and drink—what kind of stunt was she pulling?

They wrestled the wind opening the door, but with all three of them pushing, they finally stumbled out. Groans rang out from inside the pub; no one wanted the cold and rain inside. Just ahead they saw Rachel enter a shop.

"That's a local craft and clothing shop," Danny said. "Can't believe they're open."

"How did *she* know they were open?" Breanna asked.

"Let's find out," Tara said. She ducked her head and began to push through the wind that so desperately wanted to push her back.

"I'm sorry," Breanna shouted. "I should have known she wasn't your best mate. You've been here all this time, and no one from the States has visited you."

Because the last time anyone in the States knew Tara, she was the sad mom who had lost her toddler. She had a Winnie-the-Pooh tattoo in honor of her son, Thomas. At three years old, he died in a playground accident. That's when her life in the States was over. It had been years now, and although she was functioning normally, she carried him always. She and his father, Gabriel, divorced, but they'd remained cordial. But lately even they had lost touch. Sometimes it was easier to start fresh if you cut ties with the past. Or so she'd thought. Maybe she was fooling herself. Tara walked faster, not wanting to relive those horrific first years learning how to move and breathe without her son.

The last time she'd seen Rachel Madigan, Tara had been lying on her kitchen floor in her New York City apartment. Gabriel had left. He'd really tried to deal with her grief, but she was leaving him no room for his own. She knew that now. But back then, right after Thomas had died, she couldn't think of anyone else. She'd laid on the floor because halfway to the refrigerator she'd decided she was never going to eat again. And oddly the relief she felt was palpable. Just let go. The floor was cool. She decided she was never going to get up again. Her real best friend, Kate, had called everyone in Tara's roster, hoping someone could help. Rachel had come right away. Unlike all her other friends, who had stood over her, trying to coax her up, Rachel had laid down on the floor with her, eye-to-eye. "This is going to be the hardest thing you've ever had to deal with or ever will have to deal with," she said. "But I know you can do it. Because you, Tara Meehan, are a force of nature. And that's the mother Thomas knew. I bet he wouldn't like seeing you on the floor." She lifted her head. "Although these are stunning tiles. I don't suppose you'll divulge the maker." Tara didn't respond. "Sorry. Not the right time."

Tara had been furious. But she did get off the floor. And she did breathe. And drink water. And eventually she started eating. Not much—but enough to survive. It was painful to relive those days. Her life was better now. She carried her grief everywhere she went. Not a day went by that she didn't think of Thomas, or talk to him in her head, but it didn't cripple her anymore. Everyone needs a Rachel Madigan at some point in their life.

Maybe Rachel *was* a friend. And maybe she was here because she needed one too. Had Tara ever thought of that? No. She'd gone directly to accusing her of murder.

They reached the shop where they'd seen Rachel duck inside, but it was dark. They peered in for a minute and then saw a light from a torch bouncing around the space.

"Did she break in?" Breanna asked, reaching for the doorknob. Suddenly the torches swung to the window. Had it not been for the sheet of rain between them and the glare, it may have blinded them.

"I thought we'd be more subtle," Danny said.

"Not in this weather," Breanna said. She opened the door and hurried them inside. "I'm with the Galway Garda Station," she announced. "Who's in here?"

Tara was surprised. She'd never heard Breanna represent herself with such authority. Technically, she wasn't lying. Tara was proud of her.

"Garda," a woman's voice said. "What brings you here?"

"I'm making sure no one has broken into your shop," Breanna said. "We saw the torch and wondered who was in here. Are you the owner?"

"Rachel?" Tara called. "Are you there?"

"You followed me?" Rachel said. She sounded annoyed.

"We were worried about you," Tara said. "The biggest storm they've had here in ages, and you're running out of a warm pub."

"I'm Rose," the woman's voice called out. "I'm the owner, and this one had already put in an order. Storm or no storm, an order is an order."

"An order for what?" Tara asked, aware that it was really none of her business.

"Your penis cake," Rachel said. "But I suppose you don't want it."

"Is this a bakery?" Tara asked.

"I moonlight," Rose said. "Whenever anyone needs sexually explicit baked goods, they come to me."

"Good to know," Tara said with a straight face. She turned to Rachel. "I owe you an apology. I'm so sorry for how I've behaved. I remembered how good you were to me after my sweet Thomas passed. I feel terrible for how I've treated you."

"It's okay," Rachel said. "I forgive you."

"Well, let's get this penis cake and get back to the pub!" Tara said with forced cheer.

"Will ye please stop saying 'penis cake'?" Danny said.

"Do you mind if we look around while we're here?" Breanna said, removing a torch from her pocket and turning it on.

"Not at all," Rose said. "But you break it, you buy it."

When they returned to the pub, their penis cake opened the celebratory floodgates as people gathered around to have a laugh and a piece. Tara and Danny were bought drinks, congratulated, fawned over. The trad band played lively tunes as Dave danced to them, and a memorial fund had been set up for Noel that was already overflowing with cash. When the guards burst in two hours into their revelry, Tara knew immediately it didn't look good. Here, a member of their group was dead, most likely due to foul play, and they were dancing, drinking, eating, and collecting cold, hard cash. Well, the cash certainly hadn't been their idea—it had most likely come from the publican.

For a few moments, the guards watched them celebrate. Then the musicians finally copped on and stopped playing, Dave stopped dancing, and the room fell silent.

"I'm Detective Sergeant Kehoe, and I've come with distressing news. We've two members of a ferry missing—Captain Mickey and Noel Carrigan."

"My brother isn't just missing," Dave said. "He's been murdered."

A gasp was heard around the pub. Kehoe picked up the box filled with cash. "The guards will be taking possession of this until the dust settles," he said.

"It's for my brother's funeral," Dave said.

Tara was dying to ask them why they thought Captain Mickey was missing. After all, they had seen him, and they went back to the boat to arrest him. Obviously, he hadn't stayed put. Did the guards believe them now? Tara sidled up to the bar, and when the publican finally came over, she asked for the photo.

"What photo is that, now?"

"The one I just showed you. With Captain Mickey and his son and the dancing medal."

"Sorry, pet. I have no idea what you're on about." He smiled and ambled away.

Of course. They were closing ranks, taking care of their own. Other people had to know about Captain Mickey's grandson being a dancer. There would probably be something online. But it proved one thing. Tara would not get anywhere by trying to enlist the locals. She had to play it smart.

She headed for Kehoe. "Did you charge my mobile phone and see the photos?"

"Miss Meehan," he said, glancing at her jumper. "Or Mrs.—"

"Still Miss."

"I'm organizing a search party. If you'll please return to your cottage, I'll make sure to return your phone after its been processed."

Processed. They would do it by the book, wouldn't they? They wouldn't, say, destroy her photos. Would they?

"I want to be involved in the search," she said.

"Not a chance," Kehoe said. "I want all of you back in that cottage."

"You can't force us to stay there," Breanna said. "That would be considered house arrest."

"If you resist an order from the guards, we can charge you," Kehoe said.

"No," Breanna said, "it doesn't work like that. Unless we're officially charged, we're free to do whatever we like, including join the search." As they spoke, the others had gathered around—Rachel, Tom, Mark, Danny, and Dave. On this at least, they were a united front.

Kehoe shut his eyes briefly. "We're expecting a short break in the weather a few hours from now. We'll have two hours to search before another front moves in. We'll need all the volunteers we can get.

"We'll cover the most ground if we go in groups of up to four," Kehoe said. "Find your partners now."

The pub-goers, already feeling festive and drunk, all volunteered. "I'm sticking with you," Danny said.

"I think we should all stay together," Tara said.

"Because you still think one of us is a killer," Dave said.

"My focus is on Captain Mickey," Tara said. "And if he's a killer, I don't want *any* of us running into him on our own."

"Where do we start?" Dave asked.

"I've got two ideas," Tara said. "First, we search the boat. And then we find that famous cow."

"Why?" Danny said. "You know how to get a cow to talk?"

Tara laughed and gave him a kiss. "No," she said. "It's the only lead we have on Captain Mickey. But first I need to go back to the cottage. With Breanna only."

Chapter Nine

Fireside Chat

"You want to go back to the cottage now?" Danny asked Tara. "We're waiting for the break in the rain to search."

"I just . . . need to take care something." She wanted to see if she could figure out what Mark had tossed in the fire. Maybe it was nothing. But it had been the way he'd done it—sneakily—and she had to satisfy her curiosity. Danny was just as protective about his friends as Tara was hers. She didn't want to accuse Mark of anything. She just wanted to put her mind at ease.

"Then let's go take care of it," Danny said. "We can hurry and make it back before the search begins."

"Breanna will come with me," Tara said.

Danny narrowed his eyes. "What's the story? What are you really up to?"

"Girl things," she said, crossing her fingers behind her back. She didn't think admitting that she wanted to see what one of his mates had tossed into the fire would go over so well.

"Why do I get the feeling you're just saying that so I won't come?"

Because he knew her. "Hen parties are just for us gals," she said. "We'll be back before you know it."

Danny glanced at the clock on the wall. "Thirty minutes," he said. "And then I'm coming after ye."

She nodded, then kissed him, which earned them another round of applause. If only life could be that happy.

"What exactly are we doing back here?" Breanna asked, stomping muck off her shoes as they stepped inside the cottage. They were soaked yet again, but at least they'd made it in one piece, and Tara was pleasantly surprised to see the guards had returned with a box of clothing. It looked more like clothing that farmers and fisherman wear than her normal wardrobe, but at this point she'd dress like a nun if the outfit was dry.

"I saw Mark throw something into the fire," Tara said. "It's probably nothing, but I had to check."

Breanna raced her to it, and before Tara knew it, she was on her knees, pawing in the ashes. "Found it." She held up a burned scrap. "It's a photo," she said. A second later she gasped. Tara hurried over.

"What is it?" Breanna showed her the photo, most of which was burned. Still left was the image of a beautiful, smiling blonde. A man's hand was wrapped around her waist. On his ring finger was a silver band with etchings.

"Do you recognize her?" Tara asked. She had never seen the woman before.

"I sure do," Breanna said. "That's Tom's soon-to-be-ex-wife."

Tara looked again. "She is beautiful."

Breanna pointed to the hand. "That isn't Tom's hand." Breanna studied it. "It's Mark's. I noticed his ring on the boat."

"Tom wasn't the one tossing the photo either," Tara said. "It was Mark." It was also Mark who had pestered Tom nonstop on the boat about how Tom and his wife had called it quits and he needed to forget her. Was this why? And if Mark was having an affair with Tom's wife . . . had he also been in a jealous rage when he found out Noel had slept with her? Was he seeing her at the time? Was this why Noel had kept calling out "Mark" and pointing to him? Why did he confuse things by also pointing to Tom and then an empty egg carton? Maybe he was delirious. How much stock could one put in a dead man's last words?

Breanna studied the photo again. "Wow. We can't tell anyone. Tom would lose his mind."

"We're in a terrible position," Tara said. "Mark could be a killer."

"We need the rest of this photo." Breanna pawed around the fire again. But it was no use. Whoever the man in the photo was, his image had been burned.

"Tom said it himself," Breanna said. "Noel wasn't the only man she cheated on Tom with."

"We have two possible scenarios here," Tara said as she paced. "Either Mark flew into a jealous rage when he found out Noel slept with the woman he's having an affair with, *or* Mark suspects Tom of killing Noel, and he threw out the photo because he doesn't want to be next."

"And what? Both Mark and Tom carry around obscure poisons just in case?"

"You make an excellent point," Tara said. And there was no coming back from accusing someone of being a killer. "We have to keep this to ourselves, but keep digging." They pawed through the box of clothing and picked out flannel shirts and trousers to change into at the pub.

"I pictured us in boas and tiaras," Breanna said as they stuffed the dry clothes inside their jackets.

"We can wear those one day when we get back," Tara said.

Breanna perked up for a minute, but then her face darkened. "Imagine finding out your best mate slept with your wife?" Breanna shook her head. "There would be war."

"Either way I'm in a bit of trouble with Danny," Tara said. "I can't imagine not telling him. And think of how awkward our wedding would be with the two of them as his groomsmen."

"I don't envy you," Breanna said. "But at least we have a temporary plan. It's the two of us against this killer." Tears came into her eyes. "I should have listened to you. You said no hen party, and I should have listened to you."

Tara gave her a hug. "Don't give it a second thought," she said. "I'll have the best worst hen party story of anyone who ever lived."

* * *

"Did you know that Captain Mickey has a son who's an Irish dancer?" Tara said to Dave as they walked down to the ferry en masse. The rain had indeed stopped, but approaching black clouds were a reminder that the reprieve was temporary. Time was of the essence. "Apparently you and your brother beat him out of a major competition."

Dave wrinkled his nose. "We've been in thousands of competitions."

"However, this is the one that launched the pair of you into fame."

Dave seemed to be concentrating. "Val O'Grady?" he said.

"Danny," Tara called, "what's Captain Mickey's last name?"

"Last name," Danny teased. "I have no idea Ms. America, but his second name is O'Grady." Tara stuck her tongue out even though his back was to her. "Don't show it if you aren't going to use it," Danny said. He really did have eyes in the back of his head.

"Is it true that he lost out on a big competition because of you?" Tara asked.

"Because we won," Dave said. "Fair and square."

"Was there big money involved?"

"It was a nice chunk of change, but really, all the deals after that led us to our current standing."

"May I ask why you are still dancing for hen parties if you're doing so well?"

"Because we like beautiful women who are out to have a good time," Dave said. He glanced at Tom, who was walking just ahead of them. Tom pretended not to hear, but Tara noted that his entire body stiffened. He was definitely listening. "Actually, it was Noel. He was the biggest flirt. Noel was the one in charge of our schedule. Just ask our agent." He placed his hand on his forehead. "Our agent. I haven't even told our agent."

When they finally reached the dock, the squishing noise their collective shoes made sounded like something out of a horror movie. The ferry was still moored, although it seemed to have drifted sideways. It wasn't until they were closer that they could see the difference. It looked like Captain Mickey's ferry but there was no CAPTAIN MICKEY emblazoned across it in red.

"It's not the same ferry," Tara said. "How can it not be the same ferry?"

Everyone edged in to have a look. "What on earth is going on?" Danny asked.

"Let's find out," Breanna said, taking the lead. She strode toward the ferry, and just as they were figuring out how to board without a ramp, a figure appeared on deck. It was a woman. She was bundled up for the storm, but a long, dark braid hung down her back.

Tara recalled her conversation with the publican and thought she'd take a chance. "Captain Sara?"

The woman crossed her arms and glared down at them. "Who wants to know?"

Had the guards even realized they'd searched the wrong boat? When they set out, the rain was so thick it would have been easy to miss that there was no writing "on the wall." "We're looking for Captain Mickey."

"Do I look like Captain Mickey?"

"He wanted us to find you."

"Did he, now?"

"He did."

"Secret word?"

"Cow," Tara said.

Danny nudged in. "I don't think calling her names is going to win you any favors."

"Say more," Captain Sara said.

Everyone exchanged glances.

"Famous cow," Tara said.

The woman stared longer, then held up a finger and disappeared below deck.

"What is happening?" Rachel put her hands on her hips and surveyed the group. "Am I being pranked? Irish style?"

"We're in the middle of a James Bond film, are we?" Tom asked.

"That was class," Breanna said, thumping Tara on the back.

"I'm marrying a spy," Danny said.

"Second thoughts?" Tara asked.

"Are you joking me?" Danny said. "Call the priest; let's do this."

"I bet Noel would have married you," Dave said. "He could quote scriptures by heart."

"Ours isn't going to be super religious," Tara said. "But I'm glad he had his faith."

Captain Sara returned. "I'll take you on board," she said. "But only after each of you agrees to a pat down."

"A pat down?" Tom said.

"Make sure no one has any weapons. Or poison."

Poison. Captain Mickey knew full well there had been foul play. Or was this part of *his* sick and twisted game?

And if she was saying *poison* with such confidence—did that mean Captain Mickey found the poison on the boat?

"No one is patting me anywhere," Dave said.

"I thought you were used to that," Tom quipped.

Dave glared. "How do we know *she* isn't the killer?"

"You don't," Captain Sara said, crossing her arms and flashing a defiant look.

"Where would you be taking us?" Breanna asked.

"Inisheer." The smallest and eastern most of the Aran Islands.

"Guys," Rachel said, "you're not really considering this, are you?"

"We're under enough suspicion as it is," Mark said. "Didn't the guards tell us to stay put?"

"That was earlier," Danny said. "We stood up for ourselves in the pub."

Dave raised an eyebrow. "We did?"

"You couldn't hear because you were probably dancing," Rachel said.

"You're not really thinking of going, are you?" Tom asked, looking only at Danny.

Danny glanced at Captain Sara. "I'm willing to chance it. I want to know what Captain Mickey is up to."

"What if it's murder?" Mark asked. "And we're next?"

"If it's worth anything to ye, Captain Mickey was saying the same thing about all of ye," Captain Sara said. "I've never seen him so frightened."

"If Captain Mickey was the killer, he could have poisoned all of our milkshakes," Danny said. "But he didn't."

"That's our consolation?" Tom asked. "He could have killed us but didn't?"

Danny shrugged. "I'm not going with my eyes closed, lad, but if Tara is going, then so am I."

Breanna, Danny, and Tara stood in one group, while the rest remained huddled together. The holdouts.

"A three-hour tour," Rachel sang.

"The storm is coming back," Dave said. "You really want to be stuck on a different island without food, clothing, or lodging?"

"That is an excellent point," Rachel said.

"No one has to go who doesn't want to go," Tara said.

Captain Sara looked at her watch, then glanced at the dark clouds above. "I'm not waiting all day, lads."

"Why don't you lads go to the garda station and tell them where we're going," Danny said. "It will be like an insurance policy."

They glanced at Captain Sara to see if she would protest. She remained silent.

Rachel stepped forward. "What help will that be if she kills you and chucks you all out to sea?"

Breanna motioned for Captain Sara to lower the ramp. Instead, she lit a cigarette as she lowered a rope ladder. The wind immediately blew it out, but she kept it dangling from the corner of her mouth. "If you can't climb, you can't ride."

Breanna started up the ladder. A groan came from

the holdouts. Rachel joined their side. "Bridesmaids before bros," she said.

Tom let out a curse. Dave scurried over to their side. In the end, they all boarded the boat, and as the small ferry pulled out, Tara suspected that, like her, they were all hoping this wasn't the last time they'd ever see the shore again.

Chapter Ten
Shipwrecked

Inisheer, Tara knew from past visits, was a delightful island during nicer weather. Like Inishmore, there was no shortage of stone walls, rising hills, curving roads, and the stunning backdrop of the Atlantic Ocean. This island was also known for a sunken church, lighthouse, castle, and the remnants of an old shipwreck whose giant rusted carcass still sat at the edge of the ocean and attracted visitors from far and wide. The *Plassey*, dubbed "the best-known shipwreck in Galway," had been a steam freighter carrying yarn, stained glass, and whiskey when it was battered by a storm in the 1960s. It was a reminder, especially now, that storms should not be taken lightly. When the group disembarked (climbing down Captain Sara's rope ladder), they found a row of bicycles waiting for them.

"If we want to make it to shelter before the heavens

open up again, these are your best bet," Captain Sara said.

"Our best bet?" Danny said. "Are you not coming with us?"

Captain Sara shook her head. "This is where I leave you." She removed a book from inside her bulky jacket. "Are you the one with the guards?"

"I'm a clerk at the garda station," Breanna said.

"Close enough." Captain Sara handed Breanna the Bible. "Captain Mickey wanted you to have it." She saluted and climbed the ladder to her ferry. She stood on deck, as if watching to make sure they mounted the bikes and rode away.

"What is it?" Dave asked Breanna, eyeing the book.

Breanna glanced down. "It's . . . a Bible."

"Oh my word," Rachel said.

"Exactly," Breanna said.

"What kind of sick game is he playing?" Danny asked. "Captain Mickey's gone twisted."

Breanna shoved the Bible in her coat. "I'm still keeping it safe."

"Of course," nearly everyone replied.

They all exchanged glances. "We have no idea where we're going," Tara said. "Are we supposed to just ride all over the island until the skies open up and we drown?" Why hadn't she refused this trip altogether? Had she brought a murderer to the party, or had Danny? She wished she had the power to click her heels together three times and find herself back at Uncle Johnny's salvage mill, having a chat, a cup of tea and a blueberry scone as big as her head.

Danny suddenly whirled around and pointed at Captain Sara, who was still standing at the bow. "Where is Captain Mickey's ferry?"

"Look," she said, "Captain Mickey is afraid. And until we figure out what happened to that poor lad on his ferry, it's best you all are far away."

"He's on Inishmaan," Breanna guessed. But Captain Sara didn't answer. She turned around and disappeared below deck. A minute later she was pulling out, sans the horn. *Great.* Now they were stuck on this island without shelter, food, or clothing. Would the pubs be open here, like the one in Inishmore?

"We were duped," Danny said.

"I told you," Tom said. "I told you we shouldn't have come."

A lightbulb clicked on for Tara. Captain Mickey must have hid in his private quarters the minute he saw the body. Probably didn't want to be blamed.

"In some ways, that's a relief," Dave said. "But isn't it against the law to abscond with my brother?" He gulped. "Even if . . ." He let the rest hang in the wind. *Even if he's dead.*

"I'm sure Captain Mickey will have a lot to answer for," Breanna said. "Captain Sara too. But right now, we have to find shelter."

"She's right," Mark said as he craned his neck to look at the ominous clouds. "Our reprieve isn't going to last long."

"Do you think the pubs here will be open?" Dave asked. "Or an inn? A cafe? Anything?"

Danny headed for a bicycle. "Let's find out."

"Are you sure that's a good idea?" Tara said. "The roads will be slick from all the rain."

"We'll be careful," Danny said. "Walking would take ages."

They all grabbed a bike and followed Danny. It was hard to steer in the wind, and after just ten minutes, which felt much longer, Tara's legs were already burning. Fat raindrops began to fall.

"We're in such trouble," Breanna yelled.

The village was starting to come into view, and they could tell right away that unlike the pub on Inishmore, the ones here were closed for the storm. Or, if the pubs were secretly open to some, it wasn't obvious from the outside. All the establishments were dark. Not a soul was wandering about. Using the bicycles started as a good idea, but it quickly became a nightmare due to the slick and muddy roads.

"We need a plan," Tara said as Breanna cried out. Her bicycle toppled over. They all stopped to help. Danny and Tom reached her first, lifting her up. She thanked them and then kicked her bicycle as hard as she could, unleashing a few impressive curses.

"This is all my fault," Breanna wailed. "If only I had listened to you. We could be having a nice, boring time back in Galway."

"Let's find shelter, and then we'll all give out to you," Tara said, looping her arm around her friend.

"There's a ruined sunken church and a castle," Danny said. "But neither of them have roofs."

"What about the lighthouse?" Tom asked.

"It's always locked to the public," Danny said.

"Maybe we should go to the *Plassey* shipwreck," Tara said. "We could crawl underneath and at least have a partial roof over our heads."

"A roof?" Rachel said. "You're calling the carcass of an old ship a roof?"

"If it keeps you from getting soaked, it's a roof," Tara said. Now was not the time to be a diva.

"What if Captain Mickey is there, and he's just waiting to murder us?" Dave said.

"He can't murder all of us at once," Danny said.

"He can if he has a gun, you eejit." This came from Tom.

The rain was coming down harder. There was no time to argue. "I'll take my chances with the shipwreck," Mark said. "But I think it's smart to ditch the bicycles."

"Good idea," Breanna said. "If we go missing, at least they'll bring the dogs to this point."

"Comforting," Rachel said.

"Let's get to the ship," Danny said, pointing east. "It's on the coast. Given we biked at least halfway, it's probably another twenty-five-minute walk."

"We don't have that long," Tom said. "I can take someone on the back of a bike."

"Me too," Danny said.

Mark kept silent. "I'm in better shape than all of ye," Dave said. "I can ride one too."

"I can ride my own bike," Mark said. "I don't feel I can handle someone else on it."

"My bride-to-be?" Danny said, hurrying to his bike. "Would you care to join me?"

The rain began in earnest, and soon they were all doubled-up on the bikes except for Mark, who was flying solo. Danny took the lead. At least they were wearing proper rain gear, and once they had shelter, they could remove their raincoats and hopefully not freeze to death. The wind was at their backs, which made steering quite a challenge, but once they got the hang of it, it helped push them along, and before they knew it, the rusted hulk of the *Plassey* shipwreck came into view. Tara could only imagine the terror when the six-hundred-ton ship collided with Finnis Rock and was thrown by the wind onto the eastern shore of this island. But the crew had been lucky. The brave islanders rescued all eleven crew members and of course salvaged the cargo. Were the twelve hundred residents of this island in the present day still so brave and kind? Tara was sure someone would open their doors to them if they only knew they were out here. Suddenly Rachel's earlier singing of "three-hour tour" didn't seem so funny. They still didn't have cell service, and she didn't even have her phone. At least this island wasn't deserted, so as soon as they made it through the storm, they could find an inn, or a pub, or some kind soul to help them. That is, of course, unless a killer had another plan in mind.

They were indeed able to crawl underneath the shipwreck, and it was just in time. The wind howled and rain pummeled the wreck, the pinging on the rusted steel as loud as gunshots. They managed to all huddle in the same area for extra warmth. Even if one of them was a killer, the storm might get them first. Danny had his arm around Tara. "You're a good sport," he whispered. "I'm glad I'm marrying you." Tara felt a warmth spread through her. Danny O'Donnell was long on charm but short on compliments.

"Back at ya," she said.

"If any colleens want to cuddle, I've got two arms," Tom said.

"I'll take me chances," Breanna answered.

Rachel had scooted awfully close to Dave, but he didn't seem to notice. His knees were up to his chest, his hands hugging them to his body, and he started to rock and croon. Tara felt for him. First his twin murdered, now stuck with a group of strangers underneath another ship in a storm. This had to be a living nightmare.

"Why don't we all say where we were when Noel drank that shake," Breanna said.

"Like our alibi?" Rachel asked.

"I just think it might be good to talk it out," Breanna continued.

"Are you joking me?" Mark said. "What good will that do?"

"Don't we all agree by now that it was Captain Mickey?" Tom chimed in.

"I don't think it's Captain Mickey," Breanna said. "Captain Sara told us he was really scared."

"He sent us to an island in a storm to fend for ourselves with nothing but a Bible," Dave said. "If that's not indicative of a madman, I don't know what is."

With nothing but a Bible. Tara couldn't stop thinking about that. Why had he sent them with a Bible? Why did he specifically want Breanna to have it? Was there a clue in the Bible? She needed to get Breanna alone so they could see if there was anything in there.

"We were all huddled around the bar," Rachel said. "Everyone but Tara."

"I was at the stern, looking out at the ocean," Tara said. Through the giant holes in the shipwreck, she watched the wind drive the rain sideways.

"Shouldn't we discuss who had a motive?" Mark said. "I mean we didn't even know Noel." He cleared his throat. "I also overheard one of the twins telling the other he wanted to kill him."

"What?" Dave said. "And why are you talking about me as if I can't hear what you're saying, like?"

"Was it you threatening Noel or was Noel threatening you?" Mark asked.

"I have no idea what you're on about, if either of us said it, it was in jest." Dave, who had finally stopped fidgeting just a bit ago, started rocking again.

"I know what you burned in the fire, Mark," Tara said. Tempers were flaring, and technically none of them had any range of movement to speak of. Poison wasn't a woman's game. It was a coward's game. Maybe it was time to frighten the coward.

"Me?" Mark said. "What fire?"

"The fireplace in the cottage," Breanna said.

"Where we could be right now," Rachel said.

"What did you burn in the fire?" Tom's voice was low and menacing. Uh-oh. On the other hand, maybe Tara should have kept her mouth shut.

"She's making it up," Mark said.

"I'm not," Tara said. "And when I went back to the cottage, I retrieved it. Not all of it burned."

"What is it?" Danny asked.

"If someone burned something in the fire, it wasn't me." But Mark sounded worried. He knew exactly what they'd found.

Thunder rolled and something hit the hull of the shipwreck with a *thunk*. Everyone jumped.

"What in heavens name are ye doing out here in the storm?" It was a deep voice, but all they could see from their viewpoint was a pair of large black boots.

"Thank God," Rachel said, crawling out.

"Hey," Tara said, as she tried to grab her ankle. "We don't even know who it is."

"I don't care if it's Noah and he wants to take me on his ark," Rachel said. "I'm getting out of here."

Suddenly a face appeared as the person bent down to peer inside. It was Captain Sara. "Change of plans," she said. "Captain Mickey took pity on ye. After all, only one of you is a killer. Now. Who wants to go inside a warm cottage and have a nice supper?" Tara was bumped left and right as everyone crawled out from underneath the shipwreck. And just when things were starting to happen. Tara felt as if her movie had been interrupted at the very moment the killer was revealed. But at least this way, she'd be able to get her hands on that Bible.

Chapter Eleven
Say Grace

When they arrived at a thatched-roof cottage thirty minutes later, Tara was relieved to step inside and be wrapped in warmth. A fire was going, and a woman with a round face and bright smile began passing out towels, and they had piles of clothing laid out on the sofa for them to choose from. Tara had already decided that she wasn't leaving this cottage until the storm was well and past, no matter what the others decided to do. She was rifling through clothes when someone came up behind her.

"Can we talk?" She turned to find Mark behind her, an intense look on his face.

"Sure." They moved over to a quiet corner.

"About that photo . . ."

She glanced at his hand and saw the same silver ring with etchings. "I'm sorry," she said. "I should have spoken with you in private."

"Did you tell anyone else? Tom?"

"Do you think I told Tom?"

Mark looked down at his feet. "No."

"I'm not going to tell anyone," she said. "But I think you should."

"I know," he said. "I will. But I'm not a killer. You know that, don't you?" She remained silent. He shook his head and walked away.

"Where's Captain Mickey?" Breanna asked.

"He's with the guards," Captain Sara said. "Still on Inishmaan." She looked as if she had a juicy secret. "I shouldn't be saying this now, but they found a tiny piece of thallium on the boat."

"What's thallium?" Rachel asked.

"It's a poison," Captain Sara said. "A very deadly one."

"Is it silver?" Tara asked.

Captain Sara raised an eyebrow. "How did you know?"

"I saw a tiny piece of metal on the floor—and an empty vial on the counter," Tara admitted.

"What?" Dave shouted. "Why didn't you say something?"

Because one of you might be a killer. "I didn't have a clue what it was," Tara said. "I thought maybe it was metal off your tap shoes."

"Dance shoes," Dave said. "I told you it wasn't." His mood had turned sour. He turned to Captain Sara. "Did the coroner think he was poisoned with thallium?"

"I wouldn't have those details now," Captain Sara said.

Tara felt a rush of cold go through her, and it had

nothing to do with the weather. She had once designed a penthouse in NYC for a chemist. He liked to chat. And one thing he had chatted with her about was thallium. Tara knew two things about thallium. One, it was very deadly, even to the touch. Two, it didn't kill instantly. Or even in a half hour. It took time to build up thallium poisoning in the body. Days, weeks even.

"Why don't you all get changed, and I'll be putting supper on the table. A nice Irish stew," Captain Sara said.

Tara made a beeline for Breanna and dragged her to a private corner. "I need to see that Bible."

"We're safe, pet. Why the panic?"

"Please. I think there's a clue to the murder in there."

Breanna retrieved the Bible from her coat and handed it to Tara. Tara thanked her and took it in the restroom. There, she locked the door and opened it. She found no letter announcing a killer stuffed inside, no indication of where in the Bible she should look. She thought about it. She thought about everything that happened on the boat. But mostly she thought about everything Noel said. And finally, everything clicked. When she opened to the correct passage, a shiver ran through her. But what was she going to do about it?

She changed clothes and found Captain Sara at the stove. "I'm just about to dish it out, luv."

"This is your cottage, isn't it?" Tara asked.

"It is."

"Thank you so much for letting us stay here."

"You're welcome. Although you won't be staying long. The guards are on their way to take you back to Inishmore."

This was the best news she'd heard all day. "When will they be here?"

"Should be here by the time we finish supper."

Perfect.

Soon they all had changed into mismatched and ill-fitting but dry clothing. Everyone had a heaping bowl in front of them. A few reached for their spoons.

"Before we begin," Tara said. "I thought Dave might like to say grace."

Dave froze with the spoon halfway to his mouth. "Me?"

"Do you know any good ones?" Tara asked. "I noticed the cross Noel was wearing, so I assume the two of you were devout."

Dave frowned. "No. That was Noel. He was always quoting scriptures. I didn't mind it at all, and I am as good a Catholic lad as I can be—but it's me brother who would have led grace."

"I see," Tara said. "That's why Noel told us who his killer was in code."

"Code?" Tom said. "What are you on about?" Everyone stared at Tara. Dave let his spoon drop into his bowl. Given the stew smelled delicious, she realized she should have waited before ruining everyone's appetite.

"He kept saying 'Mark,'" Dave stuttered. "Pointing at Mark. Are you saying what I think you're saying?"

Mark leapt from the table. "Are you accusing me—"

Tara held up her hand. Mark glowered but sat. "But then he pointed at Tom," Tara continued. Tom looked up, then simply dug into his stew and gave a moan of appreciation. "But then he pointed at an empty egg carton."

"He was delirious," Dave said.

"You never left his side," Tara said. "He had to find another way of letting us know who he thought had done this to him." She took a breath. "Mark. Thirteen. Twelve." She glanced at Breanna, who took it from there.

"Tom was wearing a jersey with the number thirteen. An egg carton that held a dozen—12—eggs!" Breanna held up the Bible. "Captain Mickey was kind enough to lend us his Bible. Mark chapter 13, verse 12. I'm only going to read the first part because I believe that's where he was going with this." Dave's face had gone white. And despite the cold, he'd broken into a sweat. "And brother will deliver brother over to death . . ."

Danny let out a low whistle.

"You killed him," Rachel said. "You killed your twin."

"Diabolical," Mark said.

Dave began to sweat profusely. "That's ridiculous," he shouted. "You're reaching!"

"If the coroner confirms he was poisoned by thallium, it won't look good for you," Tara said calmly.

Dave shook his head. "I already told ye it wasn't off me shoes."

"I've no doubt it was purchased on the black market," Tara said. "But the reason I say it won't look good for you is that thallium poisoning is done a little at a time. It can take weeks to add up to a lethal dose. *Weeks*." Everyone stared at Dave. He opened and closed his mouth like a fish. "Captain Mickey will no doubt testify that he did not write *D-A* on the cup."

"You can't prove that!" Dave shouted.

"Your fingerprints will be on the Sharpie. You wanted everyone to think that Noel was trying to poison you. The little twin-switch scenario. But you got lucky that it could have also stood for *Danny*. Not only would it muddy the waters, it would also throw suspicion on Captain Mickey."

"Prove it."

"I don't have to. I think the reason Captain Mickey disappeared and gave us the Bible was that *he* could prove it. He must have seen you remove a plastic vial from your backpack—the one you refused to let him take with the rest of our luggage—and slip it into the milkshake, then start to write *D-A* on it. No one else would have had any reason to stop writing the name. You wanted us to be confused. So you could get away with murder."

Dave was trembling now. "If Captain Mickey says he saw me do that, he's a liar."

"You wanted to stop dancing," Tara said. "Is that why you weren't invited to join him on *Dancing with the Stars*?"

Dave was starting to vibrate. His leg bounced underneath the table. "How did you know I wasn't invited?"

"A little birdie told me." She wasn't going to put the publican in danger.

Dave threw his napkin on the table, and for a moment Tara thought he was going to launch himself at her and strangle her with his bare hands. "He wins again," Dave said. "Even in death, Noel Carrigan wins." He screeched back from the table and ran to the door. "I loved him," he said. "But we were twins. We were supposed to stick together. He should have never accepted an invitation to dance solo. I gave up law school for him, and he betrays me like that?"

"Don't run," Danny said. "You'll make it worse."

"I'm going to throw meself off a cliff," Dave said. He threw open the door. Then slammed it. He whirled around and pointed at Tara. "I should have given that milkshake to you."

Danny stood protectively. "Stay there."

Soon fists could be heard pounding on the door. "That must be the guards coming now," Tara said. "I'm sorry, Dave. I think this is your last dance."

Tara was never so happy to be back in Galway. Dave had finally given a full confession—a tale of two brothers torn between wanting to stay together and go their own ways. Tara asked Rachel to stay on until the wedding, and she graciously agreed. They enjoyed an old-fashioned hen party with just the three ladies, while Danny and Tom did their own thing. Mark had confessed his sins to Tom, and for now the pair of them weren't speaking. Mark had bowed out of the wedding. But the five of them made the best of it. They got together in their local pub and raised a pint to the adventure they'd survived, giving their thanks to the basics like dry clothes and a roof over their head.

Breanna paused with her pint in the air. "Here's to no more hen parties, ever!"

They all hoisted their pints once more. "No more hen parties, ever!"

"Except when I get engaged," Breanna said. "Then we're having a hen party. With Irish milkshakes!" The rest of them stared at her as she grinned and grinned.

MURDER MOST IRISH

Peggy Ehrhart

Acknowledgments

Abundant thanks to my agent, Evan Marshall, and to my editor at Kensington Books, John Scognamiglio.

Chapter One

"A milkshake called The Leprechaun?" Bettina Fraser lowered her menu to address Pamela Paterson. "This new cook—or 'chef,' as he calls himself—is certainly imaginative."

She raised the menu again, hiding her face and leaving only her pouf of scarlet hair visible. Pamela and Bettina were lunching at Hyler's Luncheonette, sitting at one of the tables near the big plate-glass window that allowed a view of the passing scene on Arborville Avenue.

"I think I'll have a tuna melt." Pamela spoke half to herself, but a server was standing nearby, and a few quick steps brought her to Pamela's side. Sensing the server's presence, Bettina lowered her menu again.

"The same for me," she said.

The server, a sweet-faced young woman who Pamela recognized as a recent addition to Hyler's staff, made a notation on her order pad. "And to drink?" she inquired. "May I suggest The Leprechaun? It won't be on the menu forever—the chef just invented it, and it's special for St. Patrick's Day. After next week, it will be gone for a whole year."

"Is that it?" Bettina pointed toward one of the Naugahyde-upholstered booths along the wall. There, on the worn wooden table, sat a tall frosted glass containing a bright-green liquid.

"Yes." The server nodded, and her blond ponytail bounced. "Very minty—that's where the green comes from. Do you want to try one?"

Bettina tightened her lips into a contemplative knot, but after a moment of contemplation, she said, "I'll just stick with my usual vanilla."

Pamela requested a vanilla milkshake as well, and the server collected their menus, the oversize menus that were a Hyler's trademark, and went on her way.

"In a rut, I guess." Bettina shrugged. "Both of us . . ." Her voice trailed off, and her focus shifted from Pamela, who was sitting across from her, to the view of Arborville Avenue offered by the window. "Oh my goodness!" she exclaimed. "I didn't know they were going to do this! What a spectacle!"

Pamela was sitting with her back to the window. She turned abruptly, and the legs of her chair squeaked against the wooden floor. The sight she encountered was indeed unusual, at least in the context of a suburban New Jersey town.

A small flock of sheep was making its way past Hyler's windows, jostling each other but sticking close together as they trotted along the sidewalk. They were large creatures, but dainty-footed, with wide-set eyes, jutting ears, and springy, tightly coiled fur. A faint chorus of baaas was audible through the plate glass. Leading them was a young man in jeans and a T-shirt, carrying a shepherd's crook. Visible as the procession moved past the window and continued south was a young woman, also casually dressed.

"They're students from Wendelstaff College," Bettina explained, raising her voice to be heard over the laughter and exclamations that had erupted among the other diners, some of whom had risen from their seats and moved closer to the window. "The *Advocate* got a press release. I knew about the sheep, but I didn't know there would be a parade. The sheep are part of an event the students are staging in the park behind the library."

"What's the event about?" Pamela asked, half turning to face Bettina.

"Sustainable living," Bettina said. "It was all in the press release. To raise interest in 'slow fashion'—the opposite of fast fashion—they're going to shear the sheep. I was planning to stop by later this afternoon. My editor wants a story."

The sheep by now had passed, and the diners had calmed down and settled back into their seats. Pamela had returned her chair to its normal position, from which she could see their server delivering another bright-green milkshake to another booth, along with an oval platter on which rested what looked like a hamburger and fries.

Delivery completed, the server made her way back to the counter that stretched across the back wall of Hyler's. A few moments later, she was heading toward Pamela and Bettina, laden with oval platters bearing tuna melts.

"Back in a second with your milkshakes," she said as she lowered the platters onto the paper placemats already set with napkins and silverware.

But she had no sooner turned away than a commotion drew their attention to one of the booths along the wall. It was the booth to which the server had just delivered the bright-green shake and the hamburger and fries. The shake had tipped over, and a green puddle was oozing across the table's surface, with a few green dribbles already landing on the floor.

The diner, a portly middle-aged man, had sagged forward, landing with his head on his uneaten hamburger.

Once again, the diners were distracted from their meals, bobbing up and down for a better look. Amid the murmurs, Pamela heard someone say, "That's Lionel Dunes, from St. Willibrod's."

The man who collapsed, apparently Lionel Dunes, had been alone in his booth, but the couple sitting at the nearest table had instantly jumped to their feet. The woman was now bending over Lionel Dunes while the man looked around the room.

"Is anyone in here a doctor?" he called.

Many people were talking at once, but no one responded to his question. He repeated it in a louder voice and then shrugged and picked up his phone. The young blond server who had delivered the green milkshake made her way among the tables toward the booth containing Lionel Dunes. She was followed by an older woman, also a server and a longtime member of Hyler's staff.

Pamela had been watching the commotion from her

seat by the window, craning her neck and twisting to get a clearer view. When she glanced back to check on how Bettina was reacting, she was startled to see that Bettina had disappeared—at least from the other side of the table. Bettina was instead en route to the site of the unfolding drama, her bright hair and jaunty orange blazer making her easy to pick out from the crowd.

The whoop of a siren from Arborville Avenue signaled that help had arrived. Visible through the plate-glass window, an ambulance came to a stop at the curb in a spot usually reserved for handicapped parking. A pair of EMTs, a man and a woman dressed in navy-blue pants and zip-front jackets bearing shield-shaped patches, emerged. They opened the back of the ambulance and slid a stretcher out, expanding its crisscrossed metal legs until it stood waist-high and wheeling it toward Hyler's heavy glass door.

A diner at a booth near the door hopped up and pulled the door open. Other diners edged aside and pushed tables and chairs out of the way so the EMTs could guide the stretcher toward where Lionel Dunes still sagged onto his uneaten meal. The diner who had bent over him right after his collapse was hovering nearby.

"I think he's still breathing," she reported to the female EMT, a sturdy older woman, "but his lips are blue."

The EMT nodded, and she and the male EMT set to work. The room fell silent as they aligned the stretcher with the burgundy Naugahyde bench that Lionel Dunes sat on and then lowered it so it was the same height as the bench. They gently nudged him onto his side and tugged him onto the stretcher, rolling him onto his back and securing him to the stretcher with wide straps.

Once he had been wheeled through the jumble of tables and chairs and out the door, conversation resumed. The young blond server was still standing near the booth, and she turned to the older one with a puzzled expression.

"Do we clear away . . . or what?" she inquired.

"I don't see why we shouldn't," the older server said. "It wasn't the food. He had some kind of a spell or something, like a stroke. He hadn't even tasted his hamburger." She collected the platter that held the now-cold hamburger and fries.

The young server picked up the glass containing the milkshake. "He did drink some of this," she commented. "Quite a lot, in fact. I guess he liked The Leprechaun."

Most of the diners had returned to their seats and taken up eating where they left off. Bettina, however, still lingered near Lionel Dunes's booth, scrutinizing the bench where he had been sitting. As Pamela watched, she bobbed forward, apparently reaching for something. When she straightened up again, she was holding what looked like a rolled-up T-shirt. She unrolled it, holding it out to examine it, but she was still facing the booth with her back toward the room, and most of the T-shirt was hidden by her body.

An alarmed squeal rose above the sedate chatter that had resumed. The chatter stopped and eyes turned toward Bettina. She whirled around and displayed the T-shirt. Printed across the front in large block letters were the words "Kill Me, I'm Irish."

The older server had set off with the platter, disappearing through the swinging doors that led to the kitchen, and the young server had followed her across the room with the remains of the milkshake. She, however, hadn't quite reached the doors yet, and she turned in response to Bettina's squeal. As she gazed at the T-shirt, her expression was transformed. Her lips stretched into a grimace, and her eyes grew wider and wider. Setting the milkshake on the counter, she darted across the floor until she reached Bettina.

"I had no idea," she exclaimed, grasping one hand with the other and twisting her fingers. "No idea at all. Someone . . ." She gulped and took a deep breath. "Someone left a parcel this morning—I didn't even see the person. The parcel just appeared on the counter, with a note that said to deliver it to Lionel Dunes when he came in. The shirt was inside, I guess. Where did you find it?"

"Back in the corner." Bettina nodded in the direction of the bench where Lionel Dunes had been sitting.

"Would he have left it behind on purpose, if he hadn't . . ." The young server's voice trailed off.

Diners at neighboring tables were watching the exchange with interest. One woman, a pleasant woman Pamela recognized from the bank, spoke up to say, "Maybe the note and wrappings are still here. You should retrieve them in case . . . in case, you know . . ."

"He dies and it's not natural causes," her dining companion, who Pamela also recognized from the bank, chimed in.

"Not natural . . . yes, of course," the young server murmured and then covered the lower half of her face with her hands. Her eyes, still open abnormally wide, stared out from above her crisscrossed fingers.

They were joined then by the older server, who put her arm around the young server's shoulders. Bettina was still holding the T-shirt, but no longer in such a way as to display the message across its front.

Pamela was curious about the note and the wrappings. If the EMTs had noticed the T-shirt, which must have been tucked away at the very far end of the bench, they certainly would have retrieved it, along with anything else. She climbed to her feet and threaded her way among tables filled with people more interested in the unfolding drama than in their meals until she was standing at Bettina's side. Bettina handed Pamela the T-shirt and turned back toward the booth. She peered into its shadowy recesses.

"Do you see anything?" Pamela asked.

"Something . . . but I don't think I can reach it." Bettina leaned on the bench, and her head disappeared under the table. Her voice was muffled. She groaned and inched forward along the bench, murmuring, "Getting closer . . ."

A moment later, she popped back up and eased into a sitting position. Her face was pink from exertion, but she raised a hand triumphantly. In it was a crumpled piece of brown paper with a few strips of parcel tape clinging to the edges. She laid it on the table and smoothed it out with a carefully manicured hand. Taped to the brown paper was a formal-looking note, like something printed on a computer: "This is for Lionel Dunes. Please deliver it to him when he comes in for lunch today."

"I think I should keep this," Bettina said, looking up at the two servers, who were hovering nearby. "It could be important later, depending on what happens with Lionel Dunes. I'll be talking to Detective Clayborn soon—I meet with him every week to report on police doings for the *Advocate*."

"Take it." The older server made a pushing-away gesture as if to disavow any connection with the wrapper and its attached note. "And take the T-shirt too . . . unless"—she closed her eyes and frowned—"he turns out to be okay and comes back here looking for it."

"We'll take care of it." Bettina shifted her gaze to Pamela, who was still holding the shirt. Then she reached out and stroked the older server's arm. "You have enough to think about."

The woman stared and opened her mouth. No words came out, and she closed it again.

"I mean . . . I just mean . . . that you're very busy here." Bettina folded the wrapper into a more compact shape and pushed herself to her feet. "You both take care now," she added, and offered a quick hug to the older server and then to the young one. "Everything will be fine."

Back at their own table, Pamela and Bettina studied their neglected lunches. The sandwiches no longer glistened with melted butter as they had when fresh from the griddle, and the tall glasses that held the milkshakes were no longer frosted, but rather streaked with drips of moisture. But Pamela was hungry, and food was not to be wasted.

Bettina had already picked up her knife and fork and carved off a bite of tuna melt.

"I'm not sure about drinking the milkshake, though," she commented as she raised the bite of sandwich to her mouth.

"Lots of people have been drinking theirs." Pamela glanced around the room. "And somebody at one of the other booths even drank one of the green ones with no ill effects."

Bettina nodded and gazed at her milkshake. "The milkshakes are so good here, even partly melted like this one. It would be a shame to just leave it."

Pamela nodded too. "There's no reason to think Lionel Dunes collapsed from drinking the milkshake. People collapse for all sorts of reasons." She pulled her milkshake closer and leaned toward the straw protruding from its creamy surface. A long sip delivered a smooth, cool draft of vanilla-flavored richness.

Bettina followed suit and looked up from her milkshake with a smile that reminded Pamela of a contented cat.

They focused on their meal then, chatting on and off, as diners around them chatted too. New arrivals with apparently no idea that anything untoward had happened earlier seated themselves at Hyler's tables and in Hyler's booths—even the booth from which Lionel Dunes had been carried by the EMTs. Pamela was sure, however, that Arborville's grapevine was already abuzz with news and speculation about Lionel Dunes's lunchtime collapse.

Chapter Two

Not too much later, Pamela and Bettina stepped through Hyler's heavy glass door onto the side-walk. The March day was unseasonably warm, and the sky was a clear blue.

"A good day for the sheep-shearing event," Bettina commented. "Come on along with me. It's just around the corner. In fact"—she tipped her head toward the gap between Hyler's and the hair salon that was its neighbor—"we can take a shortcut, and I can drop this T-shirt and wrapping off at my car."

A dark and narrow passageway, suited only to foot traffic, led from Arborville Avenue to the parking lot that served the library, the police station, and the town park. Bettina led the way into the shadows, and very shortly they emerged into the sunlight.

Before them lay a stretch of asphalt with cars in rows along either side, and beyond that, a wide lawn the sallow green of early spring. Roaming the lawn were sheep, almost top-heavy with their delicate legs and their thick, fleecy coats. A few were nibbling at the unpromising grass. A small cluster of casually dressed young people, presumably students from Wendelstaff College, stood at the edge of the lawn near a table whose surface was covered with piles of leaflets, cards, and flyers.

Bettina stowed the T-shirt and wrapping in the trunk of her Toyota, and she and Pamela set out across the parking lot. As they approached the young people, Bettina called out, "Did I miss the shearing?"

It seemed unlikely to Pamela that they had indeed missed the shearing, because the sheep still appeared luxuriantly fleeced. Wouldn't they look . . . *sheared* . . . if they had in fact been sheared?

A young man, the same young man who had led the sheep past Hyler's window, turned, took a few steps toward Bettina, and extended his hand. "Amos Clark," he said.

"Bettina Fraser from the *Arborville Advocate*," Bettina responded, accepting the offered hand for a brief handshake. "And this is Pamela Paterson."

Pamela shook hands with the young man too. He was medium-sized, with brown eyes and hair, and pleasant features as yet unmarked by life's challenges. Seeing his T-shirt up close, Pamela noticed that it was printed with the words "Kiss Me, I'm Irish."

"Did I miss the shearing?" Bettina repeated.

Amos's lips tightened into an unhappy grimace. "It's postponed," he said. "Till next Saturday. Aileen is at the hospital with her husband."

"Aileen?" Bettina raised a puzzled eyebrow. "I think

that's who sent the press release to the *Advocate*. What happened to her husband?"

"She's Aileen Conway, but she's married to Lionel Dunes. She teaches at Wendelstaff, and she's the sustainable living group's advisor. Lionel was taken ill while he was having lunch at Hyler's." Amos nodded toward where the back of the building that housed Hyler's faced the parking lot.

"Oh my goodness!" Bettina raised a carefully manicured hand to her cheek. "We were just in there." She glanced at Pamela to indicate that Pamela was part of the "we." "What a shocking thing that was!"

"Very," Amos agreed. His gaze, tinged with melancholy, drifted toward the sheep. "We had a good turnout right when it was supposed to start, but people didn't stick around after we announced the postponement." He took a deep breath, squared his shoulders, and brightened. "Next week, though. We'll try again, and I'm sure Lionel will be fine."

A female voice reached them from across the parking lot then, calling hello. The greeting was intended for Amos, they realized, as he turned in that direction and brightened even more. Approaching them was the young blond server from Hyler's, still wearing her uniform of white shirt and black pants. She was followed by the older woman who had been her fellow server earlier.

"Shiloh!" Amos reached out an arm and pulled her to his side as soon as she came within reach. "How are you doing?" He nuzzled her cheek.

"I guess you two know each other," Bettina commented with a gentle laugh.

Amos ceased nuzzling and said, "This is Shiloh Aston." He extended a hand toward the older woman and added, "And her mother, Dot Aston."

Mother and daughter did resemble each other, though Dot's hair was more of a dishwater blond, and her build was sturdier.

Bettina happily completed the introductions by mentioning her own name and Pamela's. "I've seen you both in Hyler's so many times," she went on, "that I feel like I know you already." Her expression modulated from sociable cheer to concern, and she extended a soothing hand toward Dot. "How are you doing after that . . . medical event?" she inquired. "How are both of you doing?"

"He'll be fine." Dot nodded. "I'm sure. The EMTs were so prompt."

The conversation veered back to the sheep-shearing then, with Amos explaining that the owner of the sheep would be coming at three to pick them up, though the shearers recruited for the occasion had already taken their equipment and gone home. The sheep had had the effect of arousing interest in the sustainable living concept, and the group had been able to give out some literature.

"Hopefully next week it will all happen the way it's supposed to," Shiloh said, and lifted a delicate hand to display crossed fingers. She gently disentangled herself from Amos, who had kept her tucked close to his side. "I've got to get back," she whispered. "We both do." She leaned in for a quick kiss. "Talk to you later."

"We've got to get going too," Bettina said, after bidding Shiloh and Dot goodbye.

But before stepping away, she turned her attention to Amos. The expression on her face—implying friendly, offhand curiosity—was an expression that Pamela knew well. Bettina employed it to good effect in her news-gathering adventures, and the curiosity it implied was in reality anything but offhand.

"Your T-shirt is just right for the upcoming holiday," she said. "Did you buy it locally?"

Amos tipped his head to look down at the shirt front as if, Pamela thought, to remind himself what wardrobe choice he had made that morning.

"Oh, this?" he laughed. "A friend makes them. I'm not even Irish."

Amos glanced around the park. "He was here before. He's a big supporter of the sustainable living concept—the basic shirts he starts with are dead stock, discontinued lines, surplus. He silkscreens the captions—all kinds of captions."

"Like 'Kill me, I'm Irish'?" Bettina's tone was still light.

Amos pulled back and a vertical crease came and went between his brows. Then he laughed, like a short bark. "I haven't seen that one," he said. "He's got a website though—just Google 'Tommy's Tees.' He sells them out of his dorm room too, and at craft fairs."

Bettina promised to return the following Saturday for the sheep-shearing, and then she and Pamela turned and headed toward where Bettina's faithful Toyota waited near the entrance to the library.

"Why did you ask him that?" Pamela inquired when they were halfway across the parking lot.

"I don't know." Bettina stopped walking and faced

Pamela. She looked into the distance, and her lips tightened into a puzzled zigzag. "It just popped out. I'm sure Lionel Dunes will be fine, but if he isn't . . ."

They walked on in silence until they reached the car.

"You wouldn't want to stop at the Co-Op, would you?" Pamela asked. "I need a few groceries—but I don't mind walking home, really, if you've got things to do."

"I'll go with you." Bettina took out her keys and unlocked the passenger-side door. "I like to visit the Co-Op every once in a while, even though Wilfred does all the cooking now."

Bettina had been a conscientious, if uninspired, cook through three decades of married life, serving the same seven meals in rotation week after week until her husband retired and enthusiastically took charge of the kitchen.

"What are you and Pete doing tonight?" she inquired, in a change of topic as she steered the Toyota toward the parking lot's exit.

Friendly, offhand curiosity? Pamela asked herself. Or anything but? The answer, however, was simple: "Nothing."

"Don't tell me he's out of the picture now too!" The Toyota lurched as Bettina pressed too hard on the gas pedal and then removed her foot completely.

Pamela had been widowed many years earlier, but had only recently started dating again, whereupon Bettina had taken a lively interest in her romantic prospects. Pete was Pete Paterson, and Pamela had met him through the curious fact that they shared the same last name and first initial.

Pamela laughed. "He's still in the picture. His nephew is getting married out on Long Island this weekend, and he'll be away till Sunday night."

"So you'll be alone. I'd invite you to come over for dinner, but we're meeting Wilfred's cousin at a restaurant."

"I'll be okay," Pamela said.

They were underway again, and the short drive to the Co-Op Grocery proceeded without incident.

Pamela set her grocery bags on her kitchen table and greeted the cats sniffing around her feet. It was pleasant to be welcomed home by housemates, even if the housemates weren't human.

Pamela and Bettina lived across the street from each other in large old houses typical of the houses in Arborville. Pamela and her architect husband had bought their house as a fixer-upper many years earlier, attracted to Arborville because, though it was in New Jersey, it reminded them of the Midwestern college town where they met and fell in love. When Michael was killed in a tragic construction-site accident, Pamela remained in the house they had so carefully restored, wanting their daughter's life to continue as much as possible as it had been. Now that daughter, Penny, was all grown up and Pamela was alone in the house, but for Catrina, Ginger, and Precious.

Groceries were quickly put away. Perishables went into the refrigerator, apples into the wooden bowl on the counter, bread into the bread drawer, and cat food into the cupboard. That chore done, she checked the clock and noted that it was barely three o'clock.

Today, in a rare reprieve, no work waited upstairs on her computer. Pamela's job required skill and dedication, but it had always been done from home, even before the realization that much work could be done from home transformed so many people's lives. As associate editor of *Fiber Craft* magazine, Pamela was tasked with evaluating articles submitted for publication, copyediting articles chosen, and reviewing the occasional book. Only every month or so was she required to travel into Manhattan for an in-person day at the office, and the job had been ideal when Penny was small.

With the luxury of a free afternoon lying ahead, a few hours of knitting seemed as nice a way to fill that time as anything she could imagine. Perhaps, given that it was such an unseasonably warm day, she would even take her knitting out onto the porch. Then, later, she would start a pot of brown rice on the stove top and slip the piece of salmon she'd bought for dinner into the oven.

By the time Pamela stepped back into her kitchen the next morning after a trip to the curb for the newspaper, the kettle was hooting so frantically that the cats had interrupted their breakfast to stare at the stove. She herself stared for a moment, disoriented, as the unfolded newspaper dangled from her fingers.

The headline, glimpsed through the flimsy plastic sleeve that contained the newspaper, had been so startling that she had pulled the *County Register* from its wrapper en route back to her porch. Then she had stopped before ascending the steps to absorb the headline and skim the first few lines of the article, which was by the *Register*'s ace reporter, Marcy Brewer.

ARBORVILLE MAN DEAD FROM CYANIDE POISONING read the lead article's headline. Below, in smaller letters, were the words, "Police Suspect Murder."

"Arborville resident Lionel Dunes was pronounced dead yesterday afternoon at County Hospital," Marcy Brewer had written in her opening paragraph. "He was taken there by paramedics after collapsing while eating lunch at Hyler's Luncheonette, a popular Arborville eatery. He had drunk half a milkshake called The Leprechaun, which had recently been added to the menu in honor of St. Patrick's Day. Though an autopsy is pending, his symptoms and appearance were consistent with cyanide poisoning."

The kettle was still hooting, and steam was erupting from its spout. Pamela took a deep breath, ordered herself to concentrate, and set the newspaper down on the table. Before stepping outside for the newspaper, she had ground coffee beans and transferred the grounds into a paper filter nestled into her carafe's plastic filter cone. Now she turned off the heat under the hooting kettle and poured a stream of boiling water over the grounds. The fragrant aroma thus released brought her back to herself.

The fresh loaf of whole-grain bread from the Co-Op's bakery counter waited in the bread drawer, but just as she was moving on to the toast stage of her breakfast ritual, she was distracted by the doorbell's chime. The cats too were distracted, and Catrina and

Ginger scampered ahead of her as she hurried to the entry.

A figure was visible through the lace that curtained the oval window in the front door—a female figure particularly recognizable by the bright scarlet of her hair. Pamela pulled the door back to admit Bettina.

"You saw it, I suppose," Bettina exclaimed as she extended a foot to step over the threshold. The foot wore a dainty kitten-heeled shoe in pale pink. "The *Register*, I mean—I noticed that you'd already picked up your copy from the curb."

She was carrying a white cardboard bakery box, which she thrust toward Pamela. In a change of topic, she added, "Wilfred went out first thing this morning so it's really fresh. Still warm, even."

Early as it was, Bettina's scarlet hair had already been styled into its careful bouffant, and her makeup was flawless. She dressed for her life in suburban Arborville with the flair of a devoted fashionista, even if her figure was anything but svelte and even if the occasion was simply a visit to her best friend's house for morning coffee. Today she had acknowledged the unseasonably warm weather by taking from her closet a pair of wide-legged linen pants in pale pink and pairing them with a striped linen blouse that combined the same pale pink with soft cream. Large pearls dangled from her earlobes.

Pamela accepted the box and said, "Come on into the kitchen. Coffee's ready."

Bettina knew her way around Pamela's kitchen as well as Pamela herself did, and she headed directly for the cupboard where the wedding china was stored. It was precious and beautiful, featuring garlands of pink roses, but Pamela thought it was silly to save pretty things for special occasions, and she used it every day.

It was the work of only a few minutes to arrange cups and saucers and small plates on the little table and add napkins and silverware. Bettina made sure the cut-glass sugar bowl and cream pitcher, filled with heavy cream, were convenient to her customary chair. As Pamela poured coffee into the cups, Bettina untied the string that secured the bakery box's flaps, folded the top back, and transferred a square of crumb cake to each plate.

The *Register* had been set aside, but so eager was Bettina to discuss the startling news about Lionel Dunes that she let her coffee languish without sugar and cream for a minute as she leaned across the table to address Pamela.

"It was the milkshake," she said. "That seems certain. Cyanide supposedly tastes like bitter almonds, but how would anyone know how The Leprechaun was supposed to taste?" She shrugged. "It was green, so mint, I suppose. Didn't that server, who we now know as Shiloh, say it was minty? If it was really minty, and really sweet, that could hide the bitter almond taste."

Pamela nodded. "Or maybe the mint combined with the bitter almond taste, and Lionel Dunes thought that was how it was supposed to taste."

"And it was just the one milkshake, like we noticed." Bettina dipped a spoon into the sugar bowl, apparently now ready to attend to the task of transforming her coffee into the sweet concoction she preferred. "Someone else was drinking a green one with no ill effects."

"Do you think Lionel Dunes was targeted specifically?" Pamela lifted her cup to her lips. The heavy cream that she kept in the refrigerator was specifically reserved for Bettina. Pamela liked her coffee black.

"That's the question." Bettina added a heaping spoonful of sugar to her coffee and stirred vigorously. "Was the poisoned milkshake meant for him? And who put the poison in? And when?"

"Shiloh delivered it," Pamela said. "She could have added the poison, probably easily."

Bettina added a big dollop of cream to her coffee, stirred again, and looked up. "But why?" she asked.

Pamela took a large sip of coffee, enjoying the bitterness and willing the caffeine to do its work. "Shiloh seems the most obvious suspect," she said after a minute. "But for that reason, maybe she isn't. If I was going to poison someone, I wouldn't put the poison in a milkshake that I then delivered to them in full view of at least fifty people."

Bettina took a long sip of her coffee, as if she too was seeking the aid of caffeine in puzzling out the mystery. "The cook could have done it," she announced after returning her cup to its saucer with a clunk, "or 'chef,' as he calls himself."

"How would he know who the milkshake was for," Pamela asked, "without an accomplice?"

"Umm." Bettina had just taken her first bite of crumb cake and was occupied chewing.

Pamela picked up her fork. The Co-Op's crumb cake was one of its bakery counter's most notable offerings. The cake itself was tender and moist, with a touch of lemon, and the crumb topping was dense, rich, and buttery, hinting at cinnamon in color and taste.

She teased off a bite, conveyed it to her mouth, and set all thoughts of Lionel Dunes aside as she yielded to its delights. But those thoughts were set aside for only a moment.

"Bettina!" she exclaimed suddenly.

Bettina looked at her over the rose-garlanded rim of her coffee cup, eyes wide.

"Anyone at all could have added the poison to the milkshake!"

"Really?" Bettina lowered her cup.

"Think about it." Pamela realized she was waving her fork like an old-fashioned schoolmarm driving home a lesson with a ruler. "Food comes from the kitchen and is staged at the end of the counter, where the servers pick it up and deliver it to the tables."

"Yes." Bettina nodded. "I've noticed that."

"What happened to distract everybody in Hyler's right before Lionel Dunes's milkshake was delivered?"

Bettina's eyes grew wider. "The sheep," she whispered. "The sheep being herded past Hyler's window."

"Of course." Pamela rested her fork on her plate. "The sheep could have been timed as the perfect distraction, and the poisoner could have been waiting near the end of the counter for the moment when no one was paying attention to the milkshake destined for Lionel Dunes."

"That doesn't mean Shiloh didn't do it, though."

"No, it doesn't," Pamela agreed. "But it opens up the possibility that lots of other people had access to the milkshake, and Hyler's has a back door too, near that end of the counter."

"Motive," Bettina murmured. "What motive would anyone have for killing Lionel Dunes? He was just an ordinary person, the husband of a Wendelstaff College professor."

She turned her attention to her piece of crumb cake then, as did Pamela, and for the next few minutes the focus was more on eating crumb cake and sipping coffee than on talking. When Bettina spoke again, it was to introduce a topic even closer to home than a murder right in the heart of Arborville.

"What do you hear from Penny?" she asked.

"Not much . . ." Pamela laughed. "Thank goodness! She's too busy with the job—and social life, I'm sure—to pay attention to what's happening here on the west side of the Hudson. I'd prefer she didn't find out that someone was poisoned at Hyler's."

"She still thinks she wants to be an architect?" Bettina's fork, bearing the last bite of her crumb cake, paused partway to her mouth.

"Following in the footsteps of her father," Pamela said, "though at present she's working in the mail room at his old firm while she waits to see if she can get accepted into a good program."

Bettina's fork completed its journey and she surveyed her plate, which now held only crumbs. She lifted the flap of the bakery box and peered inside.

"Two more pieces," she observed. "One for you and one for me."

"I'm fine." Pamela waved her hand as if to shoo away the idea of more. "But you go ahead."

"I will." Bettina folded the flap back, scooped a piece of crumb cake onto her plate, and surveyed Pamela from across the little table. "Only one piece of crumb cake, and black coffee besides. That's why you're thin and I'm not. I'll never understand why you're not more interested in clothes with that figure."

Not only was Pamela thin, she was also tall. But her wardrobe consisted of jeans and hand-knit sweaters, or casual blouses in warm weather, and her dark hair was worn simply, hanging straight to her shoulders or pulled back with a clip.

Bettina lingered for another half hour and then took her leave. Pamela warmed what was left of the coffee, refilled her cup, and returned to the kitchen table to ponder the rest of the day. A walk, for sure, to take advantage of the pleasant weather, she thought, and then laundry and house cleaning, and she'd turn the Co-Op chicken into chicken stew with dumplings.

Chapter Three

It was Monday morning, and the message, as usual, was terse. "Please evaluate the attached articles for possible publication in *Fiber Craft*," Celine Bramley had written, "and get the evaluations to me by 8:00 a.m. Thursday." Across the top of the message, short titles preceded by the Word logo hinted at the articles' contents: "Breton Lace," "Anatolian Tablet Looms," and "Molas."

The leisurely weekend had bred a taste for leisure, and Pamela was reluctant to jump back into work right away. It was only a little after nine, and she was still in her pajamas and robe. Seemingly of its own accord, her cursor roamed the upper reaches of the screen until it landed on "Favorites." She clicked, and from the drop-down list chose AccessArborville, the town's listserv.

Predictably, current discussion focused on the shocking news that Lionel Dunes had been murdered—by poison!—and the poisoning had occurred right in Arborville's very own Hyler's Luncheonette. A few people noted that he would be particularly missed by the congregation at St. Willibrod's, where he volunteered for all manner of tasks. And one person, who had been in Hyler's when he collapsed and had seen the T-shirt, noted that Lionel Dunes wasn't even Irish.

Scrolling down was like traveling back in time, to a time before the Lionel Dunes story had subsumed all other topics. Here was someone troubled by skunks under her porch, and here was someone offering a bunk bed free to anyone who would pick it up. And *here* . . . was Lionel Dunes himself—or rather, a message posted by Lionel Dunes the day before his unfortunate demise.

Under the heading SPRING CLEANING, he had written, "Cleaning out cupboards in the smaller meeting room at St. Willibrod's, I found a cache of old parish photos and papers. Who wants to help me identify the people and decide what to preserve?"

One person had responded and made an appointment to meet Lionel at the church Saturday afternoon. Pamela removed her hand from her computer mouse, rolled her desk chair back, and stared at the screen. Obviously this meeting had not been able to take place. Could Lionel Dunes have been killed in order to make sure it didn't take place?

It was the work of only a few minutes to dash across the hall to her bedroom and pull on yesterday's jeans and blouse.

Wilfred Fraser answered the door, with an apron tied over the bib overalls he had adopted as his everyday uniform when he retired. A welcoming smile creased his ruddy face as he stood aside and gestured for Pamela to enter. The Frasers' house had the yeasty smell of baking bread.

"She's not here though," he said. "She's with Clayborn, but come on in. There's coffee, and she'll be back soon. And I'm just about to take my sourdough out of the oven."

Pamela followed him through the Frasers' inviting living room and dining room to the spacious kitchen. The Frasers' house was the oldest house on the street, a Dutch Colonial, dating from the era when most of Orchard Street had been given over to orchards—apple orchards, to be precise. Bettina and Wilfred had added the kitchen, which featured sliding glass doors that opened onto a back patio. Pamela entered the kitchen to find Woofus the shelter dog lounging in his favorite spot against the wall near the sliding doors, a spot from which he could watch squirrels in the yard.

Seated at the scrubbed pine table that dominated the eating area of the kitchen, Pamela accepted a mug of coffee that Wilfred had fetched from behind the tall counter that marked off the cooking area of the kitchen. No sooner had she taken her first sip than Woofus stirred his shaggy bulk and twisted his head to look toward the front of the house.

He'd been alerted to Bettina's arrival before any sound perceptible by humans could be heard. But now Bettina called from the living room, "Pamela isn't home."

"She's in here," Wilfred called back.

Footsteps made their way to the kitchen, and in a

moment Bettina stepped through the doorway. "I thought you'd want to hear about my meeting with Clayborn," she said, focusing on Pamela. "And here you are."

Bettina had dressed for her meeting with Detective Clayborn in a jersey print wrap dress featuring shades of periwinkle and fuchsia, accessorized with bold silver jewelry and fuchsia kitten heels.

"Dear wife . . ." Wilfred greeted her with a hug. "Sit down and have some coffee. And my loaf of sourdough will be ready in a very few minutes."

"I have things to tell you." Bettina addressed Pamela as she settled onto one of the chairs that surrounded the pine table. Her eyes were bright with purpose.

"I have things to tell you too," Pamela said. "Or rather, *one* thing, but it's an interesting thing."

"You first, then." Bettina looked up and accepted a mug of coffee from Wilfred. He headed back to the area of the kitchen marked off by the high counter, returned with the sugar bowl and cream pitcher from Bettina's sage-green pottery set, and departed again. The yeasty aroma of baking sourdough was becoming intense.

"Lionel Dunes volunteered at St. Willibrod's," Pamela said, "and last week he posted on AccessArborville that he had come across some interesting old photos and papers in a cupboard. He invited parishioners to help him sort through them." Bettina opened her mouth to speak, but Pamela raised a hand and continued. "He had an appointment to meet someone on Saturday afternoon."

"After he was dead," Bettina murmured as she stirred sugar into her coffee.

"Obviously he didn't know he was going to be dead."

"Who was he going to meet?" Bettina asked, pausing as she tipped the cream pitcher over her mug. "That person could be a suspect. I wonder if Clayborn ever looks at AccessArborville."

Pamela shook her head. "Why would the person make an appointment with Lionel but then kill him first?"

Bettina took a sip of coffee and smiled, signifying that her administration of sugar and cream had had the desired effect. Then a crease appeared between her carefully shaped brows and she said, "You came all the way across the street to tell me what you saw on AccessArborville, but now you're saying it's not significant."

"It *is* significant." Pamela tapped on the table. "Think! The person who killed Lionel could have been worried about what might be revealed if the photos and papers were examined—by whoever."

"Hidden secrets," Bettina whispered. "And someone wanted them to remain hidden—at least until he, or she, could investigate that cupboard alone." She took another sip of coffee. "I guess the room is kept locked."

"Probably. Anyway"—Pamela interrupted herself to aim an encouraging nod across the table—"now it's your turn to tell me things."

The sound of the oven opening and closing distracted them, and the aroma of baking sourdough became even more intense.

"Does anyone want to sample my sourdough?" Wilfred called from his post near the stove. Without waiting for an answer, though there was little question what the answer would be, he added, "It has to cool a tiny bit first."

"To begin with"—Bettina sighed—"Hyler's is closed, and that yellow crime-scene tape is all over the place, both doors, front and back." She sighed again. "But on to Clayborn. Shiloh is high on his list of suspects, also the 'chef' at Hyler's who made the milkshakes. He's questioned them both, as well as Shiloh's mother—though he admitted motives are so far lacking in all three cases. And things are complicated by the fact that the remains of the poisoned milkshake had been discarded long before Lionel Dunes died and anyone connected poison with his collapse."

"Did you give Detective Clayborn the T-shirt and the paper wrapping with the note?"

"He wasn't happy—I mean he was happy to have them, but he said I had no business taking them. I pointed out that at the time I took them, no one had any idea that Lionel Dunes had been murdered, and that the T-shirt and the paper wrapping with the note could easily have been mislaid or even purposely destroyed—let's say, if Shiloh and/or the 'chef' are really the culprits."

"Did he say anything about Amos?" Pamela asked.

Bettina's glance had strayed toward where Wilfred was busy in the cooking area of the kitchen, apparently slicing his freshly baked sourdough loaf. Now she focused on Pamela again. "Like what?"

"If Shiloh is a suspect, I'd think Amos would be too—at least if Clayborn makes the obvious connection that we did."

"What connection?" Bettina frowned, and her lips tightened into a puzzled knot.

"That the parade of sheep past Hyler's window was timed to distract everyone while the poisoner tinkered with the milkshake."

"*We* didn't make that connection." Bettina's expression softened into a laugh. "*You* did—and it's very clever."

They were interrupted then by the arrival of Wilfred, bearing a broad wooden cutting board that held the result of his bread-making labors. The loaf had been round, with a domed top baked to a crusty golden brown. Now it was a half round, and next to it lay several slices that displayed the loaf's interior—pale and sponge-like in texture. He set the cutting board down in the middle of the table and headed back the way he had come. Yeasty vapors rose from the still-warm sourdough.

Next to arrive were plates, butter knives, napkins, and a dish of butter and a jar of jam. Wilfred fetched his own coffee and took his seat, beaming with satisfaction.

"It's raspberry jam, from the farmers market in Newfield," he explained as he twisted the lid and the jar opened with a pop. "We had one jar left, from a batch I bought last fall, made by a local jam-maker."

The focus for the next few minutes was on transferring slices of bread to plates, watching pats of butter melt into the welcoming surface of the slices, and adding thick dollops of the ruby-red jam. The taste was as appealing as the vision, with the slightly chewy bread, anointed with butter, the perfect vehicle for the sweet and acidic jam. Wilfred accepted the praise that followed the first sampling bites with a modest dip of his head.

Pamela's sips of her black coffee complemented the bread and jam with its slight bitterness. That black and bitter state seemed to intensify the stimulating effect of the caffeine as well, and her mind returned to the discussion that had preceded the arrival of the bread.

"There was one odd thing Amos did," she said, interrupting the silence that had descended on the table.

Bettina looked up, a mouthful of bread and jam reducing her response to "Umm?"

"When you asked him whether the friend who silkscreened the 'Kiss Me, I'm Irish' T-shirt that he was wearing also made T-shirts reading 'Kill Me, I'm Irish,' he seemed defensive," Pamela explained, adding, "and his 'I haven't seen that one' struck me as a little too self-consciously offhand. But maybe it's just my imagination, or maybe he just didn't think 'Kill Me, I'm Irish' was funny. And by the way, someone on Access-Arborville pointed out that Lionel Dunes wasn't Irish."

"Amos and Shiloh are boyfriend and girlfriend," Bettina observed after she had swallowed. "That complicates things too. But Shiloh's mother has worked at Hyler's forever. If you wanted to kill someone, choosing your mother's workplace as a venue doesn't seem very wise."

"And we have no idea why Shiloh, or Amos, would want to kill Lionel Dunes." Pamela took another sip of her coffee.

Wilfred had been silent, enjoying his sourdough and even helping himself to a second slice. But now he spoke. "The person who made the 'Kill Me, I'm Irish' T-shirt seems implicated somehow."

"Tommy's Tees," Pamela said.

"Maybe *he* has a motive?" Wilfred shrugged. "Though why would he advertise himself as the killer by leaving a calling card—a shirt that he had made?"

Bettina transferred another slice of sourdough to her plate. Before reaching for the butter, she commented, "He's a friend of Amos's, so there's the Amos connection again."

"Amos claimed not to have seen the 'Kill Me, I'm Irish' shirts," Pamela reminded her.

"He could have been lying—for obvious reasons." Leaving her bread unbuttered, Bettina jumped up and dashed from the room.

In a moment, she was back, carrying her phone. "Tommy's Tees, Tommy's Tees," she murmured as her fingers fluttered over the device. "Amos did say Tommy's Tees has a website." After a bit more searching, Bettina raised the phone aloft. "Found it," she exclaimed. Lowering the phone and once more bending toward it, she quoted, "Hand silk-screened tees for all occasions, sustainably produced."

"Search for 'Kill Me, I'm Irish,'" Pamela suggested.

Bettina set her fingers fluttering again, and Pamela and Wilfred watched, neither eating nor sipping coffee.

"No . . . no . . . no," Bettina whispered after a while. "Custom tees, though." She looked up. "He says he also makes custom T-shirts, and the lettering on the 'Kill Me' shirt and Amos's 'Kiss Me' shirt looked very similar."

"Why would the killer order such a thing"—a perplexed wrinkle took shape on Wilfred's forehead—"unless in an attempt to frame someone else?"

"Like Amos, who is known to wear Tommy's Tees T-shirts, or Tommy himself." Pamela extended her hands, palms up, as if offering her statement as the obvious conclusion.

"Clayborn might be asking himself some of these questions," Bettina said, "now that he has the shirt."

"More sourdough, Pamela?" Wilfred gestured toward the cutting board.

"No, thanks." Pamela smiled. "But I'd take a little more coffee."

Wilfred leaned over to peek inside his wife's mug and inquired, "How about you, dear wife?"

Bettina nodded and Wilfred hoisted himself to his feet and headed for the stove.

"I'll bet Detective Clayborn isn't asking himself what secrets the cupboards in the meeting room at St. Willibrod's might be hiding," Pamela commented as the sound of the kettle being filled reached them from the cooking area of the kitchen. "Secrets someone might be willing to kill to protect."

Bettina's lips curved into a sly smile. "I have to admit that I'm curious. And the timing of the murder seems so calculated. Let's say the killer sees Lionel Dunes's listserv message about finding the photos and papers, and he—or she—resolves to get access to the cupboard and remove whatever's in there that's incriminating . . ."

Pamela nodded and took up the theory. "But then the very next thing, somebody responds and makes an appointment to help Lionel sort through the cupboard's contents on Saturday afternoon."

From his post at the counter, Wilfred chimed in. "Oh no!" he shrieked in a comically shrill voice. "My secret will be revealed! I must get rid of Lionel Dunes before he keeps the appointment."

"Exactly," Pamela said.

"That person, whoever it is, could certainly have a motive. Amos and Shiloh don't, and I don't want Hyler's to become known as the place where one of the servers poisoned a customer." Bettina punctuated her comment by slapping the pine table.

Wilfred reappeared then, carrying a steaming carafe, which he tipped over the three empty mugs. With fresh coffee at hand and, in the case of Wilfred and Bettina, second helpings of sourdough to furnish with butter and jam, they resumed chatting—not about the milkshake murder, however, but about more cheerful topics.

Before Pamela rose to head back to her own house, she and Bettina agreed to visit St. Willibrod's the next day and see what they could find out about the contents of the meeting room cupboards. Bettina was covering an event at the library in the morning, so the meeting room errand would take place after lunch.

* * *

The visit with the Frasers had lasted a few hours, and though it was now nearly noon, the hearty sourdough bread topped with butter and jam had been substantial enough to make another meal unnecessary, at least for the present. Pamela climbed the stairs to her office, sat down once again at her computer, and pondered the short titles of the articles awaiting her judgment: "Breton Lace," "Anatolian Tablet Looms," and "Molas." All three sounded equally tantalizing, so she opened the file for the first, whose full title proved to be "Breton Lace: Regional Style in Pays Bigouden."

Numerous illustrations accompanied the article—photographs taken by the author as well as sketches and engravings dating back to the eighteenth century. They showed women wearing a most distinctive headdress, cylindrical like a chef's toque but even taller, and crafted from a type of lace particular to the Breton region in northwest France. The lace was made by embroidering patterns onto a net backing, rather than by more common lace-making techniques akin to crochet or macramé.

Pamela settled happily to work, pleased to read that the craft was being kept alive by young women who wore the traditional headdresses on festive occasions with outfits inspired by folk styles. Thoughts of Lionel Dunes and the poisoned milkshake receded from her mind.

After a break for a cheese omelet when her stomach let her know that the morning's bread with butter and jam was not going to suffice until dinnertime, she returned to her office. There she wrote an enthusiastic recommendation that "Breton Lace: Regional Style in Pays Bigouden" be published. The evaluations weren't due for two more days, so Pamela devoted the rest of the afternoon to a walk, and her evening to knitting as a sedate British mystery unfolded on the screen before her.

Chapter Four

The next morning's *Register,* however, brought the real-life mystery of Lionel Dunes's murder back to the forefront of Pamela's mind. Bettina had not been the only reporter to be granted a meeting with Lucas Clayborn. Marcy Brewer's front-page article made liberal reference to Arborville's sole police detective, as well as the "Kill Me, I'm Irish" T-shirt—making it clear, at least to Pamela, that Bettina's access to Detective Clayborn had preceded Marcy's.

SHIRT FORETOLD LUNCHTIME MURDER read the boldface headline, and Marcy went on to assert that Arborville's police were avidly seeking the identity of the person who delivered the shirt to Hyler's as well as the person who made it.

Pamela looked up from the newspaper. She and Bettina had discussed the fact that a person bent on murder would be silly to advertise his or her intentions by delivering a threatening shirt to the victim. But if the shirt was intended to point the police toward people who were actually innocent—namely, Shiloh, Amos, or Tommy of Tommy's Tees—then the person who delivered it *could* be the killer, or an accomplice. And the person who made it would likely know who bought it.

She returned to the article. Marcy Brewer went on to stress that Hyler's was now closed—for the foreseeable future, she said—and she had even consulted Access-Arborville and interviewed a few Arborvillians to come up with quotes on the order of, "I just don't see myself eating there ever again."

Pamela groaned and set Part 1 aside in favor of the Lifestyle section.

The morning had been productive, devoted to evaluating "Anatolian Tablet Looms Revisited: Recreating an Ancient Turkish Weaving Technique." The author had constructed a replica of a tablet loom preserved in a museum in Istanbul—a simple device, very portable—that consisted mainly of small, flat "tablets" typically made of wood. The fiber to be woven was threaded through holes punched in the tablets, and the weaving process resulted in long strips of fabric that could be sewn together side by side or used as-is for belts or strapping.

Now, however, Pamela's focus was on Bettina, who had begun talking before she had even stepped across the threshold.

"You saw it, I suppose!" Her tone was accusing, though it was not Pamela who was being accused. "Right there on the front page of the *Register*." Her voice took on a nasal whine, imitating an imagined interviewee. "'I just don't see myself eating there ever again.' After all the years Hyler's has served this community! And you should have heard the things people were saying at the library event, shameful things about that sweet young woman, Shiloh, and even her mother."

She stamped her foot, which was shod in a lavender pump that matched her chic lavender coat. A cold front had blown in during the night, bringing more seasonable weather, and Bettina had added a lightweight wool scarf to the ensemble.

"And I won't even go into how I feel about Clayborn," she continued, "taking credit for finding the T-shirt and then giving that story to Marcy Brewer."

Startled from her nap by the commotion, Precious, who was an elegant and aloof Siamese, leaped from the top platform of the cat climber, stared at Bettina for a moment, and scurried off into the dining room.

Pamela murmured a few comforting words before collecting her jacket from the closet. A few moments later, they were out the door and on their way across the street to where Bettina's car waited in the Frasers' driveway.

The meeting rooms at St. Willibrod's were accessed through a door that opened onto the parking lot at the back of the church complex. Bettina was familiar with the layout from many St. Willibrod's events she had covered for the *Advocate*.

"It's locked, no doubt," she commented to Pamela as they stepped through the door. "The room probably, and the cupboard for sure—otherwise anybody who didn't want secret things to be found could have come in like we did just now and rummaged to his or her heart's content. There's a custodian, though, and I can probably get him to help us."

Being well acquainted with Bettina's ability to charm even the most unwilling prospects into cooperating with her agenda, Pamela had no doubt this was true.

Bettina strode on ahead, murmuring, "Let's just see what we can see first . . ."

A short hallway stretched ahead of them, coming to an end at a T-intersection where it met another hallway that led off to the right and the left. They proceeded along the short hallway, Bettina's heels clicking against the vinyl floor, until they came to a door bearing a plaque that read MEETING ROOM A. Facing it was a door bearing a plaque that read MEETING ROOM B.

Bettina turned to Pamela. "I think you said Lionel's message specified the 'smaller meeting room'?" Pamela nodded and Bettina pointed at the plaque on the right-hand door. "This one, Meeting Room A, is where the St. Willibrod's Women's Auxiliary meets. It's pretty big, big enough to accommodate thirty or forty people."

She spun around and pointed at the other plaque. "This is probably the smaller room."

Bending forward, she tried the knob, producing a click and a rattle, but the knob didn't turn. The attempt to enter the room had not gone unremarked, though—by someone inside the room.

"What was that?" a male voice asked. "Did you hear it?"

The response was unintelligible, a low murmur, and then the first voice spoke again. "I made sure to lock it. We certainly don't want anyone finding us out."

Footsteps took the place of speech, as well as other sounds of movement, and then the footsteps moved toward the door.

Bettina grabbed Pamela's arm and tugged her along the hallway as the doorknob rattled from inside the room. A moment later they had reached the T-intersection and ducked around the corner off to the right.

"It could be the killer and an accomplice," Bettina whispered, "ransacking the cupboard for . . . for . . . whatever they're ransacking it for."

The door opened, unseen by them where they lurked, but two voices were now clearly audible, a male voice and a female voice.

"Are you my sweet kitty-cat?" the female voice cooed. "Sweetums? Sweetums?"

The response, an incongruous "Meow!" came in a pleasant baritone.

"I'll text you about a good time for tomorrow," said the female voice, "and we'll take up where we left off."

"Your kitty-cat can't wait!"

"Me neither, sweetums."

A long silence suggested words had been replaced by a more physical type of communication. Pamela and Bettina looked at each other, and Pamela was sure that her own expression reflected the same amusement that she saw on Bettina's face.

Footsteps were heard now, two sets of footsteps, with the heavier ones headed in their direction. Pamela turned away, as if about to continue down the hallway in which she and Bettina had taken refuge, and Bettina did likewise. But from the corner of her eye she glimpsed a tall redheaded man hurrying along the other branch of the hallway.

The woman had apparently left through the door that led to the parking lot, suggesting the lovers were trying to avoid being seen together, even—or especially?—in the vicinity of St. Willibrod's.

By the time Pamela and Bettina retraced their steps to where Bettina's faithful Toyota waited, there was no sign of anyone else in the parking lot.

"I don't think this was a clue," Bettina commented after she had settled in behind the steering wheel.

"I don't either," Pamela agreed. "The post on the listserv made very clear the time that Lionel would be accessing the room on Saturday afternoon, so the lovers could easily have rescheduled if they'd been planning to meet then."

Bettina nodded. "Certainly they wouldn't have killed in order to keep their meeting time sacrosanct."

"That means we still want to get into that room," Pamela said. "There are secrets to discover, secrets that the killer was desperate to protect."

The St. Willibrod's custodian was not easy to track down, but Pamela and Bettina finally found him in the church hall, a large room with doors that opened to Arborville Avenue. "Just Bill," as he identified himself, was a pleasant middle-aged man with graying hair and a craggy face softened by unexpectedly blue eyes. When they entered, he had been removing folding chairs from a large closet.

"Don't know who would've been in that meeting

room, or why," he responded when Bettina mentioned that it seemed to have been in use earlier, without specifying what that use apparently was. "I've got a key, and the parish secretary does. Nobody else does, except for Lionel Dunes—rest his soul."

"Is the parish secretary a tall man with red hair?" Bettina asked.

"A tall man with red hair?" Bill laughed. "Hardly. Maybe he's a friend of hers, though." He paused and rubbed his chin. "Can't think what anybody would be doing in that room, except Lionel, with his spring cleaning project . . . and now, of course, someone put an end to that."

Bettina's eyes widened. "Do you think someone didn't want him to be . . . cleaning?"

Bill laughed again. "Who would care? People have been stuffing odds and ends in those cupboards for decades. Clearing them out would have been a public service."

"I wonder if you'd open the room for me and let me look in the cupboards . . ." Bettina accompanied the words with a flirtatious glance from beneath a delicately shadowed eyelid.

Bill shrugged. "Don't see why not. Can't think why you'd want to, though." He stared at Bettina for a moment, then raised a finger in the air. "I know who you are now," he exclaimed. "I thought you looked familiar. You're that reporter for the *Advocate*."

A grin rearranged his craggy features. "On the trail of a story?" he inquired. "Arborville Man Poisoned to Protect Decades-Old Secret?"

"Uh . . ." Bettina looked at Pamela, and Pamela responded by raising her brows. Their theory about the motive for Lionel Dunes's murder had seemed so clever, so ingenious. But maybe it was just common sense—though not, apparently, to Detective Clayborn.

Before Bettina could answer, Bill spoke again. "I'm game," he said. "But not now." He gestured toward the open closet and the stack of folding chairs leaning against the wall. "I've got a concert to set up for, local string quartet. Come back tomorrow about ten."

Chapter Five

Pamela had been ruminating, and by the time Bettina arrived at her door that evening, she had made up her mind. If other people—Bill, for instance—saw the connection between Lionel Dunes's spring cleaning project and his death, the theory she and Bettina had developed, making that very same connection, was all the more compelling.

She explained this to Bettina as they proceeded across the porch and down the steps, en route to where her serviceable compact waited in the driveway. The Knit and Nibble knitting club was meeting at Roland DeCamp's, and Pamela was driving.

"Clayborn overlooks a lot of clues by ignoring AccessArborville," Bettina commented as she tugged at her seatbelt and clicked it into place. "And he doesn't listen when I try to help him, or"—she whirled to face Pamela—"he accepts my help and then pretends like it was all his idea anyway."

Pamela suspected she knew what was coming, and

she was right. As she backed out of the driveway, Bettina revisited themes from that morning, bemoaning the fact that Detective Clayborn had taken credit for the "Kill Me, I'm Irish" T-shirt coming into his possession and then giving the story to Marcy Brewer.

The drive to Roland DeCamp's house was not long, though the DeCamps lived at the other end of Arborville in a development everyone called The Farm. The land had once been a real farm, owned by a family named Van Riper, but recent Van Riper heirs had grown tired of farming. They had sold their land to a developer and now The Farm consisted of new houses that were quite grand, and more modern than most of Arborville's housing stock.

Roland's wife, Melanie, answered the door and welcomed Pamela and Bettina into the DeCamps' elegantly modern living room. Melanie herself was elegantly modern, svelte and blond, wearing dark leggings and a slouchy sweater in a pale camel color.

"He's in the kitchen," she explained, gesturing toward Roland's usual chair, which was empty, though the briefcase in which he stored his knitting projects waited nearby. "He's made a cake, but it's still in the oven." She held out a tastefully manicured hand. "May I take your coats?"

Pamela slipped out of her jacket, and Bettina removed her lavender coat to reveal one of her jersey wrap dresses, this one in a print that combined lavender with bright gold and orange. She was still wearing the gold earrings from that morning, large hoops with a texture like rope.

Pamela and Bettina were not the first to arrive. In fact, they were the last. Sitting side by side on the DeCamps' sofa, Holly Perkins and Karen Dowling had already taken their projects from their knitting bags. They were best friends, despite—or perhaps because—they were as different as any two young women could be.

Holly was outgoing and strikingly attractive, with flowing dark hair that she accented with streaks of bright color. She smiled often, with a dimple that came and went. Karen was quiet and shy, blond, and pretty in a delicate way.

Both the sofa and Roland's usual chair were turquoise in color, angular and low-slung in design, suited more to agile legs than to the elderly. The furnishings also included a substantial armchair, however, and that armchair was always reserved for Nell Bascomb, the oldest member of the group, who now greeted the newcomers from its comfortable depths.

Pamela and Bettina joined Holly and Karen on the sofa, which was very long. Holly and Bettina were right next to each other, with Pamela and Karen at the sofa's ends, and no sooner had Bettina settled into place than Holly turned to her and said, "What a story about Hyler's! Poisoning—can you imagine? And now it's closed!"

Melanie was on her way out of the room, heading for the kitchen, but she paused en route. "It was such a popular place, but I wonder if people will ever be brave enough to go back."

Holly made a dismissive sound, an abrupt hiss. "That sensational coverage in the *Register* certainly doesn't help—though it's tempting to think the person who made the milkshake or the person who served it is the guilty one."

"Marcy Brewer could have said more about the sheep," Bettina said. "Pamela and I were sitting right there, and along came a parade of sheep on their way to the sustainability event, and the next thing we knew Lionel Dunes had collapsed onto his lunch . . ."

Roland's voice reached them from the hallway. "He should have known better. A green milkshake strikes me as very silly," he said as he rounded the corner into the living room. "And so does all this St. Patrick's Day fuss in general. But of course silly people need their silly holidays."

He proceeded to his chair, followed by a lustrous black cat. Entertaining the Knit and Nibble group in the comfort of his own home, Roland had set aside the well-tailored pinstripes, befitting his job as a corporate lawyer, in which he usually appeared. Tonight he wore well-tailored slacks and a dark-gray V-neck sweater that Pamela recognized as one of his own creations. The V-neck revealed a flawlessly starched shirt collar anchored by a discreetly patterned silk tie. Above it, his lean face was serious.

"At least there's not going to be a parade," he muttered after hoisting his briefcase onto his lap. "We have enough of those as it is."

"There's always a St. Patrick's Day parade in the city," Holly commented.

"Better there than here." Roland snapped the latch on his briefcase, lifted the lid, and took out an in-progress work that involved four double-pointed needles. The cat, whose name was Cuddles, had clambered up beside him and stretched out along his thigh.

Pamela nudged Bettina, who tilted her head, giving Pamela a glimpse of her half smile. The smile suggested that Bettina's reaction to Roland's comments was similar to her own. Pamela, however, was almost relieved that the conversation launched by Holly's reference to the poisoned milkshake had taken the turn it had—and had seemingly stalled in the face of Roland's grumpiness.

Nell's disapproval of gossip that rehashed unfortunate events was well known, and she would doubtless have spoken up if Holly had pressed Bettina and Pamela for specifics, given that Bettina had revealed they were both present when the poison took effect.

Nell did join the conversation then, but it was to lean toward the sofa with a smile that softened her aged face and comment, "What a fortunate little granddaughter you have!"

She was addressing Bettina, whose latest knitting project rested in her lap. It was small, lacy, and a delicate shade of pink. Bettina actually had two granddaughters. The older one was being raised by academic parents who lived in Boston and had declared that they were raising a *person*, not a *girl*, and had forbade girly gifts of all sorts. The younger one, very young, had been born to Wilfred Jr. and his wife, Maxie, and lived right in Arborville—close enough to be spoiled on a daily basis.

"And you, Roland? What are you knitting?" Holly

accompanied the words with a smile that revealed her perfect teeth and activated her dimple. "It looks very complicated," she added.

"Not actually very," Roland responded without looking up. "It's a sock, and I'm trying to concentrate."

"And you've been busy in the kitchen too." Holly's smile took on an encouraging edge. "Something certainly smells delicious."

"Yes, it does," Bettina chimed in. "Cake, I'd say."

Roland's only answer was to furrow his brow and make a great show of executing his next stitch.

Sensing that Nell was a more promising conversation partner, Holly shifted her attention in that direction. Soon she and Nell were discussing Nell's latest do-good project, small blankets to be delivered to the Haversack animal shelter.

"They can be any color, even multicolor," Nell explained. "It's a great way to use up odds and ends left from other projects, just as long as the yarn is soft and warm." The blanket taking shape on her lap was a gentle shade of blue.

Holly, in turn, displayed her work. So far it was just a few inches of knitting in an eye-catching bright yellow, but she explained it was to be a sleeveless, scoop-necked midriff-baring top, hopefully to be finished in time for summer. The linen-blend yarn she had chosen would make it suitable for warm weather.

"And Karen? It looks like you have a new project too." Nell leaned forward.

"Doll clothes go very fast," Karen said with a shy smile. She was in the middle of a row, but she held up her crisscrossed needles to show off a tiny green rectangle. "Part of a St. Patrick's Day outfit for Lily's favorite doll."

Pamela herself was nearly finished with an ambitious project she had begun around Christmas, visiting the fancy yarn shop in Timberley and splurging on eight skeins of natural cream-colored wool imported from the Shetland Islands. The project was a pullover sweater in a complicated cable-knit pattern, with wide cables like multistrand braids decorating the front and sleeves.

A lull fell over the group then, with eyes focused on busy fingers as needles were thrust and yarn looped almost in synchrony. Pamela was happy to knit in silence, thinking her own thoughts, but after a bit Bettina stirred and lowered her work to her lap.

"It's very hard," she murmured, "making this lacy stitch, counting and keeping track of whether to knit or purl." She turned to Pamela. "Do you think the garden center has pansies yet?"

Pansies were an early spring ritual in Arborville, and indeed generally in New Jersey. Since they tolerated chilly weather, their cheerful multicolored faces enlivened porch planters, window boxes, and flower beds long before almost anything else, except for crocus and snowdrops, was in bloom.

"I don't know." Pamela's pattern required concentration too, and she responded in a tone not designed to encourage discussion.

Bettina took the hint and turned to Holly, and soon she and Holly were chatting happily about spring garden plans, with Karen occasionally contributing from her end of the sofa. The quiet buzz of conversation formed a pleasant backdrop to Pamela's thoughts and she knitted steadily away until Bettina turned to her once again.

"It's eight o'clock, or nearly so," Bettina said, and pointed to the chair that Roland and his cat had vacated.

In fact, the faint aroma of coffee that had registered subliminally as Pamela worked was now growing stronger. Across the room, Nell set her knitting aside and looked up to greet Melanie, who had just entered. Melanie was carrying a graceful pewter tray that held five steaming cups of coffee nestled onto their saucers and two empty cup-and-saucer sets, all pale porcelain, unadorned. She set the tray on the coffee table that flanked the sofa and went back the way she had come.

When she returned, it was to deliver a second tray, identical to the first except for its cargo: a pale porcelain teapot and a matching cream and sugar set, as well as spoons and small napkins.

"He wants to serve his creation himself," Melanie explained, tipping her blond head toward the hallway that led to the kitchen. She was about to perch on the edge of the low-slung turquoise chair, but an urgent cry from the kitchen impelled her to hurry from the room.

"In the drawer." Melanie's voice reached them faintly. "The spatula is always in this drawer."

A few suspenseful minutes passed, and then Roland stepped in from the hallway, holding aloft another tray, which he deposited on the coffee table with a flourish. Seven small porcelain plates held seven pieces of cake, cake of an unexpected color.

"It's *green*!" Holly exclaimed. Her nails, painted metallic orange, glittered as she clapped her hands.

Roland frowned slightly and surveyed the group. "It's supposed to be green," he said.

"For St. Patrick's Day!" Holly crowed.

"Yes." Roland nodded curtly. "I suppose it is."

"But you said you thought green milkshakes were silly," Bettina objected.

"Perhaps I did, but this is a cake. It's not the same thing at all."

Bettina looked more closely at the piece of cake nearest to her. It was a single layer and square, as if cut from a cake baked in a square or rectangular pan. A sugary white glaze covered the top, but the cut sides revealed that the cake itself was a vivid shade of green.

"True," Bettina commented. "It's not the same thing at all and, anyway, I never thought green milkshakes were silly."

"Your cake is beautiful," Holly assured Roland. "Tell us the secret. Is it mint flavor?"

Roland shook his head, and his lips abandoned their serious expression to curve into a smug smile. "Lime Jell-O and a box of cake mix—no harm in labor-saving shortcuts. But I made the glaze with fresh lime juice."

Roland distributed the coffee and cake to the people lined up on the sofa and made sure that the cream and sugar were within Bettina's reach. Melanie delivered a slice of cake to the small table at Nell's elbow, as well as a freshly poured cup of tea—and the sugar, as soon as Bettina had spooned as much as she wanted into her coffee.

A few minutes later, everyone was settled with coffee or tea and cake at hand. Roland had given up his chair to Melanie and fetched a straight-backed chair for himself from the dining room. He'd pulled both chairs up to the other side of the coffee table, and Cuddles had retreated to watch the proceedings from a distance.

"Delicious!" was the general verdict once the cake had been tasted, and Pamela concurred. The cake itself was moist and sweet, with a pleasant tang of lime, and the icing balanced intense sweetness with a jolt of lime's acidity.

"Will everyone be cooking corned beef and cabbage this Sunday?" Holly inquired when the pace of eating and drinking had slowed. After nods all around, including from Roland and Melanie, she added, "I certainly will. Soda bread too." She paused. "There's always the question, though—what to do with the rest of the buttermilk?"

Pamela nodded. The Co-Op seemed only to sell buttermilk in quart-size containers, and there weren't that many other uses for it—unless one was turning out multiple loaves of soda bread.

"You could drink it," Nell suggested.

"I know people used to," Bettina said, "but it's definitely an acquired taste."

Nell tilted her head and glanced toward the ceiling, as if in quest of a fugitive thought. "Yogurt would probably work just as well," she murmured. "It's cultured like buttermilk, which makes it a bit acidic."

"That settles that." Holly accompanied her words

with a dimply smile. "But then there's the question of what to do with the rest of the cabbage."

Holly had a point. A head of cabbage, Pamela had often thought, was the vegetable version of a ham, in that it lasted and lasted and lasted.

"Coleslaw," Karen suggested in her mild voice.

Nell joined in. "Waste not, want not. It's tasty sautéed in butter as a side dish with anything, not just corned beef."

Pamela was about to contribute a recipe she had once made, involving vinegar, that turned shredded cabbage into a kind of relish—but Roland was stirring. He pushed his starched shirt cuff and the ribbing of his sweater sleeve aside to consult his impressive watch, and then he stood up.

"Fifteen minutes have elapsed," he announced. "It's time to resume knitting."

Melanie allowed only the slightest smile to creep across her pretty lips as she rose. She began gathering plates, empty now but for random green crumbs, onto one of the trays, while Roland collected cups and saucers. As their hosts continued to clear away, the knitters took up their work again.

A little after nine, Pamela and Bettina stepped out onto the DeCamps' porch, followed closely by Holly. Karen and Nell were still inside, saying their thank-yous and goodnights, but they soon joined the others on the porch, and the small group made its way along the walk that led from the DeCamps' imposing split-level house to the street. Though winter had faded the lawn that the walk bisected, its even texture and precisely groomed edges testified to the ministrations of the DeCamps' landscapers.

Holly's orange VW Beetle waited at the curb, and Karen and Nell, who had ridden with her, veered toward it as the group approached the street. Holly, however, lingered near Bettina.

"I saw a few posts about the sheep on AccessArborville." She was whispering, even though Nell was far enough away to be out of earshot. "It sounds like the sustainability group got the publicity they wanted for their event—though then it had to be postponed, which was a shame. But"—she rested her hand on the sleeve of Bettina's lavender coat—"do you think the sheep and the poisoning were connected?"

"The timing . . ." Bettina hesitated. "The timing seems so calculated—create a distraction with the sheep to give the poisoner a chance to add the poison to the milkshake."

"Wouldn't that make it less likely that anyone who works at Hyler's was the poisoner?" The only light came from the streetlamp, and Holly's face was in shadow, but her voice sounded hopeful. Holly was a devoted Arborville booster who regularly described the town as "awesome" or "amazing," so it made sense to Pamela that she would want to defend an Arborville institution like Hyler's.

"Who was in charge of the sheep?" Holly asked. "Do you know?"

"Amos Clark, one of the organizers of the event," Bettina said, "but the problem is that his girlfriend is

Shiloh, the server who delivered the milkshake to Lionel Dunes."

Before Holly could respond, voices reached them from the direction of the orange Beetle. Karen's and Nell's voices, to be precise.

"Yes, yes," Holly called back. "I'm coming." With a quick "good night," she stepped away.

"We'll find out more tomorrow," Bettina commented as she and Pamela continued on to where Pamela's car waited. "I hope Bill doesn't forget our appointment."

"He seemed curious about the cupboards' contents too." Pamela unlocked the passenger-side door.

"I know you'll want to walk to St. Willibrod's," Bettina said as Pamela slipped behind the steering wheel, "but I don't. So either I meet you there or I drive us both."

"You can drive us both." Pamela laughed. "I'll see you at a quarter to ten."

Chapter Six

Pamela's first reaction was to sneeze. Bill had opened the double doors of the cupboard to reveal shelves stacked with . . . things. He had reached in and pulled out a faded cardboard box, like an oversized shoebox, and brushed a layer of dust from its top. Once opened, it proved to contain yellowed newspaper clippings intermingled with curling black-and-white photos. The clothing in the photos, which showed formally posed people smiling for the camera, situated them in the fifties or earlier, and the dates on the newspaper clippings harmonized with that estimation.

Another shelf held stacks of hymnbooks, as well as bundles of paper that Bill identified as most likely surplus parish bulletins, though from before his time.

"I'm not as old as I look," he said with a laugh.

After pulling out a few more boxes and transferring them to the large table in the center of the room, he said, "I'll leave you to it, ladies, but let me unlock these other cupboards before I go."

Once the cupboards were unlocked, he headed for the door. Before disappearing into the hallway, though, he saluted them, saying, "I'll be back in an hour—and be sure to keep track of anything mysterious that you come across."

Pamela and Bettina looked at each other, and then they looked around the room. Besides the table, which was surrounded by eight wooden chairs, the furniture consisted of a comfy-looking sofa upholstered in flowered chintz and a few matching armchairs.

"I guess we know what this sofa was most recently used for," Bettina commented with a giggle. "It even has pillows."

She picked one up, a smallish pillow but quite plump and covered in a rustic fabric that looked handwoven. She squeezed it and commented, "Nice and soft, but it has a funny smell."

She handed it to Pamela, who sniffed it. "Not bad." She sniffed again. "But definitely noticeable, and kind of familiar in an odd way." She returned the pillow to the sofa.

A door had swung ajar on one of the other cupboards, and Bettina stepped closer to peer inside.

"This one's actually a closet," she reported, pulling both doors open wide. "Choir robes perhaps." She reached in and retrieved one, holding it aloft on its hanger. "Ancient," she declared. "And I doubt the choir even wears robes anymore."

The robe had once been blue, but the fabric was now faded to near gray and was dusty as well. The long edges where the robe fastened closed in front were frayed, as were the edges of the sleeves.

"Sad." Bettina shook her head and hung the robe back up with its fellows.

She leaned into the closet, pushing the robes aside and stooping to examine the floor, then emerged to report that the closet contained only robes.

"No secrets there, I don't imagine." Pamela watched as Bettina pushed the doors closed.

Without conferring further, they set to work, Pamela continuing to explore the first cupboard and Bettina tackling the one next to it. The room was silent, except for the sound of papers rustling, occasional murmurs that didn't require responses, and sneezes.

Pamela discovered a cache of photos spanning a quarter century, formal group photos of young men in suits and young women in dignified dresses. Confirmation photos, perhaps? And on the same shelf was a pile of books, all the same, that resembled high school yearbooks. She slid the top one out to discover that it commemorated the seventy-fifth anniversary of St. Willibrod's founding—which had occurred in 1878.

A tattered manila envelope held receipts, none more recent than 1980, for things like floral arrangements, catered food, exterminator services, and gutter repair. Beneath the envelope was a wooden plaque bearing a brass plate that read "In Memory of Marietta Cooper, 1875 to 1972."

"Here's something!" Bettina exclaimed suddenly, interrupting Pamela's musing about how the plaque had ended up in the closet rather than affixed to, perhaps, a memorial bench.

In one hand Bettina held a box, like a cigar box but made of tin and decorated with a pattern of violets and lilies of the valley. In her other hand she held a piece of paper with deep creases, as if it had been folded.

"My dearest darling," she read. "The days are endless as I look forward to our escape, from this place, from my husband, from your wife."

"Interesting." Pamela set the plaque down and joined Bettina at the table, where the tin box now rested, open to reveal a pile of what were obviously letters. A few unfolded letters lay next to it on the table.

"Interesting," Bettina agreed. "But here's what's really interesting." She picked up another letter. "This one begins, 'Dear Pastor Stickleback,' but the handwriting and the stationery are the same. It sounds like Pastor Stickleback had a secret life."

"A secret life someone was desperate to keep secret?" Pamela picked another letter from the tin box and lowered herself into one of the chairs that surrounded the table.

Bettina did likewise, and soon both were engrossed in the contents of the tin box. A timeline could even be constructed, because each letter was headed with the month and day of its composition. The earliest letters, written in January and addressed to "Dear Pastor Stickleback," merely complimented Pastor Stickleback on his sermons. Compliments led to a request for counseling "on a personal matter."

Soon after, "Dear Pastor Stickleback" became "Dear Randolph," and "Yours truly, Elise Windsor" became "Affectionately, Elise." By the time summer arrived, love had been declared—mutually, to judge by the letters' content, even though the tin box contained only Elise's side of the correspondence.

The last letter had been written on the occasion of a journey Randolph was about to undertake, but Elise assured him of a loving reception on his return, at which time she would have freed herself of her "encumbrance" so they could carry out their plans.

Bettina began folding the letters and slipping them back into the tin box. "What do you think?" she asked. "Is this the secret someone was willing to kill for? Someone who knew about the tin box and its contents and was desperate to get in here and collect it before it fell into unsympathetic hands?"

"The letters seem awfully old," Pamela commented, fingering the thoughtful wrinkle that had formed between her brows. "Old-fashioned stationery, old-fashioned handwriting. After enough time has passed, love affairs—even illicit ones—can seem quaint rather than shocking."

"Let's say they were written in the fifties, though." Bettina paused and tightened her lips into a contemplative line. "And let's say maybe a child resulted from the illicit affair, a child born after the last letter so there's no reference here"—she glanced down at the stack of letters—"but maybe Randolph and Elise didn't end up freeing themselves of their *encumbrances* and marrying each other." She shifted her gaze to Pamela. "That child could easily still be alive."

"Could be." Pamela nodded. "And somehow recently aware that he is not, genetically, the person he was always taken to be."

"Or that *she* is not, genetically, the person *she* was always taken to be," Bettina added. "And these letters are the proof."

"There could bc an inheritance involved—but the connection has to be proven."

"Odd, though," Bettina murmured, "that the letters would end up just tucked away in these cupboards. If the relationship meant as much to Randolph as it seems to have, you'd think he'd have stored them in a more secure place."

Pamela didn't answer. Something had just occurred to her, and she returned to the cupboard she had been exploring when Bettina called her attention to the tin box. She pulled out one of the books that had been produced to commemorate the anniversary of the church's founding.

Back at the table, she displayed the book to Bettina. The cover showed a line drawing of St. Willibrod's as it had looked before the modern building that housed the church hall had been constructed, and before parking lots were necessary. The noble stone building, with its substantial wooden doors opening onto its wide slate porch, had been surrounded by a grassy park.

"St. Willibrod's was seventy-five years old in 1953," Pamela explained, "and they created this book to commemorate the event. Maybe we can figure out when Randolph Stickleback was the pastor."

Heads bent together, they paged through the book, which included many old photographs as well as reproductions of newspaper clippings—the originals of which, both photographs and clippings, Pamela suspected, resided in the dusty boxes that cluttered the cupboards. The book also contained lists of people who had contributed their time and talents to groups like the Altar

Society and the Women's Auxiliary, lists of babies who had been baptized, and . . . lists of parishioners who had given their lives in the two world wars that had occurred between 1878 and 1953.

An especially poignant detail involved Pastor Randolph Stickleback, who had enlisted to serve as a chaplain in World War I and was killed at the Battle of the Meuse-Argonne.

Bettina sighed. "So tragic. I almost feel like I knew him. And poor Elise—he never came back."

"That answers our question about how the letters ended up forgotten in this cupboard. He didn't want to leave them in the vicarage because he didn't want his wife to find them, and nobody goes off to war convinced that they won't return."

"But he didn't." Bettina sighed again. "And here the letters sat, until someone . . ."

"Bettina . . ." Pamela touched Bettina's arm. "I don't think these letters are the secret we've been looking for. Now we know that the affair happened over a hundred years ago. Could there be anyone still around now who could possibly be affected if the story got out?"

"Probably not." Bettina replaced the lid on the tin box. "You're right." She twisted around to look at the cupboard where she'd found the letters. "And there's nothing else in there worth murdering someone to protect—nothing that I could find anyway."

"It seems, then, that we've been barking up the wrong tree, as Wilfred would say." Pamela stepped over to the cupboard she'd been working on, returned the commemorative book to its shelf, and closed the cupboard doors.

The door to the hallway opened then and Bill peeked in.

"How are you doing, ladies?" he inquired in a jovial voice. "Ready to call it a day?"

He ambled into the room and joined Bettina, who was still standing at the table with the tin box nearby.

"Looks like you found something interesting." Bill reached for the box.

Bettina turned her head ever so slightly to make eye contact with Pamela. Her mobile features were not normally given to subtlety, but she managed by dint of the slightest alteration in lip and brow to signal distress.

"It's . . . it's . . ." She laid a hand on the box. "It's some correspondence, very old . . ."

Pamela entered the conversation. "The people involved are long gone, but still . . . maybe we should respect their privacy."

"Oh!" Bill bent closer and studied the box. "Is it the love letters that lady wrote to Stickleback? I didn't know those were still stuck away in here."

"You know about them?" Interest and relief lightened Bettina's expression.

Bill nodded. "Sad story, him dying in the war and all of that, though I can't condone him sneaking around behind his wife's back, especially being that he was supposedly a man of God and up there preaching from the pulpit every Sunday."

"How . . . how do you happen to know the story?" Bettina asked. Her hand still rested protectively on the tin box.

"That drama group, the Arborville Players. They did

a staged dramatic reading, made up invented letters for Stickleback's part. One of the people in the Players is in the Women's Auxiliary here. She found them by rummaging in these cupboards, I guess. I'm surprised she put them back, but perhaps she figured they belonged to St. Willibrod's. Very honest of her."

"Very." Bettina picked the box up.

She seemed dejected, Pamela thought. Even the scarlet tendrils of her hair had lost their buoyancy. Clearly, the foray into the cupboards had not borne out their theory about why Lionel Dunes had been murdered. And the secret of the letters, which they had in any event decided was irrelevant to the mystery, had turned out to be no secret at all.

"Might as well put it back where it came from." Bill held out a hand, and Bettina relinquished the box. It was the work of only a minute to stow the box and close and lock the cupboards.

"Ladies, it's been a pleasure." Bill tipped his head in a half bow and gestured toward the open door.

Pamela and Bettina thanked him, Bettina cheering up enough to add a flirtatious wink.

"See you at the funeral?" Bill asked, jingling his keys, after they had all stepped out into the hallway and he had locked the door to Meeting Room B. "It's tomorrow, you know—right here at St. Willibrod's. Eleven a.m."

Bettina glanced at Pamela and, taking her shrug for assent, said, "Of course!"

Since Pamela had often heard Bettina argue that, by skipping funerals, Detective Clayborn overlooked valuable clues, she suspected that, invited or not, Bettina would have been among those assembled to mourn the passing of Lionel Dunes the next day.

"There's to be a reception in the church hall afterward, just in time for lunch—but I don't think Hyler's has been engaged to cater it." A short bark of a laugh indicated that Bill had been amused by his joke.

He left them then, explaining that with tomorrow's reception on the schedule, chores awaited him in the church hall.

Back at home, Pamela brought in her mail, greeted the cats, and made a quick cheese omelet for lunch. The evaluations of "Breton Lace," "Anatolian Tablet Looms," and "Molas" were due the next morning by eight, but with a whole afternoon ahead, she would finish the work and send them off early.

The first two had been read and recommendations written. "Molas" remained, or in its full title once the Word file was opened, "A Fabric Bestiary: Animal Themes in Traditional Panamanian Molas." Tempted, as always, to study the illustrations first (and submissions to *Fiber Craft* generally included illustrations), Pamela was charmed by the images of roosters, turtles, monkeys, fish, cats, and even an elephant—all rendered in an applique process based on layers of fabric cut away to reveal the colors beneath. And the reds, blues, oranges, greens, magentas, and yellows used in the designs were juxtaposed in a way that made them fairly vibrate.

"Yes, yes, yes," she murmured as she scrolled through the images, and then again as she read the lively text that related the images to the village life of the creators—though with the caveat that images of creatures like the elephant were not based on observation.

She wrote an enthusiastic recommendation that the article be published, checked over her other two evaluations, and sent all three off to celine.bramley@fibercraft.com.

The rest of the afternoon was devoted to gardening. The garden center *did* have pansies, and two hours later clusters of cheerful pansy faces nodded at passersby from a pair of terra-cotta planters on Pamela's front porch.

The next morning, Pamela climbed the stairs to her office as soon as she'd fed the cats and finished her breakfast of toast and coffee. She was unsurprised to find that her boss at *Fiber Craft* had not been idle. Waiting in her inbox was a message from Celine Bramley, accompanied by the stylized paperclip that indicated one or more attachments.

"Please copyedit 'Molas' for inclusion in our upcoming issue devoted to traditional needle crafts and look over 'Sheep to Shawl.' I know we rejected it once, but the author has revised. I need this work by Monday at 5:00 p.m."

Chapter Seven

Lionel Dunes's funeral, held beneath the somber gaze of the saints whose lives were commemorated in St. Willibrod's impressive stained-glass windows, had been well-attended. Residents of Arborville, who knew him from his volunteer work at the church and elsewhere, had turned out in great numbers, as had his colleagues at the Timberley accounting firm where he had been a partner. His wife's colleagues from Wendelstaff College had been present as well—and many of the students involved in the sustainable living project, including Amos Clark.

At the ancient cemetery overlooking the Hudson River from the crest of the Palisades, Pamela and Bettina had picked their way over the faded grass—Pamela in sensible shoes and Bettina in elegant black suede pumps—to the grave that was to receive Lionel Dunes. They had watched as his coffin was lowered into the ground, where he joined the ranks of those who, even before Arborville became Arborville, now slumbered for eternity.

Now they were back at St. Willibrod's, in the modern appendage that was the church hall. Voices echoed off the walls and the polished floor, merging into an indistinct hum, as people greeted each other and coalesced into chatting groups.

Food was available, however—lots of food. It was laid out on long tables at the far end of the room, near the apron of the stage, whose burgundy velvet curtains were now closed. Chatting groups formed and re-formed as people peeled off to investigate the buffet offerings. Bill, standing off to the side of the tables, caught sight of Pamela and Bettina and offered a discreet salute.

"I'm certainly ready for lunch," Bettina confided, "after hiking all over that cemetery in my good shoes. Shall we see what's available?" She peered toward the buffet table.

She set off across the floor, but she had taken only a few steps before she was accosted by a woman Pamela recognized as Bettina's friend, Marlene Pepper. Marlene was a pleasant, if talkative, woman about the same age and shape as Bettina—though she lacked Bettina's fashion sense. Today she was wearing a nondescript but respectable navy-blue skirt suit, in contrast to Bettina's chic black crepe coatdress accessorized with a triple-strand pearl necklace and dangling pearl earrings.

"Quite the impressive turnout," Marlene commented. "Of course, he was a longtime fixture in the community."

She nodded toward a slender middle-aged woman garbed in a simple black sheath. The woman was disengaging herself from another woman, who had just hugged her and was now peering intently into her face.

"That's Aileen Conway," Marlene added. "Otherwise known as Mrs. Lionel Dunes. Do you know her?"

"Uh, no." Bettina raised a hand to her mouth. Her nail polish today was a tasteful natural shade. "Poor thing! What a shock she's had!"

"All alone now." Marlene shook her head mournfully. "They had no children, though of course there are her students"—Marlene paused a moment, then went on—"like him."

"Him," Pamela realized, was Amos Clark, in a suit, as she'd noticed at the funeral. He stepped out from a small group milling around near Aileen—there seemed to be no formal arrangement for anything like a receiving line—and hugged her too. A pair of young women emerged from the group, students, Pamela thought. Aileen bent toward them, seemingly enjoying the exchange as a tall redheaded man looked on sympathetically from his post against the wall.

"Have you been to the buffet?" Marlene asked, but then she noticed their empty hands and answered her own question, saying, "I guess not. Me neither, and I expect the food is really good." She led the way to the far end of the room, edging through the crowd and talking all the while, to the effect that the catering had been entrusted to Lionel's favorite restaurant in Timberley.

The buffet tables had been arranged so that people could serve themselves from either side, and stacks of plates, along with silverware wrapped in a white linen napkins, waited at both ends.

"A lot to do at short notice, to arrange an event like this," Marlene concluded as they waited for a chance to step closer to the buffet. "But Aileen does know how to organize things, and Ted Stewart has been so helpful and such a comfort. Why, you'd almost think—"

But at that moment, Marlene took advantage of a break in the crowd to reach out and seize a plate and a bundle of silverware. Pamela and Bettina did likewise and began to edge along the table, where they first encountered trays of mini quiches with delicate fluted pastry edges. As Pamela studied the selection, voices drifted from across the table.

"I wonder if the sheep-shearing will go ahead on Saturday," a woman mused to no one in particular.

"It has to," another woman chimed in. "The poor things get very hot during the summer, and summer will be here before we know it."

Pamela added a mini quiche from the tray labeled "Crabmeat Quiche" to her plate.

"Not a moment too soon," came another voice, though subsequent fragments of dialogue indicated that the focus was still on sheep. Voices chimed in, as Pamela moved along the table selecting smoked salmon with capers on pumpernickel, a stuffed mushroom cap, a grilled jumbo shrimp on a skewer . . .

"Icelandic sweaters make great souvenirs . . . they wear like iron," someone murmured.

"New Zealand wool . . ."

"Shetland Islands . . ."

She had reached the cheese platter, where the Stilton

beckoned. Now someone was talking about lambswool. Pamela settled a few crackers next to the bit of Stilton on her plate.

"Lambswool pillows," came a voice. "Really love mine—also those pelts. They make great rugs."

"So soft . . . pillows, and the pelts. That lanolin smell is nice once you get used to it."

"Look at those shrimp!" a voice cut in, a louder voice, and more familiar than those drifting from across the table. It came from Bettina, who edged next to Pamela and picked up a shrimp skewer. "Would it be horrible if I took more than one?" she inquired of Pamela.

Before Pamela could answer, a man who had just helped himself to two shrimp, accessing the platter from the other side of the table, said, "Go ahead! You only live once."

One of the woman who had been discussing lambswool spoke up to say, "Not if you're allergic to shellfish."

As Pamela moved along the table, pausing at an appealing tray of crudités, overlapping voices across the table chimed in with cautionary tales about marine creatures of all sorts.

"No meatballs." Bettina turned to survey the buffet when they reached the end of the last table. "Usually these catered events have meatballs."

"Lots of other things, though." Pamela laughed. "I don't think we'll go hungry."

Beverages were on offer too, dispensed from bars set up on either side of the room. But Pamela and Bettina addressed themselves first to the contents of their plates. Pamela didn't mind eating while standing up, but even with a finger-food buffet like this one, a hand was required to hold the plate while the other hand conveyed food to the mouth, leaving no extra hand to manage a glass.

Once they had nibbled their way through the mini quiches and the smoked salmon on pumpernickel and the skewered shrimp and the rest, Pamela and Bettina relinquished their empty plates to a server circulating with a tray. Feeling more sociable with a glass of wine rather than the encumbrance of a plate, Pamela was happy to chat when Marlene Pepper reappeared.

Soon a small cluster of people had formed, drawn by the presence of Marlene, who seemed to know everyone in Arborville. The fact that servers were now offering trays of petit-fours made it unnecessary to move from the spot. Listening more than talking was Pamela's usual habit in a crowd, and she realized she was quite enjoying the cheerful buzz of conversation—more cheerful than one might expect, given the occasion.

She confided this thought to Bettina after Marlene and her friends had taken their leave and the room had begun to empty.

"Hardly anybody here was all that close to him," Bettina said, "and even his widow seems cheerful." She nodded toward where Aileen Conway still stood near the double doors that led out to Arborville Avenue.

Aileen was smiling as she shook hands with a man whose well-cut suit suggested he might be a colleague from Lionel Dunes's accounting practice. The man who had earlier been lingering near the wall stepped forward and shook the man's hand too.

Pamela and Bettina were approaching the doors, and it seemed only polite to speak to Aileen on their way out.

"I'm Bettina Fraser," Bettina said, "and I'm so sorry about your loss." She adjusted her features to harmonize with her words and offered her hand.

"Aileen Conway." Aileen accepted the hand. "Very kind of you to come."

"Ted Stewart," the man who had been lingering near the wall chimed in with his name, as did Pamela with hers.

Hands were shaken all around, and Pamela and Bettina made their way through the heavy doors, past the church, and around the corner to where Bettina's faithful Toyota waited in the parking lot.

The next morning found Pamela, still in pajamas and robe and holding that day's *Register*, lingering on her front walk rather than hurrying back into her house with her usual dispatch. The headline had been joltingly visible through the plastic sleeve that encased the newspaper, and she'd slipped the newspaper from its sleeve to double-check the wording.

POLICE NEAR ARREST IN DUNES CASE, she read, the letters sharper but no different from what she'd glimpsed through the plastic. The article, under Marcy Brewer's byline, cited Arborville Detective Lucas Clayborn to the effect that sufficient evidence had now been gathered to definitively identify the murderer—though the murderer was not identified in the article.

Back inside, Pamela turned off the flame under the kettle, which was hooting frantically, and poured the steaming water through the freshly ground coffee waiting in the filter cone atop her carafe. She lowered a slice of whole-grain bread into her toaster, buttered it when it popped up, and settled at her kitchen table to absorb Marcy Brewer's report in more detail.

There was not, however, much detail to be absorbed, and Bettina confirmed that fact when she arrived an hour later. By then, Pamela had read the rest of the *Register*, including a feature in the food section suggesting uses for all the cabbage that didn't get cooked and eaten on St. Patrick's Day. She had also dressed and made her bed and checked for email that had appeared since her first-thing-in-the-morning visit to her computer.

Wordless and grimacing, Bettina stepped over the threshold, her manner at odds with the bright yellow of her stylish trench coat, which was fashioned from a fabric that resembled patent leather. In her hand she held not a white bakery box but a compactly folded newspaper encased in a flimsy plastic sleeve.

"He's just delivering them now," she said. "It's a wonder anyone pays any attention to the *Advocate*, given that the carriers can't be counted on even to always get it to them by Friday, let alone in time for them to read it with their morning coffee."

She punctuated that thought with a disgusted snort, and Catrina looked up from her nap in the sunny spot that appeared mornings on the entry carpet.

"Not that it makes any difference. A weekly can't compete with a daily—I know that and I accept it." She held up the newspaper. "And here's my report of the murder, woefully out of date compared to what Marcy Brewer wheedled out of Clayborn, and I've just been with him and he didn't tell me anything new at all."

Pamela slipped her arm around Bettina's shoulders and gently guided her through the doorway into the kitchen. Bettina deposited the *Advocate* on the kitchen table next to the still-spread-out *Register* and returned to the entry to shed her coat.

Meanwhile, Pamela refilled the kettle and set it to boil. When Bettina reappeared, the sound of coffee beans clattering in the grinder made conversation impossible for a few moments, but when the clattering subsided, Pamela spoke.

"I imagine Marcy did wheedle," she said as she fit a paper filter into her carafe's plastic filter cone, "and Detective Clayborn felt like he had to give her something because she can be *very* persistent—and he wants to save face. What he gave her isn't much, though."

"It's not?"

Pamela poured the freshly ground coffee into the filter and turned to face Bettina, who had taken her customary seat at the little table.

"'Police near arrest'?" Pamela laughed. "How near is 'near'? And 'sufficient evidence,' but no specifics?"

"I feel better." Bettina folded the *Register* and set it aside, along with the *Advocate*. "I know you don't keep goodies around, but will you make toast?"

"Of course," Pamela said, "and you know where the cream is."

The kettle began to whistle, and Pamela resumed her coffee making, adding the boiling water to the filter cone. A gurgling drip signaled that the water had begun its journey through the grounds. Soon the tantalizing aroma of brewing coffee was joined by that of toasting whole-grain bread, and soon after that, Pamela and Bettina sat facing each other at the little table with coffee and toast at hand. Bettina's toast, reposing on a wedding-china plate, had been garnished with not only butter but also a dark swath of blueberry jam.

"What if Clayborn really did have someone in mind when he told Marcy that the police were nearing arrest?" Bettina asked. The toast, along with the coffee transformed by sugar and cream into the pale and sweet concoction she preferred, had lifted her spirits. "Who do you think it would be?"

Pamela reached for her own cup of coffee, sipped, and let its caffeine-laden bitterness do its work for a few moments.

"Shiloh or the cook who made the milkshake seem the most likely prospects, but their motives just seem so obscure."

"Maybe Clayborn uncovered a motive, for one or the other." Bettina gazed at Pamela over the rose-garlanded rim of her coffee cup. She sipped and lowered the cup. "Maybe that's the evidence he told Marcy had been gathered."

"Shiloh links to Amos, and vice versa," Pamela said. "Detective Clayborn must have figured out that they're a couple."

"And Amos was leading the sheep that provided the

distraction right before the poisoned milkshake was delivered to Lionel Dunes."

"Too, too complicated." Bettina shook her head, setting her earrings to bobbing. They were Murano glass, large beads that juxtaposed a kaleidoscope of colors to striking effect.

"Too, too complicated," Pamela agreed. "But we'll go to the sheep-shearing tomorrow and see what we can see."

"And hear." Bettina nodded again. "Besides, I have to be there anyway because I'm covering it for the *Advocate*."

With that issue settled, both concentrated on their coffee and toast, and when the conversation started up again, the pansies now brightening Pamela's front porch were the focus.

"Wilfred is going to the garden center tomorrow," Bettina said, after expressing her admiration for Pamela's pansies, "and then we'll have ours." She celebrated that thought with a bite of toast and a sip of coffee, adding, after she had swallowed, "Spring really is just around the corner."

Half an hour later, Bettina stood in the entry slipping back into her cheerful coat. But before she took her leave, she stepped over to the little table where Pamela set her mail, both incoming and outgoing.

"What's this?" she asked as she picked up a catalog. On its cover, along with a discreetly blurred image of a nude female body, were the words "Your Sensuous Self."

"It's addressed to someone a few houses down," Pamela said with a laugh. "The mail carrier gets confused sometimes."

Bettina paged through the catalog. "Candles," she murmured, "scented oils." She looked up and whispered, "Lingerie." She flipped through a few more pages. "Cozy pillows . . . to make your love nest even more cozy." She turned a page, "And lots of other . . . sensuous . . . things." She closed the catalog. "My goodness!"

"I'm going to put it back out for him to pick up," Pamela said and held out a hand.

The catalog was returned to the little table, and Bettina set off, pausing on the threshold to say, "I hope Pete knows that he's invited tomorrow night."

"Yes, yes," Pamela assured her and added a hug.

Work for the magazine awaited upstairs: the article on molas to copyedit and the revised "Sheep to Shawl" to evaluate. "Molas" was interesting, Pamela recalled, and it would be a pleasure to study the delightful illustrations once again. "Sheep to Shawl" had already been rejected once, but the author, a docent at a reconstructed colonial village in Connecticut, was nothing if not persistent. Pamela decided to start with "Sheep to Shawl," whose full title was still "Sheep to Shawl: Shearing, Spinning, and Weaving History in a Reconstructed Colonial Village."

Her original rejection had pointed out that the article focused too much on visitors to the village, especially ill-behaved students on field trips, and not enough on Colonial-era wool production. The author had taken that criticism to heart. The new version of the article went into great detail about the shearing, sorting, washing, picking, carding, spinning, and weaving that transformed the wool garment nature had given the sheep into garments that could be worn by humans.

A long excursus was devoted to lanolin, still used as an ingredient in modern products like lipstick and skin creams, and definitely not wasted in colonial times. It was extracted from the newly sheared fleece, the author explained, by boiling the fleece for several hours in large pots of water. This was done outdoors over open fires at the colonial village. The water was then cooled and the lanolin skimmed off the top. A photo showed a bowl of lanolin looking for all the world like a scoop of expensive face cream.

"Readers of *Fiber Craft* will find most of this relevant now," Pamela wrote in her evaluation, "but I suggest that, since lanolin is tangential to *Fiber Craft*'s focus, the description of how it's produced be trimmed considerably."

The next few hours, after a break for lunch, were devoted to copyediting "Molas." When that task was finished, Pamela rolled her chair back from her desk, closed her eyes, and raised her arms above her head in a most luxurious stretch.

Chapter Eight

The shearing event's most crucial participants, the sheep, were already there when Pamela and Bettina arrived. Also present were the organizers, namely, Amos Clark and several other students from Wendelstaff's sustainable living group. Aileen Conway, who Pamela recognized from the reception in St. Willibrod's hall, was on hand as well, in her capacity as the group's advisor.

Few observers had remained the previous week, once word spread that the shearing was postponed. But now a lively crowd milled about in the parking lot, and a cluster of people browsed among the leaflets, cards, and flyers spread out on the table near the edge of the lawn. Among the crowd were children, darting excitedly across the lawn to inspect the sheep, then retreating in giggles, as their parents socialized.

The sheep themselves ambled here and there, bulky with a winter's worth of fleece, sampling the unpromising grass and occasionally gazing at the crowd.

Two burly men, not old but older than the Wendelstaff students, stood off to the side keeping an eye on the sheep and the adventurous children. Pamela counted six sheep, which she thought was the same number of sheep that had made up the procession along Arborville Avenue the day Lionel Dunes was poisoned.

Amos, at a nod from Aileen Conway, stepped out onto the lawn and raised his voice to address the crowd.

"Okay," he shouted, "we're going to get this underway. These guys"—he pointed at the burly men—"are from a sustainable community along the Hudson, and they're going to do the shearing the old-school way, no electric clippers."

One of the burly men held up a tool that looked like hedge clippers. The other man advanced toward the sheep, making comforting sounds. He singled one of them out and the others, as if they knew what was happening, edged away.

"It doesn't hurt them," the man with the clippers called.

The other man prodded at the sheep he had chosen until it sank back onto its haunches, then he positioned himself behind it, almost hugging it, as it sat upright with its forelegs extended. He reached out a hand, and the man with the clippers passed them over.

"Starting on the chest," began a running commentary as he wielded the clippers. Thick rolls of fleece began to fall away as if the sheep were being peeled, though where the fleece had been shorn, the skin was still covered by a short layer of curly fur.

"Moving on to the belly . . ." More fleece fell away,

and the sheep punctuated the man's narrative with low bleats that sounded like a foghorn.

Once the belly was shorn, the sheep was lowered onto its side, and the even thicker fleece from its flanks and back joined the pale mound accumulating on the grass.

"Fascinating," murmured Bettina, who was standing next to Pamela, "and the sheep is so obedient . . . like it just goes along with what's happening, no questions asked." She had her phone out and was taking photos of the process to accompany her article.

"Sheep are like that," Pamela murmured back.

The shearing of the first sheep was now complete, and that sheep, considerably less bulky, had hopped to its feet and ambled away. The shearer set down his clippers and smoothed the wool that had been removed out on the grass. It was so densely matted that it resembled one of those sheepskins sold as rugs.

Both of the burly men set to work then, shearing the remaining sheep. Many of the onlookers, with children in tow, moved onto the lawn to watch the process from a closer vantage point, now that it was clear the sheep were reliably docile. Bettina, meanwhile, was scanning the cluster of people near the table full of literature.

"I want to interview Aileen Conway," she explained. "I talked to Amos last week, but Aileen, understandably, had left."

Bettina continued to search, her head bobbing up and down, until after a few moments she announced, "There she is, on the lawn by the sheep. Come on!" She grabbed Pamela's arm.

Pamela wasn't sure why she had to accompany Bettina on the errand to interview Aileen, but it might be interesting to get a closer look at the shearing process, especially given the details she had absorbed from "Sheep to Shawl."

They set out, Bettina striding quite confidently in her bright-red sneakers, worn that day—Pamela was sure—with the thought in mind that tramping across grass might be on the agenda. The rest of Bettina's outfit, well-cut jeans topped by a red leather jacket with a fetching peplum, complemented the sneakers.

Bettina approached Aileen and introduced herself again, alluding to the meeting at the reception and adding her *Advocate* credentials, and soon the two women were chatting companionably about the shearing event and the sustainable living program.

Pamela, meanwhile, recognized Liadan Percy among those watching as the nearest shearer skillfully maneuvered his clippers over the forelegs of the sheep he was working on. She and Bettina had met Liadan, a local Wiccan, in connection with another of Bettina's *Advocate* assignments.

Liadan recognized Pamela too, and edged through the small crowd until she was standing at Pamela's side.

"I couldn't resist the chance to observe this," she said, nodding toward the activity taking place on the lawn. "The ancient Celts sheared their sheep in early spring, I'm sure, when they still followed the Wiccan creed and lived in harmony with nature." She fingered the voluminous shawl, anchored with an ornate knot-like brooch, that reached to her knees.

Between the dramatic shawl, thick wool dyed a

heathery purple, and the untamed salt-and-pepper curls that reached past her shoulders, Liadan herself could have passed for a Celtic priestess.

"I did debate coming, though." She leaned close to Pamela and spoke confidingly.

"Hmm?" Pamela nodded, distracted by fragments of conversation reaching her from the direction of Bettina and Aileen. Bettina seemed to be quizzing Aileen about the destiny of the wool resulting from the day's shearing.

"It doesn't belong to the Wendelstaff group," Aileen explained. "It belongs to the community that owns the sheep."

"But you'll take some . . . buy some?" Bettina suggested. "Because the group wants to make a point about valuing resources. If turning the wool into cloth is labor-intensive . . ."

"Oh, it is. It is!" Aileen interrupted.

". . . not a scrap of cloth would ever be wasted."

"No," Aileen said, "it wouldn't."

Liadan's voice became audible again as both Bettina and Aileen fell silent.

". . . Devil and Tower," Liadan was murmuring, "never a good sign, and I almost decided to stay home."

Pamela sensed that she'd made her puzzlement obvious when Liadan laughed a sudden merry laugh and reached out to touch her on the shoulder.

"The tarot," she explained. "My morning reading. Devil and Tower are never good . . . but then there was World, right-side-up, signifying completion, perhaps soon."

Pamela nodded. Liadan was a devotee of the tarot—

Pamela recalled that now. In fact, Liadan had once insisted on doing a reading for Pamela.

"Completion?" Pamela asked. "Of what?" She knew a reading applied only to the person whose hand, guided by some unconscious force, selected the cards to be read. But she herself was longing for completion. What clues would complete the yet unfinished solution to the puzzle of Lionel Dunes's death?

"Of course it has to be processed, I would think," said a voice at her elbow, Bettina's voice. "Washed, of course."

"Yes, washed," Aileen agreed. "And there's a byproduct—lanolin."

"But it wouldn't have to be woven," Bettina said. "It looks so soft. I'll bet it makes nice pillows."

Liadan reached for Pamela's hand. "I'm going to leave you now," she said. Her voice was musical, and the hand that seized Pamela's seemed to vibrate. "You are needed elsewhere," she added, and slipped away.

Curious, Pamela thought. But with a mental shrug, she shifted her attention to the conversation underway between Bettina and Aileen.

"Why would you think of that use particularly?" Aileen inquired. "Pillows, I mean."

Pamela hadn't gotten a very good look at Aileen during the reception in St. Willibrod's hall—a few glimpses from across the large room and then a closer glimpse as she and Bettina bade their quick goodbyes. Her impression then had been of a slender, middle-aged woman who was otherwise nondescript. Observing Aileen at greater length, Pamela could see that she was quite attractive in an unobtrusive way. With no cosmetic enhancement, her brows arched over large, dark eyes, and her full lips seemed tinted by nature rather than art. The streaks of gray in her dark hair detracted not at all from her appeal.

"I came across one the other day," Bettina said, "in the course of some research . . . for the *Advocate*. It had an interesting aroma, which I'm thinking now was lanolin." She laughed. "Someone's been using one of the meeting rooms at St. Willibrod's for what I suspect is an unauthorized purpose."

At that moment, Bettina was distracted by Amos, waving from a spot on the lawn near where the flock of now-shorn sheep milled about. One of the burly men who had done the shearing was stuffing huge clumps of the shorn wool into a canvas bag. Other bags, already stuffed, lay around him like giant pillows.

"Do you want to interview one of the guys from the community that owns the sheep?" he called.

"Yes! Yes!" Bettina called back, and set off across the lawn.

Pamela exchanged a few pleasantries with Aileen, about the event and about the sustainable living program, and then she set off after Bettina.

Bettina had been busy in the few hours since she and Pamela returned to Orchard Street after the shearing event. The Bettina who greeted Pamela and Pete at the Frasers' door had chosen her outfit with the occasion very much in mind. The occasion was "St. Patrick's Day Eve," as Wilfred had declared, and Bettina wore a fit and flare dress in bright kelly green, with chic pumps in the same shade. Several strands of green jade beads accented the dress's scooped neckline, and green jade earrings bobbed at her ears, a striking effect with her scarlet hair.

"Come in, come in!" she sang, waving them into her comfy living room. Woofus the shelter dog, sprawled out on the sofa, looked up and studied Pete for a moment and then resumed his nap.

"He doesn't know you very well yet"—Bettina winked at Pete—"but he can tell you're a friend."

She led the way through the dining room, where her industry was apparent in the carefully set table, also featuring green, and into the kitchen. Wilfred was standing at the stove, with a large apron protecting the slacks and green flannel shirt that he had substituted for his usual uniform of bib overalls.

"Pamela!" He turned and made his way from the cooking area of the kitchen to the eating area. "Pete! Good to see you!"

The greetings were accompanied by a hug for Pamela and a hearty handshake for Pete. Pete and Wilfred were certainly a study in contrasts, Pamela thought as she watched them together, but only physically. Both were genial, smart, and kind. Wilfred, however, was ruddy of face and bulky of figure, while Pete had struck Pamela when they first met as resembling a model in a catalog for outdoor wear. He was handsome—though not in a glamorous way—and definitely fit, which his slim jeans and sleek turtleneck made clear. That his brown eyes occasionally hinted at melancholy made his handsomeness all the more appealing.

Tempting aromas had offered a preview of the evening's menu the moment Bettina opened the front door. Here in the kitchen, where corned beef bubbled in a pot on the stove and soda bread baked in the oven, they were intense.

"Beer?" Wilfred suggested. Four tall glasses from Bettina's set of Swedish crystal waited on the high counter that separated the cooking area of the kitchen from the eating area.

Nodding as his offer was accepted, he opened the refrigerator and took out four bottles. One by one, he twisted the caps off, tipped the bottles over the glasses as he tilted them slightly, and watched carefully until the amber liquid and the creamy foam generated by the pouring came to within half an inch of each glass's rim.

He'd provided cheese to accompany the beer, Irish cheddar, as well as Irish cream crackers. They were creamy colored squares, crispy but substantial, and a perfect foil for the rich cheese with its sharp saltiness.

Wilfred soon returned to his work at the stove. The others were happy to stand at the bar, sipping their beer, eating cheese and crackers, and observing his ministrations, which were so interesting as to make conversation unnecessary. As they watched, he carved a head of cabbage in half and set half aside. He sliced the other half into thin slices that mounded into a tangle of long cabbage slivers on the cutting board. In a Dutch oven, he melted butter and added the sliced cabbage when the butter began to sizzle.

Pamela knew from past St. Patrick's Day feasts that Wilfred's twist on the traditional side dish of cabbage was like the treatment Nell had advocated. He sautéed it in butter rather than boiling it, since boiling did it no favors, as he was wont to say. But now it seemed that he had something else in mind. As the cabbage cooked, he chopped a handful of green onions and added them to the cabbage, stirring the Dutch oven's contents with a wooden spoon, adding salt and fresh-ground pepper, and stirring some more.

Cream, apparently, was to be part of the creation as well. He stepped away from the stove to fetch a carton from the refrigerator and measured out a cupful, which joined the cabbage and green onion. More stirring, and then he lifted the lid off a saucepan that had been waiting nearby. From it he scooped potatoes—peeled, quartered, and steaming from recent cooking, lowered them into the Dutch oven, and took up a potato masher.

The performance was riveting, like a puzzle. What would result from the combination of cabbage, green onions, cream, and potatoes?

"What is it?" Pamela heard herself ask.

Wilfred glanced over his shoulder, potato masher in hand. "Colcannon," he said. "An old Irish recipe that combines the two essential St. Patrick's Day side dishes into one. But just for fun . . ." With his other hand, he held out a bowl containing chunks of something that looked like potato, only yellow. "I'm serving turnips too. Steaming them takes but a few minutes."

The aroma of baking soda bread had become overwhelming. Murmuring "Time to check on this," Wilfred set the bowl and the potato masher aside and bent to open the oven, releasing a draft of sweet, warm air. Donning a pair of oven mitts, he transferred from the oven to the stovetop a flat baking pan. On the pan reposed a dome-shaped loaf with a crisscross scoring its golden-brown crust.

"Very soon, very soon." Wilfred spoke half to himself as he tipped the bowl of turnip chunks into a saucepan fitted with a steamer, added water and a lid, and set it to boil.

Some minutes later, Pamela, Bettina, and Pete had arranged themselves around the Frasers' dining room table, with Wilfred's customary seat at the table's head still vacant. Sounds of cupboards and drawers being opened and closed, pots and pans being shifted about, and dishes clanking against counters suggested that preparations for serving were proceeding apace.

The table settings that awaited the feast had been Bettina's contribution. Plates from her sage-green pottery set rested atop placemats made of a quilted fabric that featured a jaunty shamrock print. Bright-green linen napkins were tucked next to the plates, along with Bettina's sleek stainless steel flatware. Pewter candleholders furnished with tall green tapers flanked a vase overflowing with greenery and white roses. Salt and pepper, carving utensils, and serving spoons completed the arrangements.

"Who's for a refill on the beer?" came Wilfred's voice from the doorway.

Pete hopped up, saying, "Let me lend a hand," and headed for the kitchen.

Once the beer had been replenished and Pete had taken his seat again, Wilfred proceeded to serve the meal. First to arrive, on an oval platter from the sage-green pottery set, was the corned beef, a glistening slab of meat deep pink in color. Wilfred set it within easy reach of the spot that he would occupy and returned to the kitchen.

Next came two bowls. One held the steamed turnips, the bite-sized chunks now coated with melted butter. The other held the colcannon, like a mound of creamy mashed potatoes but flecked with green. On the third trip, Wilfred delivered a small bowl of mustard and a small dish holding a goodly portion of butter. And finally he brought forth the soda bread on a wooden bread platter. After taking his seat, he began carving the corned beef, revealing its juicy interior as slices rolled methodically off the edge of his knife.

"Hand along your plates," he advised. Plates were passed to the head of the table and then returned to their owners bearing generous servings of the corned beef.

The turnips and colcannon were a serve-yourself proposition, but Bettina took charge of the soda bread. She cut the round loaf in half and then sliced one of the halves and handed slices, speckled with raisins, onto offered plates. The interior of the bread was still warm—hot, even—and the pat of butter that Pamela applied to her slice softened instantly.

Wilfred surveyed his guests and his wife, his ruddy face aglow in the candlelight. With a cheery "Bon appétit!" he invited them to partake.

The corned beef, enhanced by a dab of mustard, lived up to its promise. The meat was tender, juicy, and flavorful—with brine and pepper predominating, and an aromatic hint of bay leaf. In Wilfred's colcannon, the simplicity of mashed potatoes enriched with cream was offset by the slightly bitter cabbage and the tangy green onions. The steamed turnips added the contrast of a texture that yielded pleasantly to the teeth, and a subtle sweetness.

"Delicious!" Bettina gazed at her husband from her spot at the foot of the table. "You have outdone yourself!"

"I second the motion." Pete, sitting on Wilfred's right, turned toward his host. "I don't know when I've had a better corned beef dinner, at any time of the year."

Pamela spoke up too, and after praising the corned beef and the colcannon and the turnips, she focused on the soda bread, which she had found to be exceptionally moist, with a substantial crumb.

She said as much, to which Wilfred replied, "Yogurt."

Bettina laughed. "I told him about Nell's idea, and he tried it."

Wilfred nodded. "There are many more uses for extra yogurt than there are for extra buttermilk—though of course a person could make multiple loaves of soda bread."

"And that wouldn't be a bad thing, not a bad thing at all." Pete helped himself to another slice of soda bread and Bettina cut the remaining half of the loaf into slices.

They concentrated on their eating then, with second helpings of everything all around, before conversation, other than exclamations of pleasure, resumed.

Pete turned to Bettina as the pace of eating slowed and the sage-green surface of the plates, once covered with food, began to reappear.

"Your article in the *Advocate* on Lionel Dunes's murder was very informative," he said.

"You thought so?" Bettina's fork paused en route to her mouth, and she raised her brows. "It was a little out of date, given that Marcy Brewer had weaseled that tantalizing tidbit out of Clayborn." A disgusted puff of breath punctuated the statement. She waited for a moment and then went on to quote the *Register*'s headline: "'Police Near Arrest in Dunes Case.'"

"That was Friday's paper." Pete's sympathetic manner brought out the melancholy in his eyes. "I didn't see anything about an arrest in the *Register* this morning, so I'm not sure I believe they were all that near."

"Marcy Brewer tends to exaggerate." Bettina's expression, verging on haughty, implied that she herself, as a more ethical journalist, was above such tactics.

"And anyway," Pete said, "given that you were right there at Hyler's when he collapsed, your report of the event itself certainly had claim to be more authoritative than Marcy Brewer's."

At this praise, Bettina's expression softened. Her mobile features were more suited to cheer anyway, and she rewarded Pete with a grateful smile.

Wilfred was stirring at his end of the table, checking the condition of the plates. Pamela's and Pete's were empty but for bits of fat, smudges of mustard, and streaks of colcannon. Bettina lifted one last bite of turnip to her mouth and set down her fork.

"We'll be having salad," Wilfred announced as he rose from his seat. "But first I'll clear."

Waving away offers of help, he removed the platter with the remains of the corned beef, the bowls—now empty—that had contained the colcannon and turnips, the bread platter that still held a few small slices of soda bread, and the mustard and butter and carving and serving implements. Then he began to gather the plates and flatware.

As Wilfred was making his trips back and forth to the kitchen, conversation among the three people left at the table veered back to the topic of Lionel Dunes's murder, but this time with a focus on its meaning for a revered Arborville institution.

"Do you know anything about the plans for Hyler's?" Pete inquired of Bettina, perhaps thinking that the *Advocate* had been privy to a plan unknown to the general public. "I was all set to have lunch there yesterday, but it was closed, and when I drove past this afternoon, it was still dark inside."

"Just a shame." Bettina shook her head and pinched her lips into a mournful knot. "They don't *have* to be closed, I don't think, because the police finished with the crime scene days ago, and the crime-scene tape is long gone. But if people are afraid to eat there, why be open?"

"What would bring people back, I wonder?" Pete shifted his gaze from Pamela to Bettina and back to Pamela and waited expectantly.

"Maybe if it turned out that Shiloh and/or the cook had nothing to do with the poison," came an answer from an unexpected quarter. Wilfred stepped through the kitchen doorway with a small plate in each hand.

"That would be the best conclusion," Pamela agreed, "both for the restaurant and for them."

Wilfred set the small plates, which contained the salad, in front of Pamela and Bettina and then returned to the kitchen. Once everyone had a salad and Wilfred was back in his seat, he repeated his customary "Bon appétit!" and picked up his fork.

"I don't think there's actually a traditional St. Patrick's Day salad," he said. "Until air transport made it possible to ship fresh produce anywhere at any season, lettuce would have been hard to come by in Ireland in March."

Pamela inspected her not-traditional salad. It definitely involved lettuce—butter lettuce, she thought—torn into leafy curls. Layered among the lettuce curls were slices of some pale fruit, and dotted over the top were chopped nuts. She bent closer and decided they were pecans.

Perhaps she had even murmured it aloud, because Wilfred said, "Yes." He laughed. "Not very Irish, I know. Pecans are native to North America, but I thought they'd go well with the pear slices."

They did, and the mild, tender butter lettuce, which Wilfred had drizzled with a simple oil and balsamic dressing, formed the perfect backdrop.

Pete had evidently been ruminating as he chewed. He looked up when his plate was nearly empty and said, "What if the milkshake was delivered to the wrong person?"

"Oh my goodness!" Bettina's fork landed on the rim of her plate with a clank. "I never thought of that—and neither did Clayborn, I'm sure."

"It would be bad for Hyler's," Pete observed with a sad smile. "It could mean that the cook is quite possibly the murderer."

"But it would be good for Shiloh," Bettina cut in. "If she was the murderer, surely she would have delivered the milkshake to the person she meant to murder."

"Your suggestion makes a certain amount of sense, Pete." Wilfred faced Pete and nodded slowly. "Shiloh was new on the job, the parade of sheep was distracting . . ."

The conversation came to a halt then, as Pete's suggestion set brains abuzz with implications that demanded silent pondering. Pamela was so deep in thought that she was oblivious to the disappearance of her empty salad plate and the arrival of a stemmed dessert cup, clear glass, containing a mousse-like substance the color of mocha.

She only returned fully to the present when Wilfred handed her a plate of pale oval cookies, bidding her to take a few and pass the plate along. She complied, slipping the cookies onto the matching glass plate beneath the dessert cup, picking up her spoon, and sampling the contents of the cup.

Bettina was already squealing with pleasure as Pamela took her first taste. A moment later it was clear that the squeals were justified. Like chocolate mousse, the dessert was pleasantly chilled, and the consistency was rich and creamy. But the mocha color correlated with a mocha taste, resembling sweet coffee with plenty of cream. That was just the way Bettina liked her coffee, Pamela reflected. No wonder she was squealing.

Pamela took another spoonful, savoring it in quest of a label for another flavor, an elusive flavor that complemented the mocha. The flavor combination seemed familiar, but why?

"It's Irish Coffee Mallow." Wilfred laughed a delighted laugh. "An invention of mine. I based it on an old recipe that involves melting marshmallows into coffee and stirring in whipped cream and chilling the result. But I added a bit of Irish whiskey, in honor of Saint Patrick."

"It's delicious!" Pamela said. "What a brilliant idea—all the delights of Irish coffee and most of the delights of mousse—minus only the chocolate—rolled up together."

"The alcohol basically evaporates," Wilfred explained, "but the taste of the whiskey remains."

Pete added his compliments, and Bettina noted that the cookies were the perfect accompaniment, though not homemade. They were shortbread cookies from the Co-Op bakery, tender and buttery, but not upstaging the mallow, which was the main attraction.

"We'll have coffee in the living room in a bit," Bettina suggested as spoons scoured dessert cups for the last bits of mallow and only crumbs remained on the plate that had held the shortbread cookies. "Coffee served with Irish Coffee Mallow seemed too much of a good thing."

"Please let me do something helpful," Pamela said, rising from her chair and picking up her own dessert plate and cup.

Bettina was on her feet then too. "It's only fair," she told Wilfred. "You've been working all day."

"In that case"—Wilfred leaned toward Pete—"come on down to the basement and take a look at the dollhouse I'm building for our new granddaughter." He stood up. "I know you, of all people, will appreciate what I've done."

Wilfred's idea that Pete would appreciate the dollhouse project was based on the fact that Pete himself built things—he had left a successful career on Wall Street to pursue work that he considered more satisfying, work with his hands. Pamela had been surprised when what she thought was a casual date with the man she'd hired to replace her window screens turned out to be an elegant dinner at a very expensive French restaurant, but she was enjoying the relationship that had resulted. Pete combined the confidence and sophistication of someone used to money with a humble appreciation of craftsmanship and physical labor.

An hour later, after coffee in the living room accompanied by more shortbread cookies, Pamela and Pete stood on the Frasers' front porch as Wilfred and Bettina bade them goodnight from the doorway. Hugs and handshakes were exchanged, and then Pamela and Pete crossed the street to Pamela's house, where her porch light cast a welcoming glow.

Chapter Nine

The next morning Pamela opened her eyes in her bright room and, like a projected image fading when sunlight hits a screen, the fragments of a lingering dream slipped away. The dream had been one of those dreams about trying to get somewhere—home, maybe. She had waited for a bus, but when it came it wasn't the right bus, though it could take her to the spot where she could catch the right bus, if only she had the fare, which she didn't. Other people came and went in the dream, some of them the same people, disappearing and reappearing—to the point that she almost felt she should greet them. There was one man especially, so familiar . . .

As she pushed the bedclothes aside and sat up, Catrina and Ginger emerged from the region where her feet had been. Catrina scampered toward the doorway, but Ginger dawdled behind as Pamela slipped into her fleecy robe, edging aside and waiting as she slid her feet into her furry slippers.

Catrina had reached the landing by the time Pamela and Ginger started down the stairs. She was waiting in the corner of the kitchen where the cats were accustomed to eat their meals when Pamela, with Ginger hovering close, entered.

Pamela opened a can of Tuna Treat and scooped generous servings into a large bowl for the two cats to share. Precious had joined them by then and received her own bowl with her own serving of Tuna Treat. Pamela stared at the cats as they bent avidly over their breakfast. Especially she stared at Ginger. Something about Ginger echoed with an image . . . from the faded dream.

She closed her eyes, but the image was no clearer. And anyway, there was coffee to make and a newspaper to fetch. She set water to boil and was back inside with the *Register* before the kettle began to whistle. After slipping a paper filter into her carafe's filter cone and grinding coffee beans, she extracted the *Register* from its plastic sleeve. The front-page headlines made no reference to the Lionel Dunes case.

"So much for 'Police Near Arrest in Dunes Case,'" she remarked to Ginger, who had finished her meal but was lingering in the kitchen. The kettle's whistle summoned her to the stove then, and in a few moments the aroma of fresh-brewed coffee began to fill the room.

Toast was the next step—except the doorbell's chime summoned her to the entry. Through the lace that curtained the oval window in the front door, Pamela recognized a familiar figure with a crest of bright scarlet hair. She opened the door to admit Bettina.

"I hope you haven't had your toast yet," Bettina

said. She was carrying a white bakery box, larger than those in which she usually delivered morning treats. "This showed up on my porch first thing, with a note, 'Happy St. Patrick's Day from a grateful reader of the *Advocate*.' So . . . I smell coffee . . ."

"What's in there?" Pamela asked, peering at the box as if somehow closer scrutiny would make its contents visible.

"Something that looks very, very delicious, and just in time for breakfast." She handed the box to Pamela.

"You're right about smelling coffee." Pamela smiled and nodded toward the kitchen doorway. But Bettina paused en route to bend over the small table where Pamela set her mail.

"You still have this!" Bettina giggled and picked up the catalog that had strayed into Pamela's mailbox a few days previously, the Sensuous Self catalog. She giggled again. "Are you thinking of placing an order? Pete might enjoy seeing you in one of these—"

Pamela interrupted. "I meant to put it out for the mail carrier to deliver to the right address, but I just didn't do it yet."

"Lots of interesting items . . ." Bettina flipped through a few pages.

"The coffee's going to get cold," Pamela said. "Shall we . . ."

She stepped through the kitchen doorway. But something was nagging at her, and Ginger was so persistently lingering, and that image from the dream was so . . . elusive.

Bettina followed her into the kitchen and headed for the cupboard where Pamela stored her wedding china.

"I was thinking . . ." She reached up and took out two cups and then two saucers and two little plates. ". . . about Pete's idea."

"Um?" Pamela responded from the table. She had just untied the string and flipped back the cover of the bakery box to reveal a dozen doughnuts iced with bright-green icing.

Bettina carried the china to the table and continued speaking. "Maybe Shiloh *did* deliver the poisoned milkshake to the wrong person. That would complicate things."

"A lot," Pamela agreed. "There could be all kinds of suspects and all kinds of motives, depending on who the milkshake was actually intended for."

"How could we ever know that?"

Without answering, because there really was no useful answer that she could think of, Pamela fetched the carafe from the counter and filled the two cups waiting on the table. While Bettina opened the refrigerator in search of the heavy cream, Pamela transferred the cut-glass sugar bowl and cream pitcher to the table, along with napkins and a spoon.

Once they were seated, Bettina began the careful process of sugaring and creaming her coffee, stirring the sugar in first and then stirring while dribbling in cream until the color paled to mocha.

Ginger had remained in the kitchen. Now that Bettina was no longer moving about but settled into her chair, the cat approached and began to delicately sniff at her shoes. This custom was for cats, Pamela often reflected, perhaps the equivalent of a host seeking an update on recent doings from a guest. Bettina had dressed casually this morning, in a tunic and leggings, olive green, with her scarlet hair and red sneakers providing bright accents.

As Ginger sniffed, Catrina wandered in from the hallway that led to the back door. She napped in the sunny spot that appeared on the entry carpet every morning and was probably on her way there, but she stopped and joined Ginger in the investigation of Bettina's shoes.

Bettina gazed at them fondly and extended her feet to give them better access. "It's amazing to think that this one"—she wiggled the foot nearest Ginger—"is Catrina's daughter. Catrina is absolutely jet black, and she's that reddish ginger color."

"Her father was that reddish ginger color," Pamela reminded Bettina.

Ginger was the product of an unplanned encounter between Catrina, adopted as a woebegone stray, and a roguish ginger tom.

"I remember him." Bettina nodded. "But I haven't seen him around lately."

Pamela nodded too. "He used to come and go, but now he's just gone."

"Anyway . . ." Bettina took an exploratory sip of her coffee and smiled. "Shall we?"

She transferred one of the doughnuts to her plate and nudged the box toward Pamela. Pamela reached in and took a doughnut too. The icing was thickly applied and intensely green.

Bettina lifted her doughnut to her mouth. "Mmm," she murmured. "Smells minty."

Pamela stared. The room seemed to tilt as images,

memories, impressions that she had considered random shuffled themselves into something coherent.

"Bettina! Don't!" She leaned forward, reached out a hand, and grabbed the doughnut just as Bettina was about to bite into it.

Bettina reared back, so startled that she almost tipped her chair. She seized the edge of the table to steady herself and frowned at Pamela. "I know you don't usually eat sweet things for breakfast," she said, "but that doesn't mean I can't."

"Bettina!" Pamela's voice came out more shrill than she intended. "These are *poison*, just like the green milkshake. The person who left them on your porch is trying to . . . remove . . . you before you go to the police with what you know about Lionel Dunes's murder."

"But I don't know anything." Bettina's lips puckered into a confused zigzag.

"You do," Pamela said, "but you don't realize it." She explained what she had realized, how it all came together to make sense . . . especially the sheep, then she stood up. She dropped the doughnut she was still holding back into the bakery box, and tipped the one from her plate back in as well. She flipped the box's cover into place and tied it down securely with the string.

"You must take this to Detective Clayborn immediately and explain to him what I just explained to you." She held out the box. "I'd come along but I'm still in my robe and pajamas, and the sooner he gets this the better."

"I could wait while you get dressed," Bettina said. "I

know it won't take long because you'll just put on the same thing you wore yesterday, and you never wear makeup."

Despite the shock of realizing that Bettina (both of them, in fact) had just narrowly escaped death, Pamela laughed—albeit shakily.

"Just go!" She made a shooing motion with her hands, and a few minutes later, Bettina was on her way.

Detective Clayborn was initially dubious, Bettina had reported after her trip to the police station. He had said that anonymously delivered green-iced doughnuts accompanied by a St. Patrick's Day greeting were not inherently suspicious. But when Bettina pointed out that a green milkshake called The Leprechaun was not inherently suspicious either, he agreed to have the cupcakes analyzed for cyanide.

"And what about my idea of who the killer is?" Pamela had asked.

"I don't know what he thought," Bettina had said. "You know how he can be."

Now it was Monday morning. The aromas of coffee and toast filled the little kitchen, and the *Register* lay spread out on the table. But even a very thorough reading of Part 1 and Local had turned up no new reports on the Lionel Dunes murder case—not even another "Police Near Arrest" teaser.

Pamela had spoken to Bettina on the telephone, and to Wilfred, who assured her that even if the doughnuts turned out not to be poisoned, her concern for Bettina's welfare was very much appreciated.

The copyedited article on molas and the evaluation of the revised "Sheep to Shawl" were due back by five, and Pamela checked over her work one more time before sending them off. That task out of the way, she gathered a few canvas totes from the closet, slipped on her jacket, and set out for the Co-Op.

Knit and Nibble was meeting at her house the following night. She planned to serve shortbread cookies, homemade and cut in the shapes of shamrocks. The recipe did not call for exotic ingredients, but butter was needed—lots of butter. And her pantry was nearly bare of both cat food and human food.

Pamela returned home an hour later, invigorated by an outing that had combined a chilly breeze with the promise of spring offered by drifts of crocus and snowdrops, and even a forsythia venturing into early bloom. She unpacked and stored her groceries, which included a piece of flounder for dinner and an extra pound of butter, and climbed the stairs to her office. No new assignments from *Fiber Craft* had arrived, but there was a newsy note from Penny, who either still hadn't heard about the Lionel Dunes murder case or was unaware that her own mother had gotten caught up in the mystery. There was also an email from Pete, with a link to an article about a house-moving project that the county was undertaking to save a Colonial-era structure.

The day ended with a few hours of meditative knitting as Catrina and Ginger dozed beside her on the sofa. Thoughts of Lionel Dunes receded as the motions of knitting soothed her and the genteel British mystery unfolding on the screen distracted her. She'd done what she could. Perhaps she and Bettina had really just been barking up the wrong tree.

Chapter Ten

"You were right! You were right!"

Pamela stepped out onto her porch early Tuesday morning to see Bettina in full flight midway across the street, wearing a ruffled pink robe and with her hair in disarray. She carried a sheet of newsprint.

"It's all here in the *Register*," she panted as she gained the curb and hopped onto the grass.

As soon as Pamela reached the spot at the end of her front walk where her own copy of the *Register* lay, Bettina was at her side. She waited as Pamela retrieved the newspaper, then seized her arm and steered her back toward the porch from which she had come, talking all the while.

"The killer was Aileen Conway," she panted, "just like you thought, and the doughnuts were poisoned, and a neighbor's security camera caught her delivering them to my doorstep right after dawn, and she was arrested last evening."

Though Pamela felt herself rendered a bit breathless

by the onslaught of words, she opened her mouth to speak. Before any sound emerged, however, Bettina resumed her excited narrative.

"So I'm forever grateful to you, of course, for grabbing that doughnut out of my hand, and thank goodness Clayborn had the sense to follow up on the doughnuts and find a way to figure out who delivered them." She paused, but only briefly, as she negotiated the porch steps in her high-heeled pink mules, and then went on.

"Of course, Clayborn gave Marcy Brewer the scoop"—she held out the sheet of newsprint, which proved to be the front page of the *Register*—"even though I'm the one that was almost poisoned."

Her voice had thinned to a strained gurgle. Turning to face her, Pamela noticed tears forming and pulled her close for a hug, front page of the *Register* and all, though she herself was encumbered by her own copy of the paper, still in its plastic sleeve.

"It wasn't fair." She addressed a spot somewhere above Bettina's head, given that she was so much taller than her friend. "Detective Clayborn can be very inconsiderate."

Bettina pulled away from the hug and wiped her eyes with her free hand. "That's not why I'm crying," she squeaked. "I'm crying because my best friend saved my life."

Another hug was necessary after that, and still with an arm enfolding Bettina, Pamela said, "Come inside. I'm sure the kettle is hooting furiously by now, and it will just take a minute to have coffee ready."

Bettina wiped her eyes again, blinked a few times, and mustered a smile. "I have to run home and dress."

She looked down at the robe and slippers. "I'm meeting with Clayborn this morning, and I can't go like this. It won't be a scoop, but readers of the *Advocate* appreciate reporting that comes from a reporter who lives in their community."

The kettle *was* hooting furiously when Pamela returned to her kitchen, and she was soon settled at the table with coffee and toast at hand, reading the *Register*'s article on Aileen Conway's arrest. Many details were missing, of course, details that had slowly assembled themselves in her mind and led her to realize who had poisoned the doughnuts and why.

Dressed and downstairs again, Pamela set about making the cookies she planned to serve to Knit and Nibble that evening. As she worked, creaming butter and confectioners' sugar and vanilla, and then blending in flour, the automatic motions of her hands allowed her mind to roam. She reviewed the scene in Hyler's when Lionel Dunes collapsed onto his hamburger, the parade of sheep, the visit that she and Bettina made to Meeting Room B, the funeral and reception, the rescheduled shearing . . .

The motive for the murder had only gradually become clear. A red-headed man had hurried away from the tryst in Meeting Room B, and a red-headed man, who introduced himself as Ted Stewart, had been lingering near Aileen Conway at the reception—where Marlene Pepper had mentioned how helpful Ted Stewart had been to Aileen, and had seemed on the point of suggesting that there was something . . . improper . . . in their relationship.

Moreover, as Pamela had later recalled, the red-headed man—Ted Stewart—had been present at the rescheduled shearing. But it had taken a while to realize that they were all the same red-headed man, that he and Aileen were lovers, and that Aileen wanted to be free of Lionel so she could marry Ted Stewart.

Then the cookie-making demanded concentration again. The dough had to be gathered into a ball, wrapped in plastic wrap, and chilled—and the break in baking offered an opportunity to clean the parts of the house where the Knit and Nibblers would convene.

But as Pamela ran the vacuum over her living room rug, her mind continued to roam. The sheep had been a key element in solving the crime—in more ways than one. Without the sheep, she wouldn't have realized that the woman in Meeting Room B was Aileen. The red-headed man could have been present at the reception as a platonic friend supporting Aileen in her hour of grief. Of course, as Bettina had pointed out, Aileen had seemed quite cheerful, but his tryst in Meeting Room B could have involved some whole other woman—but for the pillow.

The pillow Bettina had noticed on the sofa in the meeting room had been covered with a rustic fabric that looked handwoven, and the pillow had looked homemade. The aroma, curious but pleasant, that Bettina had remarked upon was an effect of the pillow's stuffing—lambswool that still retained a hint of lanolin. In her capacity as advisor of Wendelstaff's sustainable living program, Aileen must have had access to freshly shorn wool and the rustic fabrics made from it. She'd created the pillow to, as the Sensuous Self catalog put it, "make a cozy love nest even more cozy."

And the sheep themselves had been deployed as a distraction. Pamela had figured that out early on, but she hadn't realized who engineered the distraction. It was Aileen, of course. She must have suggested that a parade of sheep would create interest in the shearing event, and she must have told Amos to lead them down Arborville Avenue at a specific time, a time that would suit her nefarious plan.

Then she lurked at Hyler's, in a booth near the back door, which handily was also near the end of the counter where the servers picked up beverages. While everyone was fascinated by the sheep parade, she slipped from the booth, added the poison to the milkshake destined for her husband, and escaped through the back door.

Pamela put the vacuum away and commenced dusting. Once the tables and cupboards and shelves in the entry, living room, and dining room had been polished, and all the rummage-sale and thrift-shop treasures that reposed on them were dust-free, she put her dust cloth away and fetched the bin that held her collection of vintage cookie cutters.

From that collection she selected a shamrock and, just for fun, a four-leaf clover. She rolled the chilled dough out on a well-floured pastry cloth and set to work, pressing the shamrock cookie cutter into the soft dough and delicately transferring each dough shamrock to a waiting cookie sheet.

She filled one cookie sheet with shamrocks and one with four-leaf clovers, and as a final touch she sprinkled them all with green-tinted sugar, patting it gently into their pale, doughy surfaces. When the oven light clicked off to indicate the oven was ready, she slid the cookie sheets into place on the wire racks and closed the oven door.

Holly and Karen were the first to arrive, and Holly's first words upon stepping into the entry were, "Something smells amazing!" Her next words were, "Why did that woman want to poison Bettina?"

The door had remained ajar after Holly and Karen entered, and Bettina had been right behind them coming up the walk. She crossed the threshold in time to hear Holly's question, and she answered it.

"Because she thought I had figured out that she was the one who killed Lionel Dunes."

Holly and Karen stared, and Holly exclaimed, "So you're the one who solved the mystery!"

Bettina laughed. "Not exactly. If I had, I wouldn't have announced that fact to the murderer herself."

"Bettina was just chatting about possible uses for lambswool," Pamela explained, "and Aileen took that to mean . . . well . . ."

Bettina took over. "Aileen was secretly meeting another man, a man who wasn't Lionel Dunes, and they had a special love nest, and she had furnished the love nest with a lambswool pillow. So when I started asking her about lambswool pillows, she assumed I knew about the love nest. And I—we"—she nodded toward Pamela—"*did* know about the love nest—"

"*But*," Pamela chimed in, "we didn't know that Aileen was one of the lovers—"

Bettina took over again. "—until Pamela put two and two together and saved me from eating a poisoned doughnut."

"And that was a very good thing," came a new voice.

Nell had just entered, and the new voice was hers. She surveyed the group, her faded blue eyes fond and her white hair forming a disarranged halo around her aged face.

"A very good thing, indeed," she added, "but I can't help but think that more than intuition was involved in Pamela's realization that the doughnuts had been prepared and delivered with sinister intent."

"Oh, it was much more than intuition." Holly's intense gaze met Nell's. "Pamela and Bettina knew all about the love nest where Aileen and a man who wasn't Lionel Dunes met for their secret rendezvous, and—"

"Are we knitting or talking?" inquired a masculine voice as the front door, which was still ajar, opened wider and Roland stepped through. "I know it's past seven, but I was unavoidably detained when it became necessary to circle all the way back to the corner to look for an alternate-side parking sign."

He set out toward the living room, where the hassock that was his customary seat waited at the far end of the hearth. Sitting down and opening the elegant briefcase that held his knitting, he continued talking.

"Why, given the amount of taxes we pay in this

town, they can't put up more than one alternate-side parking sign in a block is beyond me."

"The parking on Orchard is always the same," Bettina said. "You don't have to go looking for the sign. It's legal on Pamela's side Tuesday morning through Thursday night."

"Sometimes they change it." Roland spoke more to himself than to Bettina. "They like the fines they collect when people get confused." He lifted four double-pointed needles and a skein of yarn from the briefcase, then closed the briefcase and set it on the carpet.

"Shall we join Roland?" Pamela gestured toward the living room.

She knew Holly had been interrupted in the course of agreeing with Nell that more than intuition had been involved in saving Bettina from Aileen's malfeasance. But Nell disapproved of amateur sleuthing, and her comment had been a subtle hint that she suspected her friends of yet another foray into that realm. So perhaps it was best that they tend to their knitting.

Soon Nell had settled into the comfortable armchair at the near end of the hearth, and Holly, Karen, and Bettina were lined up on the sofa. Pamela was perched on the rummage-sale chair with the carved wooden back and needlepoint seat. It was a pleasure to give herself over to the soothing rhythm of her needles as they shaped her special Shetland Islands yarn into the complicated cables of her sweater project.

Bettina was sitting on the end of the sofa nearest Pamela's chair, alternating between consulting the magazine page that contained her pattern and studying the few inches of lacy pink knitting that dangled from her needles. Next to her was Holly, still at work on the summery top she was fashioning from linen-blend yarn in bright yellow. Karen had a new project, a tiny one again, that was undoubtedly an addition to the wardrobe of her daughter's doll. And Nell, across the room, was occupied with what looked to be another small blanket, gray this time, for the Haversack animal shelter.

As if Holly had read Pamela's mind and thus been privy to her survey of the other knitters' projects, now complete but for one, she looked up and focused on Roland.

"Starting another sock!" she exclaimed, adding a dimpled smile in case her vocal enthusiasm wasn't enough. "You *have* been busy! Just last week you were only halfway through the first."

"They generally come in pairs," Roland replied without lifting his eyes from his work.

Bettina nudged Pamela. "Do you think he's really going to wear them?" she whispered. "Hand-knit socks hardly seem his style."

It was Holly who responded. "I'm sure he'll wear them, after all that effort," she said. "We all wear the things we knit, don't we?" She surveyed the room. "Unless we knit them for someone else, of course, in which case they wear them."

Bettina lowered her knitting to her lap. "I love to see my Wilfred wearing the sweaters I've made for him and"—she shivered with pleasure—"what a thrill it will be to see my little granddaughter in this!" She raised her knitting again.

The conversation ebbed and flowed, involving reminiscences of favorite projects, including sweaters that Nell had knit for herself in her youth and projects even older.

"My mother was a knitter," Nell said, "and she recalled that she and her friends brought their knitting to their college classes and worked away while the professors lectured."

"Weren't they there to learn?" Holly seemed startled. "When I was studying at the Haversack Academy of Hair Design, I made sure to pay attention." Holly and her husband owned a salon.

Nell laughed her gentle laugh. "They were there to meet husbands. Sadly, that was most women's career goal back then."

Roland continued to knit, perhaps relieved that the conversation launched by the inquiry about his sock had veered in a direction that allowed him to concentrate on it in peace.

After about ten minutes had passed, filled with lively discussion of women's lives then and now, Bettina nudged Pamela again. Nodding toward Roland, she whispered, "I think he's getting ready to look at his watch."

Pamela was on her feet and heading for the kitchen as Roland intoned, "Eight p.m. Time for the break."

Bettina joined her in the kitchen, where earlier in the day Pamela had set out wedding-china cups, saucers, and little plates, and everything else that would be needed to serve the cookies with coffee and tea. The cookies themselves were arranged on a platter, shamrocks and four-leaf clovers intermingling, all shimmering with a dusting of green-tinted sugar.

"The four-leaf clovers are the ones that really bring good luck," Bettina commented, "not the shamrocks, like many people believe."

Pamela busied herself at the counter, filling the kettle and setting it to boil, and pouring the coffee she had already ground into the paper filter she had placed in the carafe's filter cone. Bettina fetched the heavy cream from the refrigerator and filled the cut-glass cream pitcher.

Holly entered then, peeking around the corner from the entry first and edging in with a sly smile.

"Ladies," she whispered. "I know there's more to be told. How did you find out about the love nest, and how did you connect Aileen with the love nest?"

"Well . . ." Bettina drew Holly to the far side of the table so they weren't in Pamela's way. She began to describe the quest that had been launched by the post Pamela saw on AccessArborville. Midway into her narrative, the kettle began to whistle, and she waited as Pamela poured the steaming water into the carafe's filter cone and ran water to refill the kettle for the tea.

"*Awesome*," Holly said when Bettina was finished. "That's just awesome to have figured that out. And it really was about the sheep. Hyler's didn't have anything to do with it at all. The sheep provided the distraction Aileen needed to add the poison to the milkshake, but they were her undoing as well—because the lambswool in the pillow linked her to the love nest."

Unexpectedly, Nell stepped into the kitchen, but via the door that led to the dining room. She'd apparently been lurking there, close enough to Bettina and Holly to overhear everything Bettina said.

"So, as I suspected, it wasn't just intuition that made Pamela intercept the poisoned doughnut," she said as she attempted to control a smile. "But, since you're both so smart, what's the explanation for the T-shirt that, as the *Register* put it in one of their sensationalistic headlines, 'foretold the lunchtime murder'?"

"Aileen, of course." Pamela turned from the counter. "The creator of the shirt was involved with the sustainable living group, so Aileen would have had contact with him. Besides his website, he sold shirts from his dorm room and at craft fairs, sales that could easily be cash sales and untraceable."

Bettina took over. "Aileen dropped the shirt off at Hyler's to throw police off the trail, to suggest that the creator of the shirt was guilty—or Amos, who had a similar shirt. Or maybe Shiloh, who was Amos's girlfriend and who served the poisoned milkshake besides."

The kettle had begun to whistle again, and Pamela added boiling water to the tea leaves waiting in one of her vintage teapots.

"Roland is asking if we're actually having a break." Karen had appeared behind Nell, standing in the doorway that led to the dining room.

"Of course we are, of course we are." Bettina seized the platter of cookies and hurried from the room. Karen and Nell followed with cream and sugar and a stack of little plates.

The coffee was ready, and the kitchen was fragrant with the aroma. Pamela filled four of the cups ranged on the table and checked the progress of the brewing tea. After a few more minutes of bustling, the coffee-drinkers had been provided with coffee and the tea-drinkers with tea, and all the Knit and Nibblers had transferred cookies from the platter to their plates.

"We're all so fortunate to be safe, to be here," Nell said, gazing at the group from the depths of her arm-chair, "with such terrible things going on in the world, all over the world, and even sometimes in our little town."

Looking around the room, Pamela did not know whether it was by chance or on purpose, but every plate held only four-leaf clovers.

KNIT

Knitted Potholder

A knitted potholder is a fun project that goes quickly and isn't too difficult. For pictures of the project, including the in-progress photos referred to below, visit the Knit & Nibble Mysteries page at PeggyEhrhart.com. Click on the cover for *Irish Milkshake Murder* and scroll down on the page that opens.

If you've never knitted before, it's easier to learn the basics by watching than by reading. The internet abounds with tutorials that show the process clearly, including casting on and off. Just search on "How to knit," "Casting on," and "Casting off." You only need to learn the basic knitting stitch. Don't worry about "purl." That's used in alternating rows to create the stockinette stitch, the stitch you see, for example, in a typical sweater. If you use "knit" on every row, you will end up with the stitch called the garter stitch. That's the stitch used for this potholder project.

Use "chunky" or "bulky" yarn for this project and size 6 needles. Not-too-large needles and thick-ish yarn will produce a dense knitted effect, which is what you want. You will need about 110 yards of yarn. It's best to choose 100% wool yarn, because wool is much more heat-resistant than synthetic. You don't want your potholder to melt in use. You will also need one or two pieces of felt, each a bit less than 8 inches square. The felt will be hidden inside the potholder to give it extra insulation. Use two pieces of felt if your yarn isn't too bulky, one piece if it is. The felt doesn't have to be the same color as your yarn.

These directions will make a generous-sized potholder, about 8 inches square.

Cast on 32 stitches, using the simple slip-knot process or the long-tail process. Knit until your piece of knitting is as long as it is wide. To check your progress, fold it on the diagonal. There is a photo of this step on my website. When it makes a perfect triangle folded, cast off. Repeat this process to make a second square.

Trim your square or squares of felt if necessary to make the felt very slightly smaller than your knitted squares. Smooth out one of your knitted squares and lay the felt on top of it. Using a sewing needle and sewing thread that matches your yarn, tack the felt to the knitted square, working all around the edges. There is a photo of this step on my website.

Lay the other knitted square on top of the first knitted square with the felt inside like a sandwich. Make sure the sides, the bottoms (the ends where you cast on), and the tops (the ends where you cast off) of the knitted squares are aligned. There is a photo of this step on my website.

Thread a yarn needle—a large needle with a large eye and a blunt end—with more yarn or with one of the tails left from when you cast on or off. Use the whip stitch to sew the two knitted pieces together all the way around, catching only the outer loops along each side and the ends. When only a bit of yarn remains on your needle, pass the needle through a loop of yarn to make a knot and rethread your needle. Hide all your tails by working the needle in and out of the seam for an inch or so and snip off the small tail that remains. There is a photo of hiding tails on my website or you can just tuck them inside.

If you wish to add a loop so you can hang your potholder, you will need a crochet hook. Using the same yarn, crochet a chain about an inch and half long. Search the internet for "Crochet chain stitch" if you do not already crochet. With your yarn needle, use the tails remaining at each end of the chain to anchor the chain in a loop at one corner of the potholder.

NIBBLE

Irish Coffee Mallow

In *Murder Most Irish*, Wilfred Fraser invents a special dessert for his St. Patrick's Day Eve meal. It's a twist on an old-fashioned recipe involving marshmallows and coffee, but he adds Irish whiskey. The alcohol in the whiskey evaporates, but the distinctive flavor remains.

The mallow needs to chill for six to eight hours before serving, so if you plan to serve it for dessert, start in the morning. As a bonus, you can use leftover breakfast coffee instead of making more for the recipe. It makes six not-too-large servings.

For a picture of Irish Coffee Mallow, as well as some in-progress photos, visit the Knit & Nibble Mysteries page at PeggyEhrhart.com. Click on the cover for *Irish Milkshake Murder* and scroll down on the page that opens.

Ingredients

1 cup strong coffee
20 regular-sized marshmallows
¼ cup Irish (or other) whiskey
1 cup heavy cream

Heat the coffee in a small saucepan over medium heat. Without removing the saucepan from the heat, add the marshmallows a few at a time and stir. It might seem that they are going to bob about, remaining whole forever, but they eventually melt completely into the coffee. Remove the saucepan from the heat and let the contents cool slightly. Add the Irish whiskey. (If you want to make sure the alcohol in the whiskey evaporates, add it as soon as you remove the saucepan from the heat.) Let the mixture cool to the point that you can touch the outside of the saucepan comfortably.

In a medium bowl, whip the cream to soft peaks. Add the coffee mixture to the bowl, stirring until it's completely blended in. A wire whisk makes this process simple.

Ladle the mixture into six small dessert dishes—old-fashioned stemmed dessert cups made from clear glass are ideal—and chill for six to eight hours.

MRS. CLAUS AND THE LUCKLESS LEPRECHAUN

Liz Ireland

Chapter One

"What you need is a snowmobile," Jingles announced with a disdainful glance toward the reindeer being harnessed to my hybrid sleigh. The electric motor had proved unreliable, so I'd decided to go the old-fashioned route. My first reindeer, Cannonball, who very much resembled his name's shape, had trouble making it up Sugarplum Mountain without stopping for a few breathers. Since my home, Castle Kringle, was located halfway up the mountain, this lack of stamina presented a problem.

The reindeer before us now was Cannonball's alternate.

Jingles, the steward of Castle Kringle, considered himself an expert on, well, everything, and wasn't impressed. "You wouldn't catch me on a sleigh driven by an animal named Wobbler."

Actually, I'd been pleasantly surprised when my sister-in-law, Lucia, had brought Wobbler to my attention. Lucia was the Claus family's reindeer liaison and had a soft spot for outcast reindeer. Cannonball, for instance. He obviously hadn't worked out so far, although he'd launched himself onto an exercise program and had cut back his moss intake. But Wobbler, contrary to his name, seemed perfectly fit.

"You know how judgy and harsh reindeer can be," I said to Jingles, keeping my voice low so that Wobbler wouldn't overhear us. "Wobbler told me that they gave him his name when he was still just a calf and shaky on his legs."

They seemed sturdy enough now, if rather long. And knobby-kneed, now that I looked at them.

"Everyone deserves a chance," I concluded.

No one could deny that Wobbler was eager to make the most of this opportunity. As Salty the elf checked the tightness of the harness, the animal practically pranced in place in his impatience to get going.

Salty finished and stepped back with a little bow. "All ready, Mrs. Claus."

"Fired up and ready to go!" Wobbler stamped a hoof in his excitement.

More excitement than the task at hand warranted, to be honest. I was just driving in to Christmastown to pick up my friend Juniper and take her to the iceball match at the arena in Tinkertown, the next village over, where most of the worker elves from Santa's workshops lived.

Jingles shot me an arch glance and wrapped his long green-and-white striped scarf more tightly around his throat. He'd been very careful about keeping his throat in good condition since he'd decided to sing an Irish ballad this week for the talent show being held during the Saint Patrick's Day fair in Christmastown. Until recently, I hadn't known Jingles could sing. I still wasn't sure. The only hints he gave were some tuneless warblings he emitted when my husband, Nick, was nearby. Nick was going to judge the contest.

"Are you sure you don't want to come to the game?" I asked Jingles.

"I shouldn't risk it."

He was worried that he might get carried away by the excitement and cheer himself hoarse just days before the talent show.

"Watch out for that one," he said pointedly under his breath, nodding toward the restive reindeer.

"You worry too much." I climbed onto the sleigh, and held the reins loosely. I still felt a little self-conscious driving a sleigh pulled by a sentient animal. "Okay, let's go."

Wobbler tossed his head back, with surprise in the one large eye I could see from my vantage point. "What was *that*?" he asked.

I shook my head, confused. "What was what?"

"'Okay, let's go.'"

"A suggestion?" I said, nonplussed. A moment before, he'd been raring to go.

The reindeer puffed out a breath. "You're supposed to shout, 'On, Wobbler!' with spirit and gusto."

He was obviously confusing me with my husband. But even though Nick was Santa Claus, he didn't boom at reindeer like the Santa of fiction except at big moments, like Christmas Eve. And that was mainly for show.

"Really, we can just go," I said.

Wobbler didn't budge.

Still standing on the raised step of the castle's side portico, Jingles crossed his arms over his slight potbelly and sent me a look that screamed, *Told you so.*

"You're expected to do what Mrs. Claus says," Salty admonished the animal.

"I have expectations too." Wobbles lifted his head. "I'm not an automaton."

I cleared my throat, glad that only Jingles and Salty were around to witness this. "On, Wobbler."

He was not impressed. Or moved. "Spirit and gusto," he repeated.

Oh, for the love of Christmas. "On, Wobbler!"

A delighted Wobbler reacted as if I'd cracked a whip in the air. He reared slightly and then barrelled forward, jerking the sleigh so forcefully that I nearly tumbled backward over the seat's backrest.

Just like that, we were speeding toward the snow path down the mountain toward Christmastown. Evergreen trees lining the way passed in a blur. My grip tightened on the reins, but I hesitated to tug. I didn't want to be rude.

Besides, the speed was sort of a gas. Wobbler's long-legged fast trot was surprisingly smooth, and my little sleigh skimmed over the snowy ground with just a few jangles from the reindeer's harness breaking the silence around us.

As we wound down the mountain, every once in a while the vista would open up, and I could see all across Santaland. It was a gorgeous March day, the sky was clear, and the mercury stood at a balmy fifteen degrees Fahrenheit. Spring was coming to Santaland, and I was ready for it. Not that I didn't love all the winter activities in my adopted country—Christmas in Santaland was hard to top—but after months of freezing, my bones looked forward to even a modest North Pole warming trend.

For now I could simply appreciate the glimpses of the picturesque Bavarian-like village, Christmastown, in the valley below, sunlight glistening on the snowy rooftops. In the far distance, the high, craggy summit of Mount Myrrh looked almost cheery against the blue sky and not the treacherous peak it was, situated in the formidable frozen wilderness beyond the border of Santaland called the Farthest Frozen Reaches.

Wobbler took a curve a little too fast, raising us onto one skid. My stomach lurched, and I had to grab hold of the sleigh's guardrail. "Slow down," I said. "There's no rush."

"I'm supposed to get you down the mountain to your destination in an efficient, timely manner," he called back to me, as if he were reciting from a reindeer rule book. "Better three hours too soon than a moment too late—that's my motto!"

I was distracted by the sight of two of Nick's many Claus cousins, Clement and Carlotta, standing at the end of their driveway. This neighborhood, Kringle Heights, was dotted with chateaus where Nick's family, close and distant, all clustered. They saw me coming and waved, and I asked Wobbler to pull over for a friendly chat.

"Better not," Wobbler said, zooming past the duo.

"Hey, April!" they called as we streaked by.

"Can't stop!" Wobbler barked at them, never slowing his pace. "Appointment in town!"

I turned and raised my shoulders at their nonplussed expressions.

The trip was the fastest I'd ever traveled down the mountain without flying, which I—not a lover of heights—preferred to do only in emergencies. As we drove through the arched gate that heralded the city boundary into Christmastown, I remembered that I hadn't actually told Wobbler our destination.

"The address is 306 Turtledove Lane."

"I know where I'm going," he returned in a clipped voice. "I checked your schedule with Jingles before we set out."

No one could deny that he was a very scrupulous reindeer. Come to think of it, maybe Wobbler was just what I needed in my life. Contrary to the opinions of some, I wasn't scatterbrained, but occasionally I became so absorbed in an activity that other things slipped my mind. Having a reliable, conscientious form of transportation was probably a good thing.

We turned off Festival Boulevard, Christmastown's main thoroughfare, and wound through the smaller village streets to Turtledove Lane, where Juniper lived.

As he slowed to a halt, Wobbler announced, "306 Turtledove!" like a train conductor barking out a station stop. As if I didn't know where I was.

Juniper had been waiting on the stoop of her brick-and-timber building, which, at three stories, was the tallest on a block filled with modest one- and two-story cottages and rowhouses. She wore an overcoat, but a bright-red scarf was wound around her neck. Red and white were the colors of the Christmastown Twinklers, the iceball team we rooted for. I noticed she was even wearing red booties with little pom-poms at the curled toes.

She was lugging her euphonium case. It was almost as large as she was, and I jumped out to help her heave it into the back of the sleigh. I also introduced her to the new reindeer.

"What happened to Cannonball?" she asked after greeting Wobbler.

I hesitated. "He . . . needed some time off."

"He was too fat," Wobbler said, with typical reindeer frankness. "If you'll just get in the sleigh, we can be going."

Juniper's lips flattened into a laugh-suppressing smile as we climbed back in and took our place on the driver's bench seat. I picked up the reins and gave them a light shake.

Nothing happened.

"We can go now," I told Wobbler.

"Really?" he replied. "How would I know?"

Seriously? I sighed. "On, Wobbler!"

The reindeer took off like a shot.

Juniper glanced at me in alarm as she gripped the seat. "What's that about?"

"Spirit and gusto."

Despite his fussiness about getting started in the proper manner, Wobbler navigated the Christmastown streets deftly and with little input from me. Soon we were on the open snow path toward Tinkertown, which was about a twenty-minute drive away, across a narrow swath of the Christmas Tree Forest that ribboned through Santaland.

Juniper leaned back with a contented sigh. "This is nice. Much better than taking one of the sleigh buses. I don't have to worry about other elves being annoyed by my euphonium case."

Juniper and I both played in the Twinklers pep band. Everyone in the Santaland Concert Band, to which we belonged, played for either the Twinklers or the Tinkertown Ice Beavers, depending on where they lived and which team they supported. On nights when the game was in Tinkertown, the sleigh buses were packed with Christmastowners being ferried to their sister village, even though Santaland Transport added more sleighs to the route. A euphonium case took up almost as much space as an elf and was never a welcome sight to someone trying to squeeze onto the bus.

I played bass drum, but it was always driven over in the band's equipment sleigh by Luther Partridge, the band director, and Smudge, the lead percussionist. They both rooted for the Twinklers too.

"Best of all, we'll get home faster," I said. Waiting in the cold for the sleigh buses after the games was always a drag. Especially since our team usually lost.

Juniper turned to me, her eyes bright. "But we'll go to the Tinkertown Tavern for the celebration tonight if we win, right?"

I laughed. The winners of the iceball game always did repair to the closest tavern to celebrate with grog and hard cider, but there hadn't been a Twinklers wingding in a long time. "Sure, but like I said, we'll get home fast."

She clucked at me disapprovingly. "Oh, ye of little faith. Smudge is pessimistic about our chances too."

She and Smudge had been romantically involved before I met them. Now they had an odd friendship I'd given up trying to define. I was pretty sure Smudge wanted to rekindle something, but after a series of romantic disasters, Juniper was being cautious and friend-zoning him.

"According to the latest report on the sports page of the *Christmastown Herald*, Crumble Woolly's knee is still healing," she continued. "He might be back in the lineup soon."

The state of iceball player Crumble Woolly's knee had been an ongoing saga since he'd had a smash-up during the New Year's match. Doc Honeytree had operated, but last week it had been announced that Crumble wouldn't be playing for the next several games and had rashly turned in his uniform sweater. The Twinklers coach, Constable Crinkles, had recruited two wild elves to fill out the Twinklers bench, creating the biggest controversy to hit Santaland since the year the Candy Cane Factory had experimented with blue candy canes.

On the ice and off, there was no love lost between the wild elves of the Farthest Frozen Reaches and Santaland's more "civilized" elves. Wild elves were either the descendants of criminals who'd been exiled to the frozen north or strange elves who simply preferred living in the frozen waste.

Wild elves always trounced the Santaland teams when they brought their team down from the Farthest Frozen Reaches for a yearly exhibition game, but that was because they played by their own rules. Who was going to stop them? However, in a regulation game that counted toward the coveted Golden Skate Bootie trophy, usually called the Golden Bootie, for the year's most winning team, the wild elves would be kicked off the ice if they cheated.

"The Twinklers are going to win tonight," Juniper predicted.

"I'll keep my fingers crossed," I said.

"Everybody thinks it's the end of the world that Crumble's out. But the Twinklers weren't winning much when he was on the team either. Maybe new blood is just what we need."

In the middle of our conversation, Wobbler slowed and pulled to the side of the snow path. I didn't notice until we came to a stop. "What's going on?" I asked him.

"Lucia Claus is waving at us."

That I hadn't seen my sister-in-law showed how distracted I was. Her sleigh was unmistakable. Behind the seat, she'd installed a platform big enough to accommodate Quasar, her reindeer friend. Hers was the only personal sleigh in Santaland that held a reindeer passenger. His neck and head jutted over the back of her bench seat so that he appeared to be right next to her.

I counted it as a mark of reindeer respect for Lucia that Wobbler would stop for her. He didn't seem inclined to slow down for anyone or anything else.

Lucia pulled up alongside us. Next to her, Quasar's nose fizzled red in the gathering darkness. The nose marked him as a misfit from the Rudolph herd. "Hi, April," he greeted me.

"Hi," I said. "Aren't you all going the wrong way?"

Lucia shook her head. "I'm too bushed to go to the iceball game. I've been supervising the shoring up of the ice shelters all day."

Ice shelters stood all over Santaland so that snowmen would have cool places to rest in the summer months. In the spring, they were repaired and fortified. Though summer temperatures rarely rose enough to melt a snowman completely, they could experience severe shrinkage if they didn't have a place to shelter from the summer sun.

Knowing Lucia, she'd done more than supervise the work. To patch the shelters, elves cut ice from nearby ponds and formed bricks from them. From her exhausted look, my sister-in-law had been hauling ice bricks around herself. She was never too exhausted to look into reindeer welfare, however.

"How's it working out, Wobbler?" she asked him.

"Excellent so far!" he said.

I nodded. "He's very . . . enthusiastic."

"We're going to be late," he said impatiently.

Lucia laughed. "Well, don't let me keep you."

"I wish you could come with us," Juniper said. "The Twinklers are going to win tonight."

Lucia considered for a moment, then said, "Hope springs eternal, I guess." She made a hitching sound at her reindeer and was on her way.

I made the same noise, but we didn't move. Remembering, I commanded, "On, Wobbler!"

We shot forward and covered the last mile into Tinkertown in record time. Wobbler was like a streamline train once he got going.

"Claire's going to be selling ice cream tonight, right?" Juniper asked.

"Oh yes. She has big things planned."

"Good—I've been looking forward to getting one of those Twinkle-sicles."

Our friend Claire, the owner of a recently opened ice-cream parlor called the Santaland Scoop, had come up with the idea of selling team-themed popsicles at games, and her ice-cream cart had become a popular concession at the arena. This week she was planning on doing a big promotion for the Saint Patrick's Day fair too.

"She seems so happy." A contented if slightly envious sigh accompanied Juniper's words. "You see, you were worried for nothing."

Claire was a friend from my hometown in Oregon, and I had been both excited and anxious when she'd announced her intention to move to Santaland. Christmastown was generally a welcoming place, and its all-year festivity was a big draw, but the North Pole could also be a strange world to try to fit into. Marrying Nick had anchored me here and given me instant standing in the community, yet even I had experienced a bumpy road to Santaland assimilation. I was ecstatic about having my friend nearby again, but once the novelty of the place wore off, I feared Claire would decide she'd acted in haste.

So far, though, no regrets had set in. Her business was off to a strong start, and the ice-cream craving–inducing summer months were still ahead. Plus, detective Jake Frost—the real reason behind Claire's move to Santaland—had recently opened up a local office in

Christmastown so he and Claire could spend more time together. Lately their free time was mostly spent fixing up either his office or her ice-cream parlor, but neither of them seemed to mind what they were doing as long as they were with each other.

"Maybe Smudge will come with us to the tavern tonight," Juniper said, making me wonder if the friend zone was wearing thin.

We had to cross through the town to the far outskirts to reach the Tinkertown Arena. Tinkertown is Christmastown's more industrial sister village. Santa's workshops are located there, as well as the Wrapping Works and the Candy Cane Factory. Those plants alone employ thousands of elves, who live in charming cottage communities surrounding the various warehouses and factories.

The home of the Ice Beavers is the pride of the town. The arena is a massive circular structure with a thatched roof. Tonight it was already surrounded by sleighs and snowmobiles.

I instructed Wobbler to drop us off close to the door and then park himself wherever he felt most comfortable. Some reindeer liked to socialize while the games were going on.

"I'll need to stay at attention," he said.

I shook my head. "The game will last at least two hours. You could probably even doze off if you want."

His big brown eyes widened. "Nap on the job? No, ma'am! Not this reindeer."

"Suit yourself." I reached into the sleigh to grab Juniper's case.

As we approached the entrance, Juniper swapped

her wool elf cap for the Twinklers pep band's red-and-white beanie, which had multicolored flashing lights threaded through it. At the top, instead of a pom-pom, there was an old-fashioned plastic Christmas bulb. These were lit whenever the Twinklers scored.

She glanced at my head with concern. "You didn't forget your Twinklers beanie, did you?"

"No, I've got it in my bag." I wasn't lacking in Twinklers spirit, but I always put off changing because the arena was kept chilly. Beanies weren't as warm as wool hats.

"I brought extra batteries in case someone's beanie runs out of juice." Juniper patted her purse. "Just let me know." Her beanie was already twinkling, and there was a bounce in her step. She loved iceball.

We passed through the entrance to the outer corridor where the elves could check their cross-country skis and snowshoes, if that's how they'd traveled there. In the center of the hall stood the glass trophy case where the Golden Skate Bootie was kept. Atop the trophy was a gold elf skate, with long blades and a curl at the bootie's toe. The golden figure rested on a vertical rectangular metal column decorated with golden snowflakes at the corners. The rectangle was divided in two columns: one for the Ice Beavers, one for the Twinklers. The area under the Ice Beavers' name was crowded with engraved years to denote when Tinkertown had taken home the trophy. The area set aside for the Twinklers still had plenty of room.

Juniper and I went over to the spot in the outer corridor where Claire had set up her milkshake and ice-cream concession, just by the doors to the stands. She stood next to her refrigerated cart from which she sold Twinkle-sicles, Beaver Pops, and milkshakes to fans. The side of the cart bore the logo of the Santaland Scoop, her Christmastown store: a cheeky ice-cream cone leaning against the capital *S* of *Santaland*. Claire wore her usual uniform, red pants and shirt with a red-and-white apron that also bore the Scoop's logo over the breast pocket.

To drum up excitement for the upcoming Saint Patrick's Day fair, Claire's assistant, Butterbean, was dressed as a leprechaun. His round, compact body was in green from head to toe, with a kelly green velvet cutaway coat and knee breeches tucked into mint-green stockings. His feet were shod in dyed leather green booties with only a modest curl at the toe but with large buckles that matched the one decorating his green Mad Hatter–style hat.

There was another leprechaun too—but this one's appearance was more startling. His suit was identical to Butterbean's, but it looked to be a size too small for him. Butterbean was attempting some last-minute costume adjustments with safety pins.

"It's hard to breathe," the big bruiser of a leprechaun rasped. He had a craggy face and a flat nose that looked as if it had been broken more than once.

Juniper's eyes rounded in recognition as she stared into the elf's grizzled face. "Golly doodle! You're Crumble Woolly!"

The gruff-looking leprechaun broke into a smile in the glow of her admiring gaze. "I am."

At the name *Crumble Woolly*, my confusion cleared. I'd seen him dozens of times, but never so close up.

And he'd always been in his Twinklers uniform, never dressed as a leprechaun.

Butterbean jabbed his fellow leprechaun with his elbow. "Crumble, surely you recognize Mrs. Claus."

Crumble looked at me anxiously. "Oh, oh. I'm sorry, Mrs. Claus," he said in his gravelly voice. I couldn't tell if that was normal or the result of his sucking in his breath. "I'd bow, but I'm afraid my pants would split."

"We don't want that," I said. Truly, we didn't. "I'm pleased to meet you."

"What an honor!" Juniper said. "You're a legend."

Crumble's face turned mottled red. "I'm still in the game—or I will be, once this bum knee of mine mends. For now . . ."

He crooked his head toward the butcher paper poster someone had taped on the wall behind the ice-cream cart. It advertised the Saint Patrick's Day fair taking place in Christmastown a couple of days from now. GAMES! TREATS! TALENT SHOW! BALLOON RIDE! the poster promised. It was decorated with shamrocks that looked as if they were falling from the sky like March snow flurries.

"I hope you'll be back to playing soon, Crumble," Juniper said. "We were all sorry when you got hurt. My brother cried."

"Aw, that's sweet," the craggy leprechaun said. "How old's your little brother?"

"Thirty-two. He said, 'There goes Christmastown's best chance in a decade to take home the Golden Bootie.'"

As they spoke, my eyes lingered on that poster. I edged closer to Claire, who was handing a red Twinklesicle to a young elf. "I thought *you* were going to dress as a leprechaun for Saint Patrick's Day."

"I was, till Butterbean got the brainstorm of having a celebrity spokes-elf," Claire said. "It's brilliant, really. Who better than Crumble to build excitement for our Saint Paddy's Day milkshake concession and balloon ride? Besides, I realized that I couldn't really help out with the balloon ride *and* sell milkshakes."

"It's going to be a three-man operation," Butterbean said.

I'd been hearing about this balloon ride with a certain amount of trepidation. A milkshake concession would be a winner all by itself—but a hot-air balloon decorated like an ice-cream cone seemed like a Butterbean scheme that could go very wrong.

"Are you sure that this balloon will be safe?" I asked Butterbean.

"I'm not making it from scratch," he assured me. "I sent off for a kit."

Butterbean had sent off for a turkey once too. The mail-order company delivered a vulture instead.

Worry must have shown on my face. "It'll be safer than a ski lift," he assured me. "The balloon's going to be tethered. It'll only go up fifty feet and come right back down again." He hopped as if to demonstrate. "Nothing to it."

"Ouch!" Crumble twisted. "I thought something hit me, but I must've popped a button." He nodded toward the other side of the corridor.

I narrowed my eyes in that direction. There *was* something shiny on the ground. As I went over to investigate, Butterbean checked the buttons on Crumble's coat. "No, you're fine," he told his fellow leprechaun. "Just keep your stomach sucked in. And don't drink too many milkshakes tonight."

I located the object I'd seen on the corridor floor and bent down to pick it up. I frowned. It was a metal bottle cap. The letters *SS* were stamped on the top of the cap.

SS? I frowned up at the Santaland Scoop sign. But that wasn't Claire's logo, and nothing she sold had a bottle cap associated with it.

As Butterbean and Juniper used pins to adjust Crumble's pants to allow him to suck in some air, I caught sight of a face peering through a plate glass panel next to the arena entrance. A glaring face. It looked like an elf but with such a dark expression that a shard of fear pierced me.

When I caught his eye, the face disappeared.

I raced outside and stood outside the large double-doored entrance. A sleigh bus was letting out passengers, so the walkway was crowded with elves. None of them looked particularly sinister. Had I just imagined that face?

"Mrs. Claus! Mrs. Claus!"

The shouting came from Wobbler, who was practically hopping on his front legs to get my attention. Had he seen something?

I hurried over to him. He was standing behind a sleigh bus.

"What's the matter?" I asked.

"Nothing. I saw you at the entrance and thought you were looking for me. Are you ready to go?"

"No—we just got here. The game hasn't started yet."

"Oh." He nodded. "Well, when you're ready, I'll be here."

I looked back down the street. "Did you see a suspicious-looking elf peering into the arena a minute ago?"

"I don't have time to spy on elves, I'm concentrating on work. Unless . . ." His big eyes grew wider. "Is spying on elves part of what I'm supposed to do? Clandestine activity was not in my job description."

Getting Wobbler paranoid about malevolent elves probably wasn't the best thing. "Never mind—you're doing a great job." The compliment made his withers twitch with pride. I'd have to get him a lichen treat from the reindeer brownie concession inside.

There was no trash can nearby, so on the way back in I tucked the bottle cap into my pocket. The tiny object wouldn't strike me as significant until later, after the night took a deadly turn.

Chapter Two

I bought the lichen brownie and took it out to Wobbler, then went back inside. Claire was busy—her leprechauns were drawing crowds—so I decided to wait till halftime to buy a milkshake. I really wanted one of the Beaver Pops, which were fudgsicles, but that might have seemed disloyal.

I headed into the arena and located the Twinklers pep band in the stands. Luther had set up the snare and bass drums, but I didn't see Smudge anywhere. I hoped he wasn't going to miss the game. I didn't want him to be sick, and I also found playing snare drum more difficult than beating time on a bass drum.

Juniper was in her place at the back with the brass, next to the tuba. "Have you seen Smudge?" I asked her.

"Unfortunately, yes."

Her eyes shot daggers toward the stands on the opposite side of the rink. There, among our rival pep band, whose members all had plush, buck-toothed rodent caps on their heads, stood Smudge, behind *their* bass drum. I had to blink to believe it. He was even wearing an Ice Beavers hat.

"He's turned traitor." Even if her batteries had run out, Juniper could have powered her Twinklers beanie with rage. "He's tired of rooting for the losing team."

"Seriously?" So much for the friend zone. Smudge had placed himself squarely in enemy territory.

"I went over and confronted him." She snorted in disgust. "He spun some yarn about being upset that the Twinklers are bringing wild elves onto their team."

"But Ham and Scar live in Christmastown now."

She shot me a look. We both knew that the residency ploy was questionable. In truth, the wild elves were living in the so-called jail cell in Christmastown, which was really just a spare bedroom in the Christmastown Constabulary cottage. Since Constable Crinkles himself was the Twinklers coach, the ethics were a little dodgy, but Smudge's disloyalty to his home team seemed even worse. When I peered disapprovingly at him and caught his eye, he looked away sheepishly.

He was even willing to be demoted to a second percussion part in the Ice Beavers pep band, I couldn't help noticing. He took great pride in being the best drummer in Santaland.

"Well, it's only a game," I forced myself to say, hoping to calm Juniper down.

It didn't work. "I hope our wild elves trounce those Beavers," she declared.

That sweet, positive Juniper could be hell-bent on walloping the other team was the first hint I received of how high emotions would run during this game.

Luther hurried over to me, a fretful look in his eyes.

"Good—you're here. As you can see, we need you on snare drum and bells tonight."

The idea panicked me a little. "I've never played Smudge's parts."

The band director shook his head. "You'll just have to lace up your booties and lean into the ice paddle."

I wasn't familiar with that particular sports metaphor, but I got the idea. I needed to stop whining and rise to the percussion challenge.

The stands had filled up, and restive elves began to chant and clap.

"What's going on?" I wondered aloud.

Soupy, our tuba player, pivoted in his sousaphone to talk to me. "I heard that our usual referee was refusing to officiate at the game tonight because he thinks there will be trouble." He peered around his horn. "I don't see him down there."

When the teams finally took to the ice to warm up and the wild elves Ham and Scar appeared for the first time, a few jeers went up from the Ice Beavers side.

Someone in the stands across the arena tossed a lichen brownie onto the ice.

"I hope this doesn't get out of hand," I said as we watched the arena's old janitor, Nip, walk carefully out to sweep up the brownie debris.

While the players whizzed across the ice, the lights strobed around the arena, making it hard for the eye to settle on any one player. But then a spotlight opened up, and to my surprise Nick stepped into it. My husband was wearing a workaday Santa suit—red wool with white shearling trim, and he had black skates on his feet. Over the arena's speaker system, a voice announced, "We are honored tonight, folks. Officiating this game will be Santa Claus himself."

The arena erupted in cheers—everyone knew he would be fair—and Nick waved acknowledgment to the stands. At six feet tall, he towered over the elves on both iceball teams. He would have a good vantage for seeing the plays.

Our pep band had launched into a jaunty version of "Here Comes Santa Claus" when he appeared. The Ice Beavers band joined in during the second chorus.

It was perhaps the most sportsmanlike moment of the evening. Of course, a game involving elves skating at breakneck speed while trying to toss a hard chunk of ice into a small net using something that looked like a cross between a lacrosse stick and a snow shovel was bound to get crazy sometimes. But elves usually tried to remember their manners on the ice. This wasn't ice hockey.

Tonight was different, though.

During the game, things got wild fast. Players flung themselves and their opponents against the Plexiglas barrier protecting the spectators from a stray iceball. Sometimes elves just ended up piling into each other in a mountain of sticks, helmets, and legs. Periodically Nick had to stop to untangle a clump of elves as our pep bands played dueling Christmas carols across the ice at each other. These incidents occurred occasionally during any iceball game, but everything happening during this game seemed to be carried out with atypical ferocity.

I wish I could say that the tossed brownie was the only incident of hostility directed toward the new players, who played well and were outscoring everyone. Unfortunately, during the first half, several elves across the arena unfurled a banner with WILD ELVES GO HOME! to boos . . . although far more boos came from the Christmastown side than the Ice Beavers bleachers.

At that point Nick had to blow his whistle, stop the game, and plead with the elves to take their banner down.

"This is *friendly* competition," he reminded them. "There's no reason to make any of the players feel unwanted. Elves are elves."

"Except *wild elves*!" someone shouted.

Murmurs broke out—some sounding in agreement. Down on the sidelines, Constable Crinkles—his round body stuffed into his track suit instead of his usual constable uniform—scanned the crowd anxiously. Maybe it was a good thing that Ham and Scar were staying at the constabulary, I thought. Win or lose, they might need protection.

At halftime the Twinklers were comfortably ahead. Ham was the difference. The compact elf was a wonder on the ice, able to thread through defensive picks and flick the ball into the little basket goal as easy as you please. It was breathtaking to watch. I wasn't much of a sports fan, but even I could see that he had rare power, the Michael Jordan of iceball.

Nick impressed me too. I couldn't believe how agile he was. Of course I knew that he could skate. He'd given me a few lessons on the ice at Peppermint Pond over the years. He'd also told me that he'd grown up playing pickup games of iceball with his friends—

apparently it was impossible to reach adulthood in Santaland without having some iceball experience. But I'd never seen him actually race around a rink like this. Even when the game seemed close, it was hard for me to take my eyes off him. He skimmed across the ice backward and forward, made quick turns, and occasionally vaulted over fallen elves to avoid crashing himself.

To think you could be married to someone for three years and still not know basic information about them. I was almost as astonished as I had been when I'd discovered the identity of the enigmatic bearded man I'd fallen in love with while he was on vacation at my inn in Cloudberry Bay, Oregon. Granted, for shock value it's hard to top realizing you've developed a burning passion for Santa Claus.

During the last minutes of the game, the Ice Beavers launched a desperate offensive. It was an ugly stretch of tackling, tripping, and crashing to the ice in multiple elf pileups. The Ice Beavers fans grew more upset as we Twinklers—sensing our first victory all year—were practically hopping in jubilation. Beanie lights were flashing nonstop.

When the buzzer sounded, the evening's scorekeeper—Deputy Ollie, Crinkle's nephew—held up cards showing that the Twinklers had won with twenty-one goals to the Ice Beavers' sixteen. Our side of the arena erupted in joyful celebration.

On the ice, the players had dropped their competitive aggression and were politely shaking hands, but several fans on the other side chucked their Ice Beavers hats at Ham. Though there was no chance of the wild elf getting hurt by a plush toy, the gesture was shocking.

Perhaps the most ecstatic person in the arena was Juniper, who wasn't above aiming taunting smiles at Smudge. When he crossed over to help Luther load the drums into the equipment sleigh, she lorded the victory over him mercilessly.

"You picked the wrong moment to become a turncoat."

He scowled. "I still say it's wrong to bring in the wild elves just because you have a sick player."

She made a tutting sound. "Are you going to throw your beaver hat too?"

"Just wait till the next game," he grumbled.

Juniper laughed. "I'm looking forward to it, because we're going to win. How many times do you have to lose before you decide to support the Twinklers again?"

After Smudge skulked away, I shook my head. "Gloating much?"

"He deserved it." Her eyes were bright. "We're going to the Tinkertown Tavern now, aren't we?"

"Of course—I just want to see if Claire needs any help loading up."

But Claire, Crumble, and Butterbean had already been packing everything up during the second half. I was a little disappointed—I never had managed to get my hands on a milkshake. I supposed I could make do with a grog.

Nick found me talking to Claire. I enveloped him in

a hug. "You were fantastic," I said. "I never knew you could do that."

He smiled. "Referee?"

"Yes—and skate like a pro. And here I'd thought Tiffany was the lone champion skater in the family."

Tiffany, the mother of Christopher, Nick's nephew who was going to be the next Santa Claus when he reached maturity, had once been a competitive ice skater at the junior amateur level. Now she gave lessons and sometimes still performed herself on special occasions.

"I'm not quite at Tiffany's level," Nick said. "I've never done any kind of jump, and I don't intend to."

"You were leaping over elf piles like a gazelle," I said.

He shook his head. "I'm just glad we got through the game without any major incident."

A Twinklers player named Wick stopped by to thank Nick for refereeing the game. Wick was the captain of the Twinklers and the oldest player on the team. "If you hadn't stepped in, I don't know what we would have done," he said. "I'm only sorry there was so much naughtiness on the ice."

Nick shrugged. "Next time will be better."

Juniper blinked up at Wick. Whenever she ran into a Twinkler, she couldn't help fangirling a little. "Congratulations on the win! You were all wonderful."

He beamed a smile at her. "Thank you all for being here. The Twinklers have the best fans—and the most patient."

We all laughed.

I informed Nick that Juniper and I were headed to the Tinkertown Tavern. "You'll come too, won't you?"

He frowned. "I shouldn't. As a referee—as Santa—I shouldn't put myself in a situation where I might appear partisan."

That was Nick all over. He hated taking sides in contests. In fact, Mrs. Firlog, the organizer of the Saint Patrick's Day fair, had spent weeks twisting his arm before he'd agreed to judge the talent show. He almost immediately regretted it, because ever since word got out, he was the object of not-so-impromptu previews of acts that were going to take part.

He might not be the flashiest Santa ever, but when it came to being considerate of others, he set the bar high. The older I got, the sexier kindness seemed. I was tempted to just go home myself, but I'd brought Juniper, and she had her heart set on being part of the celebration.

I told Nick I'd see him later, back at the castle.

"Be careful," he said. "A Twinklers celebration at the Tinkertown Tavern could get rowdy."

"I think I can handle a few rowdy elves."

Claire said she was too tired to go out with us. I suspected she wanted to get back to Christmastown and to Jake Frost, who hadn't been able to attend the game because of a case he was on. Butterbean would help her get back to Christmastown and unload their supplies.

Crumble, still in leprechaun garb, was sipping at an extra-large milkshake and staring longingly—and almost bleary-eyed—out at the ice.

"Would you like to come join the celebration at the

Tinkertown Tavern?" I asked him. "It'll be a big Twinklers party."

He took off his leprechaun hat, revealing a pink scalp covered with bristly short hair and ears that were huge even for an elf. "No thank you, Mrs. Claus." He looked down at his leprechaun suit. "I was here in another uniform tonight."

The wrong uniform, his tone implied. I hadn't considered how difficult it must have been to watch his team win without him.

"I'm sure you'd be welcome," Juniper said.

"My brother, Frankie, lives in Tinkertown. I think I'll drop in on him."

Claire put her hand on his green velvet–clad arm. "I appreciate your being here tonight, Crumble. Thanks to you, the Scoop took in more than I expected. A lot of elves asked about our Saint Patrick's Day event too."

Butterbean bounced in anticipation. "It's going to be colossal!"

Wobbler was waiting for us right in front of the door, so Juniper and I joined the joyful procession the few blocks to the Tinkertown Tavern. A big crowd was there—lots of Twinklers players, the pep band, fans, and of course, Constable Crinkles.

Wick, the team captain, asked everyone to raise a tankard of grog to Coach Crinkles, who was both beaming and squirming. Victory was so foreign to him, he didn't seem to know what to do with himself.

A few Ice Beavers were sprinkled among those gathered in the tavern, gritting their teeth but being good losers. Once, when we were joined for a drink by Wick,

Juniper narrowed her gaze at someone across the bar. For a moment I thought maybe Smudge had put in an appearance, but when I looked over, I saw an Ice Beavers player getting up from a table to leave with a pretty brunette elf.

"Everybody's flipping sides tonight," Juniper said.

I didn't understand. "Who is she?"

"Crumble's girlfriend, Poinsettia." Her voice dripped with disdain. "Canoodling with the enemy. I hadn't even heard that she and Crumble broke up."

Poor Crumble. "I wonder if it was the leprechaun suit," I said.

Wick shook his head. "I'm not surprised, really. Poinsettia's an iceball groupie. Her type just wants to be with a winner."

"Then the joke's on her," Juniper said. "The Twinklers won tonight, and Crumble will be back and winning again soon too."

Wick frowned. "This season?"

"Coach Crinkles said that the wild elves are just substitutes," Juniper said.

The team captain tapped his fingers on the bar. "Doesn't seem fair to just use them and then toss them off the team."

"It wouldn't be fair to Crumble just to set him aside either." Juniper didn't understand disloyalty. "You said you're retiring after this season. How would you feel about being benched just before the finish line?"

He frowned.

The conundrum made me think of Wobbler. If Cannonball's fitness regimen yielded good results, would I be able to put Wobbler out to pasture? Even that distant, hypothetical decision made me uncomfortable.

Wick left us, but the party continued. More toasts were raised, and the Twinklers pep song was sung as everyone clacked tankards of grog and made merry. I couldn't help noticing that the wild elves, Ham and Scar—the heroes of the game—were absent. Most of the Twinklers players, especially the old ones, were so unused to celebrating that a lot of them left early to go get some sleep, but the rank-and-file fans were energized.

It was a wonderful time until the tavern's door banged open. At first I was worried some angry Ice Beavers had arrived to rumble. Then Nip, the old janitor from the arena, staggered into the room. Though he was panting as though he'd just run a marathon, his pallor was the color of gray sleet.

"Come quick," he said between panting breaths. "It's Crumble. He's dead!"

Chapter Three

"I thought everybody had gone home," Nip explained as we entered the arena.

I'd tagged along after Constable Crinkles and Deputy Ollie, not out of ghoulish curiosity but because Crumble's death sat uneasily at the back of my mind. I kept remembering the look on his face as he'd been staring at the rink the last time I saw him.

Juniper had been very helpful in trying to calm down poor Nip, but the old elf was still shaken.

"I can't believe he'd just drop dead like that. He was the best player the Twinklers had for several years," the janitor said, his voice hoarse with emotion. "Not that it did them much good."

Everyone nodded. For years, Crumble had embodied an entire town's hopes for victory; now he was an inert form in green velvet at the side of the rink. Only the overhead rink lights were on, like an extra-large spotlight on the scene of the tragedy. His body lay close to where I'd seen him earlier, when he'd been looking longingly at the ice and sipping his milkshake.

I scanned the area until I spotted a large red-and-white striped cup sitting on a bench, as if Crumble had set it down just before he took to the ice. The cup bore the Santaland Scoop logo. Had he been nursing the same milkshake all night?

Nip, still pale with shock, explained how he'd found Crumble.

"I'd already done my cleaning-up pass of the stadium, and I wheeled the trash bin out back. Then I went into my little room where I keep a little hot plate for making cocoa and fixed myself some. And then . . ." He ducked his head, embarrassed. "I might've dozed off a little."

"If you finished cleaning up for the night, why didn't you just go home?" I asked.

The janitor's expression turned mournful. "Home's not the same now without Winky."

I could have kicked myself. I'd forgotten that Nip's longtime companion had died over the winter—Nick and I had even delivered a condolence fruitcake in person. The two elves had lived together for decades. Small wonder he preferred to linger around the arena. Going home to an empty cottage was probably still achingly difficult.

"Something woke me up, and I put on my coat and got ready to leave. I was just turning off the last lights when I noticed Crumble lying in the middle of the rink. I hurried over and pulled him off the ice and left him just where he is now. First I called Doc Honeytree, and then I remembered that the constable was probably at the Twinklers victory do at the Tinkertown Tavern."

"You should have phoned the Tavern and saved yourself the strain of running over," Juniper asked.

Nip removed his striped elf cap with its ragged pom-pom ball at the tip and twisted it nervously in his hands. "Sure, I could have. Only I didn't feel like standing around with a dead body for the entire time it was going to take Doc to drive over from Christmas-town."

I did some quick calculating. If Nip had called the doctor over a half hour ago, he was bound to arrive soon.

Crinkles, who was still in his red coaching track suit, looked distressed. "I sure am sorry about all of this. Crumble was a good elf and a whale of an iceball player. Sad that his life ended when he wasn't able to take part in our Twinklers victory."

That was strange, wasn't it? I looked down at Crumble's feet, which were no longer in his leprechaun shoes. He was wearing ice skates.

"Why was he on the ice?" I asked.

The others stared at me.

"Crumble practically lived on the ice," Crinkles said.

"But he was recovering from knee surgery. Should he have been skating on it?"

The constable scratched his head. "I hadn't thought about that, but you're right. Doc ordered him to stay off the ice until that knee heeled."

"Maybe that's why he collapsed," Juniper said. "He'd gotten out of shape."

Would a few pounds cause a complete collapse?

I turned to Nip. "When you found him, was there anything odd about his appearance?"

He shrugged. "Just that he was still wearing that funny outfit. Looked to me like he must have fallen hard too. There was a nasty bump on the back of his head."

I kneeled to check for myself. Crumble's hair was shaved down to a bristle, so the bump wasn't hard to spot. His impact with the ice had left a raised bruise just above his nape. A trickle of blood oozed out of it.

That struck me as wrong too, though I couldn't pinpoint why. I sat back on my heels. Poor Crumble. There wasn't much dignity in dying in a too-tight leprechaun costume.

I glanced at the cup again. If Nip had already done a cleaning pass around the arena, that cup wouldn't have been there. It had to be Crumble's. He must have returned to the arena with his milkshake and put it down while he went out to skate.

Could the milkshake have had something to do with his collapse?

I looked out across the arena.

"You said you found Crumble on the ice?" I asked.

Nip nodded and pointed about ten feet out. "Right out there, where that iceball paddle is. It was right next to him. I guess he must've dropped it when he fell—that's probably what woke me up."

Sounded reasonable. I couldn't see anything else on the side, apart from two iceballs. There was no telling if they were left over from the game, or if Crumble had gotten them out to knock around the rink.

Putting my hand on his velvety shoulder, I leaned in closer to check to see if there was any discoloration around his mouth. I'd heard poison could turn a victim's lips or tongue blue. The way he lay there, I could only see his lips and they appeared normal—right up to the moment they moved and he emitted a groan.

I was so shocked, I fell backward.

The three behind me yelped in surprise.

In a trembling voice, Crinkles asked, "Is he alive?"

Could a dead elf groan?

Quickly, I unzipped my puffy coat to use as a pillow beneath Crumble's head. "Are there any blankets around?" I asked Nip.

"There are some towels in the locker room."

"Get whatever you can find—and some of that hot cocoa you made might be good too."

Hot cocoa was like mother's milk to elves. It might be a good restorative for Crumble.

Nip hurried off faster than I thought the old elf could move, and Juniper followed to help.

Crumble's being alive energized us all. At least we wouldn't have to piece together what had happened to him. He'd be able to tell us what he'd been doing skating around the empty arena.

Before Nip and Juniper returned with the towels, Doc Honeytree arrived. The wizened old medic in black peered down at Crumble through his thick round spectacles.

"Seems he's still alive," Crinkles said.

As Doc knelt beside Crumble, his cracking joints echoed in the empty arena.

"Of course he's alive," the doctor said impatiently. "Didn't anyone notice that he was breathing?"

"I think Nip panicked when he found him—he probably remembered finding Winky—and the rest of us just took his word for it that Crumble was deceased," I explained.

"Never assume." Doc's frown deepened. "Though I'm surprised that he could breathe at all in this ridiculous getup he's wearing. What is this?"

"It's a leprechaun suit," I said. "It was a promotional thing."

"Looks like a green sausage casing."

Together, we loosened several of the buttons on his front to allow Crumble to breathe and the doctor to put his stethoscope to the elf's chest.

"Ticker's okay," Doc declared. He then pulled a tiny flashlight out of his black bag and shone it in Crumble's eye. "Hm . . ."

It was an ominous sound.

"We need to get him to the Christmastown Infirmary," he said.

The Christmastown Infirmary was Santaland's hospital. It wasn't very big or modern, but it didn't need to be. Elves were hardy beings, and most preferred to recuperate surrounded by the cozy comforts of their cottage homes.

"Do you think he could have been poisoned?" I asked.

Doc looked at me sharply. "Who said anything about poison?"

"I just thought . . ." I nodded to the milkshake container. "He was drinking the milkshake, and then he collapsed on the ice."

Juniper, who'd just come back with Nip in tow, overheard me. She looked so shocked that I worried she'd drop her towels. "That's one of Claire's milkshakes."

Crinkles's eyes grew wide as he glanced at the cup. "Jumping jellybeans! The Santaland Scoop's milkshake killed him?"

Oh God. I should have kept my big mouth shut until I was alone with Doc. "No—I was just floating a possibility."

Crinkles looked at the cup fearfully.

"*Nothing* killed Crumble," Doc reminded us. "He's not dead. He's probably sustained a serious concussion, though."

"But what if he got the concussion from falling on the ice because he drank that poison milkshake?" Crinkles asked.

Doc Honeytree had wearied of the subject. "Never mind the milkshake. We need to get Crumble to the infirmary where he can rest. I warned the fool elf that he should stay out of the rink. I don't know what came over him."

I did. That longing look at the ice after the Twinklers won big had spoken volumes about his regrets over not being able to take part in the game. I wasn't a sports player, but I'd empathized viscerally with his feeling of having been out of uniform during his team's big moment. He was probably also wondering if the reason they won was because he *hadn't* played. Ham and Scar were the high scorers of the evening, and they wouldn't have even been there except for Crumble's being out of the game.

"I have a stretcher outside," Doc continued. "I'll need help carrying Crumble out to the sleigh."

Crinkles and Nip went out to get the stretcher. Doc Honeytree had also brought blankets, so he returned my coat to me. I put it on gratefully; the empty arena was frigid. "We should pick up Crumble's equipment too." He nodded to the paddle and balls on the ice, which Juniper and I scooted out to retrieve for him.

The two came back with the stretcher, and with effort we lifted Crumble onto it. As they were hauling him away, the rest of us followed. Doc Honeytree lingered behind the rest of us, though, and I turned to see him snatching the Santaland Scoop cup off the bench.

"I should probably check this out," he told me in a low voice that I hoped Crinkles's big ears wouldn't catch. The constabulary was often the source of rumor and wild speculation. Deputy Ollie was an even worse gossip than Crinkles.

Where was Ollie? I hadn't seen him since the game. He must have gone back to Christmastown already.

I looked ahead to make sure that Crinkles wasn't listening. "Do you really suspect that Crumble was poisoned?"

"Did I say anything about suspicions?" Doc could get spiky when crossed. "I'm just trying to be thorough." Perhaps to distract me from dwelling on the milkshake question, he said, "Crumble's family should be notified that he's in the hospital."

"He said he has a brother in town." In fact, he was

supposed to be visiting with him. What had Crumble been doing still at the arena?

Juniper jumped into the conversation. "Frankie Woolly—he runs Woolly's Furniture. He lives above his shop here in town."

Doc put his hand on my arm. "Maybe you could let him know that his brother's had an accident. It always helps patients to have visitors in the infirmary. Does Crumble have a wife?"

Juniper and I exchanged a look, remembering the faithless Poinsettia at the tavern. "Not really. But we'll go by Frankie Woolly's tonight."

Juniper lowered her voice. "We should also offer Nip a ride home and make sure he's okay staying alone."

I hadn't thought of that. I was glad I had Juniper with me tonight. She had a big heart, a cool head in a crisis, and as one of Christmastown's librarians, seemed to know everyone in Santaland.

We'd reached the arena's outer corridor where Claire's ice-cream cart had stood. For a moment I remembered the strange elf who'd tossed a bottle cap at Crumble and then run away. Coincidence?

Nip and Crinkles stopped by the large double doors leading to the sleigh parking area and turned toward us. "Should we load him into your sleigh or mine, Doc?"

"The constabulary's snowmobile would be faster," Doc said. "I appreciate your helping me, Constable. I've asked Mrs. Claus to inform his family of what had happened, so you don't need to worry about notifying anyone."

Crinkles was nodding in agreement, but then he froze. His gaze fixed on something behind Juniper, Doc, and me. His eyes widened in shock. "Holy doodle!"

We all turned to look. It didn't take long to see what had captured his attention.

The glass door of the trophy case was hanging wide open. The light inside shone bright in the corridor, but it illuminated nothing but an empty shelf.

The Golden Bootie was gone.

Chapter Four

"I must be slipping," Nip lamented as we drove him home. "I never once heard anyone breaking into the trophy cabinet."

Technically, the cabinet wasn't really broken into because it had never been locked. "All the thief had to do was open the door," I pointed out.

Juniper frowned at me. "It was still taken illegally—that's breaking in, isn't it?"

Nip looked sad. "What's this world coming to? Who would steal the Golden Bootie?"

To Santalanders, such a theft seemed unthinkable. Elves were always shocked by crime, but I wasn't an elf. I was used to assuming everything not locked up or nailed down was just asking for it to be stolen.

"Maybe it was just juvenile delinquents," I suggested.

They blinked at me in incomprehension.

"Juvenile what?" Juniper asked.

"Young elves who—" I could tell by the befuddled expressions that the idea of teenaged elves gone bad was just as foreign as the idea of a stolen trophy. Why disillusion them?

"Then again, maybe it's all just a misunderstanding," I finished.

"Golly gumdrops, I hope so," Juniper said.

Nip shook his head. "Crumble falling on the ice and nearly dying wasn't a misunderstanding. And I didn't even hear him up there, skating around."

"But you said something *did* wake you up," I reminded him. "You said you must have heard him drop his paddle. Is that the sound you remember?"

He frowned in concentration. "I'm not sure. I just remember popping awake and feeling as if something wasn't right."

"Could you have heard a door slamming?" I couldn't help suspecting that the trophy's disappearance and Crumble's accident were related. Had Crumble caught the trophy thief red-handed and tried to stop him?

But that didn't make sense, given that Crumble was found on the ice and the trophy cabinet was in the arena's outer corridor.

Nip frowned in concentration for a moment longer but tossed up his mittened hands in frustration. "I can't be sure. Maybe all I heard was Crumble falling on the ice. I feel useless."

"But you did all the right things," I said. "You called Doc and ran for help." It was amazing *he* hadn't collapsed during his dash to the Tinkertown Tavern.

"Don't doubt yourself over this, Nip," Juniper told

him. "You do a great job taking care of the arena. If something happened to you, they'd have to hire three elves to replace you."

He shrugged modestly at the compliment. "That's just because I've been at it for so long. I've got arena janitorial service down to a science."

"Nip's residence!" Wobbler announced as we stopped in front of a modest cottage.

The old elf eyed his stoop as if he were holding back a regretful sigh.

"Would you like us to come in with you for a bit?" I asked.

"No, no. You all need to get over to the furniture store and tell Frankie what's happened. He'll be shocked." He climbed down from the sleigh. "Tell him for me that I'm awful sorry."

"We will," I promised.

We watched to make sure Nip made it safely into his house before pulling away.

Wobbler got us across Tinkertown quickly. As Juniper said, Woolly Furniture took up the ground floor of the house where Frankie Woolly lived. The building, a hulking, half-timbered two-story edifice, sat on the corner of a hilly street. The lights were dim on the street, but I could make out a chair on the sign hanging above the door.

We knocked on his residence's door, which was off to the side.

"I bought my couch here," Juniper said, peering into the dark showroom window of the furniture workshop.

The door opened quickly, almost as if Frankie had

been expecting someone. "I thought you—" The elf's voice stopped momentarily when he recognized me. "Mrs. Claus?"

I often forget the reaction people might have to seeing me on their doorstep, even if I'm not dressed particularly Mrs. Claus-y. Out of respect for Crumble, Juniper and I had switched our Twinklers beanies for our usual warm knit hats, but obviously I was taller than an elf, and just by being married to Santa, I was a recognizable person in these parts.

I looked into Frankie's face for echoes of his brother and didn't detect many besides a similarity in their blue eyes. Frankie's nose was straight—it had obviously never been broken—and his build, while not what I would call scrawny, was definitely less beefy than his sibling's. He was stooped, and the deep creases in his face told me that he was no stranger to worry.

Confused, he craned his head to peer around me at the parked sleigh. "Is there something I can do for you?"

"We're here about your brother," I said. "Crumble had what appears to be an accident."

The elf's jaw dropped. "What kind of accident? Where?"

"He fell on the ice," Juniper explained. "Doc Honeytree and Constable Crinkles are taking him to the Christmastown Infirmary."

Frankie's eyes grew even wider. "He had an accident at the arena?"

"Yes," I said.

"I warned him not to go back there."

"So he did come by your cottage?" I asked. "I spoke to him after the game, and he mentioned that he was going to drop by."

Frankie opened his mouth to say something and then appeared to check himself. "Yes. He was here."

"He couldn't have stayed long," I said, wanting to elicit a sense of the timeline of Crumble's movements this evening.

"No, not long." His expression had gone vacant. I wondered what I'd said to make him so reluctant to speak. "Is there something in particular that you're here for?"

"For you," Juniper said. "If you'd like to visit Crumble at the infirmary, we can drive you there. We're heading back to Christmastown now."

"I'd appreciate that," he said. "I'll run and get my coat."

He shut the door on us so that we wouldn't follow him inside. Juniper and I went back to the sleigh.

"Where to now?" Wobbler asked.

"We'll be going to the Christmastown Infirmary."

"This has been an eventful first day on the job for me."

"We're lucky you're here," Juniper said. "You've been wonderful."

The reindeer twitched with pride at the compliment.

A few minutes later, Frankie emerged from his cottage, bundled in his coat and carrying a basket. "I packed some things for Crumble—his favorite crackers and a few drinks he enjoys. I thought he'd stay tonight to have some, but . . ."

"What happened?" I asked.

The elf shrugged. "Oh, you know. Brothers don't always agree." Looking around us, he frowned. "Aren't we going to go?"

I'd forgotten. "On, Wobbler!"

Off we went. No one could say that Wobbler lacked pep.

"Did you have an argument while Crumble visited you?" I prompted Frankie when we were out of town on the open snow path.

He shook his head. "It was nothing. I'll feel better after I speak to Crumble."

Juniper shot me a look that had more than a little disapproval in it. I'd been so intent on pumping Frankie for information that I hadn't given him a clear idea of the state of his brother's health.

"You might not be able to have a conversation with Crumble just yet," I said. "He was in bad shape when Doc Honeytree took him away."

Frankie gulped. "How bad?"

"Doc says he has a serious concussion," Juniper said. "He was completely unconscious when Nip the janitor found him on the ice. He has a nasty bump on the head."

"And that's all Nip saw—just my brother on the ice?"

It was an odd question. "Would you have expected anything else?" I asked.

He shook his head. "No, no. I was just curious about . . . the circumstances."

"Do you know why Crumble would have been on the ice at all?" I asked. "Why did he go back to the arena after leaving your house?"

"He was a little . . . upset. He's been depressed ever

since hurting his knee. He came by my cottage because he wanted to borrow my skates—we wear the same bootie size. He wanted to see if his knee was well enough to skate again, which I told him was madness. That's when he took my skates and stormed out." He blew out a breath. "I should've tried harder to talk him out of getting back on that ice."

"You probably couldn't have stopped him if he was really determined," Juniper said. "Anyway, you had no way of knowing that he'd fall."

That had been bothering me, I realized. What would cause an expert skater like Crumble to fall? It must have been the sudden loss of support from his leg to make him fall backward on his head. I was an abysmal skater, but most of the time when I fell on the ice, I ended up falling on my butt. But maybe Crumble was trying some fancy footwork and got tripped up by his stiff knee.

Silence stretched as the sleigh glided down the snow path. This section of the route was flat and barren, with only fields of white stretching out under the starry sky. Faint ribbons of green overhead were the hint of the spectacular northern lights we often saw here.

Juniper grew uncomfortable with the silence. She cleared her throat and told Frankie, "The couch you made me is still holding up very well."

"I'm glad to hear it." His face fixed in concentration for a moment before he guessed, "Blue crushed velveteen with the black piping?"

She smiled. "What a memory! Although you were right about that fabric and hair. My rabbit sheds, and the fur shows up."

He nodded absently.

Juniper's pet bunny, Dave, ruled the roost at her apartment. "I don't mind, though," she assured him. "I just vacuum a lot. Luckily you recommended the fabric protector."

"Animals are tough on furniture," he said.

The exchange exhausted the conversation between the two, and no other word was spoken until we got to town and Wobbler stopped.

"Christmastown Infirmary!" he bellowed loudly enough to wake everyone in a ten-block radius. Santaland's hospital was housed in a two-story gray stone house with a mansard roof. The building's perimeter was filled with holly bushes strung with white lights.

The nurse on duty, Nurse Cinnamon, greeted the three of us at the door. She was a stocky elf in a crisp white uniform and wore sensible white elf booties with rubber soles.

"We're here to see Crumble." I gestured toward Frankie. "This is his brother."

The nurse broke out in a smile. "I think your brother is wonderful. I'm a huge Twinklers fan myself. I usually never miss a game—except on nights like tonight, of course, when I have to work. But look what happened: I was able to be here when they brought your brother in."

She ushered us down the hall to Crumble's room on the first floor. Little about it seemed hospital-like, except for the bed itself, which was adjustable. The rest of the room was done up with carved wood furniture, lace curtains, and comfy quilts, making it resemble a cottage bedroom.

Crinkles was there, as was Doc Honeytree. Unfortunately, Crumble still seemed out of it. He'd been taken out of his leprechaun clothes and was wearing a hospital gown and a matching nightcap over his head bandage.

"Has my brother spoken at all?" Frankie asked as we all gathered around the bed.

Doc gave his head a shake. "He took quite a wallop on the noggin, but he's not running a fever, and his eye movement is okay. He just needs to rest and be kept comfortable. I expect he'll be awake soon, and we'll know more. If he seems delirious at all, call me immediately."

"I brought him some of his favorite treats." Frankie held up his basket. "Would it be okay to offer them to him when he does wake up? The big guy has quite an appetite."

Doc barely glanced at the basket. "Diet shouldn't be an issue."

Crinkles was more curious. "What'd you bring?" He pulled out one of the drinks and beamed his approval. "Spritz Cream Soda—I had one of those once. It was good, but they're hard to find."

I frowned at the little bottle, which looked like the old-fashioned mini bottles they used to sell in the United States back in the days before plastic. The stubby bottles still sometimes could be found in stores as a sort of retro offering.

"I've never heard of Spritz sodas," I said.

"It's new," Juniper explained. "Well, since last year. Spritz makes it all by hand in small batches."

Artisan soda pop. I studied the *SS* lettering on the bottle's label and then remembered the bottle cap I'd picked up off the sidewalk in front of Claire's shop this afternoon. When I reached into my pocket, it was still there.

Nurse Cinnamon appeared. "We're getting a little crowded in here, aren't we? Our patient needs peace and quiet."

Doc Honeytree's lips pursed. "The patient is out like a dud Christmas light."

"For shame, Doctor. You know that even an unconscious patient can hear things." She hovered protectively over her charge. "And an illustrious athlete like Crumble Woolly is bound to be even more sensitive to his surroundings."

Frankie stepped forward. "Will it be okay if I stay with him tonight?" He nodded to the upholstered armchair in the corner. "I can sit up in this chair here."

"Of course—I'll move it closer for you." She zipped over to drag the chair across the room before anyone could even move to help her. "The rest of you, though . . . it *is* a wee bit overpopulated in here." Nurse Cinnamon attempted to herd us all out. All except Frankie.

I hung back to speak to him.

"This is all my fault." Tears filled his eyes as he looked at his brother. "I didn't tell you the whole truth about what happened between my brother and me last night, Mrs. Claus."

"If it would make you feel better to talk about it now . . ."

He took a ragged breath. "We fought—the same

fight as always. My petty resentment over being stuck running the family business while he tries to pretend he can be an iceball hero forever."

"You've argued about this a lot?"

Frankie nodded. "But last night was worse. He'd . . . well, he'd been drinking, and I lost my temper."

"I didn't see him drinking," I said. "Just a milkshake."

He huffed out a laugh. "He's sly about it, but I could tell, and for some reason I just snapped. It was that stupid leprechaun suit! Where was the dignity in that? Did he really think it was better to caper around in that foolish costume at the arena than to come home and take his place in the family business? Why should *I* always be the responsible one?" Realizing he was getting wound up all over again, he released a deflating sigh. He swallowed, and his voice lowered. "I called him a washed-up ice jock. Then I told him I didn't care anymore if he lived or died." The elf's eyes filled with tears. "My own little brother—how could I say such a thing?"

"All of us say things we regret when we're angry."

"But what if those are the last words I ever say to him? I was so mean . . . over so little. Nothing that couldn't be fixed."

The pain in his voice made my heart go out him. But why did I get the feeling that he still wasn't telling the whole story?

I shook my head. "Doc says Crumble will wake up. He just needs rest." I smiled at him. "I think you need some too."

Nurse Cinnamon darted her head in and said in a sing-song, "Come along, Mrs. Claus."

In the hallway, Crinkles was consulting with the doctor. "Do you think he'll wake up again soon? I'm going to have to start an investigation into what happened to that trophy. I was hoping Crumble would just be able to tell us."

And I was hoping he'd be able to explain how he'd come to fall on the ice—although maybe Frankie's explanation was all that was needed. He'd felt a yen to play iceball after watching his old team win, so he'd tested his legs to see if he was ready to get back on the ice. And his legs had let him down.

Yet it seemed a strange coincidence that the trophy had disappeared at the same time.

Nurse Cinnamon shut the door to the patient's room. "You'll all be able to visit him tomorrow, starting at ten in the morning. Except you, of course, Doctor. You're welcome to see Crumble anytime."

"Thank you very much," he grumbled. "Very gratifying to be given permission to see my own patient."

"We'll have our star Twinkler up and running again," she promised, as if she hadn't heard Doc's sarcasm at all. "And next time, we'll keep him away from those awful milkshakes."

"Milkshakes?" I asked.

What did this nurse know about milkshakes?

She blinked at me. "Wasn't a milkshake the cause of all this?"

"We don't know yet," Doc said. In a lower voice he explained to me, "I'll have my nephew Algid test the milkshake. I doubt he'll find anything."

I now suspected he would. Not poison, though. Alcohol. But I wasn't going to say anything in front of Crumble and the nurse.

Nurse Cinnamon let out a huff of consternation. "I guess I was misinformed. The constable told me that the whole mishap was caused by a milkshake."

Crinkles reddened.

I should have guessed that Crinkles wouldn't be able to keep his mouth shut about my earlier milkshake suspicions. I could only hope that word about the milkshake didn't go beyond these hospital walls.

Chapter Five

"A poisoned milkshake?" Claire's voice looped up, incensed. "Where did this ridiculous idea come from?"

I cringed. I'd stopped by the Santaland Scoop this morning to check on Claire—and also because the ice-cream parlor had become my home away from home. As I sat in the bright yet empty shop, guilt wracked me. I should never have pointed out the milkshake last night, or I should have made sure that Crinkles wasn't within earshot.

"Why would anyone think such a thing?" she asked. "Crumble fell on the ice."

Here went nothing. "A milkshake cup was found nearby, and we just wondered if there was some connection."

"Of course there wasn't," she said.

"Doc Honeytree will clear this all up," I assured her. "He said he was going to give the milkshake to his nephew Algid to test overnight. Anyway, even if there was something in the milkshake, no one thinks *you* poisoned it."

She crossed her arms over her red bib apron. "Then where are all my customers? The shop's been deserted since I opened."

I was tempted to say something about the time of day, but midmorning wasn't considered too early for elves to start consuming sweet treats. Every day for the past month, there had been a steady trickle of customers coming into the Scoop. Some mornings Juniper and I found it hard to get a table.

"I'm sure the gossip will die down and elves will start craving ice cream again," I said.

My words failed to soothe Claire. "Not if they think it's going to kill them."

Butterbean sailed in from the cold room carrying a fresh gallon of ice cream labeled *Saint Paddy's Pistachio.* "Saint Patrick's Day will change everything," he predicted sunnily. "The street fair and all the fun events at the park—especially my balloon ride—will make everyone forget all about what happened to Crumble."

"Unless we lose all our customers by then."

Butterbean blinked, missing her sarcasm. "Even if that happens, we have our big balloon ride. It'll be the greatest advertisement ever for the Scoop—elves will come flocking back."

"The milkshake-vending leprechaun at the game was supposed to bring a stampede of customers too," Claire reminded him.

"And it worked! Last night at the arena, we had the highest volume of sales per hour since the Scoop opened its doors."

Claire bit her lip. She *had* sold a lot of milkshakes, Twinkle-sicles, and Beaver Pops.

"I'll ask Algid and Doc to try to speed up the testing of the milkshake," I said. "Then you can reassure people that there was nothing to the rumor."

Claire laughed. "Sure. I can put out a sign: FROZEN TREATS: 100% POISON-FREE. I'll have to give out more ice-cream tokens just to get people in."

The ice-cream tokens were a customer loyalty scheme Butterbean had come up with. Every ten visits earned a customer a free cone token. Juniper and I had them coming out of our ears.

Butterbean bobbed on his toes and punched the button on the overhead speakers. "And listen to this." Bing Crosby singing "Too-Ra-Loo-Ra-Loo-Ral" came over the sound system. "I made a Saint Patrick's Day mood music mix."

The tinkle of the bell over the store's outer door heralded the arrival of a customer. Claire turned an expectant smile toward the sound. When a slender figure in a black trench coat loped across the threshold, her smile melted a fraction. It wasn't a customer; it was Jake Frost.

Sensing the mood in the room, Jake removed his black fedora as he approached the counter. "I'd like to try the Saint Paddy's Pistachio."

Claire eyed him with affectionate exasperation. "You already had a milkshake this morning. You and April are wonderful, but the two of you can't keep my store open all on your own. You'll either pop or go broke."

"No chance of going broke," he said. "I have a new case."

She brightened. "What is it?"

"Constable Crinkles hired me to find the Golden Bootie."

Unbelievable. "The constabulary is outsourcing detective work now?" I asked.

"Crinkles feels he's too close to the matter to investigate it properly."

For Pete's sake. "Those constables have a broad definition of conflict of interest." It seemed to encompass any activity that would interfere with coaching or baking.

"Who cares?" Claire said. "When Jake finds the trophy, it will be a good advertisement for the Jake Frost Detective Agency."

I supposed she had a point. Heaven knows I trusted Jake's ability to locate something more than I trusted Crinkles's ability. Maybe subcontracting fighting crime wasn't a bad idea.

I reached for my phone to see if there was any news about Crumble. Frankie had promised to let me know if there was any change. I was still hoping that Crumble would soon be able to tell us exactly what happened. When I reached for the phone, though, I felt the bottle cap inside my coat pocket. I'd almost forgotten about it.

"Speaking of investigations, do you have any idea why an elf would toss this at your milkshake cart, or at Crumble?"

Claire's lips twisted as she studied the bottle cap. "Spritz Greenbell," she said, irritated. "That sour little elf makes soda pop, and he's angry because I was granted a cart concession at the arena and he wasn't."

"Were you in competition?"

She lifted her shoulders. "How should I know? I just applied to be allowed to sell frozen treats and milkshakes, and the elf in charge of concessions said okay. I figured they said okay to everybody, but I guess not, because the next day Spritz was here accusing me of having bribed someone or pulling strings or something. He's a lunatic."

An elf with a grudge. I didn't want to bring up poisoned milkshakes again, but on the miniscule chance that it turned out to be true, I knew who Suspect Number One would be.

Jake was frowning. "Should I have a word with him?"

Claire shook her head. "It's probably best to ignore him."

Jake appeared to agree, but I wasn't so sure. Sometimes tempers cooled after a while, but if an elf was inclined to hold a grudge, being ignored could just rile him further.

My phone pinged with a message from Frankie: CRUMBLE WOKE UP.

Under normal circumstances, it might have been faster to make my way over to the Christmastown Infirmary on foot. At this time of year, some stretches of sidewalk were actually ice-free, which made the town easier to get around, even for klutzes like me. At the moment, though, preparations were underway for the Saint

Patrick's Day fair, so the sidewalks were blocked with booths under construction and elves setting up Saint Patrick's Day decorations and stringing up shamrock lights. The whole place was being transformed from Christmastown to Irishtown.

Adding to the atmosphere, Bobbin, the piccolo player from the Santaland Concert Band, was playing "Danny Boy" on a pennywhistle. I'd never seen him busking before.

I stopped to listen. The pennywhistle was slightly off tune, but Bobbin was putting a lot of pathos into the song. When he finished, I gave him a round of applause.

"Getting an early start on Saint Paddy's Day?" I asked.

"Practicing for the talent contest tomorrow."

Perhaps Jingles didn't have to worry too much about his competition.

"And maybe making a little extra on my eggnog break?" he hinted.

I dug into my pockets, but all I came up with was the bottle cap and a few of Claire's ice-cream tokens.

"Here," I said. "This is good for a free ice-cream cone or milkshake at the Santaland Scoop."

Bobbin looked as if I'd just plopped a poisonous insect into his palm.

Poor Claire. She'd be doomed if this mess didn't get cleared up soon.

Wobbler was waiting for me down the block. I "On, Wobblered" at him, something that still felt weird and drew a few stares from passersby. But once we got going, I settled in for a relaxing ride. Wobbler seemed to have a sixth sense about avoiding congested streets. I was becoming accustomed to being chauffeured around town.

"Christmastown Infirmary!" he announced when we arrived.

Inside, I was surprised to see Nurse Cinnamon still on duty. Didn't she ever go home? Although somehow she had managed to acquire a Sprinklers sweater jersey with WOOLLY cut out in black felt letters and pinned to the back. She sported it over her nurse whites.

"Nice sweater," I said.

She beamed. "I did the lettering myself overnight."

I guess she had plenty of time on her hands. The Christmastown Infirmary wasn't exactly Cook County General Hospital from *ER*. As far as I could tell, Crumble was the only patient at the moment.

"I volunteered to do an extra half shift," she said. "What with such an illustrious patient on the ward."

"Has Crumble received many visitors?" I asked.

"A man from the *Christmastown Herald* came by. I shooed him away. Crumble's brother is here, of course, and an alleged girlfriend"—that *alleged* dripped with disdain—"dropped in for about five minutes and then said she had to get to work."

Poinsettia, I thought. "Maybe she really did have to go to work."

The nurse harrumphed. "You should see the wilted daffodils she brought. I was ashamed to put the sad little things by Crumble's bed, but his brother insisted."

"So Frankie never left?"

"Not for a single second that I ever saw," Cinnamon said approvingly. "That shows real brotherly devotion."

Or real concern for what Crumble might say when he woke up. "Is the doctor here?" I asked.

"He had some cottage calls to make this morning, but he's on his way back. He came by and talked to Crumble earlier."

"So Crumble is fine?"

"He's got a bad headache, and . . ." A worried expression came over her face. "Well, I wouldn't say he's 100 percent, but we can always be hopeful, can't we?"

After that less-than-ringing description, I approached the room with some trepidation. The bed had been cranked up so that Crumble was sitting up. His color was good, but his eyes seemed blank as he stared at me.

"Hi, Crumble," I said. "It's good to see you awake again."

He blinked at me, then turned to Frankie. "Who's this?"

Frankie's hair was mussed, and his eyes looked even sleepier from his overnight vigil. "That's Mrs. Claus."

The patient swiveled back to me, surprised. "Oh. How do you do?"

"We met yesterday."

Frankie looked at me. "He doesn't remember yesterday."

"Nothing?"

Crumble's lips twisted. "I remember being in some kind of outfit. There was a game. I guess I passed out or something, because I woke up here."

"You don't remember going to see your brother after the game?"

He turned back to Frankie, confused. "You said I was found at the arena."

"You were," Frankie said.

Crumble looked so confused, I didn't want to ask any more questions. Had he suffered brain damage? Frankie looked distressed too.

Doc Honeytree bustled into the room with his black bag. He opened it and removed a penlight to check Crumble's eyes. "How are you feeling now?"

"About the same," Crumble said. "Tired."

Doc patted him on the shoulder. "You can sleep more if you want. We're going to keep you here and let Nurse Cinnamon keep an eye on you for a few days."

From the door, Nurse Cinnamon beamed at her patient. "It's my pleasure."

Something about that elf's over-the-top enthusiasm unsettled me. Was she a super-friendly nurse, or Crumble's Number One Fan, a la Annie Wilkes in *Misery*?

Doc motioned for me to join him outside. I excused myself to Frankie and Crumble and followed him.

"He says he doesn't remember anything of last night," I told Doc.

The doctor sighed. "Acute concussion can cause temporary memory loss. It'll probably come back."

"When?"

He shrugged.

I groaned in frustration. "I was hoping he would be able to tell us what happened last night."

The doctor looked around, then lowered his voice. "I think I can explain some of it. I was just at the constabulary, telling Crinkles what my nephew Algid discovered on one of the iceballs I picked up from the arena last night."

"What?"

"Traces of blood, and a hair that I'm pretty darned sure matches Crumble's."

I froze. "You mean someone lobbed an iceball at him? Can an iceball really knock a guy out like that?"

"If it's a direct hit on the skull, sure. That's why our players wear helmets, and why there are Plexiglas guards around the arena, to protect the fans in the bleachers."

Crumble hadn't been wearing a helmet when we found him last night.

Who would be adept enough to make a lethal iceball toss? Any player on either team, obviously. But from what I'd seen, almost anyone who'd grown up in Santaland could have struck him. Everyone played the game. Even Nick could probably sling a mean iceball.

But why would anyone do that? Anger over the game? Crumble wasn't even playing at the moment. Last night he'd just been a rather pathetic ice-cream spokes-elf in a leprechaun suit. I would have thought most players would consider him an object of ridicule, not a target for murder.

To me, this seemed personal.

And how did the theft of the trophy figure into all of this? Could it have been taken to simply make the attack on Crumble *seem* as if it had something to do with iceball?

"Algid tested that milkshake too," Doc said, interrupting my train of thought.

I'd almost forgotten about the milkshake. "What was in it?"

"One part milkshake, two parts vodka."

After what Frankie had told me last night, I wasn't surprised by this news.

"That could be part of what's causing his headache this morning." His lips flattened. "Not that the whack on the head he took wouldn't have caused it anyway."

"I need to inform Claire that her milkshake's in the clear," I said.

"I doubt that will be necessary." Doc's lips turned up in amusement. "I told them all about it while I was at the constabulary."

If Crinkles and Ollie had heard that the milkshake was harmless, it was probably all over town by now.

As I was getting ready to go, a group of Twinklers players came down the corridor carrying a large horseshoe wreath made out of what looked like clover. Across the top was a banner reading GET WELL SOON.

Wick, the team captain, stopped to talk to the doctor. "I hope it's okay to visit this morning."

"Sure—but don't stay long. Crumble is awake, but he's suffered a bad blow to the head. He needs his rest."

The players assured him that they wouldn't linger.

It was nice of his old teammates to visit. I wondered if any of them knew anyone who would want to hurt Crumble. But it would be up to Crinkles to investigate now.

After they'd filed into Crumble's room, Doc escorted me down the corridor toward the exit. "Seems strange that someone would attack an iceball player who's not going to be playing anymore," he said.

I froze. "Anymore, meaning never?"

"Not on that knee."

Even though we were out of earshot of Crumble's room, I lowered my voice. "Crumble said it was getting better."

"Better, yes, but it'll never be what it was. He'll never have the range of motion he needs to play iceball competitively."

"And Crumble knows this?" I asked.

"Of course—I told him straight up. Although he might be in denial. Didn't you know?"

I shook my head. "Everyone in town seems to think he might be back, maybe even before the end of the season."

Doc rubbed his chin. "I just assumed he had informed everyone." Now he looked chagrined that he'd spilled the information to me.

"I won't say anything," I promised.

"So maybe the attack *was* a jealous iceball player," he said.

"Maybe."

But I was just as inclined to suspect a jealous beverage salesman.

Chapter Six

Before I brought Spritz to the attention of Constable Crinkles, I decided to have a chat with him myself. Going from tossing a bottle cap to a potentially lethal iceball assault was a big escalation. Had Claire's sports celebrity spokes-elf made Spritz see red?

When I phoned the number listed for Spritz Sodas, the call went to voicemail. I enlisted Jake to help me figure out where Spritz worked. The answer shocked me: he was a clerk at Sparkletoe's Mercantile, right across Sparkletoe Lane from the Santaland Scoop. No wonder he was exploding with resentment. Every day he was a witness to the success of her shop.

Until today.

Jake and I went to Sparkletoe's Mercantile, an old-fashioned emporium that sold almost anything you could want for your home and garden. The store itself was delightfully antique, with floor-to-ceiling shelves along the walls where the stock was accessed by elves on ladders. The floor was a crowded showroom of everything from children's toys to snowmobiles. Jake and I lingered outside a hardware alcove in the back of the store, where Spritz was helping a customer choose the right size of rope.

Spritz was wearing the Sparkletoe's Mercantile uniform of a green tunic over matching short pants and green-and-white striped stockings. As he measured and cut, I caught him casting a few anxious glances at Jake and me. Good. I wanted him to be unnerved.

When he was done with his customers, he approached us warily. "Is there anything I can do for you, Mrs. Claus?"

Checking that there was no one nearby to eavesdrop, I reached into my coat pocket and pulled out the bottle cap I'd been carrying around.

"You can tell me if you're as adept at hurling iceballs as you are at throwing bottle caps."

He blanched. "I don't know what you mean."

Jake crossed his arms. He looked madder than I'd ever seen him when questioning someone; then again, I'd never seen him question anyone who'd been menacing Claire. "Are you going to deny that you threw that bottle cap at Crumble Woolly last night?"

Judging from the emotions that marched across his face, Spritz was giving that tactic serious consideration. Ultimately, though, he jutted out his chin and admitted, "I have no need to deny it. It was just a bottle cap. I didn't hurt anyone. At most, I'm guilty of being a litterbug."

A peevish litterbug.

Jake looked skeptical. "So you're saying you didn't toss an iceball at Crumble after the game last night?"

The little elf shook his head. "Of course not. Why would I?"

"Why would you toss *anything* at him?" I retorted.

Frustration filled the clerk's eyes, and he began to quiver with agitation. So much that the bell at the end of his cap tinkled. "I was just so gosh-darned mad. Excuse my language, but I was."

"Just because you applied for a concession permit at the arena and you were turned down?"

"Just?" He finally boiled over. "That was totally unfair! It was bad enough when they told me that I didn't have high enough production volume to handle a busy concession. But when that ice-cream lady breezed into town and got a concession right away, I realized the whole system was rigged. It's all who you know, and pulling strings."

"Claire didn't pull any strings," I said.

He snorted. "A non-elf woman who's best friends with Santa's wife just so happens to get the concession that I, a lowly elf, was turned down for? With all due respect, Mrs. Claus, that reindeer won't fly."

"Claire's been making ice cream for a decade back in our hometown, which sees a lot of tourists in the summer. She's experienced at what she does and could easily handle the arena demands."

"While you're still making little batches of soda pop in your parents' basement," Jake added.

A little harsh, but true.

The elf's shoulders slumped. "It's a vicious circle— I can't make more money until I produce more, and I can't produce more until I have more money to invest in equipment and a real bottling facility."

I was sympathetic to his business problems, but they weren't why I was there. "So you took your frustrations out on Crumble, who was just doing a little side hustle of his own helping Claire out."

Confusion filled his eyes. "I heard someone gave him a poison milkshake"—he glared at me—"from your friend's cart."

Jake's expression darkened. "It was nothing to do with Claire."

"Crumble's in the hospital with a concussion from an iceball attack," I said.

The elf's eyes widened. "Not because of *me*. I didn't throw any iceballs—I was always lousy at iceball anyway. Ask anyone I went to school with. I was always the last picked for the iceball team at recess."

Jake was unmoved. "I suppose you didn't happen to steal the Golden Bootie from the trophy cabinet on your way out of the arena, either?"

Spritz gaped at him. "The trophy? Of course not! How could I have done that? I caught the first sleigh bus home after the game. Somebody would've noticed me carrying around a big trophy."

He was right about the Golden Bootie being too big to conceal under one's clothing.

"Why didn't you go to the Tinkertown Tavern after the game?" I asked.

His face reddened. "I figured *she'd* be there."

Meaning his nemesis, Claire.

"Look," Jake said, "I don't know if you threw that iceball or not, but you've got the wrong idea about Claire. She's not your enemy, and she didn't get special treatment. If you toss another bottle cap—or anything else—at her or her employees, I'll see that Constable Crinkles locks you up."

From the horror in Spritz's eyes, you'd have thought that being locked up in the Christmastown Constabulary was like being sent to Alcatraz, when really the constabulary was a modest, comfortable cottage, and the cell itself was a well-appointed, cozy bedroom with ensuite bath. The place was like a penal B and B.

"I won't do anything like that again." He shuddered with self-recrimination. "I don't know what came over me. I'm usually not like this. It's just so frustrating to know that I could be following my dream of delivering delicious sparkling beverages to all the elves and people in Santaland, but instead I'm stuck here climbing ladders and stocking shelves. I even offered my boss the opportunity to invest in Spritz Sodas, but that old battle-ax turned me down. So now I'll have to spend the rest of my life in this dead-end job, cutting rope and mixing paint and smiling at stupid customers all day long. Forever."

"Not forever—not even another hour."

The booming voice shocked us all. We pivoted to the stern elf woman who stood behind us, arms akimbo. The formidable Bella Sparkletoe, owner of Sparkletoe's Mercantile, was Spritz's boss. She'd obviously heard every word Spritz had spoken.

"You'd better come with me," she told the trembling elf.

I tried to intervene. "I'm sure he didn't mean what he said, Bella."

"He sounded sincere to me," she retorted.

"I mean, he was just speaking out of frustration.

Everybody's had a job that su—" I stopped myself, sensing that the next words queued up on my tongue would not be helpful to Spritz's case. "He was *very* helpful to the customer who came before us."

Bella shook her head. "I don't tell you how to run things up in Castle Kringle, Mrs. Claus. Don't tell me how to run my business."

She frog-marched Spritz away. I looked at Jake in despair. "What have I done?"

"Well, Spritz will now be free to spend more time making soda pop."

"We should have talked to him somewhere else." Hindsight was twenty-twenty, though. So now I needed to not only find Crumble's assailant but also find Spritz another job.

"At least we know that he didn't throw the iceball," I said to Jake as we left the store.

"Do we?" Jake asked. "We don't have proof that he didn't. Just his word."

"I trust him." Now that I'd gotten him fired, I trusted him.

"Trust isn't proof," Jake said.

"There was probably someone on that sleigh bus who saw him go home last night before the time Crumble was hit."

"I'll look into that this afternoon. One of the drivers might remember seeing him on their sleigh." He looked at his wristwatch. "I'm supposed to meet Claire for lunch."

"Isn't it sort of early?"

"She doesn't like to be away from the Scoop at peak hours. Why don't you come?"

"I don't want to intrude."

He frowned. "How could you be intruding? I think she's invited Juniper too."

"In that case . . ."

I didn't need much persuading to go out to eat, and the place was the Midnight Clear diner, which was one of my favorite eateries. It was a Santalander's fantasy of a retro diner, with red vinyl booths, sparkly Formica tabletops, and a jukebox with fifties pop stars singing Christmas tunes.

When we arrived, Claire and Juniper had already claimed one of the booths. I scooted in next to Juniper. The furniture was elf proportioned, so as usual I felt oversized. I envied Claire her diminutive frame.

"I'm so glad to see you," Juniper said excitedly, as if it had been years since we'd run into each other instead of twelve hours. "I want to hear all about what's going on."

I went through everything I'd learned, minus what Doc had told me about Crumble's career. That information was confidential.

While I was talking, a waitress in a leprechaun hat came by. "What'll you have?"

I started to order my usual, the Jingle Bell Rock Reuben, but she interrupted me.

"We're only taking orders from our Saint Patrick's Day menu this week."

I looked at the card next to the salt shaker. The clip art shamrocks and leprechauns on the menu outnumbered the food offerings. "I guess I'll have the corned beef and cabbage, then."

"It's actually corned musk ox and cabbage," the waitress told me.

I sighed. The inevitable musk ox. "Okay."

The rest ordered the same. Before the waitress sauntered away, something on the drinks board caught my eye. "You sell Spritz Sodas?" I asked.

"When we can get them," she said. "Right now all we have is Ginger Fizz and Bubbling Bearberry."

"I'll have a Ginger Fizz."

Claire shook her head. "Giving comfort and succor to the enemy."

"He's not your enemy." At least, that's what we'd told him about Claire. Remembering Spritz gave me a sudden idea. "Say, didn't you say you need another employee?"

"I said I might need to take on more help back when it looked like I had more customers than I could handle. Now it looks as if I'll be lucky if I can keep Butterbean on."

"Your business will pick up," Juniper predicted. "This town is just crazy about gossip. Once news spreads that the milkshake *wasn't* poisoned, you'll have as many customers as ever."

"And if you do need to hire someone," I said, "I have just the elf for you."

Claire arched a brow. "Who?"

"Spritz."

She laughed. "Have you lost your mind?"

"No, but he's lost his job." I told her all about what had happened at Sparkletoe's Mercantile and how guilty I felt for poor Spritz getting the heave-ho.

"Poor Spritz?" Claire hooted. "No. I'm not hiring an unstable elf to work in my ice-cream parlor."

"He's not unstable," I said. "He's just . . . emotional."

She shook her head at me. "No."

So much for that. Maybe I could fix something up for him at Castle Kringle.

"If you don't think Spritz attacked Crumble," Juniper asked with a perplexed frown, "who do you think did it?"

"My money's on the brother," Jake said.

"But if Frankie's so desperate for Crumble to work more at the furniture factory," I pointed out, "why would he hurt him? That would just ensure that Crumble won't be able to help at all."

"You insinuated that you didn't entirely trust Frankie," Jake reminded me.

"He spilled his guts to me, yet I sensed that there was something he was leaving out," I admitted. "But he spent the entire night at the hospital. If he'd wanted to do his brother in, he had plenty of opportunity then."

"Unless the presence of Nurse Cinnamon stopped him."

The nurse had quite a presence, I'd give her that.

"Sounds to me like you'll have to widen your search," Claire said. "Who benefits from taking Crumble down?" She shrugged. "I bet it's something to do with an ice-ball."

Juniper gasped. "I hope not—that would be so unsportsmanlike."

But it made sense, especially since it wasn't known

that Crumble no longer had a career in that sport. Who would most want to eliminate him?

The waitress came back with our meals and drinks.

"This looks wonderful," Juniper told her.

I poured some soda into a glass, took a sip, and sat up straighter. "That's delicious." I pushed the bottle across to Claire. "Try it."

Her nose wrinkled.

"It's really good, I swear."

Hesitantly, she took a sip straight from the bottle. Her eyes widened. "Nice and gingery."

"See?"

"I'm still not hiring that elf to work in my ice-cream parlor," she said.

I was about to argue when a couple walking in caught my eye. It was one of the players from the Ice Beavers, and on his arm was none other than the lovely Poinsettia. I nudged Juniper with my elbow.

She glanced up from her plate of musk ox. "Snowball Berrytree."

"With Crumble's erstwhile girlfriend." I looked at Jake. "Talk about a motive for taking out the competition."

"Crumble's well rid of her," Claire said.

"He doesn't know he's rid of her yet. How could he? She took him flowers this morning."

Before I could think better of it, I was on my feet and ignoring the little tug on my sleeve that Juniper gave to hold me back.

Whether by design or by chance, the lovers were seated at a secluded table in the back, scooched in side-by-side. They'd wasted no time get right down to public displays of affection, as if this were a drive-in theater instead of a restaurant.

I slipped into the opposite seat, surprising them. "What do we have here?" I said. "A clandestine love affair, or is this a planning committee for your next assassination attempt?"

Snowball pushed away from his lady, and Poinsettia, reddening, blinked her long lashes at me. "I don't know what you're talking about," she said.

"I'm talking about the attempt on Crumble's life."

"The idiot fell on the ice," Snowball said.

"Turns out that he might have had a little help with that. From an iceball to the head."

"What makes you think that?" Poinsettia asked.

"Evidence from the crime scene, which you would have found out about yourself if you'd bothered to stay by his bedside more than five minutes this morning."

She bristled at the criticism. "There was no reason for me to go at all. I only did so out of the goodness of my heart."

That tracked. Five minutes of sympathy for anyone was probably a stretch for her little walnut of a heart.

"You can't blame me for whatever happened to him," Snowball said. "I was at the Tinkertown Tavern last night after the game. You probably even saw me there."

"Right. I saw the two of you leave early—around the time Crumble was attacked."

Snowball crossed his arms. "Not by me. Why would I want to hurt Crumble?"

I gestured toward the two of them.

He laughed. "Does he think Poinsettia belongs to

him? That might be a good reason for him to kill me, but not the other way around. I'm the winner here."

Right. He'd won himself a real prize.

Poinsettia huffed out a laugh. "Crumble probably won't even care when he finds out about Snowball and me. He's been so preoccupied with that knee of his, he's barely noticed me for months."

As much as I disliked this couple, every word out of their mouths deflated me a little. I should have heeded Juniper's tug on my sleeve and not rushed over. Their points made sense. Neither of them seemed honorable—she didn't seem to have the least care about what Crumble was going through—but they were right: Snowball didn't need to kill Crumble to steal his girlfriend. Poinsettia had been perfectly happy to jump ship.

"If you're going to blame someone for whatever Crumble says happened last night, the ones you ought to be looking at are those two wild elves," Snowball said.

"Ham and Scar?"

"*They're* the ones who don't want Crumble to rejoin the Twinklers. Once he does, they'll probably be out."

Poinsettia straightened. "They shouldn't be playing on the team anyway. They know they aren't wanted here."

"The Ice Beavers fans made that pretty clear," I said.

Snowball shrugged. "We can't help how people feel."

"They're elves," I said. "It's not like the Twinklers have snow monsters playing on their team."

Snowball's lips turned down. "That'll probably be next."

I got up, offended for the wild elves. I knew something about how they must feel. A few elves and people had told me that I didn't belong here either.

"Elves are elves," I said, echoing Nick's words of the night before.

Snowball's expression remained stony. "So where were Ham and Scar while Crumble was attacked?"

Not at the Tinkertown Tavern, I remembered. No one had expected them to show up, and in fact their presence at the victory celebration could have been inflammatory. But what if their absence had a more nefarious reason behind it?

I slunk back to our booth.

"What did they say?" Claire asked.

"I don't think either of them was Crumble's attacker." I gave a summary of the exchange I'd had with Snowball.

Jake tapped his fingers on the table in thought. "He has a point about the wild elves. It would be a good idea to talk to those two."

I reached over to pour myself some more Ginger Fizz, but the bottle was empty. I looked pointedly at Claire, whose cheeks colored slightly. "It really *is* good," she admitted.

"So maybe—"

She cut me off. "I'm not hiring that envious little elf."

"Who are you going to get to be your second leprechaun at the Saint Patrick's Day festivities?"

Her frown deepened, and then she turned hopeful eyes on Jake.

He drew back. "Oh no."

"Please?"

"Even love has its limits."

I had a hard time imagining Jake Frost as a leprechaun, and the vision that I could conjure of him in a goofy green suit wasn't one likely to attract ice-cream customers.

The same thought seemed to occur to Claire. "I'll think of something," she said, looking doubtfully at the empty Ginger Fizz bottle. "I hope."

After we finished lunch, Juniper had to go back to the library, and the rest of us returned to the Santaland Scoop. I wanted to go to the constabulary, but I needed to pick up Wobbler and my sleigh, which had been parked outside the ice-cream parlor for a while now. One could never predict when the constable would tire of thinking about iceball strategies and decide to start handing out parking tickets. When I'd left Wobbler there, the spaces in front of the Scoop were deserted, so he would be a sitting duck if the constables decided to start handing out parking tickets again.

When we turned the corner onto Sparkletoe Lane, though, the sight that greeted us stopped us in our tracks. Elves were lined up two deep outside the Santaland Scoop.

"What's going on?" Alarm propelled Claire forward. She pushed through the queue and entered the store, where a harried Butterbean stood behind the counter, simultaneously arguing with an impatient elf customer and running the drink blender. His tense expression collapsed with relief when he spotted Claire.

"Thank goodness you're back!" he said over the angry buzz of the blender. Beads of sweat stood out on his brow, and his cherub face was tense with panic. "It's been madness here."

"What's happened?" Claire asked.

"Everyone's heard some crazy story about Crumble getting tipsy last night from one of our milkshakes. Now all the elves in town want to try one."

Chapter Seven

Like all of Christmastown, the constabulary had been transformed for Saint Patrick's Day. Green lights were strung around the picture windows of the cottage, and two leprechaun statuettes stood sentry at the front door. As I crossed the threshold, the smell of a freshly baked treat drew me toward the dining area, where a toasty fire warmed the room from the hearth. On one wall where two paintings of winter scenes used to hang, there was now a large whiteboard with diagrams of iceball plays scrawled across it. Ollie, in the Saint Patrick's Day spirit, had drawn shamrocks in the whiteboard's corners with a green marker.

Their lunch was almost finished. The constables and their wild elf residents sat at the table, Crinkles with his napkin tucked into the collar of his navy-blue wool uniform. Ham and Scar looked as if they'd simply been using the sleeves of their rough-woven tunics as napkins.

Seeing me, Ollie hopped up, ready to fix a plate for

me. "There's some shepherd's pie left over if you'd like a helping."

Corned musk ox was sitting heavily in my stomach. "No, thank you."

"At least join us for dessert," Crinkles urged. "Ollie made a special cake."

If there's one credo in life I live by, it's that one should never pass up an offer of cake. I thanked them and took a chair next to the constable. I had to suppress the urge to slump to make myself seem less conspicuously large among the elves. The wild elves, especially, were small but scrappy.

They were still cleaning their luncheon plates, using chunks of bread to mop up every bit of food from the constabulary's everyday china, which was decorated with a wintry scene pattern. As they gobbled down food, I noticed the cascade of crumbs and drips radiating from their place settings. Table manners probably weren't a priority north of the border.

Ollie returned bearing a crystal cake server with a gorgeous three-layer cake iced with white buttercream and dripping with green-tinted white chocolate.

"It's green velvet cake," Ollie announced. "For Saint Patrick's Day. I know it's not till tomorrow—this one's just for practice."

"It's spectacular," I said.

Scar reached for the cake plate as if he might just claw himself off a piece, but Ollie blocked him. "Hang on—I'll serve it up for you."

The wild elves waited impatiently, forks in their fists. When wedges of cake were set in front of them on dessert plates, they used a combination of forks and fingers to scoop up cake and swallow it down. It was like watching feral creatures gulp down their food out of fear that someone would come and take it from them. Slurping and smacking emanated from their side of the table. It took effort to keep my expression neutral.

Crinkles smiled indulgently at them, like the proud parent of twin toddlers. "They sure like to eat, don't they?"

The two wild elves grunted.

I cleared my throat to change the subject. "I don't know how far you've gotten into your investigation . . ."

"About the trophy?" Crinkles asked. "Jake Frost is on that."

"I'm talking about Crumble. Doc says he was hit by an iceball."

"Well, sure, but that could've been self-inflicted."

If anyone besides Constable Crinkles had said this, I would have assumed he was joking. "Would it be possible for Crumble to hit himself on the back of the head with an iceball?"

Crinkles pondered this. "Maybe he was just enjoying a pickup game with someone and there was an accident?"

"So why didn't that someone come forward? Why did they run away, leaving Crumble for dead?"

The constable ruminated some more, then said slowly, "If it was on purpose, that sounds like an assault." Realization struck, and the lawman's jowls quivered. "Maybe attempted murder!"

The constable's brain was not a quick-draw mechanism. But at least the situation had finally sunk in.

"Who would do such a thing?" Ollie asked.

"Especially to a former star Twinkler!" Crinkles added.

"I'm beginning to think that his being a Twinkler might have been the reason for the attack," I said. "The culprit could be another player who holds a personal grudge against him, or someone who simply doesn't want him ever to be on the ice again."

Crinkles took a moment to eat—and to think. "Who wouldn't want Crumble to play again? He was our best player once. The last time the Twinklers won the cup was Crumble's first season."

I nodded subtly toward Ham and Scar, who were still going at their cake like two goblins. Ham grunted with pleasure as he stuffed the last bite into his mouth with his hand. Although I could sympathize with the desire to cram as much cake into my face as quickly as possible, the wild elves were a little disgusting. Also, Ollie's green velvet cake was exceptionally good. It deserved to be savored, not inhaled.

"Everybody likes Crumble," Crinkles said, not wanting to believe it.

"Yes, but he poses an obstacle to elves who might be hoping to take his place in the starting lineup."

"Like who?" Crinkles said.

Did I need to draw him a diagram on the whiteboard? I took a breath. "Like, for instance, Ham and Scar."

I was worried my bombshell might create a mini riot here—or at least cake smashed in my face—but the wild elves kept hoovering down their dessert.

Crinkles, however, was scandalized by the insinuation. "Ham and Scar were the high scorers at the last night's game!"

"Yes, I know. But they were brought in to replace Crumble. What if Crumble rejoins the team?"

The constable rubbed his whiskerless chin. "That's always been the plan." Apparently even he didn't know the particulars of Crumble's health situation—or if he did, he wasn't saying. Discretion wasn't the constable's watchword, though, so I guessed that Crumble had kept his prognosis a secret from his coach.

Then the constable's gaze sharpened—as sharp as that round-eyed countenance could ever seem.

"Did some of the Tinkertown players put you up to this?" Crinkles asked me.

I wanted to say it was my own brilliant deduction, but I had to be honest. "One of them suggested it, yes."

Crinkles slapped his hand on the table. "Dollars to donuts *he's* the one to want to get rid of Crumble. What's his name? I'll have a word with him."

"What he said made sense."

Ham burped. "It wasn't us," he said in a deep voice that was almost indistinguishable from his belch.

"Not us," Scar echoed.

I was shocked. They'd been gobbling down cake, making grunting noises, and licking icing off their fingertips with such gusto, I just assumed they weren't following our conversation.

"Where did you go after the game last night?" I asked them.

"We came here," Ham said.

"Here," Scar chimed.

"Why didn't you go to the celebration at the Tinkertown Tavern?"

"Not wanted, I think," Ham said. "Elves held signs for us to go home. Not good sports."

Scar nodded. "Not."

"They didn't want to rock the boat," Crinkles explained to me. "So I had Ollie bring them back here. He made them cupcakes to celebrate."

"Good cupcakes," Scar said.

Ollie could bake a mean cupcake—I could vouch for that. That would be worth skipping the tavern for. I could also see how the wild elves would have assumed that their appearance at the celebration last night would have caused conflict. It showed surprising tact . . . for wild elves.

And who had just been lecturing Snowball that elves were elves?

Crinkles shook his head. "Fact is, I assumed that if anyone might get attacked last night, it would be Ham and Scar."

"Funny that they're being accused now of attacking Crumble." Ollie frowned. "Well, not *funny* funny."

"No one's accusing them," I said. "But we have to ask questions, right?"

Crinkles, who had the job to ask questions and investigate, looked more befuddled than usual. "Investigating our players could wreak havoc with iceball season. And I'm the Twinklers coach. How would it look if I arrested an Ice Beaver?" His expression grew even more troubled. "Or one of my own players."

Before I could argue, the constabulary's landline rang.

Ollie jumped up to answer it. He stood stock still with the receiver at his ear, eyes opening ever wider as he listened. "Hold him for as long as you can—we'll be right there."

He chunked the phone onto its cradle and spun toward us, all Barney Fife alertness. "Galloping gumdrops! That was Nip. He caught the trophy thief red-handed."

Crinkles was on his feet and reaching for his tall constable hat that strapped around his chin. "He's at Tinkertown Arena?"

"Outside the players' changing room. Says the trophy thief's locked inside."

I was jumping up to follow them, but that last detail gave me pause. "How could he have caught the thief red-handed when the trophy was stolen last night?"

Crinkles frowned. "I guess we'll find out when we talk to him."

Whether it was intentional or not, I took that "we" as an invitation. We were all almost out the door before Crinkles remembered Ham and Scar.

"You fellows can clean up here—but don't work too hard. We've got a practice tonight." He looked worried. "I hope I can wrap up this trophy business by then."

The wild elves remained at the table with the leftover cake as we left.

Outside, Ollie sighed. "I doubt we'll ever see any of that cake again."

Crinkles was in such a flutter over catching the trophy thief that he couldn't even lament the loss of the cake. "Are you coming with us, Mrs. Claus?"

"Yes—I'll be right behind you. I'll alert Jake Frost too."

He'd been hired to find the trophy. He would probably want to be there when the thief was collared.

I texted the essentials to Jake and then hurried over to where Wobbler was waiting. "We need to get to the Tinkertown Arena."

Wobbler gaped at me. "But we're scheduled to pick up a dress at the Order of Elven Seamstresses this afternoon, and then we're supposed to return to the castle."

My adrenaline was still rushing. "Plans have changed. We're going to catch a criminal."

The reindeer froze. "A real criminal, who committed a crime?"

"Yes," I said impatiently. "We need to hurry."

I hopped onto the sleigh like Batman jumping into the Batmobile. Except my engine didn't rev and zoom off from the bat cave. It didn't move at all.

I'd forgotten. "On, Wobbler!"

The sleigh still didn't budge.

I jumped off to see what was wrong. The animal's knees were locked, and the whites showed in his terrified eyes.

"What's the matter?" I asked.

"I'm sorry." His voice quavered. "Dealing with violent criminals was not in my job description when I agreed to do this."

For heaven's sake. "You won't have to do anything involving risk."

He snuffled skeptically at that. "I am not a crime-fighting reindeer."

"You don't have to be. Just drop me off in front of the arena."

"And what if the criminal escapes and takes us both hostage? He might decide to use this vehicle as a getaway sleigh."

He'd chosen a bad moment to panic and dig in his hooves. How was I going to get to Tinkertown?

I was about to start pleading when I heard a motor buzzing down the boulevard toward us. It was Jake Frost—and his snowmobile had a sidecar.

I flagged him down.

"What's wrong?" he asked.

I didn't waste time explaining, I just jumped into the sidecar and told him to keep driving.

Wobbler called after us, but his words were lost to me. I twisted and called out, "I'll be back!"

Jake gunned it all the way to Tinkertown, and I filled him in on the few details we'd received from the old janitor.

The detective looked puzzled. "The story doesn't make sense. Do you think Nip's confused?"

"He had Ollie convinced that he'd caught the guy we're looking for."

When we arrived at the arena, Jake pulled in right next to the constabulary's snowmobile by the door. We hopped out and ran inside. I glanced at the still-empty trophy case along the way to the locker rooms.

The locker rooms were downstairs. In a dim corridor, an agitated Nip's arthritic fingers sifted through the many keys on his large ring, seeking the right one. He trembled from the excitement of it all. He'd clearly already explained the situation to the constable, but when he saw Jake and me, the story bubbled out of him again.

"I was just having my sandwich for lunch when I thought I heard something," the old elf said. "I wasn't asleep this time! So I crept down the hallway, following the noise, stealthy-like, until I came to this door. I peeked in and saw a figure moving around in there, and I caught a glimpse of the trophy. So before whoever it was could hear me and make a run for it, I slammed the door shut, threw the bolt, and then locked the deadbolt with my key." He frowned as his shaking fingers sifted through the pile. Only now I can't remember which key." There seemed to be a hundred on his big ring. He held one up an inch from his face and squinted at it. "I think it might be this one."

Crinkles and Ollie stood at the ready. Ollie had his nightstick out, which made the constable frown. "What do you think you're going to do with that?"

"Catch him?" Ollie said.

The constable clucked in disgust. "Put that thing away. We can't go around hitting folks."

"But what if he's the same elf who attacked Crumble?" Ollie asked.

Foolishly, I hadn't been thinking about that possibility, but Ollie was right. We didn't know what kind of elf we'd be dealing with when Nip unlocked that door. Suddenly *I* wished for a nightstick.

It took a few moments for the janitor to fumble the correct key into the lock. By the time he finally did open the creaky old door, we were all rigid with tension.

Crinkles called out in a shaky voice, "Whoever you are, just put the trophy down and come out with your hands up."

"I didn't steal it," came the nervous reply from inside the dark room.

I frowned. I knew that voice but couldn't place it at first. Then Crumble's brother, Frankie, stepped into view. He was wearing his work clothes—a dark-green tunic with a leather apron over it. He set the trophy on the ground and then raised his hands in surrender. Ollie rushed forward and grabbed the Golden Bootie as if he were rescuing a kidnapped child.

"Frankie?" Crinkles appeared more perplexed than usual. "What would a furniture maker do with an iceball trophy?"

"*I* didn't want the thing," Frankie said. "I was just returning it."

"From where?" I asked.

He looked at me, then at Jake Frost. Red climbed into his cheeks. He hadn't expected there to be so many people witnessing his capture. "It was at my place—Crumble took it."

"Crumble!" we all exclaimed.

"Why?" Crinkles asked.

Frankie expelled a long breath, making him appear to shrink two sizes. "He'd hit the sauce and got morose over never winning any more trophies or playing again. Said he just wanted to have the trophy for a little while. I told him that he needed to grow up and accept that he wasn't the Crumble Woolly of ten years ago." He looked at me. "That's when we had the argument about him coming to work more at the furniture store. I tried to explain that the challenges and triumphs of the handcrafted upholstered furniture business could be as satisfying as the glory of the iceball rink. But as I said, it was no use. The fight escalated, and he threw the trophy at me and ran out the door. I guess he went back to the arena then."

I was trying to work out whether their fight could have made Frankie mad enough to follow his brother to the arena, but Crinkles was more concerned about whether the trophy had been damaged. He examined it closely.

"Why didn't you tell the constable this last night?" Jake asked.

Frankie sighed. "Crumble's been having enough troubles lately. I didn't want it to get out that he was a thief as well and that he'd been drinking at the iceball rink. I thought I could just sneak it back to the arena, and no one would be the wiser."

Once a protective older brother, always a protective brother.

"So why didn't you just put the trophy in the case?" I asked.

"I thought someone might see me out there, so I snuck in the back way and was just going to leave it here, I swear." He blinked back tears. "I'm very sorry."

Crinkles seemed satisfied that the trophy was unharmed by the brothers' tussle.

"Am I going to jail?" Frankie asked.

The constable was momentarily stumped by the question. "Well, you didn't actually steal the Golden Bootie. We could hardly arrest you for returning it."

A glimmer of hope shone in the furniture maker's eyes.

Crinkles continued, "Of course, Crumble did steal it, but the Golden Bootie's back, so there's been no harm done. Getting conked on the head seems punishment enough."

Frankie exhaled in relief.

"We can't arrest anybody now anyway," Ollie said. "We're all full up. Ham and Scar are living in the jail cell."

We all left the locker room area, climbing the stairs back up to the arena level. Nip seemed buoyed by the afternoon's events. There was a bounce in his arthritic step now. "I guess I'm still doing okay if I can catch a thief." He glanced apologetically at Frankie. "I *thought* you were a thief."

"I understand," Frankie said.

"You were even trying to be quiet, and I heard you with my own two ears," Nip bragged. "Even though I had the radio on."

"You did good," Ollie said.

Jake patted him on the shoulder. "You should hang up your broom and come work for me."

The old man laughed and shrugged modestly. "Nah—somebody's got to look after the old arena."

The trophy was returned to its rightful place. Crinkles closed the cabinet firmly. "That's that. Feels good to have everything sorted out."

"Except the attempted murder," I reminded him.

"Oh. Right." He looked up at a large clock on the wall. His eyes bulged. "Suffering sugarplums! We better get back, Ollie, or we'll be late for iceball practice."

The deputies tore off.

In the parking lot, Jake sighed as we watched Frankie trudge off in the direction of his furniture store. A little voice in the back of my mind wondered if we all still weren't taking too much at face value.

"Do you think that argument could have made him mad enough to attack his own brother?" I asked Jake.

"I doubt it. An elf who worries so much about his brother's reputation that he'd risk getting branded a thief himself probably doesn't want to kill him."

"That takes us back to square one." Who attacked Crumble?

If only he would regain his memory.

"Speaking of taking you back . . ." Jake nodded at the most recent sleigh arrival in the parking lot. A remorseful Wobbler stood in front of my sleigh, his head hanging low.

"I guess I can get back to Christmastown on my own," I said to Jake. He nodded and ambled off to his snowmobile.

Almost before I was within hearing distance, Wobbler was apologizing. "I'm sorry. I panicked. I do that sometimes."

"It's okay," I said, patting his furry neck with my gloved hand. "I sprang a surprise on you, and you weren't prepared."

"That's my problem, though. I panic. I told you a lie too—during my interview I said that the reindeer made fun of me because of my wobbly legs when I was a calf, but that's not why I was declared a misfit. It's my nerves that get wobbly, not my legs."

"I never noticed that before today."

"Because I was overcompensating, trying to appear self-confident and bold. I was faking it."

"Well, there must be *some* kernel of confidence in you. You fooled me."

"Oh sure," he said, rolling his eyes. "For a whole day." He shook his head, setting his harness bells to jingling. "I deserve to be put out to pasture now—or worse, to be sent to the Farthest Frozen Reaches to be eaten by a polar bear."

"Don't be ridiculous."

"Why not? You could choose any reindeer, and you've already got Cannonball. Once he hears about what happened today, he'll probably insist on stepping back into the harness."

"He won't hear about it," I promised. "No one will. You're doing fine—we all get panicky sometimes. And if Jake hadn't come along, you probably would have worked up your courage to bring me here anyway."

I wasn't entirely sure that last part was true, but it seemed to make Wobbler feel better. He stood a little taller, assured that I wouldn't fire him and he wouldn't end up as polar bear dinner.

I checked my phone. "We probably still have time to make it to the Order of Elven Seamstresses."

He pawed the ground. "Right you are."

I climbed onto the sleigh. This time, for his sake, I didn't hesitate to say the words. "On, Wobbler!"

Chapter Eight

"Have we thought about expanding Santa's workshops lately?" I asked at dinner that evening.

The table fell silent. All six of the Claus castle residents—plus Quasar—were present at the table. I was sitting at one end, Nick on the other. In between, Tiffany and Christopher were at their usual places on one side, and my mother-in-law, Pamela, and Lucia were opposite them. It created quite a contrast: the friendly side versus the imperious side.

Quasar stood in the corner behind Lucia, munching from a bowl of grain. At my unexpected question, even he stopped chewing and lifted his head.

Nick eyed me curiously. "Right now we have more than enough to keep us busy. What do you have in mind?"

"Soft drinks," I said.

Santa's workshops made toys and games, but there were other enterprises that fell under the Santa's workshop umbrella and were overseen by members of the

Claus family. The biggest were the Wrapping Works and the Candy Cane Factory. Given that, my suggestion didn't seem too outlandish. At least to me.

Pamela, who was sitting erect in her perfectly tailored ice-blue suit, her hair pulled back neatly in a bun, clearly held the opposite opinion. She narrowed her gaze on me. "What do soft drinks have to do with Christmas?"

"Don't people drink soda pop during festive occasions?" I asked.

"I do," Christopher piped up. "But elves like eggnog."

"Or grog," Lucia put in.

I agreed that most elves preferred eggnog or hot beverages, but didn't Claire's success prove that cold drinks could catch on?

"Well, there's an elf who makes really good soft drinks, but he can't afford to open his own factory, so . . ."

Tiffany groaned. "You're talking about Spritz Greenbell, aren't you?"

I admitted that I was, and my sister-in-law, uncharacteristically, could barely contain her irritation. I hadn't expected anyone else at the table to know Spritz, but Tiffany owned a tea shop in town and had apparently had a run-in with him.

"He came by my shop last summer and wanted me to sell his sodas."

"What did you say?"

"That my business was tea, not sodas." She shook her head. "That's when he got angry. He called me narrow-minded and anti-fizz."

Pamela's mouth pursed into a moue of distaste. "He

doesn't sound like the kind of elf we'd want to do business with."

I wasn't giving up yet. "His sodas are really good. He's just had a hard time raising capital."

"I just don't see why the Claus family should get involved," Nick said. "How does it fit in with our family business?"

I'd thought of this. "Maybe we could rebrand them: Santa's Spritzers. We could do special Christmas flavors too, like Christmas Cream Soda or Jolly Ginger."

Tiffany looked doubtful. "Did Spritz agree to this?"

"Well, no. I've been thinking of this on my own. I didn't want to raise his hopes only to dash them if there was no chance."

"There's no chance," Lucia declared, and no one seemed inclined to contradict her. "We're overextended as it is. We don't have nearly enough elves working on the snowman shelters. At the rate we're going, we won't get the new one by Peppermint Pond finished in time for summer."

"Couldn't we spare some elves from the workshops for the snowman shelters?" Pamela suggested.

"We don't want to fall behind in Christmas production," Nick pointed out.

Lucia grunted. "The problem is all these distractions. Halloween, Thanksgiving, Valentine's Day, and now Saint Patrick's Day. The elves get so sidetracked by all these nonessential, piddly holidays that other things are falling by the wayside, like vital Santaland infrastructure projects."

Her words riled me up. Like most Clauses, she assumed Christmas was the only holiday worth celebrating. I had to force myself not to pop off. We were in Santaland, after all. And though I was Mrs. Claus, I was relatively new to the North Pole. Some of the holidays Lucia was grousing about were ones I had introduced to the country after Nick and I were married. As Lucia well knew.

Christopher, who was thirteen and was nearly a decade away from taking on the mantle of Santa Claus from Nick, put his fork down. "I have a lot of elf friends, Aunt Lucia, and they don't think these holidays are piddly or nonessential. Maybe you spend too much time around reindeer. To elves, festivities big and small are as essential as working and singing and breathing."

Listening to him, I felt like jumping up and whooping like Juniper did when the Twinklers scored a goal. Contradicting Lucia took guts, and he'd done it articulately and calmly.

"Well put," Nick agreed.

Lucia rarely let anyone else have the last word, however. "It won't seem so festive and fun in a few months' time when Santaland's frozen citizens have a melt-off. Next to that, all this leprechauning around will seem like a big time waster."

I had to give Lucia credit: she was the master of the buzzkill.

Jingles wheeled in the dessert trolley and handed around plates with a lovely green cake in the shape of a shamrock. Each cake was a sweet masterpiece.

"This is what I mean." Lucia nodded at her plate in disgust. "Think of all the elf hours Felice and her helpers in the kitchen spent making these goofy little food fripperies—and we'll probably gobble them down in five minutes."

Pamela bristled in her chair. "No elf hours were wasted. *I* made the cakes. I figured we'd all be eating out tomorrow at the Saint Patrick's Day street fair, so I prepared these as a special treat for tonight."

An awkward silence fell, and two red blotches appeared in Lucia's cheeks. It was beautiful to see.

I caught Christopher's gaze and smiled.

"The cakes look great, Grandma," he said.

"Thank you." She picked up her dessert fork. "Go ahead and gobble them down, everyone. See if anyone can beat Lucia's five-minute prediction."

I probably could have, but this cake demanded savoring. My mother-in-law could be challenging to deal with sometimes, but the woman knew her way around pastry. Her desserts rivaled the best cake shops in town, and this cake was no exception. It was even better than Ollie's green velvet cake.

Then again, my favorite dessert was usually the one in front of me.

"Are you ready for the talent show tomorrow, Jingles?" Tiffany asked the steward.

Serving at dinner, Jingles usually did his best to be what he never was the rest of the day: inconspicuous. He stepped forward now, clasping his white-gloved hands modestly in front of him.

"Yes, ma'am. Thank you for asking. But of course I shouldn't talk about how hard I've prepared, since Santa can't show favoritism"—his gaze slanted pointedly at Nick—"even if he knows how diligently I've rehearsed my song and how much positive affirmation winning would give me."

Nick met my gaze across the table. I knew he'd be happy when the talent show was over and Jingles stopped dropping passive-aggressive hints about how much he wanted to win.

"Warm up on your coffee, Santa?" Jingles asked, silver coffee pot at the ready.

Nick waved. "No, thank you, Jingles."

The steward retreated and went through the door back to the kitchen, humming "Kathleen Mavourneen."

"I hope Jingles does well," Tiffany said. "He's going to be impossible to live with if he loses."

Lucia agreed. "It'll be hard enough to live with him if he wins."

Despite my best efforts to restrain myself, my cake was gone too soon. As my second dessert of the day hit my bloodstream, I felt a pleasant sugar high. My thoughts started percolating, and a solution to Lucia's problem occurred to me.

"If you need more workers for the snowman shelters," I said to her, "why not talk to Ham and Scar?"

Her brows rose. "The wild elves?"

"They're really not doing much at the constabulary, and two elves from the Farthest Frozen Reaches would probably be great at ice construction."

And then they'd been living and contributing work in the town instead of simply taking up space in the constabulary.

To my surprise, Lucia gave the suggestion serious consideration. "You know, that's not a bad idea."

"You could at least give them a trial run."

She nodded. "I'll go talk to them tonight. All the other elves will be at the Saint Patrick's Day celebration tomorrow. Might be a good time to see what the wild elves can do without ruffling the feathers of the native worker elves."

Later that night as we were lying in bed, entwined under the covers, Nick pulled me close. "You did a good thing."

The bedroom was dark except for a faint glow from the fireplace grate and the faint, soothing constellation of twinkle lights in the ceiling. This was always the best part of the day—those blissful moments of alone time with Nick, when we both set aside the worries of the day and just relaxed.

Or tried to.

I couldn't quite expel all the uneasiness from my mind. After all, whoever had attacked Crumble was still at large.

"Telling Lucia to hire the wild elves was a clever idea," he said. "If Santalanders see them doing vital work, they'll feel a lot better about their being here and playing for the Twinklers."

I shrugged. "It also seemed like a natural solution to Lucia's problem."

"And you were very kindhearted to think of it. And to want to help Spritz too."

I glanced up at him. "But you still aren't interested in starting a soda pop factory."

"No, I'm not," he said.

"Then I really didn't help Spritz, did I?"

"You can't solve everyone's problems." He kissed the top of my head as he drew me closer still. "But I love you for trying."

The amazing thing was, I *had* solved Spritz's problems. I just didn't know it yet.

Chapter Nine

"I had to find someone to be the second leprechaun," Claire said to rationalize her change of heart as we waited for Spritz to finish dressing.

When he emerged from the back room of the Santaland Scoop, it was hard to keep from smiling. The velvet suit had been laundered since Crumble's accident, but the way it hung on Spritz's thin frame was almost comical. The hat was two sizes too large, as were the stockings drooping around his ankles.

"You look incredible!" Juniper said, tugging the hat back so it didn't fall over Spritz's eyes. "Just remember to keep your pants up."

The elf tried to view himself in the chrome siding of a cabinet. It was probably just as well that he couldn't see his reflection. "There's so much to remember," he said worriedly.

"You'll be fine," Claire assured him. "You're just taking tickets. Butterbean will be the one actually taking customers up in the balloon."

Juniper and I were there to help Claire ferry the last of her supplies out to Peppermint Pond. Jake and Butterbean were already at the park working on getting the balloon inflated. Claire had come back for the large wood placard displaying her menu and prices that would hook onto the side of the ice-cream cart. Juniper and I were going to pull a little wagon full of other supplies.

The Santaland Scoop was going to serve Claire's Saint Paddy's Day mint milkshakes, cones in several flavors, and shamrock pops—pistachio popsicles shaped like a four-leaf clover.

"I was up half the night making sure I had enough," Claire said, double-checking that she had everything before we set out to the park. I peered into the supply wagon. In addition to cups, napkins, and straws, I spied several cartons of Spritz Sodas.

Curious, I eyed the menu board again. Two drink offerings had been added: a Rainbow Fizz and an Irish Float.

"What are those?" I thought I'd tried everything on the Santaland Scoop's menu.

"Two late additions," she explained. "Spritz and I came up with them last night—one's a float made from rainbow sherbet mixed with Ginger Fizz, and the other's a more traditional float with vanilla ice cream, chocolate syrup, soda, and a shot of Irish cream."

"Your cart is going to be *very* popular," Juniper predicted.

"I worried about competing with Sniffle's Grog Wagon," Claire said, "but he said he wasn't worried about losing business."

Sniffles had good reason to feel confident. Nothing lured elves away from their grog.

I could see now why the normally proud Spritz had agreed to don a leprechaun suit. He had sold several cases of his sodas to Claire, whose cart and balloon ride were going to be the sensations of the Saint Patrick's Day event. If the specialty floats went over, she might decide to invest in his soda business.

Just how big a sensation the Santaland Scoop would be that day became clear when we turned the cart into the parkway and saw Butterbean's hot-air balloon rising above the evergreen trees around Peppermint Pond. The balloon was decorated like a vanilla ice-cream cone, with a Santaland Scoop logo on the cone. Elves crowded around to watch the bursts of flame inflating the balloon, and a few were already queued up to take a ride. Brave souls.

Elves were also waiting for milkshakes, including a familiar face. I gave Juniper a nudge. "There's Smudge."

"Really? I didn't notice." She folded her arms.

From the line, Smudge glanced over at her, smiled sheepishly, and waved.

The balloon aside, there was so much going on in the park, it was hard to take it all in. The Swingin' Shamrocks were in the band shell playing "When Irish Eyes Are Smiling"—the first of many times we'd be hearing that tune, I imagined. Their rendition had the crowd singing and swaying. As we helped Claire get her cart ready, Juniper and I looked around at all the other booths. All the treats of Santaland were represented, along with booths selling novelty toys, crafts, and the ubiquitous leprechaun hats. Along the fringes of the park, elves were practicing their various artistic skills in advance of the talent show, which was going to take place on a specially built platform under a huge banner announcing SANTALAND'S GOT TALENT! If the elf next to me juggling multiple sparkling pins was anything to go by, Jingles was going to have some stiff competition this afternoon.

"We couldn't have asked for a better day." Shading her eyes with her hand, Juniper looked up at Butterbean's balloon against the blue sky. Two thick ropes tethered the balloon's basket to the ground. The balloon passengers would only go to the top of the treetops and back down again, but even that prospect seemed exciting to the elves, especially when Butterbean, at his most exuberant, was promising, "Who knows? You might find that pot of gold at the end of the rainbow!"

He was like a pint-sized P. T. Barnum, and the crowd loved it.

"Will you go up?" Juniper asked me.

I laughed. "You know me better than that."

"I think I'll go up later." She checked the time on her cell phone. "Right now I want to relieve Candy at the library booth. We're displaying children's artwork. You should come by."

"I will, but I'm going to run by the hospital first. I thought I'd take Nurse Cinnamon a milkshake." I also wanted to see if Crumble had recovered any memory of his attack.

And, to be honest, the thought of Crumble alone in that hospital with Nurse Cinnamon made me uneasy.

I stood in line, bought a mint shake, and set off.

Wobbler, who was waiting on a side street off the park, moved toward me. "Where are we going?" he asked.

"I'm going to the hospital, but you don't have to bother. I'll walk."

"Walk?"

You'd have thought I'd said I was going to walk on my hands.

"It's not far."

"I know, but what will people think if I let you walk?"

"They'll think I felt like stretching my legs. Just chill out. Would you like me to find you a lichen brownie? I'm sure someone's selling them around here somewhere."

"I don't need to eat on the job."

"You're a ruminant," I reminded him. To show how free he was, I undid the buckles that attached Wobbler's harness to the sleigh. "There."

He seemed paralyzed, as if I'd undressed him in public. "You just want me to stand around, cooling my hooves?"

"Yes. Just relax and enjoy yourself."

Asking Wobbler to relax was akin to asking him to tap dance. Walking away, I sensed his eyes following me. I felt like a mother dropping her forlorn toddler off at daycare. Was it so bad to want to walk somewhere?

Before heading through town, I turned back to look once more at the park. Even more elves had arrived. Butterbean was loading his first passengers into the balloon's basket. Across Peppermint Pond, I could just make out the snowman ice shelter rising in the shade of two tall cedars on the sloping bank in the distance. The snowmen who summered there would have an incredible view of the park and the town.

I hoped Ham and Scar were working out. Getting the shelters finished would take a load off Nick's mind. Lucia's too.

In contrast to Peppermint Pond, the area of town around the hospital seemed very quiet, almost deserted. Most businesses either had closed for the day or were operating with a shoestring staff.

The hospital was also quiet. On the way in, I passed Jolly, one of orderlies, taking an eggnog break outside. He looked wistfully out toward Peppermint Pond. "I can see the balloon from here," he said.

He was right. The giant ice-cream cone was up in the air, hovering above the trees. I could make out Butterbean in green, and three passengers waving down at friends on the ground.

Inside the infirmary, Nurse Cinnamon was sitting at reception reading a magazine called *Elf Health Today.* The lead article was "Getting More Refined Sugar in Your Diet."

"I can help with that," I said.

Nurse Cinnamon looked up at me, noting the Santaland Scoop to-go cup I was holding out to her. "For me?" she asked, as if no one had ever given her anything in her life.

I nodded. "How's the patient today?"

She sighed. "Still headachy. He's finally resting peacefully, though, and his color's better. Doc gave him a sedative to help him sleep."

"Has he recovered any more memory?"

"Not so far. These things just take time." She took a tentative sip from the cup's straw.

I looked down the hallway at an orderly going into Crumble's room. "Funny when there are two orderlies for every patient," I said.

"No, just one today," she replied. "This milkshake is delicious."

I frowned. "I talked to Jolly outside, but someone I don't recognize just walked into Crumble's room."

Nurse Cinnamon was on her feet instantly, and both of us ran toward Crumble's room.

As we opened the door, an elf wearing hospital scrubs and a ski mask was standing with a pillow over Crumble's face.

"Stop!" Nurse Cinnamon called out.

Seeing us, the imposter elf dropped the pillow and bolted for the door. The nurse rushed to check on Crumble. I ran after the elf.

The fake orderly was half a corridor ahead of me. I was gaining on him though, and he was headed for the hospital entrance, where I hoped I could engage the help of Jolly to catch him.

At the entrance, however, the two elves met at the exact moment the door opened. The imposter plowed right into Jolly, knocking him to the ground. The orderly groaned, writhing on the linoleum.

"What was that about?" he said, sitting up and cradling one hand to himself painfully. "That lunatic elf broke my wrist."

"Nurse Cinnamon's in Crumble's room," I said. "She'll see to you." I took off running again.

The collision had put the elf a half block ahead of me. I kept running, although the terrain was more slippery out here than in the infirmary. Elves were more agile on the mix of ice and snow on Santaland sidewalks than I was. He was getting away from me. Worse, he was heading for Peppermint Pond, probably hoping to lose himself in the crowd there.

Halfway to the park, I passed Wobbler standing at the ready. He had evidently not followed my advice to chill out.

Now he trotted down the street, parallel to me. "What's happening?" he called out.

My lungs were already tired, and I had to shout between huffs, "Crumble's assassin! Ahead!"

We'd reached the edge of the park, which was twice as crowded now as it had been when I'd left. The sleigh buses had brought loads of elves from Tinkertown, and there was yet another one unloading right in front of us, which stopped Wobbler and slowed me down considerably. I threaded through the disembarking elves, but as I stood on the sidewalk at the edge of the park, I worried I'd lost the elf I was chasing. Then I saw a ripple of disturbance—elves turning in annoyance and shouting at someone running. I plunged back into the chase.

"Mrs. Claus! Be careful!" Wobbler called after me.

I probably should have heeded his warning. Although I yelled, "Stop him!" as I ran after the elf, my yelling just made elves turn toward me, not the elf who was deftly zigzagging through the many booths and clusters of visitors. Whoever this was, he was definitely in good shape. He moved through the crowd like an agility dog going through an obstacle course. I, on the other hand, was colliding with elves and half slipping on the packed snow underfoot. At one point I nearly plowed into a snowman in a leprechaun hat.

"Watch it!" the snowman shouted after me.

"Sorry!"

I was tiring out, but I knew the elf couldn't escape. There was nowhere for him to go.

Nowhere but up.

Spritz was just letting passengers into the basket for the next balloon ride when the fake orderly yanked the boarding elf out and slammed the basket door closed. He pulled a knife on a terrified Butterbean, whose blue eyes bulged in fear. He had no option but to let out a blast of air, and the basket began to rise.

"No!" I yelled. He was getting away.

Spritz, shocked, tried to hop to get hold of the basket, but he was too short to make it. I took a running leap and managed to grab hold and swing my leg up over the side.

It was not the wisest thing I've ever done.

Even though he was trapped in a basket with a knife-wielding maniac, Butterbean pulled me in. As I flopped onto the basket's floor like a beached fish, he whispered, "Why did you do that? He can't get away—we're tethered."

"Not for long."

I nodded to the masked elf, who was unhooking the clasp of one tether.

"Oh crumbs," Butterbean said.

On trembling legs, I rose to my feet, hugging the side of the basket. Now that he'd seen Butterbean do it, the elf released another blast of hot air from the canister, causing both Butterbean and me to jump. In response, the basket swayed, and Butterbean and I grabbed hold of each other.

Because it was only tethered on one side now, the basket was tipping as it rose. Also, the sides had been constructed with elves in mind, so I had to crouch to keep from feeling as if I was about to pitch over the side. I was practically on my knees.

I peeked over the basket's lip. The crowds below were a receding mass of gaping, upturned faces. Once our hijacker unclipped the other rope, the balloon would soon be on its way across Santaland, headed toward who only knows where. I could see beautiful Castle Kringle on Sugarplum Mountain, and I was pierced with a sharp longing to be there, back in my toasty bedroom with Nick. Yet the light breeze seemed to be drifting the other way, which would carry us toward the distant, craggy peaks of Mount Myrrh. Was that where we would end up, off in the wilds of the Farthest Frozen Reaches? Assuming that any of us could manage to land this thing.

My stomach roiled.

"Why are you doing this?" I asked the masked elf.

"Shut up." He worked to get the second tether unhooked before the basket ended up being overturned by the imbalance.

That voice struck a chord in my memory. I'd spoken with this elf before today. "You're Wick," I guessed.

"Shh." Through tightly sealed lips, Butterbean whispered, "He told us to be quiet."

The rope was finally unclamped, the basket pitched,

and the hijacker elf turned back to us, whipping off his mask. It was Wick, all right. I should have guessed it was an iceball player by the way he'd tackled Jolly and then moved through the crowd.

"I'm only doing this to escape, Mrs. Claus."

"But why hurt Crumble? He's your former teammate."

"Right. And I wanted to keep him former. Without him, we finally had a shot at winning this year—my last year—but *he* wanted to come back."

"*Wanted* to," I said in disgust. Was that what all this had been about? Winning the Golden Bootie? As the balloon started to float over Peppermint Pond, I couldn't bring myself to care about abstract ideas like patient confidentiality anymore. "Doc told Crumble that he couldn't play. Ever. You attempted murder for no reason at all."

The elf's face fell. "Doc said he couldn't play?"

"Yes—but even so, was a stupid trophy really worth someone's life to you?"

"I've been playing my whole life," he argued. "We finally had a shot with those two wild elves. They're really good."

"So you followed Crumble that night and decided to kill him."

"No! I'd gone back to the stadium because I forgot my gym bag. I saw Crumble skating. It was a spur-of-the-moment thing."

Spur-of-the-moment attempted murder I could almost believe. "There was nothing spur-of-the-moment about your trying to smother him today, though."

He hung his head. "I talked to Doc this morning.

He was saying Crumble was bound to start remembering more. Crumble might have seen me at the arena. I couldn't risk it. Then I would have been out for the rest of the season."

"Guess what. Looks like you're out anyway."

That obvious, salient point hadn't seemed to occur to him. As it sank in, his eyes looked even more frantic, and he let out another blast of fiery air. Seeing flames shooting up toward a swath of canvas holding our little basket in the air made my stomach flip. I knew that was how balloons worked, but I couldn't stop the mental vision of the whole thing going up like a match, or the Hindenburg.

Butterbean groaned. It was a sound that said *We're doomed.*

I had to think. *Talk Wick down.*

"It's lucky for you that Crumble is going to be okay," I said. "You *didn't* murder him, Wick. There's a way out for you."

"Yeah, I found a way out. This is it."

"I mean, you could go back and turn yourself in. I know Judge Merrybutton. He'll be merciful."

He snorted. "He exiled an elf for selling reindeer."

"Because it was barbaric," Butterbean blurted out.

I glared at Butterbean. He wasn't helping, even though he was correct. Hunting or trapping reindeer and selling them was considered an unforgiveable crime in Santaland.

I was at a loss for what to do next. Could Butterbean and I overpower Wick? Probably not . . . or we might die in the attempt.

"Mrs. Claus!"

At the sound of the disembodied voice close by, Butterbean and I exchanged confused glances. That sounded like . . . Wobbler?

I turned and leaned over the side to look down. Unfortunately, so did Butterbean and Wick. The imbalance almost caused me, the tallest, to tumble out. I grabbed hold of the basket and bent my knees farther to lower my center of gravity. My legs ached, but I barely noticed. I had hope again.

Below us, Wobbler was flying, and just behind him, Nick, dressed in his best Santa suit for judging the talent contest, was at the reins of his everyday sleigh pulled by a team of elite reindeer. My heart leapt at the sight of them, although I couldn't imagine how on earth they were going to rescue us. Especially Wobbler. I worried he might get hurt.

Not to mention, having a reindeer-drawn sleigh flying toward us like a missile was slightly terrifying.

Like a rodeo cowboy with a lasso, Nick spun a rope over his head, and as soon as he got close enough, he let it loose. The rope had a pick at the end of it, a piece of emergency equipment that could secure rope in ice or some other surface to achieve purchase. The pick landed on the floor next to us, and Butterbean and I immediately fell on it to hook it to the edge of the basket. Nick and his reindeer team began towing us back toward the earth. The pressure was tipping the basket so that we all had to cling to the edges.

"Let that go." Wick made a lunge for the pick.

But as he did, Wobbler let out a yell and looked as if he was going to dive-bomb us from the other side. Butterbean and I screamed, and Wick whirled. But of course Wobbler didn't hit us. He just buzzed around us like a mosquito, distracting Wick.

My heart lifted. We were really being rescued—I wasn't going to die on the crags of Mount Myrrh.

It took all the effort of Nick's team to tug us down, and as we approached solid ground, we were far from where we'd taken off. For a moment, it looked as if we were headed for a crash landing on the snowman shelter. We would have to get ready to jump off as soon as it was safe.

Wick had the same idea, except he decided to take one last dash for freedom. When the basket was twenty feet from the ground, he leapt over the side. He plummeted like a stone, hit the ground, and then rolled back to his feet. He was hop-running; he'd obviously hurt his leg. Before I could take in what was happening to Wick, Butterbean unhooked the rope, took control of the pressure valve again, and pulled something that eased us down the rest of the way. It wasn't a soft landing, but the abruptness of it wasn't enough to break any of our bones. It just left me rattled.

I looked out at Wick running—he was heading north on foot now. He passed close to the snowman shelter. As he came even with it, two elves streaked out and tackled him in the snow. Ham and Scar had caught him.

Lucia strode out with a rope and bound Wick's hands behind his back.

After parking his sleigh, Nick hurried to find me. "April."

I threw my arms around him and buried myself in his solid, woolly warmth. I'd never been so happy just to have my feet on the ground. Standing with my arms around Nick was unbearably sweet.

Beside us, Butterbean fell to his knees and looked as if he might just kiss the snowy ground. I knew exactly how he felt. I kissed Nick instead. "Thanks for the rescue."

"You should be thanking Wobbler," he said. "It was his quick thinking that came up with the idea of lassoing the runaway balloon."

I wasn't going to kiss Wobbler, but I gave him a huge hug and made a mental note to make sure he had the swankiest digs the Santaland stables could provide.

"I didn't choke," the reindeer said, amazed at himself.

"Of course you didn't. You were a hero."

He shook himself modestly. "It was nothing. I guess I just tapped into that courage you were telling me about."

The Christmastown Constabulary's snowmobile buzzed up, and Crinkles and Ollie got out to make the arrest. I'd never seen Constable Crinkles looks so shaken as when he had to take his team's oldest player and captain into custody.

"Why did you do it, Wick?" Crinkles asked. The anger in his voice was the constable speaking, the hurt was pure coach.

Wick hung his head. "This felt like our big chance to finally leave our mark in iceball history."

I couldn't predict what would happen with the Twinklers this season—no one could—but Wick certainly had left his mark. Unfortunately, it was a black one.

After the constables hauled Wick away, the two wild elves, heroes of the hour, were taken back to the festival to cheers. The hubbub over the balloon hijacking didn't die down so much as shift gears into a celebration. Ham and Scar were given a mosh pit lift as the Swingin' Shamrocks did a rousing version of "The Irish Rover."

This was the Santaland I loved—the one that, as Christopher had said, worked hard but enjoyed festivals and frivolity.

"I can't believe there was so much conflict over a game that's supposed to be fun," I said, shaking my head.

Juniper, standing with Smudge, seemed to have put aside at least one iceball conflict. "One bad snailfish doesn't spoil the whole bucket, April."

Apparently snailfish were the opposite of apples.

Smudge nodded as he watched the new star players being feted by the crowd. "Now that Wick's going to be out of the iceball game forever, it means we have even more of a need to keep Ham and Scar on the roster. Maybe our team really will win this year."

Juniper poked him. "*Our* team?"

His shoulders lifted in a sheepish shrug. "My heart never was with the other side."

She nodded in understanding. "Once you're a Twinkler, it's hard to shut off that twinkle light."

Luckily, Juniper wasn't an elf to hold a grudge—even against someone who'd temporarily gone over to the dark side of Ice Beavers fandom.

"And now," Christmastown's Mayor Firlog announced

through a megaphone, "it's time for our Saint Patrick's Day talent show!"

The crowd went wild with renewed cheers.

Nick, who had been in the same celebratory mood as everyone else, suddenly looked less enthusiastic. In all the excitement, he seemed to have forgotten that he still had to judge the talent show.

"Smile," I told him. "There are bound to be some great acts."

As I said it, though, the elf clogger company was climbing onto the stage, all in green, ready to do their version of *Lord of the Dance.*

Claire looked at him in sympathy. "Here, Nick. I'll make you another milkshake with Irish cream in it."

Behind us—yet close enough to be conspicuously within earshot of Nick—Jingles spritzed his throat and warmed up with an off-key scale.

I laughed. "You'd better make it a double, Claire."